D0425355

The Survival of Margaret Thomas

The Survival of Margaret Thomas

Del Howison

FIVE STAR
A part of Gale, a Cengage Company

Farmington Hills, Mich • San Francisco • New York • Waterville, Maine
Meriden, Conn • Mason, Ohio • Chicago

All scripture quotations, unless otherwise noted, are taken from the King James Bible.
Five Star Publishing, a part of Gale, a Cengage Company

LIBRARY OF CONGRESS CATALOGING-IN-PUBLICATION DATA

Names: Howison, Del, author.
Title: The survival of Margaret Thomas / by Del Howison.
Description: First edition. | Farmington Hills, Mich. : FIVE STAR, 2019. | Identifiers: LCCN 2018044048 (print) | LCCN 2018050666 (ebook) | ISBN 9781432851163 (ebook) | ISBN 9781432851156 (ebook) | ISBN 9781432851149 (hardcover)
Subjects: | GSAFD: Western stories.
Classification: LCC PS3608.O95727 (ebook) | LCC PS3608.O95727 S87 2019 (print) | DDC 813/.6—dc23
LC record available at https://lccn.loc.gov/2018044048

First Edition. First Printing: July 2019
Find us on Facebook—https://www.facebook.com/FiveStarCengage
Visit our website—http://www.gale.cengage.com/fivestar
Contact Five Star Publishing at FiveStar@cengage.com

Printed in Mexico
1 2 3 4 5 6 7 23 22 21 20 19

For my mother and Jay Patton, two people responsible for getting me started. Also, for George Willis, who kept me going when times and circumstances would have ended it all. The three of you have been there without request. You will never know how much it means to me. For my father, who passed on his love of Westerns to me. Also, I dedicate this to my wife, Sue. Now you know what has been bouncing about in my head for the past several years.

ACKNOWLEDGMENTS

The writing of a historical piece of fiction requires research and saddlebags filled with factual material, some useful, some not. I'd like to acknowledge my main beta readers, Rachel Sibucao and Mike Uggla, for reading the raw words and giving much needed feedback.

This book would not exist without the cynical and extremely talented eye of Lisa Majewski. Her time and effort on this novel as both a first editor and story consultant allowed the birth of this baby. May she live in a world surrounded only by clowns and chocolate.

I cannot miss this opportunity to thank two fellow authors—C. Courtney Joyner, who helped point me in the direction of my eventual publisher, and Joe R. Lansdale, who should write an entire series of books entitled "Chicken Soup for the Doubting Writer." His knowledge of the business and solid encouragement over an extended period of time made this book possible in ways he may never know.

Last, but in no way least, a thank you to editor Hazel Rumney, who tightened and strengthened my novel. We haven't met face-to-face but there must be something wrong with her as she gets my sense of humor.

I love you all and will always cherish this entire experience.

Love, like the wind, cannot be seen, only felt.

The writer, now that his work is concluded, is not inclined to dwell on the difficulties under which he laboured in the preparation of the present volume . . . The facts and anecdotes brought together in the following pages were found to be very widely scattered, and frequently accompanied by details which on no possible pretense could now be openly published.

No apology is offered for what is recorded in this book: it was neither compiled for the prurient nor the prudish, the writer's sole aim being to give (to the best of his ability) a true history.

—*Reverend William M. Cooper*
Flagellation and the Flagellants, *1870*

If I whet my glittering sword, and mine hand take hold on judgment; I will render vengeance to mine enemies, and will reward them that hate me.

—Deuteronomy 32:41

★ ★ ★ ★ ★

The Beginning

★ ★ ★ ★ ★

"I have always been willing to take the blame for the things I have done."

—Lillie Langtry

Chapter One

There are things that fix themselves in your mind; the blue smoke of multiple weapons discharging, the flash of an evil woman's smile, or the repulsive beauty of a bloodstained silhouette on a dry wooden sidewalk. How quick it soaked into the thirsty timber. An ugly discoloration of violent history now set like paint.

Wrong place, wrong time.

I am guilty of at least two sins, although there are many more I may have forgotten along the way or have never acknowledged. But as I live and breathe, I am guilty of the sin of distraction and the sin of being egotistical. The result of these sins was murder, the murder of my husband. I might not have loved him had I known that I was to be his harbinger of death. I have thought this for a long time through the ache of loneliness. The emptiness within me is not in my gut but in my heart.

I swear that outside of a couple of morning aches and pains, I do not feel any different than I did back in the seventies. But the mirror tells another tale. I look aged. I look like I have lived hard through the decades. The crow's feet are webbed now and laugh lines have become deep creases that hold the echoes of calloused work and laughter long since gone. My skin is more weathered and alcohol-wearied than it ought to be. My breasts don't sit as high on my chest. The gravity of life has pulled down on me, inside and out, physically and emotionally. I'm a bit slower than I was. Actually, I'm a lot slower. But I swear I don't feel any different inside. When I look in the mirror and a much older woman than myself is staring back at me, I feel as if I've been hoodwinked a little by life. But for now, I feel fine. I really do. Considering.

I pour the one cup of coffee I boil myself at home each morning—any more on an empty stomach gives me the jitters. I think about my journey to becoming a useless curmudgeonly fart. That is what happens, isn't it. Can't have coffee. Can't have sex. Can't have a good laugh because then you will end up piddling in your pants. Yeah, there are lots of wonderful things to look forward to in growing old. I cringe at these thoughts, stare back at the old woman in the mirror, and think *but I feel fine.*

I pull down a bottle and stir a shot of whiskey in the coffee with my finger to smooth out the shakes. Not the alcohol shakes, the emotional shakes.

Wrong place, wrong time.

I walked to the window and looked out at what I own, what we owned. Fields stretch towards a rise and just over the crest is the property line. Even though I may sometimes wander beyond it, my land stops there, just beyond a couple of rows of crops that I've done nothing with except let them set, to gradually work their way back to their natural state. It's been very much like the way I have treated myself excepting I didn't pour whiskey down the plants' throats.

Maybe I should tell you the story of my life. But there's not much there. One mistake, *wrong place at the wrong time,* and James was dead. My whole life is wrapped around that incident.

It not only killed him but it also seemed to snatch the living out of me. Maybe I'll tell you the story of my death and reincarnation.

After James's death, when I created my Jericho, that was pretty much it. I put up the walls and huddled inside. When you work the land for yourself, you cannot make the choice to slip away and have time to yourself. One day you just stop being productive. I took care of the house and did field work right alongside James, when he could join me, maybe more sometimes when he was in town keeping the peace. I came to feel that the land was mine to shape. But it never was. The land shaped me. The seasons have buffeted both of us, the land and I, worn us pretty smooth like shoreline rock. Life has surely taken the fight out of both of us.

I let the curtain drop down over the window and watched the light dance with the shadows through the lace as I sip my coffee. The taste is fine despite the cheapness of the added rotgut. I use it to mellow the taste of Gina's burnt coffee.

The land has an inherent sense of right and wrong. I enjoy the pleasure of looking at something through the window that is unspoiled, something reverting back to the way it's meant to be. My dog sighs and rolls over. I wish it were me lying there on the rug. What do you do with what's left when you feel like you really hadn't done anything with what was there before? But now I am free to start again. The tale I am going to tell you is behind me now and I am still here.

I shit the bed last night. Blood. I shit blood. It didn't hurt. I didn't even feel it coming. Surprise. Maybe it was a one-time incident, something I ate. What did I eat? Probably not much. But my drinking has drastically slowed in volume since I fought face-to-face the devils who haunted me. Whatever it was last night, it looked a lot different coming out than it did going in.

But, in all other things, this morning was an easy morning. There was no hangover. I don't have those to wrestle with anymore. As I said, my drinking has slowed. Company and companionship help fill the space created by James's absence, one temporarily filled by a daily intake of liquor until I was able to repack some things back into my Pandora's box.

On the morning that changed my life for the better, the sun had that golden ore look to it. I had nothing to do and nobody to look forward to, pretty much like every day for the past couple of years. I thought that maybe I would go into town and stock the cupboards a little. I needed more drink. I constantly needed more drink. The water from the well tasted like the ground it sits in. I think about how much easier it might be with a man around. I believed that the dangerous days were behind me, worrying if we would make it, and I've settled down. I owned the land, for what it's worth. I receive a stipend from the town that I pick up once a month in lieu of James's pay. But now I felt I had nothing to offer any man but the opportunity of being my nurse or me theirs. There ought to be a whole parcel of males just wanting to jump at a chance like that.

Maybe I'm pushing the "poor me" thing. I'm sure I still have a few good years left even with me slowing down. I should walk into town. The exercise would do me good. Keep me tough. But coming back with the staples would be a problem. I decided to take the buckboard. It's better to have four wheels underneath me and the room to cart things.

I set my morning coffee cup in the sink and went over to the stool where I sat and pulled my boots on. I wear the hide vest out of habit now, his vest; it's warm against the wind and it still smells like him. I miss that smell, that warmth. I grabbed my hat off the peg as I headed out the door.

"Guard the house, Slocum," I said behind me to the dog

without turning my head.

He didn't move, acted like he didn't hear me. Be somebody, aside from me, who decides to come through the door sometime and Slocum will tear your heinie clean off. For a mutt, he is pretty damn smart. Mostly he lies around with his belly showing in case I feel the need to scratch it. I occasionally do.

I had to stop by and see James first. He is lying there waiting for me every morning and does not know my thoughts about having another man around the house. I can't tell him. I wouldn't want to hurt his feelings. It's not serious on my part, just laziness. But I do occasionally miss having somebody to share the day with.

As I walked up the hill, the air on my face did more to wake me up than the coffee. The cross had tilted in the soil and I straightened it up, and then crammed some dirt around the base of it, packing it tight with my boot. The grass on the mound had about become sod with the roots intertwined like they do. I let it grow like that because he liked green and growing things. I am no fool. I know he is helping the plants live. He would have liked that. Even the lilac bush I planted to the side of the site is doing well. It's a little hard to tell right now, though, because the leaves have bumps and curls as they anticipate the coming of autumn and the colder weather.

I stooped down and brushed some leaves off of him. He always said I was too fussy. But it was the way I kept order in the house and fields. It was the way I carved out my little piece of life. If I mostly caught up on things in general, I would occasionally go clean up in his office. Made it easier whenever the marshal came down from Springfield to collect a prisoner and James needed to find some paperwork. Yes, sir, the neatest sheriff in the state. He went to his grave with that little gem hanging over him. I smile to think of it. Wish I could clean up for him just one more time.

When I stood up from the grave and took my hat off, I could feel the change in the air. Summer was leaving. But there were still a bunch of good weeks left. I had to start thinking of putting up food and getting staples ready for the long cold run toward next spring. I needed to fill the barn with hay and get fresh straw for the stalls' bedding. There were plenty of things to keep me busy and sleeping hard at night, if I decide to do them.

I looked down at James and wiped my hands on my pants.

"I've gotta go, honey. I'll come back from town with all the gossip. I'll let you know tomorrow morning what is going on down there."

I put my hat back on and walked down the hill towards the barn where my buckboard chariot awaits.

Town seemed to just be waking up even though it was well past seven in the morning. There were a few farmers hitched up outside the feed store down near the end of the street. Well, it used to be the end of the street but the damn town keeps growing. Now there's another barber and some kind of a material shop where ladies can buy frilly things. We hadn't any need of that before more families started moving in. I guess I will have to claim some of the blame for that one, having been married to the sheriff. People like a safe place to live. He was a good lawman.

My stomach was beginning to gurgle a bit. I wasn't too sure whether it was from my medicinal coffee or the fact that Pop Manders had stepped off the wood and onto the street, heading straight for me. He seemed all fired up about something important. You could tell by that chicken walk he gets with his elbows thrown back for speed. I guess he thinks it makes him move faster. He's rail thin, doesn't have enough fat on him to make a candle.

"Morning, Pop."

I touched the brim of my hat in salute the way I had seen James do a thousand times.

"Margaret," he came right at me. "Margaret, you've got to do something about those crazies at the Bloated Goat."

The Bloated Goat is our largest saloon. People stay late and get a little hog-wild when they're liquored up, especially the younger ones trying to prove they're not younger.

"I'll do something, Pop. I'll go out to my place and ignore them."

"That's fine for you. But there are some of us who have to live in this town with all that going on."

He now pointed a finger at me, getting himself all worked up. The veins rippled in his neck, jaws got tight.

"Talk to the new sheriff, Pop. I'm not married to one anymore, haven't been for a couple of years now."

Pop shook his head.

"Oh, sheep dip, Margaret. That new guy is no good and you know it. This place was a lot quieter when James wore the badge."

"I'd love to help you out, but it's not my place. Besides, I'm just a woman who was married to the sheriff. You'd best be talking to the proper authority. Things have changed. Remember, it was the town council that appointed him."

I looked across the street towards the diner.

"Now, if you'll excuse me, I think I'll grab my second cup of coffee of the day."

I left Pop to steam and fume in the middle of the street. He was right about the new sheriff being different than James. That's what happens when you grow older—things change and not necessarily in the direction that pleases you. If I thought about it long enough, I would begin to feel useless. Then I would be depressed. Then I would want to drink some more and that all leads to no good. I shook it off and went into the diner to have myself that second cup of coffee.

The café was on the same side of the street as the bank. So I had to cross the street to avoid the spot, and then cross back over to go to the restaurant. People who were watching me must have thought I was nuts crossing the street twice like that.

As I walked in the door, a young kid with enough whelks on his face to resemble a mountain range with snowcaps nearly knocked me back outside with the tray of dirty dishes he was carrying. It looked like I had missed the breakfast rush. I took a weekly paper from the stack by the door and found a table near the window. I liked watching the town pass by.

"Hey, Peg. What can I get you?"

Jenny smiled down at me. It's her place and she runs a clean shop. She's pretty in a fresh kind of way, a little broad in the beam, but would probably wear comfortably. She's got a real fine shape for childbearing. She will make somebody a nice wife if she ever decides to settle down and quit running a business. She was holding a pot of the magic elixir in her hand.

"Just a coffee will do me."

I nodded towards the busboy pushing through the kitchen door.

"New kid?"

"Yeah, that's the Harris's boy."

She smiled and poured me a cup of the beautiful dark stuff that is so much better than the mud I brew and didn't ask me if I wanted sugar or cream. She knew I liked it straight, like just about everything else in life. Coffee is one of the few things a person can still get that way.

"Why, the last time I saw him he was still running around in wet drawers."

Jenny laughed. It was a good laugh, good teeth.

"Yeah, they grow up fast; too fast these days, Peg. How's everything with you? Everything okay out at your place?"

I knew she meant am I doing okay living alone. James has been gone a couple of years now, but people still worry.

"Fine, Jen—and you?"

"Busy," she said, looking around the restaurant. "I have to keep hiring people just to stay up with it. I'm honestly thinking of expanding this building or moving to a larger one."

"That could be expensive," I said.

She sighed.

"We'll see. It's the cost of success. Who am I to complain? I could have worse problems. In the meantime, you enjoy your paper. I've got to get back to work."

I smiled at her and she walked away, talking to folks on her way through. She is solid from walking all day and cooking. Hard worker, that gal. She's done a hell of a job turning this café into a moneymaker.

Although I'm not big on socializing, I do find that I like being around people. It's kind of like Slocum. He likes to lie down wherever I'm at, inside or out, being near and keeping an eye on me. He's not up for conversation either, just likes being around. I cracked open the paper and settled in for the morning read.

I was really living it up on my second cup of Jenny's coffee and fifth page of the six-page paper when the door of the restaurant crashed open against the nearest table and Ronnie Heiks stepped inside. He tipped his hat in apology to the big guy who was sitting at the disturbed table wiping water off of his lap and then spotted me. Ronnie was out of breath, like he had run all the way from the telegraph office. He headed over to my table.

"Mrs. Sheriff Thomas, this wire came for you."

I cannot get it out of people's heads that I have my own name too.

"Thanks, Ronnie," I said and gave him two bits.

"No. Thank you," he said, setting the quarter back on the table. "You saved me a trip comin' all the way out to your place."

I took the letter from him.

"You're welcome."

Ronnie tipped his hat to Jenny as he passed her on the way out. I think he is smitten. At least the kid has good taste. Jenny smiled as he went out the door. She paused at my table to refresh my coffee. I saw the question in her eyes as she poured it, but she is too polite to pry. Fact was I didn't know myself since I hadn't opened it.

The dispatch was a little battered and beaten from its road trip all the way across the street in Ronnie's sweaty hands and somebody's handwriting seemed as if it could use a little help. That was the old schoolteacher training in me kicking in. I unfolded it and read the missive. It was an official letter from a sheriff out in Arizona. The writing was abrupt like any telegram but it said all it had to say.

> *Margaret Thomas STOP information only STOP Have captured a member of those believed murdered husband STOP Trial August 27 when state circuit judge arrives from Phoenix STOP Welcome to attend to testify STOP Other charges pending STOP Contact Sheriff Roy Bannon San Pueblo Arizona*

It was a cold feeling that washed through me. I didn't realize how much I had gotten used to living this way. It might have been better, not knowing, never knowing. They say the devil you know is better than the devil you don't know. But right now, I was not so sure.

James had been caught in the middle of a bank robbery here

in town, gunned down trying to shove me out of the way, saving my life.

Wrong place, wrong time.

Now there was a person to match one of the faces that have continued to live in my nightmares. I just was not so sure I wanted to see any of those faces again. Maybe this would put a period on everything and break the chain of not knowing. Maybe. I figured I had better take care of business and go home to think on this awhile.

I dropped a coin on the table and went out the door. Behind me I could hear Jenny call my name but I didn't turn around. I had no time to explain anything. I would not have known how to, anyway. I didn't even know what I was thinking. All I knew was that I could not think here, in public. I had to get home. I needed to get back to James.

After grabbing the few sack things and a couple of bottles I needed more than ever from Lynerd's store, I jumped up on the buckboard and headed back out of town for the ranch. I had a lot to think about if I was to leave. The few crops I had were three-quarters grown and there were a couple head of beef to take care of. Plus, I was still having trouble wrapping my head around the whole idea that the killers were not ghosts of some vague but unforgotten memories.

The day seemed grayer and colder as I sat on the ground next to James. Slocum laid a ways off looking toward the house. He was trying to be polite, I guess. I didn't even know how to begin talking to James. Odd, since I have spoken to him every day for two years in this very same spot. I had dreamed of getting those sons-of-bitches. I blamed myself for James's death. What if I had been home? Or had not paused to speak with James that day in town? Or if I had not kept James standing talking with me for so long like some kind of needy wife? What if? What if? I had not been myself since he'd been gone and deep down I was convinced it was my fault, even though they were the criminals. The one regret I had in life was a whopper and it had been punching me in the gut even when I tried to banish it to an old trunk somewhere in the back of my mind.

Now here was my chance. I could see him hang, maybe. But what if he got off? What if the rest of the gang found out that I had testified against their cohort? How would my life be then? It probably would not be worth a plug nickel. I didn't know how Sheriff Bannon knew this was one of the guys. Maybe he was wrong.

Maybe it was a terrible idea to even consider going. The truth was that I would not get any answers to my questions if I stayed here. I had to go. I could ride Horse up to Kansas City and take the train from there to the closest station near San Pueblo, somewhere in the Arizona Territory. Then Horse and I would ride the rest of the way. It could work. I would be there in plenty of time. But I could be riding into a trap, getting myself killed.

Hell, there was no point in getting all juiced up about this. What the hell was I hoping to gain, anyway? An ending? Did I need it? I'd come to accept things the way they were. I was not one for change. But I was always big on completion. So tar and feather me, this was going to take more thinking.

After I finished arguing with myself in front of James, I stood up and wiped my hands on my britches. Slocum stood up from where he was but didn't move towards me. He waited to see where I was going. I was going into the house to think some more. There was some of that whiskey I had picked up in town stashed behind the plates.

Chapter Two

The next morning, I leaned in toward the mirror and looked at my face. For a moment, I appeared younger. I'd stood there, confused, looking in the mirror, wondering if I'd reverse-aged and was becoming younger looking, losing some of the weather in my face and looking like I'd spent more of my life indoors instead of fighting all those years with the dirt and the sun. But it was just my eyesight going bad on me. It was like looking through the curtains I had put up in the kitchen. Those had been my only girlie touch and James's only concession to my decorating attempts. They were thin, but when you looked through them, the lace smoothed everything out. They killed the detail. Hell, yeah, I don't look half bad if you put a layer of curtains in front of me.

I pumped out some cold kitchen water and splashed it on my face. The headache would go away with time. It would be all business in town this morning. I had decided last night, deep inside the clarity of cheap whiskey, that I was going to make the trip. Now I needed to iron out the details. I had a little running around to do and a few tasks to accomplish. My first stop would be Jenny and some of that good coffee I knew I'd miss on the road. Having never been further than Slackville since coming out from the East, I had no idea what to expect. Jenny would give me the silent comfort and support I needed to push myself over the edge into final action. Then I would go to the telegraph office and let Sheriff Roy Bannon know that he could look forward to seeing me.

A wind puffed and caught the tops of the long grasses, making them dance. As I moseyed my way back up the hill to see James, I squinted my eyes against the sun, but it still hurt like tiny needles. My hair tossed straight back and then to the side but the breeze felt good against my face. It helped clear my thoughts. I could look at my choices from a distance. That was how I figured things. I would place all the thoughts on a table in my mind and stand back to look at them. I could rearrange them, could put them in some sort of order. I needed to figure out the house business, get supplies, and head to Kansas City to take the train west. Once I was at the other end of the line, I would ride Horse the remaining distance into San Pueblo and meet with Sheriff Bannon. Not much planning beyond that until I got there, heard what he had to say, and figured the lay of things.

But first there was James. I had to break the news to him. I wasn't too sure how he would take it. His hill looked good. I wanted the plot to be much more like a stepping stone to heaven than a prison of final resting. Some of the grass around him was flattened down where Slocum had been lying. He had taken to doing that in-between spending time with me, especially when I drank too much. When I would go into town he would come up the rise and wait, keeping James company. Slocum was a good friend. After I climbed the hill, he stayed a little ways off acting like he had an eye out for intruders, but giving me a moment to be alone with my husband.

"Hey, James," I knelt down on one knee next to him.

I smoothed the grass with the palm of my hand and fiddled a little with the rocks in the dirt.

"You've probably gotten word of what's going on, with my thoughts spinning around like they are," I said.

Slocum turned and looked at me when I started speaking. If

it hadn't been for that, I really would not have known if I was talking out loud or just in my head. I wiped my arm across my runny nose and watched a flat-bottomed cloud change shapes as it blew across the sky.

"They seem to have caught one of the fellas that . . . the ones who . . . put you here. I'm going out there to see if I can finish what they started way back then. Since it's in Arizona Territory, I'll be gone a spell."

I lay down in the grass next to him.

"I'll miss you. I'm going to arrange for somebody from town to drop by occasionally and keep things looking good here until I get back."

The wind blew my tears into the corners of my mouth and the saltiness ran across my upper lip. I sniffed and looked at that cloud running the sky until the wind dried my face.

"I'm not ashamed to tell you, I'm scared. Guess folks are scared about trying new things. I will be back. I promise you."

A sudden gust picked up and brushed my face with a gentle hand. The smell of our land, of our home, the taste of my tears was overwhelming. I just laid and cried. I stood up and wiped the dirt from my knees and the dried tears from my face. Slocum continued to look in my direction, waiting to see if I was finished. I walked back down the hill to take care of business. After I passed him, he slowly stood up and followed me down.

The Harris boy danced with joy to watch the place and keep the cow milked for some extra spending money. Kids his age could always use money. It took me about a week of fiddlin' about to get everything ready to go, including the telegram letting Sheriff Roy Bannon know I was coming.

All that week I never went back up the hill. Odd for me but I don't think I was ready to say goodbye. My heart was corking badly and it had taken the week to get myself used to the idea of traveling without becoming flushed and sweaty with anticipation.

The saddlebags contained most of the things I needed: a couple of changes of clothes and a few sundries. I didn't much like the idea of carrying a bunch of loose money with me. The bills were a regular size, nothing too large. I also had some coin, not wanting to attract any undue attention in unfamiliar territory. I had plenty of ammunition for both of my guns. I carried a .45 Schofield revolver. James had spent lots of time showing me how to use it. I could open the latch for reloading with one hand. I loved the automatic ejector and could perform the action with my eyes closed. I'd cut the barrel from seven inches to five so it fit a holster I owned. With all the practicing, it didn't interfere with my aim. I knew how to cock and fire at a pretty good pace. I also carried a Winchester High Wall rifle in a side sleeve on Horse. Just a single-shot, it provided me more distance than I could get with the revolver.

It was a full three-day ride to Kansas City, so there was going to be at least two nights of camping. Slocum had to go with me. Not quite ready to go alone. I couldn't stand the thought of him being left alone with a stranger caring for him. I was also afraid he might get a hankering to taste the Harris boy's hide. So he would travel with me. While there was still some daylight, I went up the hill to see James one last time.

Something didn't look right as I approached his bed. The shape of the ground was wrong and the dirt had been flung about. As I neared the gravesite, I could see that an animal had been digging, trying to claw its way into the ground and the small pit below. It probably smelled the body even though it had been some time and I had lined it with stones and rocks. Whatever had been there had not broken all the way through to James. Slocum might have scared it off. Now I needed to fix it before I left. This attack, as it was on my final day, proved a bit unsettling for me. Maybe James was trying to tell me not to go.

I spent time replacing the dirt and patting it down, all the while talking to him. I even sung him his favorite song, "The Old Gray Mare." He used to sing it to me and tease me with it when my first light hair showed up.

Oh, the old gray mare, she ain't what she used to be,
Ain't what she used to be, ain't what she used to be.
The old gray mare, she ain't what she used to be,
Many long years ago.

Then he would laugh and wrap his arms about my waist, twirling me to the point of dizziness. We would drop on the bed and I would feel his warm breath on my neck when he kissed it, ever so lightly. Even though I knew it, he would explain that he was only joking and we would end up making love till the rest of the world disappeared. Then, that one day, the rest of the world did disappear.

I finished fixing him up real nice when I was overcome with a very strange notion. Something tickled at the back of my brain that this had not been a coyote or other kind of animal trying to get in to him. It felt more like James was trying to get out, pushing up from underneath and heaving the dirt up and out from his grave. It was a very strange thought, impossible even, but I couldn't shake it, nonetheless.

I missed him so much. My world had crumbled with James on that afternoon sidewalk outside the bank.

After it was all fixed, I stood up and stared at the countryside. The sun had darkened by a passing cloud and a single large drop of water hit my forehead, followed by another, like tears from God. This might be the last time I would ever visit this place.

The rain let go about the time I got to the door of the house.

Slocum was right behind me, shaking his coat as we reached the dry interior. Then he stopped and dug at something on his side with his hind foot. I had a long trip to face come morning. I realized there was no reason to leave behind some perfectly fine whiskey for the kid to find when he puttered about the house. I pulled the bottle out from under the pie cupboard where a drawer held a few of my essentials, with the whiskey being my favorite.

I sat down in my chair and Slocum dropped at my feet. I didn't even bother to light a lamp or knock off my boots. I drank the whiskey straight from the bottle, took no pains to eat anything, and it was not long, beneath the rhythmic roof drumming and the spell of the alcohol, before the bottle slipped from my hand.

I woke to the bad breath of Slocum as he licked my face. There was a crick in my back you couldn't straighten out with a hammer. The dog needed out and I'd have to stand up to accomplish that.

"Pail full o'peach pits!" That movement smarted some. I shuffled over to the door where an overly excited dog waited for me to open it. I did and he was out like a shot, barking behind him about how it took me too long to accomplish the job.

"Yeah, yeah, yeah," I said after him.

I looked at the saddlebags packed and ready to be belted to the horse. I wasn't very swift this morning about getting my shaky thoughts straight. My sight stopped on the bottle lying on the floor. It had been my last hurrah.

The door creaked shut behind me at the end of my preparations. I buckled the bags tightly around the gelding's hind quarter. I slid the Winchester into the side sling and swung myself up into the saddle.

Holy cow that hurt!

I grunted from the effort and thought I might wet myself, but after a pause everything seemed okay. I gave a whistle for Slocum and nudged Horse with my heels. No dog, but he'd show up. On my way out, I rode around past the barn to make sure it was shut up but accessible for when the Harris kid came to do the chores. He would enjoy that, I thought. Probably roll himself a stick and play big shot where nobody could see him. I knew that's what I did at his age.

There was still no dog as I pointed Horse toward the road and moved on. I rounded the hill and gave one last look up to James. From my angle the sun sat behind the crown of the hill and I could see the shape of his marker against the brighter sky. I could see Slocum watching me watch him. I pulled up and looked at him.

"You can't sit there the whole time," I hollered up. "You'll starve."

He whimpered once and turned back to James. There were a couple of back-and-forths and then he came down the hill to join me.

"You are more sentimental than I am, you stupid dog."

He barked once and we began our journey.

Chapter Three

It was a long three-day ride to Kansas City. Thank God, there would be a train to sit down in once we got there, Slocum and me. These long straddles on horseback made my butt ache. Even though it had tended to spread out and feel a little more comfortable, if somewhat unsightly, in these last couple of years, I surely knew how sore I would end up by the time we arrived in Kansas City.

At the last minute I had decided to forgo stopping in town, fearing it may be my last chance to change my mind. I might have taken it. Slocum walked head down for the first mile or so. At the fork he perked up once he realized we weren't headed into town. He started paying a lot more attention to our direction and to the things around him. We had traveled far enough out that the smells had changed. Slocum started picking up scents of things he didn't recognize. I would talk to him every now and then from my mount to keep him close to the horse. He minded me all right, but I didn't want him to get all worked up over some field animal and take off running through the tall grass. I couldn't waste time looking for him. That train moved on a schedule. We needed to catch it or we could end up waiting another entire day before we would get out of the station. I didn't have the money to linger in Kansas City.

I wanted to push as far as possible this first day to get as much behind me as I could. There was the occasional stopping for Slocum to mark some territory, like piss bread-crumbs to find his way back. Otherwise, except for a mouth full of deerflies, the day was hot, sticky, and uneventful. Horse and I were sweating like stuck pigs. The water in the air felt like somebody had tossed a wet, hot Indian blanket over my head and shut out my breathing.

I could see that Slocum was also struggling, but in this part of the country, there were plenty of watering holes to help us get through. The more Slocum drank, the more he had to stop and take a pee. After a while, I just kept Horse walking and knew that eventually Slocum would catch up huffing and puffing and ready to drink again.

Come evening, we settled into a cool tree-canopied spot just off the trail. We were far enough away from the road that travelers could pass without seeing us. I cleared away some brush so that I could build a small fire if I needed to. I didn't plan on it, though, figuring jerky would get us through the evening and tomorrow night we would almost be near enough to Kansas City to buy us some real food. That would be a real treat for me. I gave Horse some food and water and wiped him down. Then I took care of Slocum and me. It appeared that Slocum liked jerky too.

I drank water that evening and convinced myself that in the morning, I would start a fire to make myself some coffee. It seemed like a good plan. After a hearty meal of dried, salted deer meat, I lay my head on my saddlebags and drifted off to sleep.

I walked up to James with some fine material in my hands. It was a new pattern I wanted to show him, special from the East. I couldn't complain about the cost and wanted to prove to him just how frugal I had been with purchasing the new curtain fabric.

There was the sound of a lot of boots clomping on the

sidewalk. James looked past me. Three fellas were backing out of the bank, their pistols drawn. I noted two riders on the street holding reins to a few mounts. All were garbed in dirty white long-rider coats. One of the riders was definitely female. She looked at me and the hate was palpable. As a robber on the sidewalk fired into the bank, another turned and looked at us frozen in place on the wood. His skin was rashy with evil red blisters shining in the daylight. A boil the size of two bits clung to the side of his neck.

Time slowed, accentuating every movement, every expression. I watched as his eyes moved up to the badge on James's chest. He smiled a busted tooth sneer. James stepped forward. With one arm he shoved me to the side behind a post as the thief's gun fired. Moving backwards and off the sidewalk out into the street, he wasn't such a great aim. But he was too close to miss James completely. The shot went to the inside of me. I heard a loud grunt. James fell against the post and collapsed onto the walk. I bent down, reaching for him and he fired back at the same time. But I'd knocked his arm and the bullet struck the porch post next to the scum's head. I turned my face away from the splintering wood. The noise, smoke, and wood chips exploded in the air by my face.

The woman on horseback yelled, "Kill him!" The second guy ducked and made for his horse, grabbing the reins from her. The first man, who seemed a bit chuffier than his cohort, fired again into the bank. He turned to James on the ground. I folded my body over top of James. The weight of the fat fella's foot on my back was holding me down. I felt the total of his press even though I was wriggling about under his boot.

"I said kill him," the woman shouted again.

He bent down and shoved the barrel of his gun against the top of James's cheek beneath his eye socket.

"Hello, Tulip," he hissed in my ear and made a kissing sound.

I froze for an instant and in that moment the scum fired. The smoke that pushed out with the bullet helped to obscure part of James's face. The front wall of the bank splattered red. I screamed and squirmed out from under the foot. The third man exiting the bank turned and shot, drawn by the sound of my scream. It took out a chunk of my calf and flipped me completely off James.

"Let's go, Willy," the woman commanded.

He ran to his horse, mounted with the toss of the reins from the second killer, and rode quick as sin down the street to join his already fleeing friends. Banker Cecil Jameson came out his door with a shotgun in hand. His hair, which he kept combed over the bald spot on top, was hanging down, like half of a horse's mane, to his shoulder. His face had blood-spatter on it and it looked like he had been hit in the shoulder. His shirt was glistening red. He got off one blast but yelped from the recoil and dropped the gun. The back rider's hat flew off into the street. He did not slow down.

Cecil picked up his shotgun and came staggering over to where I'd fallen next to James. I saw it all from a distance as if I was another person standing on the street with this entire fight being played out in front of me like a theater act. I cried James's name over and over. Cecil knelt down next to me.

"Peg, Peggy," he said grabbing my arm. "Let go of him so we can see if we can help."

Townspeople had gathered at this time and the other ladies were attempting to help. But I had crawled back to James and stuck to him like a tick. I just wanted him to cry or cough or do something.

"Peggy, back off. The doc is here and he needs to see to him."

Cecil pulled me up and away by the shoulders. Doc knelt down. With a delicate touch he rolled James up onto his side and I could see blood pouring through the back of his hair where the bullet had left his skull near the top of his head. It ran down onto the sidewalk and soaked into yards of my new material.

The things you see that freeze into your memory are so odd. As Doc leaned him back a little farther I could see the raw meat that had once been the side of his face. Small bits of him clung to the cotton of his shirt and were splattered on his vest. The hole appeared burnt dark around the edges from where the lead ripped away at his features as it was passing through.

He lay there without response and the doctor turned to me. I knew what he was thinking. He was thinking I had pushed James into the bullet. If I left him alone or just stepped away so that I had not been his concern, he might still be alive. The entire town was looking at me and I knew they all felt that. Doc shook his head indicating James was gone and motioned to a couple of the men standing there.

"A couple of you pick Jim up gently and take him up to my office. Cecil, you come too so I can take care of that shoulder."

He watched the men pick James up and then turned back to me.

"Sorry, Peggy. I don't . . . Sorry, Peggy. Let me help you walk with that leg. Hang on tight to me. Come on up to the office with us and get that bandaged up."

We headed for his office. As the two men started walking with James, his head turned, fell, and stared dead at me. In his eyes was the fire of accusation. It was me. It was my fault.

I jerked awake sweaty despite the cool breeze. I was one day's journey towards Kansas City and I had just passed through the entire killing in my dreams again. Slocum stared through sleepy red-rimmed eyes. He'd been through this with me many times before. I splashed water on my face from the canteen to clear the images out of my mind. I wasn't surprised that this trip had picked open the scabs of some mental wounds.

Slocum eyed me one last time and then dropped his head back down like there was a thirty-pound rock tied to it. I would have read something from a book in my bags to help settle me down but without a fire there wasn't enough light. I felt content to lie back and stare at the stars. The moonless cool night eventually lulled me to sleep.

Second day out my hind end could feel the ride. Every bump, every step Horse took shot through my butt like the point of a knife. That train sounded better all the time. You can't sleep while riding a horse. I tried it once. But after wiping the ground with my face, decided never to try it again.

Although painful, the day had been uneventful. Slocum and I found a better campsite this evening. After eating, drinking coffee, and staring at the stars, I smothered the fire and went to sleep.

I woke up to the sound of bells. My original thought was that they were part of my random dreaming and the angels were coming to take me away. But as I gained consciousness, I realized they were coming from down the road. Something was odd about them. They didn't sound like regular bells. They tolled in no particular rhythm, sometimes louder, sometimes softer. Sometimes they would stop completely. But they seemed to be headed in our direction. I crept out to the roadside, keeping myself low, hidden, and watched the approach of God knows what. Slocum gave a little whine. I shushed him, not wanting to give away our location.

As I looked down the dark road in the direction of the bells, a team of two big horses pulling a wagon slowly crested the mound in the road. The wagon was painted. The objects or colors I could see along its side seemed to be gray and black splotches in the night. It was enclosed like a stagecoach or, better yet, a traveling medicine man's rig. But much too fancy, with scrolling fringe work along the top edges of the wagon that jutted out and stood in shadowy silhouette against a clear night sky.

The horses were huffing and puffing. They either had pulled a long day or the wagon held some exceptional weight. As it got closer, I could see foam around their mouths and the glistening sheen of sweat on their flanks. The driver appeared to be wearing a blanket like an Indian, which was draped over his shoulders and fell into his lap to keep his arms free while he held the reins. The bells hung everywhere, from the fancy-pants scroll work at the top to the edges of each corner of the wagon. There were even bells hanging along the harness straps to each horse. As it approached, I could hear shuffling in the trees and undergrowth about me as beasts of one kind or another moved in the opposite direction.

It came up alongside of where I was hidden and the driver gave a grunt, pulling the horses up in their tracks. The bells swung for a moment and then stopped their clanging. The silence was sudden and deep. In the pause, nothing moved. I dared not breathe. Slocum lay silent following my lead.

The driver's head was tilted skyward and I could see the silhouette of a strange looking hat as he sniffed the air like a wolf, first one way and then the other, turning his head back and forth, trying to locate the source of what he smelled. I feared it was me. I could hear my own breathing and hesitated, not moving, to keep from rustling some dry leaves. Sweat was running down my back. I didn't know how he could smell anything as I could smell him and his horses. Even from my position off the road, the fetor was quite strong. The smell was foreign to me like a perfumed musky sweat or herbal plant of some sort.

He sat for a moment peering into the darkness ahead. Then, with a cluck and a snap of the reins, began to move forward again. The bells resumed their caroling din, swinging and clanging with the bumps in the road. I hoped that would be the end of him, strange as he seemed, but he had noticed the widening of the road ahead and pulled the wagon up there. He was different and he bothered me with his presence.

Dropping the blanket from his shoulders onto the bench, he pulled back the brake and then climbed down from his perch. As he dropped from the bottom step and hit the road, I could see the dust cloud rise from his feet. His shirt was blousy, filled with some sort of design that I could not make out from my distance in the darkness. His pants too were wide and baggy, almost like those funny English riding pants I had once seen. He stood stark, still smelling the night air once again.

He eventually walked around the front of the horses, patting them both on the rump and whispering low. He tethered them to a tree at the side of the road. Only after that did he let them loose so that they could move away from the wagon's tongue. He walked to the back of the wagon where a good-sized feed box clung to the side, which he opened, scooping out some of the contents into two feed bags. He placed them beside the back wheel and pulled a large jug from the rear of the wagon. He poured water from the jug into two buckets and walked them over to his stock. They drank readily. He allowed them that drink and then a little nibble at the foliage next to the road before picking up the two feed bags and strapping them over their faces. Satisfied that they were taken care of, he stepped back and brushed his hands on his pants.

"The horses, they are my life. It's important to keep them first before I keep myself," he said quite loudly in a distinctively female voice and turned to look where I was secluded in the shadows.

She removed her hat and I could see the hair drop to her shoulders.

"I smelled the smoke from your dead fire. I was hoping there was some heat left for me to warm my water for tea."

I froze, stuck where I crouched like quicksand, trying to embrace what I was seeing and hearing. She still stunk that strange odor. But I had no idea how far she had traveled that day in the humid heat.

"You may come out," she coaxed in a very strong accent. "I don't attack like some wild animal."

A bullwhip hung from the side of her bench seat and I had seen a knife sheath on her belt when she'd walked around the front of the wagon. A sizable knife sheath. I saw no evidence of a pistol, however, and I already had mine naked. Feeling my concealment was now akin to a joke. I decided to stand and step onto the road. I wanted to face her. She didn't scare me. It was just that I wasn't all-fired sure of what was going on here.

"The bells are pretty," I said, feeling rather foolish standing in the road in the darkness.

She looked at me.

"No, they're not. They're loud and brash and frightening to little children and wild beasts. They are atonal musical gargoyles used to drive away evil shitheads who may want to do me harm."

"Do they work?"

She walked toward me and extended her hand.

"Usually. You don't see any shitheads around, do you?"

The aroma of the strange spice or maybe her body chemistry preceded her as she approached me. It was no longer foul, only foreign now that we had spoken.

"Gina," she said and I could see her white teeth in the moonlight.

"Margaret," I said, smiling in spite of myself. "Peggy, I mean. Call me Peggy."

She laughed in that acknowledgment between strangers who are meeting on a common thought.

"A woman alone is a hard road to go."

Although her hands were calloused from the reins and other work she must have done on a daily basis and her grip was firm, it was still the hand of a woman. She nodded in the direction of the woods, nose up, lupine in instinct and movement.

"Mind if I join your fire?"

"Please," I said stepping to the side and gesturing in the direction of my camp. "I don't have much food. Just a few days' ride on this trip. But I'm willing to share the flames."

She gestured at what I could tell in the daylight would be a magnificent wagon, the likes of which I'd never seen.

"The wagon will be safe," she said. "I've put a curse on everybody who tries to enter without my agreement."

"How will you know?" I asked.

She stepped up onto the front board. The bells jangled when the wagon rocked, and behind me the horses snorted through their feed bags. The sound was a strange cacophony of pitches and tones as metal clappers met metal housings on creaking wood. I looked at Slocum. He was beginning to uncurl his tail from under his body.

"You see," she said, spreading her arms wide as if showing me her girth. "The wagon, it will be safe."

She held up one finger and then pointed at me like she was coming up with an idea.

"I have some very different coffee for you. It is my treat. Give me one moment to retrieve it from the wagon. I'll meet you at the fire."

With that, she laughed and ducked into the wagon. Though different, there was something about her I liked. I decided to forsake my one cup of coffee rule; being a little awake on a road trip isn't such a bad idea. I made my way back to the fire to stoke it up. She was a woman alone, traveling the roads, but she seemed more confident than I. Maybe she had been roving longer. Maybe she was one tough woman who had seen more than I and knew how to handle it? Either way, it was company for my second night alone on the road and I welcomed her presence.

We made a strong strange coffee and spoke well into the night. Slocum lay off to the side with his chin flat on the ground watching us through the tops of his eyes. Only once did we hear a traveler on the road above. Although our fire was small and we knew they would see the wagon to the side of the road, we kept quiet until we felt they had passed. Sound moves far in the darkness and increases in volume. The sound of women's voices drifting up to the road may not be a smart thing to offer a passerby.

"Why are you alone?" I asked her after we'd talked a while. "Did your man leave you?"

She gave a husky cackle and then leaned back against a tree.

"You might say that. Although, it really wasn't of his own accord."

I took another sip of the dark bitter coffee and watched her look off into the night. Her mind seemed to be at another place and another time.

"It's hard being alone, huh?"

She looked at me, studying my face in the firelight.

"Harder at first." She seemed to smile in resignation. "But as time goes on, it gets a little easier. After a while it's like a chore you do every day and don't even think about how or why."

I said something intelligent like "Mmmm" down deep in my throat.

"My James passed some time ago and I haven't gotten to that place in my life yet. Every day is more effort than not."

"It'll come," she said and looked back at the stars. "One day you'll be walking and realize that you didn't think about it for an hour, and then for two. Then a day goes by. It will come."

"Did your husband pass suddenly?"

She turned to me and broke into a laugh with those magnificent white teeth shining in the firelight.

"He did, but he lay around for a while, that son-of-a-bitch!"

I was aghast.

"How can you speak of your late husband that way?"

"Baul was a son-of-a-bitch," she said, becoming lively. "He smacked me. He beat me. He treated me like a pack mule. He was all-over dog shit. People knew what he was doing to me. They saw what was going on. But nobody lifted a finger to help. But God saw him. He got what he deserved."

"Nobody helped my James either," I said "including God."

She studied me a moment and then continued her story.

"We lived in a mud-and-sod farmer hut in the middle of no place. No place! Only other people around were gypsies like us. We're a dirty word to 'civilized' people. They're scared of our ways, of our colors, of our music and bells."

She looked back up towards the wagon.

"One day Baul went out to the small house to shake his snake and his heart stopped. Just like that. God must have poked him in the chest with his finger because Baul dropped dead."

"Oh, that's terrible," I said. "I am so sorry."

"No, that's good," she said and Gina's smile grew even wider.

"The fact that he was standing in the waste house meant that when he dropped forward he landed on the seat and then the weight of his own body carried him down through the hole in the bench. With a splat he lay dead, six feet down in the patties and pies, crumpled up like a maggot.

"I found him in the morning when I went out to do my business. He was lying down there; face up, eyes wide open, covered in shit. He always loved lookin' at my backside. So I let him look and then covered him up a little more, that son-of-a-bitch."

I gasped.

"That's where he stayed, day after day, and the smell of the rot stayed down there and mingled with the smell of everything else and nobody knew the difference."

Gina slapped her legs.

"After a few weeks, you could hardly tell he was there anymore. I tried to see him but," she waved her hand, "I couldn't. Now he was rotten inside and out."

She stopped there and looked at me very serious, sipping from the edge of her cup. We locked eyes. Then, from deep inside, it started. I tried to stifle it. The urge grew and grew until the laughter burst from me in waves and tears rolled. Gina joined the laughter good and strong and for that moment in time we were one. Slocum even raised his head in wonderment of these two crazy women. It felt good.

Then we talked again with occasional spats of laughter as she told her tales of the road and tried to convince me of her lack of need for a man. I wanted to join hearts with her philosophy but I still held an ache for James. Nevertheless, we passed our time in the darkness until we could no longer hold our eyes open.

I stood and began to lay out my blanket for sleep. It was only after I set the saddlebags down for my pillow that Slocum decided to step out of the flickering shadows. I don't think he disliked Gina. He just wasn't too sure of the smell of her. When she rose to go to her wagon, he stood, leaning against my leg.

"You build the fire in the morning and I will provide *desayuno* to give you a good start for the rest of your trip."

She smiled down at the dog, hands on her hips.

"I'll bring a little something for you too."

Slocum whined once and then lay down next to my bags. Gina laughed and walked back towards the wagon.

"Come wake me when you're ready. I have no special time to

get up, only when I am sleeping no more!"

The leaves and twigs snapped under her feet as she walked up the rise and then the distant gentle creak of the wagon and the clang of metal. It was comforting. The second night would be okay. Despite my tired state and easy drift to sleep, I remembered hearing Slocum snoring as I nodded off. He would wake before me also.

Chapter Four

I woke before Gina. Slocum and I were tired. The wet tongue and Slocum's damp hot breath on the side of my face told me that eating would be his favorite thing to do right now. I shooed at him, told him to go chase a rabbit. The ground seemed to have gotten harder while I'd been sleeping on it. I could feel tender areas on my hips where the earth had been pushing back at me. There were deep morning shadows retreating into the woods as the sun sat just below the treetops. It was going to be a nice day.

The gaudy paints that decorated Gina's wagon burst at me in the sunlight, almost blinding in their outlandish designs. The closest I had ever seen to something like that was a traveling preacher's wagon. He'd set up just outside the town limits on a dusty stretch along the stagecoach run. Although his tent was white, there were brightly colored banners and signs hanging inside and out. He was redemption-ready. A fiery red wooden cross shot up from the top of the large center pole. It towered over the congregational gathering grounds, radiating out for all to see that there was some of God's business going on inside. Gina's multihued wagon was brighter and more colorful. I stared at the rainbow-painted collage.

Slocum rubbed up against me. No rabbit, same old hot breath. I would have to feed him. There were chores to do. I had best get to them right then or I might be standing in the same spot come evening, still staring at those painted perplexities. I stirred up the fire. It caught back with the help of a few more dried sticks. There wasn't enough coffee for both Gina and me. I knew some coffee was hidden in her saddlebags, somewhere.

As I got closer to the wagon, I noticed it was moving slightly, the bells barely tinkling as the easy rocking of the wagon indicated Gina was up and awake. I stepped onto the first step to tell her I was putting on coffee when I heard her moan, low. Gina might be awake but it sounded as if she was having some problems. James had taught me to err on the side of caution, so I unsheathed my pistol and slipped up the steps, leaning against the solid of the wall. It was more stable so as not to alert the bells. Thinking an intruder may have entered the wagon, I flattened myself against the wall of the wagon. Slowly I slid around to the corner of the opening. Her low vocal sounds continued and I feared I would only get one chance at surprise. I removed my hat so that the brim would not precede me and carefully eased my head around the jamb.

Gina lay on her back in bed. Her knees were bent, tenting the blanket. Her hands were pushed down under the blankets, apparently between her legs. Her back was arched and her eyes closed. A final moan slipped out from between her lips. She collapsed back down flat and turned to look at me. Her teeth flashed in contrast with her dark skin. She started laughing, that big throaty laugh of hers. Sweat beaded her forehead. She did not remove her hands. I could see them still moving lazily underneath the bedclothes as the laughter shook her body.

I jerked myself upright from my crouched firing position. My breath was lost and I backed against the jamb of the opening. Faking emotional composure, I looked only at the floor so as not to embarrass her. I needn't have bothered. I was the only one embarrassed.

"You see," she said, then hitched her breath once as her

undercover dalliances caused her to jerk. "You can do everything you need to do without a man."

I was caught off guard, fidgeting and stammering like some virginal schoolgirl. Sweat ran down the side of my face.

"I heard you moan and thought that maybe you needed help."

She smiled again.

"Not that I wouldn't accept it, but as you can see I need no help."

Gina looked at my hand.

"Why is your barrel sticking up?"

I realized I still held my naked gun in the air. My arm dropped down in a quick attempt to holster my weapon.

"I'm putting the coffee on," I said too loudly. I headed back down the steps of the wagon.

"I will be out in a minute," she said from behind me.

I could hear her laughter as I crossed over to retrieve the coffee from the saddlebag.

The morning coffee was spent in silence as Gina looked at me and I dared not make eye contact with her. She could contain herself no longer. She picked up a stick and poked me in the shoulder.

"What?" I said, faking agitation at her.

She cocked her head to the side, but I still refused to look at her.

"Don't tell me you've never taken the time to make yourself happy?"

"Not really," I muttered.

I took another sip. The coffee was too hot and the sip was too large. I choked a little and coughed, spitting out the chicory.

"Happened by accident once," I said, wiping the coffee from my chin.

She laughed.

"Accidentally on purpose. Sometimes you have to take matters into your own hands," she said holding her hands up and wiggling her fingers. "You can't depend on somebody else to handle all of your problems for you."

"I can handle myself," I said defiantly, then caught the connotation. "I mean I can take care of myself. And it's not a problem."

I pulled my pistol back out to show her what I meant. She laughed and tossed the final sip of her coffee in the fire. It hissed on the burning wood.

"Hsssss," Gina said through those white teeth and laughed. "You'd better put that thing away before you accidentally shoot somebody."

Then she stood up and walked back to her rolling circus wagon. She was humming to herself as she climbed in, the bells responding with their usual cacophony of clanging.

I spent the next little while talking to myself and cleaning up camp. I fed Horse. Slocum was treated to some jerky I kept in the bags. There was no telling what he'd already scrounged up this morning. By the time I was ready to continue on, so was Gina. She came down from the wagon and gave me a huge bear-hug. I could still smell her muskiness, although this morning it was a little different. She pushed me back at arm's length and, holding on to my shoulders, looked hard at my eyes.

"I'm leavin'. But you take real good care of yourself, widow. I hope you find justice or whatever it is you are looking for. It ain't easy out there."

"Thank you," I said. "And I really hope you find you a good man."

She laughed and climbed back up on to the wagon bench, grabbing the reins.

"Don't need 'em," she said. "But I sure don't mind 'em either."

She snapped the leads and the bells bumped in a clangor of

noise as the wagon rocked back onto the road. Quite a lady, I thought to myself. I mounted Horse and turned his head around in the direction we were going.

Chapter Five

As I passed the many travelers moving in both directions, I was reminded of the fairy tales and fables my parents told me in my youth. I smiled to myself, the warmth of my mother's arms wrapped about me as she held out the tattered book she read to me from, and the strength of James guiding me to a final closing where justice would be served. My mother had taught me to finish a story once it was started and to follow through on whatever I was doing. Guess I was doing that now, following through on something for James.

It felt like I must have been getting closer to a town, as the traffic on the road was increasing. There were vendors who had set up shop along the thoroughfare, including a few trugs who either wouldn't be allowed in the nicer brothels of the tenderloin in town or were finishing their time here on the outskirts. They blatantly hawked their wares from their wagon stands. Most of them seemed to be eaten up with consumption or some disease. They were far from tallow, as were the fellas who came to see them. But everybody has to eat and I figured it wasn't any of my business.

Slocum stayed closer to Horse now. With all the distractions going on around us, he seemed to have developed a minor protective streak, which had as much to do with protecting himself as it did with protecting me.

"Well, if that don't take the rag off the bush," somebody shouted from the roadside. "Mrs. Thomas! Is that you?"

I pulled Horse up and stared down into the dark interior of an open tent flap sitting at the edge of the road. A face illuminated itself, as a man no taller than a pickax standing on end stepped out into the daylight. His arms were spread wide with his fat little fingers splayed like he was acting out the Second Coming. Sidling Horse up, I looked down at him, feeling oddly out of place seeing a familiar face.

"Hello, Bantam."

I looked at the tent and could see light reflecting off bottles of some sort. They were more than likely filled with bug juice. The display of them was stacked up on crates. Bantam was holding a quirley he'd rolled and he lit it with great flair, blowing the smoke upward toward me. Horse snorted and turned his head from the intrusion.

"Looks like you're up to your old tricks," I said, indicating the glassware.

"Now don't go jumpin' to conclusions or getting your knickers in a knot, Missus Sheriff's Wife. I'm first class all the way. Land's sake, I used my time in the pokey as a wake-up call. I've gone legit. Indeed, I am an honest businessman these days."

"That so?" I asked.

"Yes, ma'am."

He darted back into the tent and came out holding one of the bottles.

"First class all the way," he said, slapping the bottle like the rump of a horse.

I leaned down closer to get a better look at the bottle.

"Make it yourself?"

He looked aghast, as if I'd committed the greatest sin by even thinking such a thing. He walked a quick small circle like he was gathering his thoughts. His body was disproportionate and his face somewhat large for his carriage. But he had a head built to wear a hat. He had chosen a bowler, which he sported quite nicely.

"I import this from a genuine manufacturer down south of here. It's Simon-pure, not some cheap dog hotel bathtub concoction."

He almost appeared hurt.

"Well, I'm glad to hear you've straightened yourself, even if I don't fully believe it. I thought you were an odd stick and you know it. What kind of man gets himself all roostered up and tries to sell a sheriff's wife pots and pans he'd stole from the café? You weren't the sharpest arrow in the quiver, you know."

He smiled at his storied past.

"Yeah, well your husband sent me away to stew in my own juices and I think . . ."

He looked up at me with the sincerest of dog-eyed expressions.

"I think it cured me of my wicked ways."

I laughed in spite of myself.

"I can tell," I said, "by the delightful neighborhood you've decided to set up business in."

A quick glance told me that there wasn't a soul in sight whom I would feel comfortable in ushering through my front door. He stepped out on to the roadside and looked down the way I'd come.

"Just where is the esteemed Sheriff Thomas? I believe I'd like to shake his hand. You know, thank him for my rebirth as an honest and God-fearin' businessman."

I sat silent on Horse a moment while Slocum decided to size the dwarf up by sniffing at his legs. I nodded.

"He stayed home this trip," I said.

"Uh-huh," Bantam said, trying to figure out what was actually going on. "And just where is it that you, my lovely lady, are going off to?"

"Kansas City. To the tea pot, to rail it westward and take care of some business."

He squinted up at me even though the sun was behind him.

"That's still a day's ride. A person could get powerful thirsty," he said, "and hungry with a full day ahead of them. It's getting late and, as you seemed to notice, you aren't exactly in the finest purlieu. Why don't you climb down and join me in a libation and some food. We'll talk over the past, maybe find you a place to sleep. Then daybreak tomorrow, you'll be on your way to the grand city."

"Hmmm," I said skeptically.

He shook his leg at Slocum, trying to shoo him away.

"I'm small and, now being rehabilitated, relatively harmless. Besides, you've got your mongrel here to protect you."

He shooed at Slocum again. Slocum knew he was being talked about and took a step back, standing perfectly still—almost eyeball to eyeball with Bantam. Neither one wanted to give in and blink so I broke the contest by stepping down out of the saddle. I took the reins in my hands and looked for a hitching place. Bantam stepped toward me so as to speak quieter.

"I wouldn't tie him up out here, Mrs. Thomas. He'd likely not still be here in a quarter of an hour. Walk him around back, away from the road."

"All right," I said. I followed Bantam's rocking gait behind the tent.

A small alley ran parallel to the road behind the canvases and wagons. Garbage, slop pails with various and sundry other unidentifiable items, had been tossed out there to rot in the sun and be trampled in the mud. The stench was almost overbearing and everyone seemed to keep their back entrances closed to help quell the odors. A woman, I knew not whether she was dead or alive, lay sprawled in the thick muck with part of her upper half up out of the few inches of water so if she were merely passed out, she could still breathe. The dirt that covered her face hid any hint of age. From what I could tell, her skirt was hiked up about her waist and her lower extremities lay bared to the elements, splattered with the ooze. One man knelt over her and was just hitching up his drawers while another stood nearby laughing.

"I told you they're good when they begin to ripen," he cackled.

I started to move towards them when they turned and looked in my direction. Bantam grabbed my waist. I looked down at him in protest.

"Mrs. Thomas," he said sternly, "in these parts it is best to avoid conflict if at all possible."

I started to bluster and pull away, but he held fast to my pants.

"They'll get theirs, ma'am. She's a dead lady of the line and up under her rat trap is disease and death. Those men will be eaten alive and die of their sins. If you go creating a row you will only cause more problems than we already have."

I looked about and realized I was the stranger here in Bantam's house. He had to survive here. So I backed off. The men turned back to their business at the other end of the alley.

"You're right. I'm sorry. But I need to tie Horse so close to the back of your tent I can feel his breath."

"Not a problem," he said. "You may tie him up next to mine."

Once Horse was secured near Bantam's mount, Bantam helped me carry in the saddle, bags, and rifle; I trusted nobody in this sulfur pit of a town. His floor was only straw but dry and I sat my things to the side while he opened a bottle of his hooch for us.

"There is a hook shop just down the row. When the whores get too old or too washy from consumption or any disease that destroys their privates and their appeal, they are tossed out."

He spit in his glass and wiped it clean. When he picked up

mine I made a noise. Bantam hesitated and looked at me. I shook my head and he left my glass the way it was.

"Many times, what becomes of them you've just seen. The closer to the city you get, the better health the girls have. There's more money there and they demand younger, healthier women. When you are this far out in the sticks, there are no lower rungs on the ladder. They call that alley back there the *Pena de Muerte.*"

Bantam poured a splash in each glass, swirled it about, and tossed the contents into the alley. Then he added a couple of fingers worth into the *cleaned* glasses.

"What does that mean?" I asked.

"Death penalty," he said.

I considered it for a moment and then took a shot from the offered drink. The hot sting in my throat helped wash down the bile that I was feeling. It tasted like kerosene with a hint of coal but it removed the road dust. Then it hit. For a moment I thought I was going to go blind. The right side of my face felt numb. The tent was instantly hot to the point of stifling and I wanted to strip out of my clothes to let my pores breathe. When the billiard balls in my head stopped smacking together, I saw that Bantam was watching me. He smiled and took another sip of his.

"Good, huh? I meant to tell you not to throw it all back at once," he smirked.

"Had I been sipping it, I wouldn't have gotten past the first taste."

I held up the glass and looked at the residue left on the sides.

"You don't make this yourself?" I asked.

"Originally," he said and leaned towards me with the bottle for another pour.

I waved him off.

"Though now I have passed on the very delicate and secret

recipe to a trusted cohort of mine who can create this fine elixir in larger batches than I am capable of."

I looked at the jugs piled high in the tent.

"Are you really going to sell all of these?"

"It's been working out so far."

He filled another two-finger sip for himself.

"This is a fine little settlement we've established along the roadside. The folks that pass through here are powerful thirsty. I am a businessman just trying to help them in their time of need. There is no way I would ever leave this lovely little place. Why, I might be responsible for changing people's lives. Maybe saving their lives! Imagine that."

I nodded my head.

"Why, Bantam," I said, still catching my breath, "you're almost like St. Francis or some other saint, the way you minister to the needs of your flock."

He leaned forward smiling, his face glowing either from the cookfire or the bug juice. It was probably a little of both. Glass in hand, he pointed at me with his pinky and spoke.

"I have often thought that were I to receive a calling from heaven itself, I'd make a damn fine traveling preacher. I'm fairly charismatic, if I do say so, and my stature brings me a sort of oddities revelation that could seem divine."

With that, I fell to my side laughing. He sat back. I could tell he was hurt. I wiped my tears and sought to make amends with honesty.

"Bantam, you are nothing but a short crook. I don't know. Maybe you are one helluva actor. But you haven't got me fooled."

He was silent a moment.

"An ex-crook, Mrs. Thomas. Remember I told you I'd reformed. I saw my own destiny in the pokey, a kind of light. It may not have been religious but it sure as hell packed a punch to me. There is no way I'd ever go back to that place. No way."

He shook his head.

"No, sir."

I lowered my voice and spoke softly.

"All right, Bantam, I'll give you that. You've done your time as required by the state and paid your debt to the citizenry of Missouri. You have been reborn as fine as if you'd taken the Lord into your heart. You are as fresh as a newly laid egg and I was wrong to judge you."

He still looked down, fiddling with his glass, spinning it around in his hands.

Eventually, he looked up.

"I forgive you," he said.

Then he broke out into a huge laugh and fell off his box of jugs.

"I got you, Mrs. Thomas. I got you good. You thought you'd hurt my feelings. I'm a good actor, ain't I? I'm a damn good actor! Heaven help me! I could be a preacher! That's for sure."

Then Bantam jumped up, clapping his hands and hooting. He put his hands on his hips and did a little Irish jig dance kicking about the place, delighted in his devilishness. When he'd tired himself out, he plopped back down on the box and poured himself another two-finger twist. He closed his eyes to feel the burn and then popped them open again, looking straight at me.

"Ahhhh," he said, wiping the sleeve of his filthy shirt across his mouth in a grand gesture of satisfaction.

Now it was my turn and I sat back and stared at him until he had quieted himself down sufficiently. I don't know why, but I felt the need to impart some of my information to him. So, I leaned back in towards him in a gesture of imparting a secret and held out my glass for another dollop of courage.

"As long as we're on this course of conversation, I think I'd better let you in on a thing or two about me."

He cocked his head ready to hear what I had to say. Maybe he was listening too intently. Maybe I was going to make a mistake in telling him my story.

Chapter Six

"After you were sent away to prison, our lives, James and mine, were also changed forever. There was a shooting in Bleak Knob. A gang of . . . thieves, robbers . . . murderers were on the prowl for something to take and they lit upon our small-town bank. They must've figured there would be little resistance and they were right."

Bantam slammed back another finger of lightning.

"Easy pickings," he snorted and looked at the empty glass as if amazed it was empty again.

"Yes, indeed it was, except for James. Nothing illegal was easy pickings if James was around."

"He was a straight arrow," Bantam mused while pouring for himself.

I could feel myself starting to choke up so I kept talking to keep from crying.

"He was walking with me down the sidewalk when they burst out of the bank shooting their guns. James pushed me out of the line of fire and before he could turn back, they shot him where he . . . They shot him and he dropped right next to me."

I paused a moment before going on and Bantam watched me, silent. When I didn't continue, he gave me a prod.

"Kilt him?" he said with the delicate touch of a hammer hit.

I nodded.

"Second shot. Put the muzzle against his head and . . . Yes. My fault."

"How so?"

"Bantam," I said exasperated. "If I hadn't been there he would have been . . . He would have done what he has always done and still be alive today. I took his mind off of his duty and that distraction killed him!"

I was out of breath just remembering it. There was a long pause. I could see Bantam mulling it over in his mind.

"Hell. That's all beer and skittles," he said after a long pause.

He finished pouring a drink and then held up the glass to inspect the hooch in the firelight. He seemed happier with it filled again. Then he reached over and poured a little more in mine.

"Drink that," he said gesturing at my glass, and then watched me until I took a sip under his stare. "You've been carrying that feeling around with you ever since? That's dumb, blaming yourself."

He thought about the whole scenario a little more.

"Sheriff Thomas ain't above snakes. He was a good man."

He said this more to himself as if he was trying to make it stick in his mind. He looked at me and smiled.

"The things we do to ourselves. We can't change what is."

He took another swig and set the glass aside.

"But that don't explain why you're riding through my filthy neck of the woods. Why ain't you home, minding the ranch?"

I shrugged and set my glass down in front of me.

"I did stay home for quite some time."

I nodded at Bantam to put some more courage in the glass and watched him as he poured it. He handed it to me and I took a worthwhile swallow. It burnt. But it was burning better.

"I buried James up on the hill from the house. Slocum and I make our way up on a daily basis."

Slocum looked up at me when I mentioned his name. I saw the tragedy replay in front of me like a picture flip-book.

"The entire time after he passed was like living inside of a fog. I was just shuffling around like I was in a mist where everybody was moving real slow. I wasn't going anywhere and I wasn't getting anything done. I think I was dying inside.

"Then, I received a telegram from a Sheriff Roy Bannon out in the Arizona Territory. He said he thought they'd caught one of the men what had killed James and wanted to know if I could come out for the trial. But I didn't know if I wanted to go. I didn't know if I could go. God almighty, Bantam, I didn't know anything."

I bucked up and took another swig, followed by an instant refill.

"Anyways, next day I woke up and realized that if I didn't go, I would never have nothing, not even myself."

I got the shakes and had to put both hands on the glass to keep it steady. Bantam stared at me. His eyes reflected like glass marbles in the firelight. He cleared his throat before he spoke.

"Mrs. Thomas, you're a brave woman to just up and cut your suspenders like that. I admire you."

"I can't truthfully say that I'm not a little afraid of this whole operation." I fought the quiver in my voice. "It's a long trip and I don't know what's waiting for me at the other end. Hell, I don't know what's waiting for me tomorrow."

Bantam stood up and began shuffling around, moving boxes and bottles to clear a space relatively close to the fire. I believe he didn't want me to notice that he was a bit teary himself so he kept his face turned away.

Bantam brushed the area as clean as he could with the side of his foot and picked up any rocks or stone-sized objects he found and tossed them toward the tent flap. When he finished, he smacked his hands together to get the dirt off and then rubbed them on his pants, looking real proud at what he'd done.

"Sorry I don't have a private bedroom or anything like that for you, Mrs. Thomas," he said, indicating the cleaned area. "But you're more than welcome to drop your bedroll there and spend the night inside the tent near the fire. You don't have to worry as I'll be over there on the other side."

I stood up and smiled at him.

"I'm not worried. That's mighty nice of you, Bantam. But I really should make a few more miles before I call it quits. It's still quite a ways to Kansas City."

His voice rose a bit as he tried to make his point and he began to speak more with his hands.

"It's already dark out, Mrs. Thomas, and you really shouldn't be on the road at night alone. There isn't a hostel or an inn or a room of any sort for many miles. A lot of powerful bad could happen to you."

I knew he was probably right.

"Oh, I don't know . . ."

He put his hand up and stopped me.

"Ma'am, I owe it to your husband. Fact is, he probably saved my life in the long run by saving me from me."

He gave me a hopeful look, waiting for me to take him up on his offer.

"Thank you," I said.

Some hollering and yelling erupted outside on the street. It went on for a couple of minutes, growing in intensity. The screaming reached a pitch and then a couple of shots rang out. Everything got real quiet. Bantam didn't budge but kept right on staring at me. I cleared my throat and glanced at the tent flap. I hoped nobody would be coming through it.

"I'll need to feed and water Horse before I can rest," I said.

Bantam helped and took care of his own. When we'd finished, I called Slocum over and had him lay down next to my spot near the warm glowing embers. I would have his body warmth on one side of me and the fire on the other. If somebody came through that flap they'd have to get past one of those two obstacles. I didn't trust Bantam all that much but I trusted the street even less, so I stayed with the devil I knew. By tomorrow night I'd be at the train station, safely through the first part of my sojourn. Bantam nested up some flour sacks on the other side of the fire and sunk into the fabrics. He scrunched his small body down, almost hidden, and looked over at me through the firelight.

"Good night," I said.

He winked at me and exhaled a sigh of comfort.

"Just sleep. Everything will be fine."

Bantam closed his eyes and almost immediately began a snoring that belied his stature. I reached out and wrapped my arm around Slocum's warm body. His dog smell and heavy breathing was comforting, reminding me of home and what I'd left behind. After a short time spent staring into the darkness, imagining I could see the little hill out back of the ranch house, I dropped off into an exhausted, hard sleep.

Chapter Seven

Sleep can be an evil bunk partner. Pieces of things you know and pieces of things you never thought imaginable are mixed together and tossed at you like a sort of mental regurgitation. I awoke from a rape-filled nightmare of the girl in the alley with such a start that Slocum jumped up with a huffing noise, startled from his sleep. I looked at him and he looked at me as we both swept the cobwebs out of the dream corners of our minds. Once we had each decided that the other was indeed who we thought they were, we settled back down. I watched him turn a nest circle once or twice and then lay back down in his warm spot. He picked his head up one last time and looked at me as if to say, "You crazy woman," and then lay back down with a sigh.

I did feel crazy. I didn't even realize I was crying until Slocum lifted his head up again and sniffed at my face. I heard Bantam snort something in his sleep and roll over. At least I hadn't awakened him. I would have had a hard time explaining to him why I was lying in his tent in the middle of the night, sobbing for no apparent reason.

Maybe it was an omen telling me not to continue this trip. The odd thing was that I really didn't want to go home. I knew that what I needed was west, not home. If I turned back now, I'd might as well curl up in a ball and die alongside James. This was the first time since he had passed that I had a goal, a reason to go on.

The crying must have drained me. I settled back into a sleep because I realized I was dreaming. It was one of those dreams where you're awake enough to know you're dreaming but too sleepy to pull yourself out of it.

The wind blew across the face of James's grave and I could see Slocum lying off about fifty yards away with his head down. I was home in the room where I'd awoke the other morning after killing a bottle of coffin varnish the night before. It was dark in there but I felt like I wasn't alone. Something evil was close by.

The sound of boots on gravel was growing louder outside the door. My wild thought was that they must have seen the chimney smoke and wanted to get their hands warm so they could shoot. Why do we think these things when we're floating about in our subconscious? The sound stopped when it became so loud as to burst through the wall. I thought that Slocum must surely have heard it but there was no sign of the dog. In the blackness of my dream I reached around for a weapon but my hands connected with nothing. Desperation grew in my chest. I feared the worst. I stumbled and groped and knocked things about looking for salvation while my mind kept telling me to keep quiet so that Old Scratch outside wouldn't know anybody was about. I heard the door creak, and then it flew open with a loud bang and I awoke.

There was just enough light inside the tent for my eyes to adjust to the darkness as it still had the benefit of the glowing embers. My heart was trying to hammer through my chest. A deep growl rumbled from Slocum's chest and I turned to see the shape of a large man standing between me and the open tent flap. His weapon was drawn and cocked.

"You must be a new one," he said and motioned at me with his pistol. "You seem well-aged from what I can tell, but you're pretty and not too fat. I'll bet you're death on when you put your mind to entertaining. Take that blanket down and let me see."

"I'm afraid, sir, that you must have me mistaken for one of the ladies of the line. I'm actually here on business and merely passing through."

"I'm on business too, lady, and there ain't no mistake. You don't look like you'd be bringing me no French pox either."

He wiggled the gun dead at me.

"Now drop the cover so I can have me a look-see. Oh, and if that dog of yourn makes a single move I'll drop him where he sits. So you'd better tell him that you and I are really close friends."

Slocum knew he was talking about him and released a grumble. I looked at him and did my best to remain calm while frantically thinking of a way out.

"I'm fully dressed. So there's really nothing to see."

"We'll do this in stages then and the first stage is you dropping that blanket, next . . ."

The words caught in his throat, his eyes grew large. I could see him rise up a little on the balls of his feet. From behind him came the sound of Bantam's voice as flat and low as he could make it.

"Next, what you're going to do is drop that pistol," he said, "and Mrs. Thomas will pick it up. Then you're going to march like a good soldier to the flap and right on outside. Do not stop. Do not turn around. If you stop, we will be blasting your gonads into pebbles. Now move!"

The shape hesitated a moment and then held his gun out to the side and dropped it. Like a ballet dancer, he began walking tiptoed, and slowly, towards the street. I could see that Bantam had a sawed-off shotgun jammed under the man's buttocks up against the underside of his measuring stick. When he moved too slow, Bantam would prod the weapon against his privates to speed him up.

"If you stop moving, if you try something, if I don't particularly like what I perceive that you are doing," Bantam pushed with the shotgun. "I will blow your balls out into the middle of the street and you'll be able to join the working ladies to earn a living. Do you understand?"

The man's *yes* was sort of swallowed into the back of his throat but he nodded. Bantam nudged him again and the man kept moving until he was outside. I picked up the pistol and followed until just outside the tent where I threw it as far as I could down the street. Bantam backed away slowly. The man did not turn.

"Now git before I change my mind!"

Bantam scooted back to me, grabbed my hand, and pulled me into the tent.

"Grab your things and load up your horse," he said. "We've got to skedaddle."

"Why?" I said. "He's gone."

"For now," Bantam said as he began to gather armfuls of stuff and pack it into his saddlebag. "He'll be back full chisel. I don't want to be here when he returns."

He stopped and looked at me. I had not moved a muscle.

"And neither do you, Mrs. Thomas. Now hustle up your things and load your horse. We haven't any time to spare."

Slocum ran in circles for a minute and then sat off to the side, probably wondering what in the hell was going on. It didn't take me long to gather up my things. We cinched on the horses' saddles, Bantam stepping up on a large rock and tossing the small altered children's saddle over his horse's back and me trying to tie things up as fast as I could. It all seemed to take too long. I looked back in the tent and saw all the bottles of liquor stacked up in the center.

"But what about your product, Bantam? That's your new life."

"Mrs. Thomas," he said as he hoisted himself up onto the horse like a mountain climber. "That is merely my livelihood. I've got my life and I'd like to keep it. Outside of the few bottles I've brought with me, I'm afraid it doesn't travel well."

I pulled myself up onto Horse and swung his head around in the alley.

"But what will you do? Where will you go?"

Bantam veered his mount about in the alley and I began to follow him through the mud, past the decaying body of the whore.

"I don't know what I'm going to do, Mrs. Thomas. But, for now, I'm going with you."

I stopped Horse dead in the dirt.

"What?"

Before he could answer, somebody swore at the top of their voice from behind us. A shot was fired and the entire tent exploded. I was nearly knocked from Horse by the blast but managed to grab the nubbin. He spooked and took off like his butt was on fire. Bantam was already in front of me, hanging onto his horse's mane to keep from getting grassed. He lay kind of half-cocked across his horse's back, not having had time to properly seat himself. We turned at the end of the alley and shot out between some tents onto the road. I looked to the left. The stranger was standing on the road in front of our tent firing more shots at the exploding alcohol. He was screaming something that I couldn't make out over the roar of the flames. People were coming out to watch the spectacle. A few of them took sticks to try to scoop out a jar or two of lightning before they all exploded. The commotion masked our escape and the horses ran like bees were nesting in their hinders towards Kansas City.

Chapter Eight

By the time we had ridden far enough to feel safe, our mounts were dragging their back quarters. We were out of breath. Coming upon a small stream, we decided to stop and let the horses drink. Slocum's tongue was hanging about a foot out of his mouth. He lapped at the cool water for a good while. I could see his sides thumping from the run. I splashed my face, soaked my bandana in the water, and then wrapped it about my neck. Bantam began to laugh like a crazy man, falling over on his side, cackling uncontrollably. I was too mad and aching from the romp to put up with his foolishness.

"What the hell is so funny?" I snapped at him.

He looked at me with dirt streak tears weaving his cheeks.

"That juice had a lot more alcohol in it than I thought. I should have been charging more per jar. Kaboom!"

Then he went back to laughing and rolling around like some sort of demented child's toy. I left him doing his roly-poly while I filled my canteens and hung them on my saddle, one on each side. When I turned back, Bantam was tipping his head up towards the sun, drying his face in the warm air. He pushed his hair out of his eyes and looked at me.

"That's a story we'll remember for a while. Yessir."

"So now what?"

I sat down next to him and stretched my legs out, moving my toes in a circle to keep the blood flowing. I was really stiff.

"What do you mean?" he asked. "There's a train to catch if

you're going to make that trial."

"No, I meant what's next with you?" I said.

He looked at me a moment, then shook his head.

"You going deaf too? There's a train to catch if you're going to make that trial."

I stared back at him. I could tell he was serious.

"You're not going with me if that's what you're talking about."

He stood up and brushed the dirt off his pants.

"Well, just what do you suggest?" he said. "That I go back there and get myself kilt by some waddy who's all full of piss and vinegar? I understand I'm short but I'm still above snakes now and I intend on staying that way."

"Well, you can't go with me."

"Why not?"

He was starting to raise his voice and it got a little squeaky, like a pimply-faced boy trying to talk to a pretty girl.

"I've got to play a lone hand on this one and that's it."

Bantam was silent for a time, thinking, and then perked up.

"Well, I've got to get to Kansas City now anyways, don't I? I don't see how there would be any harm in us riding together for this final day. Have you got any problem with that?"

He looked at me like his words were a challenge. Damn if I could not think of a good reason to turn him down. Frankly, I was happy for his company—any company, actually—on the ride. It would be nice to have somebody to talk with on this last day's journey into town.

"No," I said. "I guess that isn't a problem."

I stood up and whistled for the dog.

"Come on, Slocum. Let's go!"

I stepped in the stirrup and swung myself up and into my wood. The saddle was beginning to fit my hind end comfortably about right now—or the other way around. Maybe it was that being this close to the city brought my spirits back up. I whistled again for Slocum and saw him finishing up a pee into the very same water we'd been drinking. I tried not to think about it and gave Horse a slap to get us going. Bantam came up alongside my flank and Slocum kept pace while investigating the side weeds. The sun was rising fresh and it felt like the real journey was finally beginning.

I had to stop dead still and look at the cityscape in front of me. Our arrival in Kansas City made so many emotions run through my body at the same time. Simply astounding. It felt like there was a steam engine pounding away in my heart. Slocum seemed a little unnerved and hung close to Horse's legs. I believe the number of people moving about spooked him. I had never seen so many carriages in one area in my life. People, my Lord, there were more people than I even knew existed. They looked like beetles from my vantage point on the rise, all scurrying and running about. I couldn't imagine that many folks all having something they had to attend to in the same place and time. Then—oh, my God—a train car filled with people moved down the center of the street, and it had no engine! I butted Horse up sideways against Bantam's mount and grabbed his arm. He looked at my face and burst out laughing.

"Is that the first time you ever seen one of those?"

I nodded, mouth open, unable to form any words. I just stared at this most wondrous thing.

"Mrs. Thomas, that is a cable car."

"A what?"

"A cable car. Used to be, because there are so many folks in the city, they would move groups of 'em around in a large carriage pulled by horses. But with so many people and so many horses, it left quite a mess in the streets. So, they kept coming up with ideas and this is the latest. They've been using them for a few years now."

"But," I pointed at the magical machine. "There isn't a steam engine or a horse pulling. How does it move?"

"Look underneath there at about the same spot the horse's traces would come down and fit into a regular wagon. There's a cable hooked there that strings way down the street. It goes around a giant pulley down at the end and as a gear turns that wheel, it pulls the wagon with all the people. Since they don't have to worry about any horses getting tired it can pull all day and more weight too. Plus you never have to feed it."

"If that ain't some kind of ballyhoo," I said.

As I watched one cable car go off away, another one came back towards us from the other direction. It, too, was filled with people in all kinds of dress. This was much like a free circus that you snuck in under the tent to see as a kid. I was truly marveled.

Bantam heeled his horse a little and made him skip. It broke my concentration.

"You gonna stare at the cable cars all day or should we find you a place to stay the night so you can make that train in the morning?"

"I guess we'd better git," I said. "You know which way the depot is? I should probably stay someplace near there."

"Just head toward that steam cloud on the other side of those buildings," he said, nodding his head off to our right. "Maybe you might get a chance to buy your tickets tonight. With all these folks around here, I wouldn't be surprised if each train sells out."

He had my feelings roped there and we headed off towards the sound of the distant train whistles.

The station district had one main difference from the rest of what I had seen of Kansas City. Everything was covered in soot. Bricks on the sides of the buildings were streaked with black and it ran down their sides like the makeup of a sweaty medicine show performer. One couldn't lean against anything or touch railings or doors without coming away with blackened hands and dirtied clothes. The handle of the door, probably due to constant use, was the only thing one could touch without feeling sullied. Many a day I have come in from the field and felt cleaner than I did an hour in the railroad area of this city.

The Union Depot was in the West Bottoms area and, I was later told, had been built near the end of the last decade. It was a long bustling place with a clock tower in the middle and a mixture of architectural styles. A blue-tiled roof made the entire building stand out from everything around it.

Horse-drawn carriages lined up in the muddy street loading or unloading passengers who seemed to come from every class of society. I knew I looked a bit rough and tumble from my ride, and I pulled my coat tight in front of me self-consciously as we rode past some high-flaunting society types. The ladies with their hair pulled up on their heads and dainty hats could hardly have accomplished a full day's work or kept up with me on my daily tasks. Still, my sense of awareness caused me to turn away when I was beside them and I nudged Horse along at a quicker pace.

We found an empty space along the hitching post and tied up. I told Slocum to stay and he lay down on the wooden walk.

I found myself in a large square waiting room with people knocking into me and giving mean looks in an attempt to get around whilst I stood dead still, wholly engaged by my surroundings. Dirty glass sections of the ceiling let in a streaky sun and a long hallway stretched out in front of me with a sign reading *To Tracks* with an arrow. On each side of the hallway were rows and rows of church pews with many people sitting and waiting. For what, I could not imagine, as surely there were far too many folks to be able to board whatever train was coming next. Bantam grabbed my clothes and pulled me to the side of the room.

He pointed to a counter with a cage at the far right of the room where a line of people waited patiently. A clerk faced them from the other side of the grilled barrier. We wandered over and stood at the end of the line. Soon we had additional travelers lining up behind us. Bantam pointed to a destination board on the wall above the clerk.

"Which town are we traveling to?"

I looked up at the board, studied it, and then back down at him.

"Where I'm headed is not on that sign."

The clerk gave me a disgusted look and thought it over.

"Then why are we here?"

"Because, I have to ride all the way to the end of the line. Then I get off and have a day's ride before I get there."

He stared at me a minute as if I really was that dumb rock in the middle of the stream. He pointed up at the sign board.

"How do we know which town is the end of the line?"

"I guess that would depend on which way we're going."

I looked down from the board and saw that we had moved ourselves to within one person of the ticket counter.

"I hope it's not sold out," Bantam said.

I shushed him.

"You know you are full of questions, like a little child," I said. "All of your doubting does not make the purchase of this ticket any easier. Now, please be quiet—you'll only make me lose track of what I'm thinking."

I turned away but he couldn't keep still.

"Just some things I figured you ought to know before you git up to the man, that's all."

I turned back at him sharply.

"You know, for a little man you've got some mouth."

"Next, please!"

I stepped up to the clerk to purchase the ticket and heard no more from Bantam. I believe he was sulking. I put on my biggest, brightest smile and plunged right in. Pulling out the telegram I'd received from Sheriff Bannon I laid it on the counter and began flattening it with the palm of my hand nervously while I thought of what to ask.

"Yes, ma'am? May I help you?"

The clerk's eyes were quite large in the magnification from his round eyeglasses, and his mustache twitched while he stood there waiting for me to answer. I didn't know if it was from a nervous tick or a ticklish hair off of that handlebar, but he seemed to become agitated with my silence.

"Ma'am?"

Bantam stepped on my foot.

"Oh, I'm sorry. I, uh, I need the train to San Pueblo."

"Where's that, ma'am?"

His eyes seemed to grow larger and completely fill the lenses. I was stuck staring at his pupils until Bantam stepped on my foot again.

"Arizona!" I blurted out.

"Oh," he said and leaned back. "It don't go there, to San Pueblo I mean."

"I know that," I said.

"Then why'd you ask?"

"Because that's where I need to go."

"Can't take a train," he said and looked down, beginning to fiddle with the ticket papers. I could sense the people behind me in line growing antsy.

"I need to take the train as close as I can. End of the line."

"Well," he looked over at the map taped on the wall. "The end of the line in Arizona is Yuma. That's as far as I can get you."

I smiled.

"That will do just fine."

He stared at me with a mouth that appeared to be fighting off the aftereffects of a lemon chewing.

"If that was where you wanted to go, then why didn't you ask me that in the first . . ."

"Because that's not where I want to go. But it will have to do."

He just kept staring at me.

I, in turn, said nothing.

"Pshaw," he said and starting pulling tickets.

"I'll have my horse with me," I said.

He stopped and looked back up at me over the glasses.

"Of course you will."

Bantam stepped on my foot again. I swatted at him backwards with my hand trying to push him away.

"Will you stop doing that?"

The clerk looked back up.

"Stop doing what, ma'am?"

I smiled.

"Not you, him."

"Him who?"

I looked down at Bantam.

"Him."

The clerk leaned over the counter and looked down. Bantam gave him a toothy smile and a salute.

"Hello," he said.

The clerk opened his mouth in surprise and then leaned back, looking at me suspiciously.

"Oh," he said and went back to pulling the tickets. "There will be a freight charge for the horse."

Bantam shouted up from the floor.

"Two."

The clerk looked back up at me.

"Yes, ma'am?"

"I didn't say anything and you aren't going."

I directed the last of it down to Bantam.

"I'm not staying here!"

I crossed my arms.

"Well, you are not going with me."

The clerk took a chaw of tobacco and stuffed it in the corner of his mouth. Somebody behind us cleared their throat real loud to let us know they were growing impatient. The clerk nodded his head down at Bantam.

"The kid going with you?"

"No, and he's not a kid."

Bantam spoke up.

"Yes, and I'm not a kid."

"Not a kid, huh? Doesn't really matter to me what he is. Then that will cost you two adults," the clerk said.

"Wait a moment," I said.

Then the man behind me said, "Lady, please!"

When I turned to look back at the man, Bantam slid up some more money on the counter. The clerk palmed it into his drawer, counting it at the same time.

"That covers two horses too," he said and slid me the papers.

"Wait a moment," I said.

"Unless you are riding tandem?"

"No, we are not."

I could feel my face turning red.

Someone behind me said, "What is going on up there?" and the line began to murmur.

Bantam grabbed me by my clothes again and pulled me away from the counter. He continued to push and pull me away from the ticket booth.

"You were really starting to get that crowd's dander up," he said.

The door out of the station was in front and Bantam whisked us through the opening.

Chapter Nine

My hopes were that a place to spend the night would be more easily acquired than the railroad tickets. I was a bit flustered just being in this city and that last engagement with the ticket clerk hadn't helped to calm me any. As we came outside, Slocum stood up, acknowledging our arrival. I looked about but saw nothing that reminded me of a boarding house back in Bleak Knob until Bantam pointed out a yellow two-story structure. I could see a sign board over the porch and, although I couldn't make it out from this distance, I figured it said *Rooms.*

I clucked at Slocum and pulled Horse's head about. Bantam untied his horse and then, in his gruffest voice, said, "Up." I was amazed as the horse knelt down his front quarters, knees to the ground, so Bantam could climb on. Then with a cluck and a shake of the reins it stood with Bantam in the saddle.

"That's service," I said.

"There ain't always a stool for the little guy," he smiled.

The sign said The Daisy and beneath that it said Rooms with the addendum: *We serve Arbuckle's Coffee.* Bantam slapped the side of his leg and turned to me smiling.

"That's some damn fine joe. I had it in Joplin once; put a campfire pot to shame."

"Well, that's certainly one way to choose a place to sleep. I never heard of just offering coffee out in the open like that if you're not a restaurant."

I could only imagine what Jenny back home might think

about this. She made her own coffee and I never did know what type it was. Coffee is coffee. Corley, who owned the general store in Bleak Knob, sold me a small sack that said COFFEE on it. I never paid much more attention to it than that.

Bantam jumped down off his horse and began to tie the reins on the hitching rail.

"We're not going to get a room by sitting out here jaw-jacking about a sign. Let's go in."

"Slocum, stay," I said and he dropped down in front of the horses. I tied off and followed Bantam up the porch steps. The closer I was to the building, the more dragged out it looked. Its peeling paint was camouflaged from a distance since the top coat was the same color as the previous one. But up close it looked a little less fresh than a "daisy." I removed my vaquero and slapped it across my thigh. The dust clouded up. I guessed I shouldn't slander an old gal like The Daisy, who probably had a few years on me.

Once inside, I stopped and checked out the faded drapes and lobby furniture while Bantam proceeded to the counter. It was done up in a style somewhat reminiscent of a lady's boudoir. It was tasteful, if overly worn. Yes, she seemed to have seen better days but still had a few strong breaths left in her.

Bantam was at the counter talking with a fellow who looked to be between hay and grass but was obviously old enough to work there. Bantam completed the transaction and turned to me as I approached.

"Don't worry. I got us two rooms," he said and handed me a key with a wink. "But I'm right in the next room."

He was waiting for some sort of reaction, I imagine. But I gave him none.

"There's a stable three buildings down where we can put up the mounts. Slocum has to sleep with them in the straw."

The clerk seemed to want to clarify that point.

"We don't want any rooms overrun with fleas. We get enough bugs as it is," he said officiously.

Lovely, I thought, and took the key.

"He'll manage sleeping with the horses. Where are the rooms?"

The clerk leaned over earnestly and pointed off down the hall. We may have been his only company today.

"Just down there. You are on the left, ma'am, and the dwa—the gentleman is in the next room along the hall."

Bantam shot him a mean look and pointed his finger like a pistol.

"The facilities are at the end of the hall for all to use for washing up and there's a modern flush device with a hinged seat in there for your comfort. Each room is also equipped with a basin chair in the event that you would rather not leave the comfort of your room."

He gave a winsome smile.

"Don't let the faded facade of this building fool you."

He directed this last bit at me. Evidently, he had noticed my visual inspection of the structure.

"Thank you, that's very nice," I said. "I think I'll freshen up a little before taking Horse down to the livery."

As I walked to my room followed by Bantam I could hear him murmur "fart head" under his breath.

"He's just trying to please," I said.

"Hell, he's downright perky," Bantam said. "I hate perky."

As I walked out of the stable, I had four things on my mind: feed Slocum, feed me, sneak Slocum into the room, and get some rest before I had to wake up and make it to the train tomorrow. I figured I could do both of the first things in one stop at the local eatery, so Bantam and I headed off on foot towards the busy area of town that seemed most promising in terms of some food.

We found a spot not too far from the boarding house under the moniker of ***Robert Ford's—Where you can get food and a shot.*** I laughed at this obvious advertising takeoff on the Jesse James legends. It had been claimed that he and his gang robbed the Kansas City Exposition ticket office of $10,000 in 1872. He also had married his first cousin Zerelda Mimms in Kansas City two years later in 1874. But death at the hands of Bob Ford took place in St. Joseph. Nevertheless, it was a chance for me to see city commerce at work.

While Slocum waited on the sidewalk in front, Bantam and I had good conversation. I ate a nicely aged thick cut of steak. I ate all of it, as I was famished. Bantam had buffalo, something he claimed to have "grown a fondness for" while working on the prison farm. I never knew about him. I believed he was blowing smoke up my pant legs about half of the time. But our conversation was genial and he made me smile. He had paid for the rooms so I purchased the meals as a thank you in return to him.

Eventually, I was full and put my scraps in a napkin, which I fed to Slocum outside. The walk back to bed was slow and enjoyable. The warm weather and light night breeze had the smell of approaching autumn in it.

It was on this gentle breeze that a sound came to me, lightly, from a distance. I knew what it was but the distance and the in-and-out wafting of the wind made me doubt my own senses. I stopped, hoping to hear it again.

"What?" Bantam asked.

"I don't know. I thought I heard . . ."

"What?"

"Ssshh. There it is. Do you hear it?"

Bantam cocked his head like a dog.

"What? Nope. I don't hear nothing," he said. "We'd better

shake a leg before it becomes pitch dark."

"We've got Slocum with us," I said.

Bantam looked up at me.

"Who do you think he'll protect first?"

He grabbed my arm and turned me back towards the rooms. I didn't hear the sound again but I was sure I had heard it at least once. It was the sound of bells, not tolling as in a church tower, but clanging as if they were strung on rope and lashed about a moving wagon.

Chapter Ten

For every beginning to engage, you must have an ending of some other condition. At one end of the pendulum swing, the rod comes to a complete stop and then returns back down in the direction from which it came. Like the beautiful brass pendulum on the grandfather clock that stood in the foyer of my father's house, the disc swung back and forth on the end of the metal baton, reaching and ending and starting a new beginning as the restoring force of gravity pushed down on the disc and caused it to return to where it had come. Over and over the pendulum is pushed back down towards the middle, always moving past and never quite stopping in the center. Our lives operate on the same principle.

When James was murdered, my center was completely lost. I was pushed far away over to one side. I went through the gamut of emotions from blame and self-loathing to anger and revenge. One particularly strong swing led me to the edge of suicide. I was fluctuating between mannered thought and wild feelings. As I passed through my center I couldn't grasp anything to stop myself. Those passions and sensations coursing through my body seemed to take over again just when I felt like I was going to get a hold of myself. I grew nauseous with all of the fervency and vehemence (and alcohol) flowing through my body. Blaming myself, I lost my way.

The days were merely keeping time. I saw nothing. I felt nothing. I assume I was clothed but could have been naked for all I knew. Oddly, I was aware of my nothingness but had neither the desire nor ability to pull myself up out of my dark state of being. I was angry at myself, at James, and damned angry with God. I was too busy blaming everyone else. Yet it was the killers, alone, who were at fault.

Then one day the telegram from Sheriff Roy Bannon arrived and pushed me back into the center of life. I knew I had better take this trip. Slowly, I began to blame the right people. All of my anger and hatred has focused itself into a single purpose. I need to see the devil and spit in his face.

Neither of my parents had ever raised their voices or hands in anger. They are buried under a piece of sod with less of a marker than James. I love James so very much that I will not let him turn to dust without some type of retribution for his soul.

Vengeance is mine saith the Lord. That may be true but I am going to be the avenger who sees that it is exacted by the courts. Because right at that moment when the telegram arrived, I was feeling chewed up and not all sure fired that the Lord was paying any attention to my plight.

As I laid in my bed in the darkness I could see the metallic leaf of the wallpaper pattern reflecting the moonlight from the window. I could actually hear Bantam snoring in the adjoining room. The walls were merely thin planks, while he seemed to have the lungs of a bear. I stood up and stepped to the window, allowing the moonlight to bathe me with its silver elegance. I pulled my nightclothes closer about me, as the early autumn night coolness seeped through the glass. I walked back to the bed and pulled myself under the covers, into the deep nest. While wondering how I would cope with not resting that night from all of the excitement I dropped into a deep dreamless sleep.

I awoke the next morning completely refreshed.

CHAPTER ELEVEN

The rain slapped against my window like a flock of birds pecking at the glass. I knew Slocum had to go out but I dreaded the stink of a wet muddy dog traipsing back into the room. I also had to sneak him out past the front desk first. Slocum was on the oval rag rug not ready to pester me yet but I knew the time was close. He started by raising his eyebrows every time I moved and then when I let out a sigh he lifted his head to let me know he was awake. I already knew. I was just taking my time. In a minute, he would be sneaking up near my head and letting out little puffs of air like he was on his last breath.

"Fiddlesticks," I said to nobody in particular and tossed back the bed coverings to feel the cooler morning air surround me.

Slocum came over to help me gain some momentum. I wasn't too sure whether I could just let him out the door of the hotel like I would have at home. Damn these rules. I didn't think he would run away but I wasn't too sure about what he would do. A sudden crack of thunder rattled the glass and lightning flashed the room. Slocum turned and faced the window and then back at me as if nothing had happened. Having to relieve oneself takes on a particular precedence in the morning that not even thunder can dissuade.

"Well, I guess you'll be all right," I said fastening up my trousers and getting ready to slip into my boots. "Not like I have a lot of choice. Hell, what are they gonna do, kick me out?"

I opened the door into the hallway and Slocum, staying tight to my side, followed me down towards the front desk. Nobody was there so I figured we may have timed it right. Opening the front door, it appeared there was a slight lull in the rain. Slocum was not waiting any longer and shot through my legs and out into the muddy street.

"Slocum!" I hollered from the dry safety of the door.

"Don't worry. He'll be all right."

I spun around and saw a pretty but plain girl behind the counter.

"I'm sure he will be. It's just that it is a strange place. I don't want him to become confused. Look, I'm sorry about the rules but he is my traveling companion."

She waved me away with her hand.

"Don't you worry about Mr. Prissy from last night. I won't say anything."

She looked out at the street.

"Thank you," I said and pulled the door up to the frame to keep the rain from splashing inside.

"You must be Mrs. Thomas."

"That's right. How did you know?"

She indicated the book.

"The guest register. You signed in last night."

"That's right."

I think I flushed a little from not realizing that. But she didn't seem to notice.

"I'm Lilith. I work the mornings here. Let me grab one of the used guest towels and we'll wrap him up the moment he comes in so that he doesn't give us a shower."

She disappeared into the room behind the counter and came back a minute later with a towel. She shook it out large.

"This ought to do," she said. "Somebody else has already used it to dry off from a washing but I'm sure that . . . I'm sorry. What's his name?"

"Slocum."

"I'm sure that Slocum won't mind a bit being second on this towel."

I laughed.

"No, probably not."

"Slocum is an interesting name. What was he named after?"

"Nothing," I said.

She seemed to want to make conversation. A lot of people like to talk in the morning. I am not one of them. I figure I have all day to talk and that I may as well wait until my brain wakes up.

"What's the name of your horse?"

I paused.

"Horse," I said.

"Oh," she said and we fell silent.

A scratching on the door alerted us that Slocum had finished his business and wanted back in. Lilith positioned herself just inside and gave me a nod. I pulled the door open and Slocum couldn't help but run right into her arms.

"I've got you, boy."

She wrapped him up good and rubbed Slocum down before letting him go. He still tried to twist and shake off water but at least we didn't catch it.

I patted the side of his head and said, "Come on, Slocum. Let's creep back to the room."

"I've just put the coffee on and it will be ready any time," Lilith said. "Come down and have a cup when you're ready. I may even have some scraps from last night to pass on to a hungry dog."

"Thank you. That's very kind of you," I said.

I looked down at Slocum.

"We'll be back shortly."

A crack of thunder and we headed down the hall to our room. I knew Slocum would spend the next little while trying to groom himself from his morning constitutional. I wanted to make sure I was all packed up and ready to go. It was a late morning train today but being this close to departure had me a bit edgy. I needed some time to pull myself together.

A particularly large orchestra of thunder rattled the room. I heard Bantam, in the other room, yell out, "What the hell?!" A quick crazed rustling of covers was followed by the whomp of a body landing on the floor.

"Jesus H. Christ!"

The rest of the profanity was a bit muffled as if he was still wrapped up in his bedclothes but I could make out some of the words plain enough.

"Well, shit the bed," he yelled out. "I paid good damn money for this room and it sounds like a freight train is coming through the wall!"

Just then another clap of thunder shook the walls and all the talking ceased in the adjoining room. I waited knowing he could not keep quiet for long.

"Christ on a cracker."

He raised his voice so I could hear him.

"Mrs. Thomas, did you know it was raining out?"

"Yes, Bantam, I did," I said projecting my voice towards his room.

He began muttering "Damn, damn, damn" and I heard his room door slam and he padded down the hallway towards the lavatory. I smiled and continued my work. At least he didn't have to go out in the mud like Slocum.

We drank the coffee and I have to admit it was as good as Bantam had indicated although Slocum seemed to be enjoying his scraps a hell of a lot more. By the time he'd finished with those, it didn't appear as if Lilith would have to send the plate back to be washed. Bantam was still cranky from his rude awakening but the coffee seemed to be helping his mind become fully functional.

"Train's at eleven," he said to me over the top of his cup.

"Yes, and we have to unstable the horses and load them onto the train well before that. I'd like to be at the stalls no later than 9:30."

"About nine now," he grumbled.

"I'm ready to head over there as soon as you are," I said.

I sat my empty cup down and waved Lilith off from her offer of another. I wanted to give Horse some good grain and a chew in the bucket for about a half-hour before walking him over. If he had just eaten before I tried to load him, he would be a lot calmer. I needed to get on the train and get moving. The closer we got to the actual train time, the edgier I was feeling. Maybe it was because it would be the point of no return. I no longer wanted one last chance to change my mind. Now I needed to nab Slocum and see what lay ahead.

I was surprised to find that the smithy's boy had already strapped the feed bags on our mounts. They were inside and dry so they did not care a hoot about the weather. I paid the blacksmith and then wandered about the stable waiting for the rides to finish breakfast. Bantam sat on a bale by the door with Slocum next to him and watched the city roll its population past for his viewing pleasure. The musty smell of damp hay and horses was comforting. It felt kind of like home.

I walked to the far wall and looked out into the side yard. The rain had begun to pick up in ferocity. Although it was like a water curtain, there was no mistaking what sat over in the yard's far corner. I pulled my hat down tight to my ears and traipsed out in the weather to look at it. It was leaning at such an angle that I first thought it was in a ditch on one side. But upon a quick closer inspection I could see where some of the axle support on one side was busted and the weight of the wagon caused it to list. At first, I was afraid to climb up figuring it might collapse underneath, such was the state it was in. I put my hands to each side of my mouth and shouted out.

"Gina!"

If there was a response, I didn't hear it with the rain pounding all about.

"Gina!"

I tried again. Still nothing.

I saw the bell ropes dragging on the ground and, still reluctant to board, grabbed a handful of rope and shook them as hard as I could. The clanging cut through the background thunder and surely made itself known inside. No noise came from within. I took a deep breath and walked up to steps that were oddly angled enough before the wagon had leaned. I hitched up my foot to climb when the blacksmith yelled through the rain from the stable.

"Get off that! There's no one in there!"

I looked back at him and he shook his head in a large motion to make sure I could see him across the yard. One glance back at the wagon and I ran for the shelter. Once under roof, I took off my hat and dumped the brim water. The smith pulled a rag from his back pocket and wiped at me with little effect.

"Kinda wet out there," he said as if talking to a three year old. "You're soaked through!"

"Right down to my inexpressibles," I said.

"Ha! That'll teach you. Why are you messin' with that old rig anyway? It was owned by a gypsy lady. You'll never get that smell of those spices out of the inside even after a bath like this."

He indicated the rain with his hand. By this time Bantam had sauntered over.

"I don't want the wagon. I'm looking for the owner."

"That would be me now," he said. "I paid her fair and square. Probably gave her too much. It wasn't going to make it much farther anyhow. She was lucky she got this far. Something or someone fairly powerful tore up the inside of that wagon. It was like there was a fight in there.

"I got the horses too. Not that those dobbins were a bargain. The taller one there has a touch of laminitis and is going to have to stay still for some time if it's to heal properly."

I turned and looked and damn if those weren't her horses in the stalls next to Bantam's Isabella. I hadn't even recognized them.

"Where is she now?"

"Oh, I don't know. She grabbed my money and some of the belongings out of the wagon that she wanted and said, 'It's all yours,' marching off towards the depot."

I turned to Bantam.

"Let's get these feed bags off the horses and head down to the train."

I started over to Horse and Bantam scurried alongside.

"What's going on? Who is this person? What do you want to see her for?"

"Long story," I said as I popped open the stall gate. "I'll tell you as we move out of here."

The farrier put his hands up like it was a lost cause.

"With that cash I gave her, she could be anywhere."

I stopped and looked at him.

"No, sir. With that wagon out there, she could have been anywhere. Without it, I'm betting she is completely lost."

Bantam had finished strapping his horse together and walked him up beside me as I completed my task.

"Who is she, Mrs. Thomas?"

"Just an acquaintance who could probably use a friend right

about now."

I swung up into the saddle and squeezed Horse into moving. At the door I pulled up and looked down at the owner.

"We all paid up in full or are you still in want of something?"

"No, ma'am," he said. "We're square as soap."

"Well, then, sir, I thank you for your hospitality and we'll be on our way. Let's go, Bantam. Hunker down, that rain is coming hard."

He pulled his hat down to let the water roll off to his right and moved off into the weather.

"Just where are we off to at the moment? We don't have a clue where your friend might be."

"Nope," I said riding up alongside of him, "only a feeling. But I know we can't be riding all over tarnation in this weather. We don't have a lot of extra time either. First, let's take these animals and get them loaded up and our gear stashed away at the railroad. Then we'll just pray my hunch is correct."

Chapter Twelve

Even though we had bought our tickets ahead of time, it took a while to get the horses loaded and our tack stole away. We were told that there was going to be a delay because of a washout on one of the tracks the day before. All the trains were being rerouted and we would have to wait our turn. That would add a few extra hours. We figured the horses would be fine in the boxcar.

We kept a few of our essentials with us in our yannigan bags as it was going to be a long ride with some train changes along the way. We weren't sitting ace-high, but the seats would be okay as far as comfort goes. Both of us were riding on our own dollars and there'd be rooms to pay for along the trip. We left the boxcar after making sure everything was in order.

My first thought was to roam the depot some and see if I could locate Gina. We entered the same large lobby room we had been in last night. There were people in line waiting to buy tickets. Bantam gave me a smug look. Of course, he didn't know what train they were purchasing tickets for but took the opportunity to be smug anyway. I wasn't going to tell him he'd been right. Slocum stayed right by my side in this sea of people. I searched for Gina as we walked straight through. The next room was larger by far than the first area. There were long benches like church pews and people sitting all about talking or reading newspapers. Some were even sleeping in their spot with their heads leaning to one side or the other. There was a flutter and a bird flew past me and up into the ceiling beams. Above them, large areas at the top of the pavilion had been replaced by stained glass windows on the roof and the colored but muted light that came in through the glass was quite awe-inspiring. The shades and tints would actually change when a darkened rain cloud would float past and filter away the light.

"What does she look like?" Bantam asked.

Good question I thought.

"The last time I saw her . . ."

Had it really only been a couple of days back? So much had happened in that time frame that it felt even further back in time. I was feeling a bit dusted and this was only the beginning of the trip.

"The last time I saw her we were saying goodbye from having shared a campfire. She is strong with long hair that she kept up under her hat. Her clothes were bright colorful prints and patterns. She was . . ."

I thought for a moment trying to put Gina into words. Bantam listened as he scanned the crowd for somebody who might meet my miserably light description. He just shook his head.

"Well, I hope we come to an eventuate quickly. Because if we don't get on that train before it leaves us we'll be at sea trying to figure out what to do."

"It should be fine. The train is on hold for a bit while they clear up those track problems."

Bantam didn't respond but hawked into a brass spittoon setting against the wall. At the end of the waiting area, large wide hallways went off in different directions as if legs of some giant beast. We stood at the intersection figuring a way to take our best bet.

"Since I can't look in the ladies privy, why don't you go that way," Bantam said. "I'll go check out the eating place. We can meet back here."

"That's as good a plan as any," I said and headed off to the right as Bantam padded down the hall to the left.

The crowd began to thin out a little in the direction I was walking. As I pushed through the door, I again was marveled at the size of the chambers in this building. Multiple basins lined along one wall of the area while individual stalls for each woman took up the other. Women entered and exited these and by just waiting, I saw most of the stalls clear out or fill up, which eliminated the idea that Gina was inside any of them. The other few, which no one went into, lay empty the entire while with their doors open. Before I left, I did turn on the spigots and let water splash over my hands. It felt good and I made a note to myself to find out what it took to get one of these for my own stead.

Stepping outside of the bathroom, I looked down the way I had come and saw that Bantam had not yet returned. I continued walking in the opposite direction and the crowds pretty much dropped off behind me. The door at the end of the hallway opened to the outdoors where I found myself in a side area that was used by people who had just arrived on the train and could be picked up by wagon with their luggage. Some empty benches were placed about for folks while they waited on their families. I scanned the clearance and was turning to go back inside when I caught the form of somebody sitting over on the far side of the looped drive in the shadows. The clothes the person was wearing were anything but colorful. The posture was slumped as if sleeping or curled over. Something inside told me it was Gina.

Her face was turned away and I didn't speak as I approached. Her clothes were new or at least spanking clean ones I had not seen before. They didn't seem to be of her style. I came within about five feet of her and there was no animal odor or scent of odd spices. Her beautiful hair hung long and clean, shining in the morning light. I wanted to touch her but I dared not, fearing there was more to what I saw before me than met the eye. Overcome by emotion from a reunion with somebody I barely knew, I didn't want to spook her. I stood there a moment, ill at ease, before making an approach. I could only say her name in a husky whisper.

"Gina?"

There was no reply and no movement of any sort. I edged a little closer to her. Again, I had the urge to reach out but held myself back.

"Gina, it's Peggy."

I heard the door behind me squeak open and somebody come out. I kept my eyes on Gina.

"Is that her?"

I raised my hand to Bantam to keep quiet. In my desire to embrace her, I touched her shoulder. She spun like a wolf.

"No!"

She screamed, jerking her body away from my touch, and slid as far on the bench from me as she could get, curling herself into a sort of ball. Her eyes pulsated anger and even though they were puffy and swollen I could see the fear with the hate. The bruising easily covered a large portion of her face. Treated cuts and scratches covered her skin. She seemed confused and disorientated and I thought she might lash out at me in her daze. Quickly she rose and leaped at me, catching me off guard. Her arms wrapped about me. Her sobbing broke through like a dam letting go. Were she to squeeze any tighter I'm sure some of my ribs would have given way. Her entire frame heaved and gasped and it took some time for the waves to flush through and settle her into a calmer place. I dared not move and let her take the lead.

When all was quiet, she pushed me at arm's length and held

me there. A smile broke and then the sobs began again. She pulled me back close and we stayed like that for some minutes. Then she pushed herself away again to get a look at me. When she spoke it was like sunlight during a rain.

"I sold the wagon," she said.

"I know."

"And the horses too."

"Yes," I said and smiled at her.

"I took the money and I got a room. I bought some new clothes. When I got back to the room I bathed."

I nodded.

"I bathed and then I dumped the water out and I bathed again and I dumped the water out and I bathed again. I scrubbed and I scrubbed and I couldn't get the smell of him off of me no matter how hard I scrubbed."

She pulled me back in close and the sobbing began again. I heard the sound of the door as Bantam went back inside. When she had finished crying she looked down and saw Slocum sitting at my feet. She knelt down to him. She grabbed his face in her hands and hugged and kissed him. I'm not sure that he liked it but he didn't pull away. When she leaned back he licked at the tears and made her laugh.

"I was hoping you might be here, that I hadn't already missed you."

I helped her up.

"I leave in a couple of hours."

Bantam came back out and walked up to us.

"I mean, we leave in a couple of hours."

She looked around me at Bantam. They sized each other up, a little unsure. She looked back at me quizzically.

"Don't ask," I said.

"Hey," Bantam shot back.

"It's a long story. I'll tell you on the trip."

I smiled.

"You're coming with us?"

Gina took another look at Bantam. He gave her his tough guy grimace.

"Got nowhere else to be," she said.

I took her by the hand.

"Grab your bag there and I'll see about getting you a ticket."

Bantam grabbed my pants.

"Just a minute. Don't I have any say in this?"

"No," I said and walked Gina off towards the ticket counter.

"You look almost citified in those new clothes," I told her.

She looked at me and smiled.

"I've never punched a woman," she smiled, "but in your case I may make an exception."

We laughed and wrapped our arms around each other. Slocum followed right behind us with Bantam bringing up the rear, griping and complaining to himself. Gina looked back a couple of times trying to get a handle on him.

"Peggy, when we were camping the other night?"

"Yes."

"You didn't have him stuck in one of your saddlebags and just not tell me, did you?"

"No, he's new."

"Just wondering," she said and gave him one more glance.

Chapter Thirteen

We must have appeared strange to the fine city people of Kansas City. The stares we collected as we walked through the depot would have struck me as rude at any other time. But right now, we were one big posse and could not have cared less about what a bunch of high-falutin' strangers were thinking. There was a sense of bonding, a feeling of unity between us. We were just a group of misfits that had something in common.

Gina's wound was freshest. Every misfortune she had a brush with at some time in her life was somehow attached to a man. Now she was attached to a group that included a man (diminutive in size but certainly not in spirit) who got equal voice with her. I would have to adjudge any issues or disputes that might come from this relationship. She hated men and for good reason.

Bantam was born having been dealt a rotten hand and had to live with years of taunting and embarrassments. One way or another, he did make a go of it and Gina would work out her problems also. I thought that, in the long run, they would probably be good for each other.

We now had our tickets in hand and a couple of hours to kill so we decided to get something to eat. There was a diner right inside the depot, so after telling Slocum to lie down and wait outside the door, we went in. It was a chance to breathe and relax a moment as we had done everything we could and now were at the mercy of God and the rail line.

"I'll be right back," I said.

I walked out of the café and across the waiting area to a place where they were selling candy and newspapers. I'd felt the sudden urge to read. It seemed to calm and center me. In times of uncertainty you dip back into the old ways, they say, and this is what I was used to when I went to Jenny's place in town. I paid for both a *Kansas City Star* and a *Kansas City Journal* and took them back over to the table where Bantam barked at me.

"What are the papers for?"

"To read," I said. "You ought to try it sometime. It might help pass the time on the train. Plus, being we are in a strange place, it might be nice to see how these folks think around here."

Gina sat very prim sipping some coffee.

"That's very nice," she said.

"Thank you."

I flapped my paper stiff upright so I could scan some headlines.

"I guess it's my way to see what everything is about."

Bantam snorted.

"Bunch of fiddle-faddle if you ask me."

"Well, I didn't. You asked me."

Gina put down her cup and wiped at her mouth with a napkin.

"Read it to us. I'm interested."

"Oh, that is just peachy. I might as well be in school," Bantam said.

I nodded towards the door.

"You could do with a little schooling. But you can go out and sit with Slocum if you aren't interested," I said.

"Too tired to move."

Bantam folded his arms.

"Go ahead but I won't be listening much."

I snapped the paper over in half to make it easier to read.

"There's an article here about the railroad washout."

Gina leaned in.

"Do say!"

"Well the headline says the bridge collapsed."

I continued to read the article.

"Further particulars of the wreck of the westbound passenger train on the Cherokee branch of the Memphis railroad have been obtained. Twenty persons were seriously hurt and some are feared missing and possibly dead.

"The wreck occurred at Lightning Creek, about a mile west of Monmouth, and was caused by the breaking of an axle on the rear coach after crossing an area of track that had been knocked out of alignment by a flash flood. The breakdown occurred at a point 400 feet from the bridge. The car broke loose from the train after being dragged 200 feet and rolled over into the ditch, which was filled with backwater from the creek.

"The accident caused the other cars to pitch and rock so badly that when the bridge was reached the baggage car struck the side timbers of the bridge and caused the whole structure to give way, thus precipitating all the other cars into the fast-moving stream below, which is swollen from recent rains. The front coach followed the baggage car into the stream and rested partly upon the baggage car, which kept it from sinking into the water. The smoking car turned completely over and is now lying bottom-up in the creek. The cars and bridge are completely wrecked."

"I feel sorry for those people," Bantam said. "Well, that certainly explains the delays and all else. The railroad probably has to reroute a lot of their trains."

I frowned. The idea of a rail delay could be problematic.

"I thought you weren't listening?" I shot at Bantam. "I wonder just how many choices of track you think they have? I really don't have a lot of extra time with this court date."

Bantam waved his hand around.

"In a depot this size, for a city this large, they have quite a few. They probably have a couple coming in from each direction: North, South, East, and West."

"No!"

"Yes, he's right," Gina returned. "I've ridden over multiple sets of tracks a lot of times in my travels, especially around big cities. They'll have enough different ways to get us around the accident. That's the secret of life, you know. Anytime you have trouble in one direction, you need to slip over onto another track and try a different direction."

Bantam actually laughed for the first time in a while.

"Words to live by," he said. "Enough with the paper, a hungry stomach can't listen."

"I think maybe something would taste good right now," I said. "What about you, Gina?"

I could see her completely fold right back into herself. Her voice became very quiet and she sort of stammered out her words.

"I'm not sure I could right now. I . . . I think maybe this cup of coffee would do fine for me."

And then she was gone, completely inside of her head. I wondered where she went when the wave washed over her.

★ ★ ★ ★ ★

THE TRIP

★ ★ ★ ★ ★

"Starting out ahead of the team and my men folks, when I thought I had gone beyond hearing distance, I would throw myself down on the unfriendly desert and give way like a child to sobs and tears, wishing myself back home with my friends."
—Diary of a young woman on the trail in 1860

Chapter Fourteen

After another hour, we managed to board amongst the grumbling groups of people. But, somehow, with all the pushing and shoving going on, the populace still did their level best to avoid us. It was like we were a lower class of humans whom everybody wanted to glance at from a distance. We were those people that other folks whisper to each other about or point at and tell their children to look at but not to get too close. What is so odd about two women, a midget, and a dog traveling together?

When we camped in some seats, we found the area around us was the last to fill up. I wasn't sure why. It was probably the feeling we gave off of not being one of them. We were not citified. We were rag proper, clean and fairly commonly dressed. Gina had traded in her colorful fabric palette for some fairly utilitarian clothing and Bantam wore what every other man on the train was wearing if they weren't wearing a suit. I was maybe a touch masculine in my bent but I wasn't about to lug an uncomfortable wardrobe across the country.

I sat facing toward the front of the train against the window with Slocum next to me. In the seat facing me was Gina. She would be watching the world she was leaving behind once the train started rolling. Bantam sat next to her, feet pulled up under him, hat pulled down, in a very determined posture that said he was planning on sleeping through as much of this train ride as he could and to leave him the hell alone. It took about thirty minutes for the cars to load and then we continued to sit there.

"Why don't we get moving?" I asked.

Bantam spoke from under his brim.

"Fewer tracks for the engines. We'll have to wait until we have enough room to make a run where we can reach a side by side. Until that's clear, here we sit."

Gina just sat and stared out the window. I could hear the conductor coming down the aisle punching tickets. Bantam pushed his hat back off his forehead.

"I think I'll use the quincy before this thing starts rocking back and forth. They don't build those things for folks like me so it may be a little easier without all the swaying."

He hopped down and made his way towards the end of the car. Slocum's head was down but his eyes were open watching Bantam walk away. After a mild snort he seemed to settle himself in for the long haul. Outside the sky was gray but the rain had stopped.

"I love rainbows," I said after a few minutes to make conversation with Gina. "I hope I see one."

She flicked a look at me.

"I'll be fine. You don't have to talk with me right now."

She looked back out the window.

"My thoughts are speaking and I need to let them finish."

She turned and flashed me a smile and then went back to staring out the window.

"Fine," I said. "But I just want you to know that you can talk if you want to."

"I don't want to," she said without moving her eyes. "Maybe later. Maybe never."

"Tickets!"

The conductor was at the seats just before us. Bantam scooted around him and hopped back up into his seat. He let out a deep sigh and looked at me.

"It's always a fight," he said.

"Tickets!"

The conductor stopped in front of us and took a moment to set us all in his head. He seemed to make a judgment call on the group with a quick "Hmm." He pointed at Slocum.

"Whose dog?" he questioned.

"Mine," I said.

"If the train fills up he'll have to sleep underneath you on the floor."

"Okay," I said.

He took the ticket from my hand.

"Otherwise he'll be good there."

"Okay," I said.

He studied the ticket before punching it.

"Long trip," he said. "Three trains. Your first switch is in Fort Worth."

He handed me back my ticket and reached his hand out to Gina for hers.

"You all going to the same place?"

Gina watched him punch hers.

"Yes, sir," I said.

She took her ticket but he hesitated a moment before releasing it, studying her face. Satisfied, he released it. He took Bantam's and punched it with learned efficiency, handing it back in one fluid motion. He indicated the back of the train.

"Food is that way."

He gave us a last look.

"Long trip," he repeated, then moved along. "Tickets!"

Bantam worked himself back into a sleep position again. Gina seemed to disappear back deep inside of her head. Slocum began to snore and his skin didn't even twitch when I ran my hand along his back. The last couple of days had been a long walk for him, way more than he was used to. He deserved a good rest. I figured I would take a snooze myself and leaned my head against the window. This was actually the first chance I'd had in a while to catch a breath and think about what lay ahead of me.

I jerked awake when I heard the conductor coming back through the car and decided I needed a little information. As he came by I stuck my hand up.

"Excuse me."

He stopped and looked at me.

"Yes, miss? What can I do for you?"

"When will we get moving?"

"Anytime, ma'am. We're waiting for the eastbound train to pull alongside here at the station. That will open the track up for us."

"Oh, that's good," I said. "How fast does this train move?"

He leaned down so that his talking wasn't disturbing the other passengers.

"Well that depends."

"On what?"

"How many cars we're pulling, whether or not we're on flat ground, how full the train is. There are many variables."

"Hmmm," I said. "That doesn't help much."

"Well, now, I've heard tell of the Santa Fe having a specially rigged engine and pulling only one car being able to get its speed up to one hundred miles per hour. At least that's what they say."

I put my hand on my heart.

"I don't know if I could take that or not."

"Don't worry, ma'am," he said. "That was only for a trial experiment. They were trying to set a record in some sort of speed run from Los Angeles to Chicago. More than likely on the flat prairie we may get up to a top speed of sixty or so miles per hour. But we won't be able to keep it at that. There are quite a few stops along the way."

"Goodness, I hope not," I blustered out. "How distant is this trip?"

He stood back up to let somebody easily pass behind him. He smiled at them and tipped his hat.

"You're getting off at Fort Worth, which is about 550 miles. That's a full day's ride with the stops and all. You should get there about this time tomorrow."

He patted the back of my seat and looked around at the group.

"You folks just sit back and enjoy the trip now. Like I mentioned, if you need any food, it's back that way."

"Thank you," I smiled. "You've been most kind."

"Long trip," he said again and walked on.

I leaned my head back, closed my eyes, and was just falling into a sleep in rhythm with Slocum's breathing when the east bounder came sliding in beside us. The squeal of the brakes, the vibration of the cars passing by, and the steam hissing out from under the sides of the train made a racket that even caused Bantam to grumble and shift position. At first the people inside the other train were a blur from the quick passing of the cars but they slowly came into focus as it slowed down to stop at the station. I could pick out faces and then watched as they all jerked in unison with the suddenness of the final stop.

Seeing them stand and begin pulling out bags they had brought with them had me wondering where they'd been and what their stories were. I enjoyed a bit of fancy as I imagined their backgrounds, using their clothing and groups to make up scenarios of their lives. Their train seemed about as full as ours and I could pick out the conductor helping people and showing them where to step down from the cars.

Not everybody had risen from their seats when our whistle

blew and the train gave a lurch. The engine struggled, metal wheels slipping on metal tracks, trying for momentum. We were officially off and the engineer seemed to be making no bones about wanting to catch up on a schedule he was already late on. The motion of our train made some of the folks in the other train look at us. A few smiled and some just stared. How interesting it was that life was going on everywhere.

The steam rose up from under our train and blew clouds across the window. Black smoke from the engine drifted down the side of the cars, its sooty sheets obscuring the other train for seconds at a time. As we began to slowly jerk and chug alongside the platform, we passed one car in particular. In one quick motion, I saw a woman turn her head and look at me. She was crying. Something about her was familiar looking and as the smoke cleared, my breath left my body. I was stunned. It was me!

A sane person would think I made this fancy up. But I swear on my husband's soul. I pushed my hand against my chest to keep any more of my air escaping. She (or was it I?) moved her head as if weary and, in looking back at me, mouthed something. A gasp left my mouth and I rose from my seat involuntarily. I pressed my face against the window to try and look down the side of the car as we slipped past. Then her window disappeared in the steam and I sat down hard, cryin' out like I'd seen a haint. She didn't just look like me. She was me. I was in two places at once. I shook all over and did my best to convince myself that it wasn't true. But I knew it was an omen, and I feared for the worst.

Gina, resting her head against the glass, lifted her eyes up and had turned her gaze on me. Neither of us spoke. I believe the gypsy passed something with her gaze and transferred it into me. Its calming effect settled me down for a moment. We looked hard at each other's eyes. In that instant I realized that something inside of me was struggling to emerge. I didn't know what it was but I did know that I had been the one to stifle it. It would be tamped down no longer. Gina took a long slow blink and turned her eyes back outside.

"You know," she said slowly as she watched the station pass by. "That in the cards—"

"The cards?"

"The Tarot. The seer deck."

"Seer?" I asked. "What do they see?"

"Your destiny," Gina said.

"You can do that?"

Gina seemed a might put out.

"I'm a gypsy. I don't sell shoes."

"Of course," I said.

"In the Tarot, if you pull the Hanging Man, it symbolizes death. But it is a death that is only the ending of one condition so that the birth of another nature may begin."

Did she know? Had she seen? The rest that I needed so badly now would probably not come right away.

She kept looking at me. I sat back in my seat and looked outside. As we rounded a bend in the tracks I saw the city of Kansas City disappearing off to my left. Confusion and wonderment played games with my emotions. My mood began to match the long gray day. Gina's words played in my mind.

"Of course, on the other hand, it could just mean that somebody dies," she said and closed her eyes.

Chapter Fifteen

What was Horse thinking as he stood there in a big darkened box, swaying to and fro, smelling coal smoke as the train clacked through the miles? I thought that maybe there was a way I could walk back through the train and comfort him a little. He was probably nervous, having never been on a train before. The sounds, the smells, and the surroundings were so foreign that I didn't need him to get riled up and injure himself.

I rose and stepped out into the aisle. It felt good to stretch my legs. The others on the bench slept with their heads tilted in opposite directions. Slocum hadn't shown any signs of being awake but I could tell by the twitching of his eyebrows that he was watching my every move. As I walked away, I heard his nails on the wood when he scrambled down off the bench. He was following me on my expedition. As I passed people in their places, some watched me, some slept, and some seemed to be engaged in lively discussions. Many stopped as I approached and then continued on in a more guarded and whispered manner after I passed. What was it about me? Maybe I'm just imagining my role as an outsider, somebody who doesn't belong here.

The loudness of the train on the rails increased dramatically when we passed through the doorway into the connection between cars. The walking aisle was reduced to merely a couple of metal plates, one sticking out from each side. The cars had independent movements of their own and the scissoring plates slid back and forth. One would sway left while the other would push to the right and then back again in opposite directions as we moved along the tracks. Some places off to the side of the flooring left and right were actually open air. I could see all the way down to the sunlight on the tracks and hear the clacking below in an ear-splitting cacophony. This was sort of like a fun-house obstacle course at a traveling carnival that needed to be conquered.

I reached across and grabbed the U-shaped bar that was attached to either side of the next car's doorway. Not wanting to actually step upon the shifting plates I pulled myself across with a quick step. It really was not all that difficult. It just looked that way at first appearance. I suppose it was like getting your sea legs on your first adventure shipboard. What I found to be easy after doing it once completely spooked Slocum. I turned around and looked at him frozen on the far side. He stared at me with his eyebrows cocked in question.

"Hey, buddy," I called and slapped both hands against my thighs at the same time.

He just stood there looking at me, then down at the moving floor. I opened the door behind me to show him the car where we were headed. He seemed to consider it a moment and then, trusting me, stepped forward. Just as he did, the train crossed a coupling that sounded like a gunshot ricochet in that little vestibule. Pop-Pop! Pop-Pop! He backed up whining as a passenger opened the door behind him.

"Excuse me."

The passenger stepped around Slocum, startling him, and with a dirty look pushed past me on into the next car. Back Slocum went through the open door, running all the way to our bench. I could see him turn and jump up onto the safety of the seat before the car door closed between us. It seemed as fine a place for him to be as any. At the next stop I would take him out so he could sniff around a little to get some air and maybe relieve himself. I continued on towards the baggage cars using the backs of the seats to steady myself as I walked and the train rocked.

After passing through two more cars, the last being the dining car, I reached a dead end. The boxcars only opened from their sides but not their ends. They were impossible to directly access from the train. There was no way I was going to be able to check on Horse while we were moving. With all my thinking about him I had gotten myself quite worked up about it. I supposed he was fine but the air was muggy and there were no vents that I had seen when we loaded him. Although I could see daylight between some of the wooden siding, I knew it was nowhere near airtight.

"May I help you?"

I spun around and came face to face with the conductor. His grizzled features reminded me of something out of a bad whiskey dream. I smiled sheepishly.

"I was worried about my horse and thought I would check in on him. It's apparent that I am unable to do so from here."

"You're correct, ma'am. The next stop will last almost an hour. We have to wait for a dangler to come through before we can head on. You can walk back and have them slide the door open for your reassurance if you'd like. I'm sure that would be no trouble as they may be loading or unloading more livestock into the car."

He stepped to the side and swept his arm back in the direction from which I had come.

"Now, if you would be kind enough to leave this area. Passengers are not allowed back here. We wouldn't want you to get hurt, would we?"

He smiled a crooked smile at me.

"Maybe you would like something to eat?"

"Possibly. How long until we reach the next stop?"

He pulled out his chained pocket watch and popped it open by pressing the fob.

"We'll be in Wichita in about forty-five minutes, ma'am."

"Why, thank you, sir," I said. "I think I'll go back to my seat and see if my traveling companions would like to join me in a late lunch."

Slipping his watch back into his vest pocket, he smiled at me and nodded.

"That would be fine."

I could feel his eyes on me as I headed back to my car thinking that this dead meat was awfully creepy, especially in uniform. But then it seemed like a lot of things were very strange. I still had not shaken the image of myself in the other train. But the further I was from the incident, the easier it became to convince myself that I had been mistaken.

When I arrived back at our seats, everybody was awake. Gina continued to stare out of the window and Bantam was people-watching while flipping a deck of cards around in his hands. Slocum knocked his tail against the back of the seat like a small hammer, happy to see I had returned from my difficult walk between the monster railroad cars. I thought a little change might do us all good.

"Conductor says we have an extended stop in Wichita. We'll be able to get off and walk about. I'm sure Slocum is ready for an outhouse break.

"I was thinking that, in the meantime, we could get something to eat or drink. How does that sound to everybody?"

Bantam put his cards in his top pocket and rubbed his hands together.

"I don't know about the rest of you," he said. "But I am ready for a little chuck myself. Maybe some chick biddy or chitterlings."

I laughed.

"You're awfully countrified in your food choices. I didn't look at the menu to see what they had. But it smelled mighty fine when I walked through there just now."

"Good enough for me," Bantam said and jumped down.

I asked him, "Where the hell do you pack it?"

"I just might hibernate this coming winter. You never know. A drink wouldn't hurt my constitution either if you ask me."

I turned to Gina.

"You haven't had anything but coffee back at the depot. I think it would do you good to put some food inside of you."

She gave me that smile I know that I used on the do-gooders right after James had passed.

"I'll be fine. You go on ahead. Maybe I'll get something later."

"You have got to eat something, Gina."

"Maybe later," she said and turned back to the window.

"Then is it okay if Slocum stays with you?" I asked. "I'll bring him back a little something after we've finished."

She nodded. Bantam and I headed off for an adventure in food. Not only was this my first train trip but it was practically my first taste of any restaurant prepared food outside of Jenny's place. We navigated our way between the cars and arrived at the dining wagon. It was nice, a little fancier than I believe either of us was used to. A genial Negro man in a white jacket with black pants motioned to us.

"Have a seat at any open table, folks," he said.

We found an empty table for two and sat facing each other with the windows to our side. The waiter approached us with a couple of menus under his arm and turned to Bantam.

"I'll be your waiter, folks."

He looked down at Bantam.

"Meaning no disrespect, sir, would you be more comfortable with a pillow on that seat for you to sit on?"

Bantam gave him that squinty-eyed look like maybe there was trouble brewing.

"What do you mean," he sort of snarled out.

Without missing a beat, the waiter continued.

"Only that some of the chairs, such as the one you are currently sitting in, are not as new or nice as they could be. The padding has been squashed, flattened over time by some mighty large behinds. A nice seat pillow would make the experience much more comfortable."

The waiter held both his stare and his smile while engaging him. I could see Bantam was thinking about it. Then he smiled.

"Why, thank you. That would be very nice."

"Not a problem," the waiter said. "I'll return in just a moment with two glasses of water with ice cubes and your cushion."

Ice cubes, I thought. How fancy! The food came and went and the scenery flew past. The timing for us was perfect as we were wiping our faces when the train began a noticeable slowing and the conductor walked through announcing our impending stop at Wichita. He smiled at us and it gave me a chill. We paid and I took a small bag of scraps and meat that the waiter had been kind enough to put together for me to give to Slocum. He would be able to go outside and stretch, eat, and do his business all in one collective visit. Bantam figured he would mosey around the stores near the depot and stretch a little also. I knew he meant he was going to the saloon. I was hoping I could get Gina out of her mood. I knew how a tragedy could pull you into a rabbit hole that was difficult to climb out of.

Chapter Sixteen

I walked back to our seats to retrieve Slocum. What was it with this dog? It's like he had this extra sense telling him that whatever you were carrying was food meant for him. He jumped down from the seat ready to follow me into Hell if need be to get at whatever morsel I was holding. But how did he know it wasn't something for me that I was planning on eating later?

Gina watched him as he moved around me in circles. I bent down a little so I could look out the window at the depot and the few shops in view. I saw Bantam as he rounded the corner and walked down the main street.

"We're gonna be here a while," I said to Gina. "Might feel good to get out and stretch your legs a little like Bantam. Grab a taste of fresh air."

She turned to watch Bantam.

"Or stretch your little legs depending upon who you are."

"Bantam's all right if you give him a chance," I said. "Come and walk with me."

She gave me that fake smile thing.

"I'm fine. Thanks."

"Well, I'm taking Slocum out for a break and checking on Horse. You're welcome to join me."

"Thank you," she said and made no effort to move.

"I may even follow Bantam's lead and poke around the town a bit to see what they have to offer."

She smiled again.

"Great."

"Okay, then. We're off," I said awkwardly.

"Okay," she said making no attempt to imply that she was in the least bit interested.

I looked down at Slocum.

"Come on, boy."

With his tail wagging like a flag, Slocum followed me down the aisle. There was a moment of hesitation near the coupling, but he followed me out and onto the platform. We crossed the wooden dock and I sat down on a bench that was against the front of the station house. I tore open the bag and laid it on the ground. I don't believe Slocum tasted anything or even chewed, but that food was gone in no time. I stood up and wiped my hands on the bag. I could see the train windows where we'd been sitting. Gina was upright in the bench with her head leaned back. Her eyes were closed. I looked back down and Slocum was staring at me.

"All right," I said. "Let's find you some water and check on Horse."

It was further down the line to the stock car with Horse in it. By the time I arrived, both of us were thirsty. The side of the car was open and a couple of men were leading some stock ponies down the ramp to the platform. I approached the fella nearest me. He had been with the train in Kansas City so I figured he would probably recognize me.

"Mind if I step in and check on my horse?"

"Be my guest," he said tugging on one of the pony's cheek pieces urging him to move. "There's a bucket inside the door and a pump right over there on the edge of the platform."

"Much obliged," I said and stepped into the car.

Horse had turned, looking at me from hearing the sound of my voice. I grabbed the bucket from next to the wall and carried it back to the pump. Setting it beneath the curved iron spout, I began working the handle. It must have looked like it was going to take me some time, because Slocum dropped his butt onto the platform so he could watch from a more comfortable position. I was beginning to work up a little sweat when I heard a gurgle from deep inside the piping and felt a vibration in the metal handle. A couple more good full pumps and the water began to gush into the bucket.

Evidently that was Slocum's cue. He rose up and wandered over to begin drinking the water from the bucket as it was filling up. The water that hit the side of his snout did not deter him. That pink tongue worked for a full five minutes. I quit pumping and cupped my hands under the spout to fill them up. Then I splashed the cool liquid on my face. If it tasted to Slocum anything like it felt to me, he had been getting a real delight. A couple of more pumps as I wanted to make sure I had a full bucket. Horse began nickering when he smelled the water. He seemed to be as thirsty as Slocum had been. It required one more trip with a full pail before he was satisfied. I made a third trip for Bantam's mount who'd begun to fidget after smelling water buckets.

I patted him down to see if he was overheated. He didn't feel sweaty. His favorite spot at the base of his jaw was crying out for a scratching so I had to oblige. Then I whispered in his ear that I had to go. He returned a snort and moved his head up and down.

"Atta, boy," I said and Slocum and I walked down the ramp out of the car.

The pony boys were just finishing tying together their newly unloaded horses. I noticed a bucket of oats sitting to the side.

"Those yours?" I asked them.

"Yes, ma'am, but we're finished with them. You are welcome to anything left for your own mount. Bucket belongs to the railroad. You can leave it in the car for them."

"Much obliged," I said.

I knew oats were a little too rich for Horse as a regular feed but this was a special occasion. I was hoping they would serve to keep him calm. All it took was one sniff. Horse dug into them as soon as I had set the bucket in front of him. Another pat from me, which he ignored, and I was back outside. As I headed back towards the passenger cars, I passed the creepy conductor.

"About twenty more minutes before we have to board, miss."

He tipped his hat and continued on in the opposite direction. I decided to go looking for Bantam to see what he was up to and let him know just how much time he had left. He wouldn't be too hard to find. I didn't figure he'd had a particular destination in mind since he didn't know his way around Wichita, just the closest saloon to the train. I could see the top of Gina's head leaning against the glass as I passed our passenger car. It was eating at me but there was nothing I could do about it.

Slocum walked right alongside me as we turned the corner and made our way down the wooden sidewalks of Wichita. I would have given cows to feed that Bantam was in the local skink getting liquored up and trying to make some sort of a deal.

Chapter Seventeen

The sound of an insanely out-of-tune piano rattled from behind some swinging doors and into the street as I approached the first saloon. Since I wasn't a hall girl or an entertainer, I really wasn't sure how to do this. The saloon isn't the place for a woman. I stopped outside the doors and looked in over the top edge to see if I could see Bantam. As short as he was, he would not be easy to spot. I only had a partial view of the room from outside. The smell of old wood, smoke, and spilt hooch wafted out from the place. It teared up my eyes for a second.

Two men making their way inside pushed past us, surprising Slocum. He growled at them and one fella turned and said, "Hey!" The back swing of the door nearly knocked me down so we stepped to the side to prevent a reoccurrence. I bent down and rubbed Slocum's head.

"It's all right, guy," I said. "Don't worry about it."

I wasn't ready to venture inside just yet. I could only savvy up so much courage per day and this trip had pretty well put me at my maximum usage. I changed my game plan and decided to start at the saloon farthest from the station and work my way back towards the train. I figured that if I didn't find him, he might be back on the train by the time I returned. We made our way down the main stretch of street to the end of the three blocks and then turned around. I didn't figure that Bantam would have ventured beyond the station part of town. He wouldn't walk past that much drink without stopping.

Along with the first saloon I had looked in, there were three others in this stretch, plus a sundries store, a small café, and a couple of boarding houses. If one was caught here overnight for any reason, they would be able to eat and sleep until they could move on towards their destination. The first saloon pretty much looked like the one up the street but seemed a little calmer. There was a crowd of cowboys inside. I looked at them and them at me. Slocum watched them from under the doors. I could hear him sniffing the air. The bartender shouted out, "No dogs or women in here!" We moved on down the street.

They may have taken me for some girl who had wandered down from the local vaulting house or somebody off the train who was wamble-cropped and begging for money. It didn't matter what they thought, Bantam wasn't there and I needed to move on towards the train. I was sidetracked along the wooden sidewalk for a moment by the smell of peanuts as I passed the doorway of the General Store. I stepped inside and bought a small bag and a large dill pickle. I'd had them both before but not nearly enough times. I bit off a chunk of the pickle and tossed it to Slocum. Pretty much if I'll eat it and he can fit it into his mouth, he'll eat it also.

Of course, I hit the jackpot at the next saloon, being as my hands were full of food stuffs. I could hear Bantam's voice ringing from inside above the sound of a couple of other angry male voices. From what I was able to decipher as they screamed over each other, Bantam thought their liquor was of an inferior quality. The house or the customers didn't seem to agree. I had a deep feeling it wasn't going to be settled by yelling and that Bantam's best shot was to get the hell out of there before they realized he was all mouth.

"Tastes like vomit," Bantam declared. "Tastes like vomit and now somebody is just airing the paunch back into the bottles and you addle-headed back-door trots are drinking it a second time around!"

I heard a deeper voice say something, not very nice by the tone, and then a general shuffling of chairs scooting on a wooden floor. Evidently Bantam wasn't moving.

"What are you gonna do, stick me with your apple peeler?" he said.

Then he laughed his high-pitched giggle. I knew that had to make their jaws tight. There was a metallic clack like the barrels of a shotgun dropping down into place.

"Now that's different," Bantam said. "Don't get too riled up, fellas, as I'm just speaking my opinion."

"Not sure we asked for one," the deep voice said.

I figured I needed to act now if he was ever going to get back on the train alive. I stepped inside with my half pickle, as if I belonged there, and took a quick survey of the scene. Immediately to my left was a table of chuck-a-luck players who didn't seem to be letting the circus at the bar interrupt their cards. A richly grained mahogany bar with a highly polished brass foot rail was directly in front of me. A considerable ol' fella with a mustache the size of an oxen yoke was on the left side holding, what I took to be, a rather small knife for his size. The barkeep was dead center of the bar, holding that double-barrel pointed directly at Bantam, who had prudently decided to defend himself with one of the mustache towels from the bar. He had rolled it up tight, holding it taut, with two hands as if he was going to snap somebody to death with it.

"Stay back or I will take somebody's eye out with one flick of this," he was saying as I stood there leaking peanut shells and pickle juice onto the floor. The bartender motioned with the muzzle of the shotgun.

"Your opinion ain't welcome here, Button. Our liquor is fine as gravy and we don't welcome some cow's udder coming in here and disparaging our commodities."

The guy with the toothpick took a step forward. He waved it as menacingly as possible.

"You got that right," he said. "I'm gonna engrave a little remembrance of me so you'll never forget who bested you."

The bartender turned toward him without realizing his gun turned with him when he did.

"Gordy, will you shut up! You've been drinking all day and you're full as a tick," he said. "Just put that pimp sticker away and let me handle this."

Gordy's head kind of dropped defeated as the bartender had taken some of the steam out of him.

"I was just trying to help, Ray." He motioned toward Bantam. "That little horse turd spit his drink on me first."

Bantam gave him a threatening towel gesture and I couldn't tell if the growl had come from him or Slocum.

"Now that was by mistake," Bantam said. "It came out of my mouth all a sudden. I'd just never tasted anything that poorly before in my life. It kinda took me by surprise is all."

Ray the bartender swiveled the gun back at Bantam.

"Now there you go insulting my goods again."

Bantam seemed to be raising his mustache towel up like a white flag of surrender. I took another step inside and for the first time they noticed me. The men froze like statues when they saw me standing there with a pickle in my hand. I fanned myself with my peanut bag and gave another piece of pickle to Slocum. I did my best impression of flirting with my eyelashes fluttering although it was a tough sell with my hands full like they were. I felt a little dumb in the attempt but it must have worked since none of them moved.

"Bartender?"

I gave him my best drippy look and even touched my cheek with my index finger. I saw that pose once in a magazine advertisement and figured it must be beguiling. He turned the gun up and brought it down beside him.

"Yes, ma'am?"

"I hate to interrupt your talk but you wouldn't happen to have any cold cactus wine, would you? I asked somebody at the station and they said you had the best in town."

Bantam was at least smart enough to take his cue and disappear around behind me and on out to the street while the frozen figures gawked. Ray fumbled for a few words but managed to spit it out.

"I'm sorry, ma'am, but we're not allowed to serve ladies or," he nodded down at Slocum, "curs."

"Oh, my," I said. "I guess I'll have to survive upon whatever the railway line can provide. Please excuse me."

I started to leave and then, popping the balance of the pickle in my mouth, turned back.

"Carry on, gentlemen."

I walked out with Slocum at my heels. I was nearly ten steps outside the door before I heard the first person ask where the runt had gotten to. Bantam had ducked into an alley. He stuck his head out around a corner and beckoned me.

"I didn't need your help, Mother."

I was thinking about the boys back in the saloon.

"Just keep walking," I said.

He stood still, looking at me with a why-did-you-show-up look on his face and his hands on his hips.

"I could have handled it myself. I am not," he spit this last word, "incapable."

By this time, I had almost reached him.

"What were you going to do with the towels, dry the angry lather off of them?"

I spun him around and pushed him towards the train.

"Start walking!"

Behind me I heard the swinging doors slap open and people

run out on to the wood. Bantam's eyes grew large. He began hightailing it for the train as fast as his legs could move. It wouldn't be fast enough. I grabbed one arm and began running with him, hoping my added size would help power both of us. It sped him up in kind of a sideways, scampering, dragging thingy but it slowed me down. The train whistle blew, meaning time was retreating. Little did the engineer realize how short time actually was. The sound of scuttling behind us was mixed with the various voices of "Let's git 'em," "There they are," and "They will get theirs."

"Faster, Bantam. This one may be for both of our lives."

He looked up at me with sweat pouring down his face as we dragged and ran for the safety of the train.

"I would need four legs or wings to travel any faster."

I looked back over my shoulder and saw that Gordy had pulled his knife out again. He was joined in his pursuit by four others who seemed to slow down enough so that the big guy was the front runner. Scared or not, any kind of a mob is dangerous. Get a group of angry people together and logical thinking goes the way of manners in a pack of drunks. The distance between us and the train seemed much greater than the distance back to the drunken hoard. We wouldn't make it and I feared for the worst. I swore I could smell their whiskey breath.

Bantam had come to his senses and kept shouting, "I'm sorry. I'm sorry. I'm sorry."

At the moment that I was sure they were upon us I heard a loud scream and the sound of a large mass dropping on the wooden sidewalk. Not wanting to slow down to investigate, we continued to scramble like our asses were on fire. The voices behind us were raised in shouting but it was a different kind of shouting. It was not until we got to the end of the street, with the screaming a half a block behind us, that we dared stop and turn around.

Gordy was down on the wood with Slocum's head buried between his legs. I could hear Slocum snarling and pulling while screaming Gordy sounded like a little girl having her pigtails yanked. The other men, fearing that Slocum might be rabid and would take after them, danced around Gordy like a hoedown.

"Grab my knife," he screamed. "Kick the damn dog!"

I could see the knife lying a dozen feet or so away in the street. One of the men understood what Gordy was saying. He ran over to pick it up. I whistled for Slocum and he detached himself immediately and ran up to us. Instead of following in hot pursuit, Gordy curled into a fetal position while making a muffled whimpering sound.

Bantam, back to his old self, laughed as if it had all been a joke.

"Now that is what I call a crotchety old fool."

"You know," I leaned down, "you could have ended up outin' both of us on that one."

Bantam looked at me all proud. He was still laughing at his own word joke.

"If there's one thing I know about, it's hooch. If you wouldn't drink it yerself, you shouldn't serve it to anybody else. If they think that tarantula juice they were pouring was any good they got a slate loose."

The train whistle sounded again and we hurried across the platform to board.

"Was it really that important to make such a commotion about it?"

"Pride of ownership," he said. "I know what I am talking about."

"What about the bartender's pride of ownership?" I asked. "He has feelings too. After all, it's his establishment."

Bantam hauled himself up on the railcar steps.

"It's all piddle if you ask me. He wouldn't have known a good drink if I had forced it down his throat."

And Bantam kept right on talking about the finer merits of liquor all the way to our seats. That was the second time I had almost died from a combination of Bantam and alcohol.

Chapter Eighteen

Gina gave Bantam the evil eye as he walked up to our seats still flapping his gums about the terrible drinks that crooked bartender had been trying to foist on him. He was furious but seemed to have forgotten the part of the story where he was lucky enough to still be in one piece.

"I guess that temper of yours is another place you got that name from," Gina said. "Cock-a-doodle-do."

"Don't know what you are talking about," he snorted. "I was just standing up for my rights. I should be assured of having a glass of something palatable. Not piss water."

He sat with his arms crossed, stewing in his own hot oil. About that time the train let out another whistle and gave a jerk. We were back on the move. I felt a sense of relief as the wheels spun, grabbed hold, spun again, and started us on our way. Slocum curled up best he could on the bench, ready to ride it out until his next break. Gina smiled at him.

"Glad to see you are back communicating with the rest of us. You feel a bit better?" I asked.

Her body moved from side to side with the motion of the train.

"The farther I get away from there, the better I feel."

She gave Bantam a quick look.

"I still don't care for men, though," she said. "Any men."

He ignored her and mumbled something about all that time spent and still not a decent drink to be had. I turned and looked out the window, watching the flat Kansas countryside roll past.

"I wonder where the next stop is."

"Conductor said it was a water stop about three hours down the track along the North Canadian River," Gina said. "I think he called it Oklahoma station. Fairly new stop from what I could get out of him."

"Hmmm," I said, not discouraging conversation but letting her take it at her own pace. "Are you feeling hungry yet?"

"Don't really know, but a drink wouldn't hurt."

Bantam turned his head up and looked at her to see if she was teasing or for real. She nodded at him.

"Yes, I mean it," she said.

Bantam smiled at her.

"I happen to know the way to the dining car as I have personally been there."

Suddenly wide awake, he jumped down from the seat.

"Follow me."

Gina stood up and pushed past him.

"I'll follow no man," she said and started towards the rear of the train. "And do not think for a moment that you can ply me with liquor and then make a pass at me."

Bantam was right behind her.

"Make a pass at you? I don't have enough money to get that drunk. Although I do like a woman with spirit."

"Oh, God, don't you even try to touch me you urchin!"

Gina was passing from our car into the next and I could still hear her chattering at Bantam. People turned their heads and watched them as they walked away arguing.

"You know you would, little man. It's in your nature. It's in all men's nature to try and take advantage of helpless women."

"Helpless!" Bantam shouted at her. "You're far from helpless."

Then, with the shutting of the railcar door, they were gone.

Goodbye you two, I thought. *Slocum and I will just wait here.* Actually, I knew this was the best thing that she could be doing. Their jousting would help her escape if just for a short time. For now, I was content to lean my head against the window and take a nap. I reached over and gave Slocum a scratching behind his ears. He moaned deep in his throat and dropped his head down on his paws. I think we were both ready for a little sleep.

I awoke to the light of the moon shining on my face like a lantern. The countryside was glowing with a silvery outline. Slocum's head was resting firmly in my lap. My two compatriots were missing. I had no idea what time it was. I considered getting up and looking for them. But how far could they have gotten? I figured I would try to get back to sleep. In my fog, I thought that perhaps I was dreaming anyway.

Through half-opened eyes I watched the shadowy landscape float past the window. The beauty of the moon edged the trees and ridges with white while extending the shadows, stretching them into long black pools that probably hid all manner of things. I thought I could see the moonlight dancing off of ripples of water occasionally peeking and reflecting the ashen light between the dark scenery in the distance. The entire scene made me think of a black-and-white piece painting. It was beautiful yet stark in its edging and collected puddles of darkness.

Then it dawned on me. That must be the North Canadian River coming up to meet the tracks at the Oklahoma station where we were going to stop for water. I wondered if a jerkwater town had built up around it. Any kind of timely layover and I was sure that Bantam would be off the train and down the street to the nearest saloon. Well, I was not going to fetch him this time. He was grown up and could figure this stuff out all by himself. As for me, I closed my eyes as the train began to slow and thought about keeping them shut all the way to Guthrie, just outside of the Cherokee Outlet.

I woke slowly from a dreamless nap. The rhythm of the train and its musical clacking had wormed its way into my body and enveloped me much the way being immersed in warm water extends the boundaries of your body. I shifted my head against the glass and cracked open one eye to look at the darkness outside of the window. In the reflection of the car interior I could see Gina's face. She was staring straight outside but not seeing anything. Her cheeks were wet with tears. I started to speak a couple of times but didn't know where to start.

"I think it was the drinking," she said without turning. "When I stopped, I started feeling all folded up inside like a bucking bronc."

There was a long pause as we both watched the mystical shapes travel past the windows. I could see the squares of light from the train cars sliding along the ground outside. They would catch a tree or a bush, light it up, and then plunge it back into dark as we clattered along. The whistle went off with a double blast. I jerked. It felt close, next to my head, not that long mournful sound I've heard at night in the distance. Gina never moved.

"I thought having a drink or two might make me forget."

She turned and looked at me. I smiled in recognition of my own failings.

"It did too, for a while. But it all comes back when you've got nobody short and stupid to distract you. Your thoughts dig in to what is really disturbing your soul. Mine is mightily disturbed."

"I know it's hard, Gina," I said.

"Do you? Has it ever happened to you?"

Her anger was trying to dump itself out on me.

"No, but I can imagine."

She made a guttural sound in her throat and turned away with disgust. We sat silent for another while. Bantam was asleep in his seat and Slocum was breathing heavy next to me. I needed to let her know that she was not alone.

"Gina."

She looked at me.

"You can't stop trouble from visiting. Trouble is going to happen to all of us one way or another. The important one in my life was losing James."

She was still with me so I kept talking.

"You can't stop it from visiting you in life. But you don't have to offer trouble a chair to sit down and stay."

She sniffed and wiped at her cheeks with her fingers.

"Is that what I'm doing? Inviting it in to stay a spell?"

"Maybe."

"Actually," she said, "seems more to me like it doesn't want to leave. I'm not sure I know how to kick it out. I think I would if I could. Damn near anything is better than this pain inside of me."

I reached across and picked up her hand from her lap.

"You'll get it. Honestly, you will and we will be right here to help. We do care about you. I care about you."

She squeezed my hand and smiled.

"I told you that men were no damn good," she said. "You know I would just like a fair shake from one sometime. But the way I see it, most of them are just a bunch of flannel-mouthed liars, thieves, and women beaters. Even that short one there."

She cocked her head at Bantam.

"Tried to ply me with liquor, you know."

"I'm sure he did, a fine-looking woman like you."

I was smiling now, encouraging her, and agreeing with her in my posture.

"And the longer you stay upset with them," I said, "then the longer they have control of your soul. It's time to fish or cut bait, honey."

I let go of her hand and leaned back in my seat. She watched me, watched my eyes, seeing if I meant what I said. At first there was just an upward shrug of her shoulders. Unexpectedly that deep husky laugh came rolling out of her belly like an earthquake. A combination of laughing and crying shook her body.

"Fish or cut bait?"

She shook her head no but could not stop sputtering. She was rushing like the river. By the time the whistle blew again, I knew that Gina was on her way back.

She rested her head against the window and got into a comfy position to sleep. I turned toward the interior of the car and caught Bantam staring at me through slitted eyes. He watched me a moment and then smiled. I wondered how much of the conversation he had heard. Then he pulled his hat brim down, nestled himself into the corner of the seat, and went back to sleep. Before my dozing off, I remembered thinking that this was not the trip I had envisioned when I was sitting back on the hill speaking with James.

Chapter Nineteen

When we arrived in Guthrie, it was dark as pitch. But the lateness of the hour seemed to have done nothing to quell the enthusiasm of the rowdy townsfolk. People were whooping and hollering and riding fast in the streets. Music or yelling seemed to be pouring out of every doorway in town. We had to disembark here and switch to another rail line. Our next train didn't leave until midmorning. It was a small connector that just ran from here to Dallas where we'd pick up another major railroad.

Our bags in hand, and with Slocum by my side, the three of us stepped out into the human stew before us. We walked back to the stock cars for our mounts. I hadn't seen Horse since that last stop and the other one had not been checked on at all. I knew that getting them out of those cars would be nothing but good for them. I wanted to do that as soon as possible. I prepared for any skittishness that might append their disembarkment.

Bantam stopped and surveyed the goings-on of our surroundings. He shook his head at the partying of the town.

"They are havin' themselves one hog-killin' time," he exclaimed. "It looks like there must be some kind of party going on."

The piano music from a nearby saloon rattled out into the street. It obviously had not been tuned in a long time but from the sound of the voices, nobody seemed to care. Bantam smiled his three-by-nine smile. It was almost as if I could hear him salivating for his next glass of hooch. I could have predicted his conversation.

"Since we have to be here all night, I may have to figure out what all that shouting is about."

"First we get your horses and find ourselves some rooms," Gina said. "I plan on sleeping, but you can carry on all you want. I think I had enough to drink on the way here."

I knew he was going to get into some kind of trouble.

"Let's make sure we know what time the other train leaves in the morning and get back here at least an hour early so we can load the animals."

He tipped his hat at me.

"Yes, ma'am. Don't you worry, I will be there teetotal."

I looked up at the car we were in front of.

"This is it. Maybe we can line up a mount for you too, Gina."

The door was just being slid open by a station boy. He stopped for a moment when he saw us in front of him. He jerked his thumb at the interior of the car.

"The three in there yours?"

"Two of them," I said. "And I think they'll be mighty happy to get out of there."

We stepped up to the car and waited. There was no door ramp so the only way in was us having to climb up. He noticed our dilemma, especially for Bantam.

"Sorry folks," he said. "The station is so new we haven't even built a ramp yet."

Bantam was looking around.

"It does seem a little sparse. You able to step down and give me a lift up or is there something I can climb up on?"

The kid pointed behind us.

"There's that rolling freight cart you can push over here and use it to step up with," he said.

Gina stood looking at him like she might want to punch him out.

"*We* can do that?"

It took him a second to catch on. He jumped down and ran over to it.

"No, ma'am," he said. "Here let me fetch it for you."

He rolled it over to the entrance and slid it alongside the opening in the train car. Gina shot me a wink on the side. He reached down and set a brake on it.

"There. That'll keep it from rolling out from under you."

I stepped up and into the car.

"That wasn't too bad."

I stuck my hand out to help Bantam. He gave a quick look at the celebrating town and waved me off.

"You go ahead, Mrs. Thomas. I'll be right behind you."

Horse nickered when he saw me. I walked over and scratched his ear while talking to him. Bantam put a knee up and pulled himself onto the cart. He turned and looked at the kid.

"Say, what is this entire fandango about? The town seems a little fun happy."

"Well, it hasn't been too long since the land run and we're right here on the edge of the Cherokee Outlet. All around us is land that was given free and clear if you homesteaded it."

Bantam finished pulling himself into the car.

"These don't much look like homesteaders to me."

"No, sir," the kid said. "They ain't. They are what follow."

Bantam nodded his head as he watched the town. A couple of shots rang out and somebody yelled. People ran around for a moment and then it all settled back down into a dull roar.

The kid didn't react to the sound.

"That kind of thing goes on a few times a day," he said. "Nobody pays much attention to it until people start crying."

"I believe you may have a couple of men for breakfast come

daylight with all this shooting and such," Bantam said.

"Not far-fetched," the kid said. "It wouldn't be the first time we've woken up to bodies in the street."

"No, I suppose not," Bantam said and turned to untie his horse.

I had Horse by the lead and walked him over to the opening of the car. I stepped down first onto the cart and then the ground. Horse seemed a bit cautious about the exit strategy. I spoke gently to him. He trusted me. We had not failed each other yet. After he stepped down, I gave him another good scratching behind the ear.

Bantam took a different tact. After saddling his kneeling mount, he climbed on and rode his horse down while it was being led by the kid. I guess it was easier than trying to climb back down. Slocum watched all of this from the side with Gina. I threw my saddle and gear up on Horse's back but continued to walk him. I turned back to the kid.

"Where are we going?"

He pointed down the street.

"About a block down on the left is the Smith's place. Then two more buildings past the livery to the hotel."

"It's late," I asked. "Will somebody be awake?"

"Someone is always there," he said.

"Do you know where we might purchase a third horse?" I asked.

"Same place," he smiled. "There is usually extras for sale."

Gina said, "Thank you," and we headed away.

"Oh," the kid had more to say. "Be careful."

Bantam stopped. "Why's that?"

The kid was walking back to shut the stock car door.

"Building in between the stable and the guesthouse is the burg's largest saloon," he said.

"How convenient," Bantam smiled and rubbed his hands together.

Gina snorted like she knew exactly where that news was going to lead us.

"What time does the morning train pull out for Dallas?"

"Eleven-fifteen twice a week," kid said. "Tomorrow's it or you wait three more days."

I jerked Horse a little to keep him facing towards the train while I talked.

"How early can we load up the stock car?"

"Really anytime from about eight o'clock. The train will pull in early. I'm sure you will hear it from your rooms."

I tipped my hat brim.

"Much obliged," I said and followed the others as they walked down the street.

Gina looked at Bantam as we walked toward the stables.

"You know, you keep popping your mouth off in some of these friendly neighborhood saloons and you just might be that man we find lying in the street come morning."

"And what would you know about it," he shot back at her. "I saw the way you couldn't hold your liquor on the train last night. I can hold mine and I'm half your size for crissake!"

"A quarter of my size, if you wanted to be honest about it. And I was a bereft soul when I was drinking the other night," she said.

Bantam laughed and threw one hand up in front of his face. He turned his horse away from her.

"Don't you be giving me that evil eye! You and all your damn mumbo jumbo. Bereft, my ass." He laughed. "Well, now, you're no longer bereft, you are just hungover."

He kicked his horse and ran in front of us. Oh, god, I thought, here we go again. I was right too. The bickering and prodding continued all the way to the stables. I felt like a mother hen with two fighting chickens. They were wearing me out with their bickering. All I was thinking of was a bed with clean fresh sheets on it and my head resting in the hollow of a feather pillow. The stable was open, as was everything else in this town, it seemed, despite the lateness of the hour. The stablemen looked us over as we walked in and kind of snickered. Gina, already mad at Bantam, took offense.

"What are you grinnin' at?" she asked him.

She stared him straight.

"I've seen some unique groups come into town since all this land grabbing started but I have never seen a group quite like you people."

Bantam had pulled up and was ready to get his two bits into this conversation. He jumped down from his mount. Horse and I joined them just to serve as some sort of middle ground and barrier in this hole the stable man was digging for himself.

"A couple of women, a dog, and a midget. You don't look any like settlers or homesteaders," he said and gave a glance over to me. "Don't look like gamblers or people who would like to get unshucked for a living. I'm not sure what you are. I must be slipping. I can usually paste folks on the first guess."

Gina kept staring at him like she had him in her rifle sights. I interrupted the moment with some common sense.

"We'll be by about eight o'clock to pick up the horses. Could you make sure they are fed good because I'm not too positive they eat much while traveling. I'd like them to be fortified for the next leg of the trip. Also, do you have any for sale?"

"Yes, ma'am, I've got those two in the corner," he said.

He stepped up and took the reins. Then he walked over and grabbed them from the other horse.

"What do you want for that roan?" Gina asked.

The stableman wrapped the two horses' reins he was holding to the rings on the wall.

"Let me think. What do I have into that one?"

He turned back to Gina and scrunched up his face as if he was trying to think of a good deal.

"Two hundred," he said.

"I'll give you one hundred."

"Split the difference and it's yourn," he said.

Gina smiled.

"Deal, one fifty."

Bantam watched in awe as she peeled off some bills. She looked at him and then stuck the small purse back between her breasts.

"Is that me or the money you're looking at?" she said. "It better be the money."

The livery man took the roan's reins and started walking to a stall.

"What's the name?" he asked back over his shoulder.

"Thomas," I said after him.

He turned and looked at me with a cocked eyebrow.

"That's the last name," I said. "We'll be staying at the boarding house just up there if they've a room."

He opened one stall gate and led Horse in. He picked up a feed bucket and locked the stall door behind him.

"There's room," he said.

He led the other horses to the next pen and locked them in.

"How do you know?"

He gestured towards a large pen with about five horses in it.

"Those fellas came in this week. Owners went down to Lora Lee's and never came back. Not a lot of customers just want a room to sleep, not in this town. Poker, land money, carpetbagging, sometimes they just disappear."

He walked the buckets over to the grain bin.

"Is Lora Lee the owner of the guesthouse?"

"Nope," he said, setting them down and scooping in some

grain. "She owns the dance hall in between it and us. Agatha runs the guesthouse. Sisters. Came here together. Agatha is very churchy. Laura Lee is . . . not so much."

He stopped and looked up at us.

"I'll see you in the morning," he said.

"You'll be here?" I asked. "What do you do, live here?"

He looked up at me and then went back to scooping more grain.

"I will see you in the morning," he said.

Sharing a look between us, we decided to leave well enough alone and headed off towards the boarding house. As we came upon the dance hall, the music that shouted from the interior was more raucous than that from any of the town outside. The doors were open wide and pinned back against the interior walls. We stood in the opening. I was amazed at all we were seeing. Women in large skirts, with variously bright-colored undergarments visibly displayed, danced upon some of the table tops in their kid boots to a three-piece grouping of piano, banjo, and drums. The trio created some of the loudest music I've ever heard. Many of the girls had dyed their hair vibrant colors and wore face paint to accentuate their lips and eyes. Bright rosy circled cheeks gave them a clownish appearance. The men in attendance seemed to be totally entranced with them, cheering and having a good time while the women pranced upon the stage and tables. They would shout at these painted ladies and the gals would playfully kick back at them and tease. This would cause another round of drunken laughter and spilled beer.

I'm no prude but I felt some apprehension for these women, with their low-cut bodices, that their bosoms would be set dancing at any moment during their performance. I stated as much to Gina. She laughed at my remark.

"That's what all these boys are hoping for," she said. "Don't worry. It ain't gonna happen. They are secured in there tighter than a sausage casing."

"Are these ladies soiled doves?"

"Soiled doves? Where the hell did you ever hear that, in church?" She laughed. "These are not sporting girls. They are working women in the truest sense of the word. Their job is to get the men to stay here as long as possible and spend and drink as much as they can. The *Nymphs du Prairie,* of which you speak, would be located in a different part of town. This, despite how it may look to you, is an upscale classy establishment. It is a place of shows and entertainment, not the type of joint where the ladies of the line ply their trade."

"Land sake! I've never even seen a building this colorful just for fun."

"Me neither," said Bantam and he headed past us towards the bar. "This is the largest dance garden I have ever had the pleasure of entering."

Gina grabbed his collar and pulled him back.

"Not yet, whelp. We have got to check in at the guesthouse and find our rooms before you start traipsing around with the nightlife."

He pushed her arm aside.

"You have your priorities and I have mine."

He looked back inside and rubbed his hands together.

"The entertainment is calling me and I do not want to disappoint these fine ladies."

He had a toothy grin on his face. Gina gave me a look. We each grabbed an arm, spun him about, and rode him out the door. He started squirming up a storm trying to escape us.

"Let me the hell go. I don't wanna miss anything."

Gina was almost lifting her side of him off the ground.

"Believe me; they will still be here when you come back."

"What do I need to go for? Just check me into a room."

"We need you to see the room," Gina said, straining to keep

a grip on him.

"Why?"

"So you'll know where to crawl to when you run out of money," I said. "Also, I want you to give me most of your cash. I don't trust you and I'm not covering for you from here on out."

He quit struggling for a moment and looked us both over. He could tell we were serious. Then he gave one last pitifully hopeful glance back at Lora Lee's.

"Dammit."

He began strutting on his own to the guesthouse, mumbling to himself as we followed close behind.

Chapter Twenty

The check-in was fairly easy but not quite as simple as the stableman had made it seem. Luckily, there were two rooms left open by the time we arrived so Gina and I bunked together while Bantam took the other room. That way, at least, we felt we could sleep peacefully without being awakened in the middle of the night by a little drunk staggering blindly into our room spewing profanities and who knows what else. If he didn't make it through his door and slept on the floor outside of his room, it wasn't our concern. We'd done all we could to make sure he knew where he was sleeping.

After we had settled ourselves into our room and did a quick washup we stepped out into the hallway. Bantam was already headed for town. I yelled at him.

"Hey, where are you going?"

He shot me a look over his shoulder and kept walking.

"Honestly, you have to ask?"

"Gina and I are going to get something to eat. We thought you might want to go with us."

"I think they have peanuts where I'm headed," he said and rounded the corner out of sight. By the time we got to the end of the hall he was outside and gone.

"Peanuts, huh? Maybe for dessert," Gina laughed. "I want some real food first."

We stepped out into the street to meet the late-night revelers. We decided to head in the opposite direction from Lora Lee's for more reasons than one. There seemed to be less life in that direction although we weren't aware that we were headed into the doggery part of town. The walking felt good and we really wanted to put on a feed after just having train food. Meat was sounding awfully good to us right about now. The only thing Gina didn't want was beans. Life on the road had sort of done her up on beans.

"If I have one more whistleberry," she said, "I believe I will explode."

That started us to laughing and soon we were hanging on each other, exhausting ourselves by our juvenile humor. Road weary and a little goofy-minded from hunger, we enjoyed the night air and each other's company immensely. Things being open all night, we were able to spot a lady-friendly-looking establishment. We took our laughing bender inside and sat down. The waitress approached and we ordered two beers immediately, which I'm sure, raised a few eyebrows.

"I hope your dough-belly can cook," Gina said to the waitress.

The girl remained stiff as if Gina had insulted her instead of having just made a casual remark.

"Our cook is one of the best in town I am proud to say."

"That's a good thing," Gina said and leaned toward the waitress as if readying to tell a secret. "Because if I'm going to give up beans I don't want to go runnin' out of here with the backdoor trots as a substitute."

That started her laughing, which started me laughing, which sent the waitress on her way to fetch the alcohol. This evening turned out as bawdy and fun as I've ever seen, although I'm sure others would have considered it quite conservative. We ended up having a grand meal and a grand time and a grandiose amount of alcohol. As we left the establishment, the waitress was smiling probably from both our imminent departure and her lovely tuppence. Gina and I stepped into the street arm in arm, tossed our heads back, and began to sing one of the saloon songs we'd been hearing pour out of the dance halls. We stumbled our way toward the rooms, alternating lyric lines and holding the endings until they sounded like a coyote howling at the moon.

There are ladies and ladies and some of them fine
While others are ravaged by work and by time
They work in the roundup and work in the fields
Some are just drunkards, you see what that yields

Into my cups and my sight ain't so keen
But close put at hand is my old carbine
Should outlaw or injun attack this sweet pearl
I'll shoot out their eyes I ain't no sweet girl

Outlaws are evil and savages worse
They'll cut off your hair and steal your purse
A headdress is purty but hides a mean heart
They'll kill when they see you; the end of a tart

It wasn't until after we had trumpeted out that last line that we realized quite a few of the people sitting along the sidewalks and on the benches lining the fronts of many of the stores were Indians. Suddenly the streets did not feel so safe or as fun. I was starting to miss Slocum right about then. It had been my bright idea to let him stay in the room and sleep.

"I wonder where Bantam is," I said.

Gina gave me a pull to hurry me along even faster.

"Don't know and don't care," she said.

Then she whispered, "You want to keep your hair attached you'll just hurry along."

We clutched each other tightly and scurried towards our rooms. It would feel mighty fine to pull ourselves behind closed doors and shut them tight behind us. I'm sure there was probably a cloud of dust rising up behind us and I thought I could hear the sound of laughter following us down the street.

Chapter Twenty-One

After a period of nightmare-laden sleep, I jerked awake in sweat-soaked sheets. Slocum sat next to me on the bed staring in an attempt to bore the thought into my brain that despite whatever hour in the night it may be, he had to relieve himself. He had to relieve himself now. I attempted, after a moment, to reorient myself to my surroundings and decided that the wisest course of action would be to allow him to complete his call of nature.

Gina was snoring like a drunk, moaning that deep comfortable sound of having fully succumbed to the sandman. If she had been awakened either by my nocturnal jerking or Slocum's brain-boring stare, she was doing a damn fine acting job, pretending to be asleep. The minor shaking of the bed was not nearly enough to wake Gina up. What a faker. We would easily be back in bed and sleeping again in a couple of minutes without disturbing her world.

It was still dark and I had no idea of the hour of the morning. As I opened the door and stepped outside into the coolness I noted that the street had quieted down considerably from the earlier rowdiness. There were still people moving about. They just were not singing at the top of their lungs like that odd pair of drunken women earlier. I felt relatively safe stepping back outside with Slocum by my side. Down in the direction of the rail station, I could hear a train pulling out. Slocum walked away from me to sniff the ground and determine the best spot to do his duty. He only looked up once when a tinker's wagon rolled past with pots and pans clanging.

I stepped out onto the dirt street and took a deep breath of the fresh air, which happened to carry the aroma of horse poop from the stable. A large drop of water hit me square on the forehead. I'd brought Slocum outside just in time. I wasn't keen to be in the same closed room with a wet dog so it would be nice to get him back indoors before he was soaked.

The rain started to fall harder and I whistled for Slocum to come back up under the porch roof. He had taken care of business by now, in multiple spots just to prove that he'd been here and was the current king of the corner. I call it the dog newspaper, read a message and leave a little bulletin of your own. But instead of coming back up to join me, Slocum stayed where he was and started barking.

"Quiet! You'll wake everybody up," I whispered as loudly as I thought I could get away with. "Get in here."

But he continued his barking. I figured he had a squirrel or a rabbit so I walked around the corner of the house to yank him back. His nose was down at the crawl space under the building. I grabbed him by the scruff of the neck and tried to pull him away. Slocum held fast.

"Come on. Get away from there."

The rain started to come down in a heavy drizzle and I knew I was losing my battle with the stinky wet dog problem. Slocum would not budge. He put his nose low to the ground up against the latticework. A deep guttural tone moved from the far end of his belly through his throat. I knelt down to see if I could get a look at what was causing him all of his consternation. There was something there, in the darkness. Though it was hard to make out what the shape was. The last thing I wanted was for some frightened trapped animal to figure that the only way out of this predicament was to charge through us.

Maybe I would be able to scare it away. I looked about for a stick or something to run along the latticework, hoping the sound would frighten him back towards the other side of the house. I spotted a small branch on the ground near the rear of the house. The size was small enough to fit well in my hand yet large enough to get in a couple of defensive swipes at whatever it was, should it come charging out.

Slocum had quit barking but was still guarding the crawl space as I ran back beside him with my weapon. I dragged it back and forth a couple of times on the lattice, hoping the rattling noise would drive the thing backwards. It shuffled and moved a bit. There was some sort of lip smacking noise that did not sound promising. I tried running the stick along the wooden lattice again with even less results. I put my left hand on Slocum's chest and tried to push him back.

"Look out boy," I said. "Back up."

He wouldn't budge. I couldn't figure out how that dog was able to dig his butt and feet into hard ground and hold fast. I took the smaller end of the stick and poked it through a hole in the latticework at the creature. I think I hit a leg or a foot. It jerked up and back into the darkness. I pulled the stick up in reverse. I tried again to push Slocum out of the rain towards the front door. But he was still insisting on his way. The sound of shuffling came from under the house and Slocum was riveted on it.

That was it. I'd had enough. Kneeling in what was hurriedly becoming mud from the rain, I was wet and getting wetter by the moment. With a deep breath I decide to give it one last shot. I turned the stick around so that the fat end was pointing towards the beast. It barely fit through the hole in the lattice. After it was about a foot inside I jammed it at the creature with a single sharp stab.

"What the hell!"

Bantam's voice rang out from under the house. It scared me

so badly that I yanked the stick back instinctively, losing my balance and sitting backwards into the muck. A branch nub caught the lattice and tore a chunk of the wood out of the framing. Bantam's head appeared out of the darkness in the large hole I had just broken through in the guesthouse foundation.

"What are you poking me for?"

I pointed at him and stammered.

"Wh . . . what are you doing under the house?"

"Sleeping," he said and crawled the rest of the way out. "As if it's any of your business."

He studied me a moment.

"I'm dry. What are you doing out in the rain? You're all muddy."

I stood up, stick still in hand. I felt like beating him with it. Instead I pointed at the house.

"That is what you have paid for a room for."

He wiped his hands on his pants.

"You need a key to get in the front door. I think I lost mine somewhere along the way."

I started wiping the mud from myself. Bantam looked up at the sky.

"Shit, it's raining."

That was when I hit him with the stick.

"Ow!"

"I'm sleeping double in a bed so you can have your own room and you end up under the house and me in the rain!"

I tried to punctuate my words with more swings but he jumped out of range. With a final shriek, I threw the stick down and stomped toward the porch. Bantam ran along beside me pleading his case.

"You see I was over at Lora Lee's talking to this fine lady who I believe was a school graduate, very learned type, and there were these two guys who . . ."

At the porch I turned on him.

"I don't want to hear it. You're just damn lucky I'm letting you in with my key. If I was you, I would shut my mouth, go to my room, and shut my door."

"But you don't understand," he said.

"Oh, I understand all right. I understand you're lucky to be alive. I don't mean from somethin' out there. I mean from someone standing right here in front of you."

He looked at me a moment, the wheels turning in his head. Then he walked on ahead of me grumbling under his breath.

He opened his unlocked room door. *Real smart,* I thought. He stepped inside and shut it behind him. I needed to head back into my room, strip down, and dry off. Maybe I could get another hour or two of sleep.

Since the hallway was empty, I shucked off my shirt and wiped my feet with it. There was no reason to bring any more of the outside in than I had to. Slocum was as wet as I was, only much stinkier. I wiped him off with the shirt, also paying special attention to his feet. I tucked my wet, muddy shirt under my arm just as I heard a doorknob click down the hall. Damn, I was practically naked! I opened our room and pushed Slocum inside with my foot. I jumped in and shut the door behind us just as the one down the hall opened up. Someday I was going to kill that little guy.

Chapter Twenty-Two

Gina stretched out her arms while still lying in the bed. First one arm as far as she could reach, including spreading her fingers, and then the other. She made a noise like she was really fighting gravity, struggling against some invisible force pushing back at her. This silliness was followed with the same actions to her legs and toes. I was not in a particularly fine mood after my wet sleep interruption last night. So naturally Gina felt this was the perfect time to give me a nature lesson. The wise gypsy spoke.

"If you watch animals when they rise from a sleep, they stick their front feet out as far as they can and hunch their backs, getting limber for the day's activity. You can even see them digging with their toes to get maximum pull."

She felt that she needed to mimic these actions as she told her story.

"Stretching, stretching, stretching until all of the kinks are popped out. It keeps them loose and limber with their spines all pulled out."

She was way too chipper. I wished I still had my stick from last night. Slocum watched her from the floor like she was crazy and keeping a wary eye on me. Gina grinned.

"You should try it."

She swung her feet down off the bed and went out the door to the bathroom.

"I'd like to try *something* right about now," I said.

"What?"

She shouted this from out in the hall.

"Nothing," I said. "Just singing to myself."

I pulled my shirt up and looked at its mud-stained front. It was already getting warm and muggy outside. I wasn't too sure if I soaked it down and wrung it out that it would be dry by the time we were ready to leave for the train. Then I thought of something.

"Come on, Slocum," I said. "I've got a mission. We wouldn't want little Bantam to oversleep and miss breakfast, would we?"

I was whistling as we walked out the door and tiptoed to Bantam's room. Sometimes I've had a mean sense of humor, which I seemed to be suppressing less and less these days. Outside the door to Bantam's room I bent down to Slocum.

"Hey, wet dog," I said.

He cocked his head and looked at me.

"When I open this door, I want you to go running in and jump up on Bantam's bed. It would also be wonderful if you could roll over on your back and scrunch about. I'm sure he would love that."

I took the doorknob in my hand and braced myself. This was going to be a swing-about-and-shout type of operation. I looked down at Slocum.

"Ready?"

I turned the knob and shoved the door open with my shoulder in one quick movement. That damn little piglet had locked the door. The force of slamming my shoulder against an unmovable object threw me off balance, right over Slocum's back and into a heap on the floor. At the same time, I hollered at the top of my lungs.

"Gooooooaahh!"

Slocum shot out from under my feet and stood watching me from across the hall. He obviously wanted to be out of harm's way should I have another brilliant idea. I had crumpled into a pile and knocked my head against the wall.

"Shit," I said, very unladylike, and lay still for a moment to see if anything hurt like it was broken.

Bantam's door swung open and he stepped out into the hallway in the smallest pair of long johns I had ever seen. He looked at me like I was a nuisance.

"What in tarnation are you doing?"

Then Gina opened the bathroom door and joined the party. She put her hands on her hips and started laughing. Soon she was bent over in her fit of hilarity.

"Don't you know it is early? Some people might still be trying to sleep," Bantam said.

"You've got that right," came some man's voice from behind another room door.

This was too much for Gina who was practically doubled-over as she went back inside and shut the door. I could hear her muffled laughter behind it. Bantam gave me a *Harrumph* and went back inside his room, shutting the door behind himself.

"Soon as I put some pants on, I'll join you for breakfast," he said from behind the door. "That is, if you've finished with your little acrobatic demonstration."

Even Slocum went back down the hallway to our room, leaving me on my own to untangle myself from my mound on the floor. So far, the day was not starting out on the high end of the scale. I was thinking that breakfast had better turn out to be tasty or I might be having me a female moment of emotional frustration.

Despite my self-inflicted funk, the rest of the morning sailed past without a hitch. Bantam was watching my every move like he was waiting for me to do something else stupid. It was starting to get to me. After we had loaded the horses into the stock car and had boarded the MKT railway car, I found myself unnerved by his gawking. I stared at him a moment in an attempt to get him to look somewhere else.

"You know what?" I said to him. "You're not right in the upper story."

He bit off a piece of jerky and held it out in an offering to Gina. She made a face and shook him away.

"I'm all right. But I believe you had better look in the mirror."

"Me?" I said raising my voice.

"Yeah, you. What kind of damn fool stands out in the rain at o'dark thirty in the morning poking beasts in the blackness of a crawl space with a stick? You could have been killed."

"Huh?" Gina looked back and forth between us.

"I wasn't poking any beasts," I said crossing my arms and looking indignant. "I was letting Slocum relieve himself and poking you."

"But you didn't know it was me!"

I stood up and pointed a finger at him.

"But it was you!"

Slocum flattened his ears. He never was one to care for yelling. Bantam jumped down from the seat to match me standing but actually ended up being shorter than when he was seated.

"But you didn't know that! I could have been a bear or a coyote or a wild opossum or damn near anything."

"But you wasn't," I said way too loudly, causing other passengers to turn and look at us.

Gina broke into laughter again. Bantam looked up and down the aisle.

"I hope this train doesn't fill up so I can go sit somewheres else without some fool across from me."

"You just go do that," I said.

But I was the one who turned and walked away. I didn't know where I was going, but you can't go too many places on a train. I didn't look back. I had a feeling it might have destroyed my dramatic exit. As I stepped onto the plate connecting the two cars, the train started up with a lurch, throwing me to the side. I caught myself and stood perfectly still hoping that they were not watching. But I heard Gina wind up her laughter again and knew I had been spotted. I proceeded on to the next car with as much dignity as I could muster at the moment while pouting like a five year old. It was kind of early for a snort of anything, but a cup of coffee would eat up a little time and possibly calm me down. A snort of something would have been better.

"Do you mind if I sit with you?"

A damn handsome man in casual traveling clothes stood in front of me. He was carrying a large book. In his other hand was his hat, one of those round flat-brimmed things that looked like the rim circled around an upside-down bowl like a halo. He smiled at me and the lace of wrinkles showed he enjoyed the sun. But when he stuck his hand out it was softer than a rancher's so I reckoned he was not used to doing a lot of labor. As I shook his hand he introduced himself with what sounded like a Scottish accent.

"My name is Theophilus Barton Fanning. I'm a traveling servant of the Lord and believe I'm looking at a lost lamb."

"Pleased to meet you, Preacher. But I really don't need any saving right now."

The planted smile never left his face. There was no flicker of hesitation in his eyes and he sat at the table despite my lack of invitation. He placed the book to the side and hung his hat on the post of the chair back that stuck up behind him. It took a couple of attempts due to the fact that the crown of the hat was not all that deep but he eventually got it hung on there.

"Why don't you just set it on the book there so it doesn't get knocked off? There is plenty of room."

"Oh, no, my child," he said leaning forward. "You must never place anything upon the scriptures. They are above all else."

The idea of having coffee to drink was starting to shift a little in my mind. When the waiter came up to the table I had already altered my order in my mind.

"I would like a cup of coffee with a shot of corn juice on the side."

The waiter stood there, glancing back and forth between the preacher and me.

"Ma'am?" he asked.

I looked at the preacher and figured that if this conversation was going to be for the long haul, I wouldn't take it upon myself to make the trip any smoother for him.

I said to the waiter, "You're right. Just pour it into the coffee and stir it up good."

I looked over at Theo.

"Anything for you, Converter?"

He smiled a quick sheepish grin and for a moment I caught a glimpse of what he must have looked like as a young boy.

"No, no thank you," he said.

The waiter took his cue and turned back to the kitchen to fetch me a powerful coffee. I had a feeling it was going to taste especially fine this morning.

"Are you getting off at Dallas?"

He looked up at me and I noticed that his eyes were someplace between the color of sand and prairie grass. He smiled again.

"Yes, ma'am."

"Because you live there?"

The waiter returned with a large steaming mug of coffee and set it down in front of me. I could smell the whiskey in the vapor. I picked up the spoon and stirred it a little.

"No, ma'am. Because it's the end of this line."

I felt as foolish as a schoolgirl. He didn't seem to be one to take advantage of that. I kept stirring and pretty soon I was chuckling to myself. I looked up and he was giving me a knowing smile.

"Yes, it is," I said shaking my head. "Yes, it is."

"You . . . ah . . . you are quite a conversationalist, ma'am. Could I have your name?"

"Not if you're calling yourself Theophilus. Mine would be completely different."

When I realized that he hadn't caught my humor I sat my spoon down and stretched my hand across the table.

"It's Peggy."

"Theophilus Barton Fanning."

"That's quite a mouthful."

We shook hands over the table and with the slight giddiness, I felt I was thinking that the coffee was working wonders even though I had only smelled it. I blew on the cup and took a nice sip. The waiter had not been stingy in his portioning. I looked over to the side and saw him smiling at me. I scowled and he ducked behind the wall to the galley. There was one of those long pauses that make folks scramble for words but Theophilus just sat there watching me drink.

"The way you drink that coffee, ma'—Peggy, makes it look like the tastiest drink on God's green earth."

"You'd be surprised, Theophilus," I said working on my second sip.

"You can call me Theo. That's just fine and a lot nicer than many of the other names I have been called in my life."

"Great, Theo. I will do that."

With that talk out of the way, I commenced to taking my third sip. I thought I might require a refill. I took a quick glance for the waiter but he seemed to be laying low at the moment.

"What about you, Peggy? Are you stopping at Dallas?"

"Only to change trains. I'm continuing on west to take care of some business."

I actually think I licked my lips between sips four and five and maybe even made a yummy sound. I have no idea what make of liquor they were pouring but I felt like a little kid tasting strawberries for the first time. I was warming to this preacher fella and our conversation. Actually, I was warming in general.

"Oh, you're a businesswoman. I like females with an independent spirit."

He had really been chopping wood until that last comment. Right about then, his axe began to dull a little. I really didn't want the conversation to go there.

"Family business, near Yuma."

"That is quite a trip for a single lady."

His words sort of prodded me like a nagging spur in the flank. I took another sip of the magic black elixir.

"Widowed. I'm traveling with some companions."

I said throwing as much weight behind the comment as I could muster to let him know I wasn't alone. The smile deserted his face and he gave a quick glance around.

"They're back at our seats, probably sleeping," I said beating him to the punch. "It is still quite early."

He placed his hand upon the Good Book and rose from his seat in a smooth effortless motion. He placed his hat back atop of his head.

"Well, God has granted us the serenity of another day and I am called to duty. I do hope that we will meet again. For now, I must continue on to spread the word of heaven."

"You do that, Deacon."

As he turned and walked away, I curled my finger at the

elusive waiter and indicated that another mug of their fine coffee was in order.

The rest of the trip to Dallas was uneventful. The group talked and laughed, argued, and slept. Basically, we got to know each other. James was the only family I had ever really had once I'd moved West and it had been a small family of three, James, Slocum, and me. Now I had inherited a new family and a motley crew at that. We were broken people. But we were brothers and sisters in life, fighting and funning like siblings do just without the common blood ancestry. We were creating our own world and our own family. It felt good. It made me more determined than ever to face down James's killers and bring an end to a part of my life that had held me back from living for so long.

Chapter Twenty-Three

Our stay in Dallas would last a couple of days. I was looking forward to some real time off of the train and some good food, but there was something I immediately didn't care for in this Texas town. Maybe, despite the Trinity River, the place was ugly and brown and flat or maybe, I was just not taking to the territory. From what I saw on a map, there was a whole lot of Texas not to take to. Despite some clumps of trees, to me it was desert. It seemed as if the farther west we traveled, the more the scrub and dirt became the prominent topographical features. I wondered if the draw to California gold would have been worth it to ride in some hard, wooden wagon over this land. There were tales recounting an average of one gravesite for every mile of overland gold-seeking wagon train trails.

Cotton and cotton mills seemed to be the main industry along with cattle, which nobody seemed to care about since they roamed aimlessly everywhere. This was also my first look at oil derricks. Their wooden towers rose into the air as if they were monsters sucking the black money out of the ground. There were a lot of people here so there had to be money. I suspected it was in the oil, not the cotton, but it may have been the combination of both. One followed the other back and forth in a drive to get rich. It's very hard to pan a fortune in gold or punch a hole through the earth in the right spot for oil. When things became too much work, some people looked for shortcuts, quick routes to easy fortune. That was how James had died.

The worst parts of town, almost any town, seemed to be the east and south sides. Maybe because the east side was settled first and was the oldest. The south was probably the first area of expansion. These parts also seemed to surround the depots, stagecoach stops, and roadways. People just passing through town were kind of stuck in those areas during their travels. The real townsfolk moved farther north and west, creating more Dallas. Churches and schools built up, away from the rowdy street life and entertainment parlors that offered diversion for the waylaid passenger.

We would have two days before our journey continued west aboard the Texas and Pacific Railroad. After looking about the area through the dust and the heat from a bench on the porch of our hotel, I started to think it would be too long. I had only been here a couple of hours. I was itching to get moving, even if it meant getting back aboard the train. The others had been getting hoary with the constant rocking of the train. They liked the respite of not riding the rails.

In actuality, I was quite grateful for their company. Even Slocum seemed to be enjoying just lying on the porch in the shade and letting the town roll past. But I had something waiting for me at the end of the line.

Somewhere in the back of my mind I hankered to get back to teaching school. If I could find a way around dealing with children, I enjoyed the idea of being needed, making a difference in somebody's life. Well, I almost had taught. I had studied for it and trained and then on the month before I began I met James and pushed it all away to help run the ranch. All the while, I secretly hoped that someday our little town would need me. But it never happened. I held that feeling in my heart too long and too hard despite how much I loved him. Now I was most probably too bitter, and the thinking too self-centered.

I settled back on the bench to wallow in my pity and allow myself a deep breath. I must have been lost deep in thought because Slocum picked up on the noise much sooner than I did, though it was plain to hear, a rumbling and slamming like somebody was driving a stagecoach across a loose wooden bridge deck. It was approaching quite rapidly along the blind side of the building to my right as we sat on the porch. A mite before its appearance, I saw a lady scurry off the sidewalk into the street. Slocum turned and jumped up onto the bench with me. He nearly knocked me off the end.

Then they came shooting around the corner of the boarding house and straight towards us like a mob of crazy children. There were at least six of them. They were whooping and hollering at each other, yelling at the top of their lungs. Some of them had their arms flapping like they were attempting to take flight. Others had their hands in the air, leaning and bobbing, trying to keep their balance as they raced at breakneck speed over the uneven wooden sidewalk. When people would jump out of the way the youths would laugh and point at the poor soul who likely as not ended rump up in the dusty street. It was rude and unwarranted. They seemed to have frightened the public enough to send them running, although they were being followed by the verbal assaults of the adult populace.

Slocum looked rapidly between me and the approaching disorderly throng and gave off his whine of uncertainty. I knew this must be brought to an end. I believed that I was the one to do it. My mind raced for a plan, which was solved when Bantam walked out the front door of the hotel in time to be physically greeted by the swiftly moving pack. In that last split second, when they saw each other, their eyes grew bigger than buckets and then *wham!* It was over.

Explosions seemed to occur. Bodies went flying in every

direction. The only thing missing was the sound of the cannons. Children sailed like they had been catapulted off the planks and into the street in every direction. Most of them landed in heaps, crumpled up raggedy doll style, like a pile of spare body parts for the picking. Long lanky kids were holding themselves in fetal positions and bleeding from a multitude of different orifices, some of which were newly created. Noses were broken, an ear ripped partially away from a head, and limbs and digits broken and twisted. A few got away clean, other than some bruising, but all of them were moaning like cows in labor, some even crying.

The only one involved to escape without injury was Bantam. The moment before impact he had dropped into a ball. The first child caught his feet on Bantam's side like hitting a bale of hay. The kid went sailing and Bantam was knocked under the bench I was sitting on. Slocum looked down at him through the slats in the seat, wondering what game he was playing.

People rushed to the hodgepodge of bodies, picking them up and brushing them off, generally checking them over. Some of the youths were having trouble standing, wobbling all about. I thought it all was from the collision when I noticed some sort of contraptions on their feet.

Bantam was crawling out from under the bench staring at their feet. With a groan, he managed to stand up. I looked at him as he gathered himself.

"Are you okay?"

"I'm a little all-overish from getting smacked," he said. "But I'll be all right."

He walked out into the street and stood tall over a boy who was still plopped down in the dirt. He pointed at the boy's feet.

"What are those?" he demanded.

The boy moaned and rolled away from Bantam. He grabbed the boy, turning him back in his direction.

"I asked you a question."

Bantam, puffed up like a fighting cock, was even scaring me. The kid had better answer him or Bantam would likely smack the snot out of him. I didn't feel that Bantam would have any compunction with smacking a child. The kid was speaking neither clearly nor loudly as his mouth was bleeding and he seemed to be missing a tooth or two.

"Roller skates," he said.

"What?" Bantam yelled.

"Sir!" the kid said hopefully.

"No, no! What did you say?"

Bantam was turning a little red from his emotional outburst.

"Roller skates, sir."

Bantam knelt down next to the boy and lifted his foot up to examine the little wheels attached to his shoe.

"How do you steer the damn things or slow down?"

"You put them on and you can slide around, as long as the ground is hard enough, or the spaces between boards on the sidewalk aren't too wide. You kinda lean to make them turn. They get you to places in a hurry."

"Hmmm," Bantam said dropping the boy's foot back to the ground, causing him to wince in pain.

"Like having metal wagon wheels on your feet. And just where were you going in such a hurry?"

"No place, sir."

"No place? You were just in a hurry to get no place like the Devil was on your tail?"

"Yes, sir. I guess so."

Bantam stood up and brushed his hands together.

"You make those yourself?"

"No, sir. I ordered them in from the east. We were just having fun, sir."

Bantam looked at the other people. A few of the kids were

still sprawled out but most had gotten to their feet.

"You could have kilt somebody, you damn fool! How did all that fun turn out for you, son?"

"Not too well, sir."

"Not too well, indeed," Bantam said. "Seems like you got a few people hurt. It could have been worse. I think we ought to do something about that."

An old woman up on the sidewalk shook her finger at the boys.

"They almost knocked me clean over last week."

Bantam listened to the woman and turned back to the boy.

"So this isn't your first time. It seems that you didn't learn from your past mistakes."

He held out his hand towards the boy.

"Give me your rolling skates."

"Roller skates, sir."

Bantam pulled his arm back like he was going to slap the boy and then seemed to think better of it.

"Don't back talk me! I'll beat you over the head with your own mechanical device. Now give me your skates."

The boy looked at the crowd that had gathered, appealing for help. He was met with silent stares even from his friends, who were beginning to back away from this mad midget.

"Sir, those skates cost me . . ."

"A beating!" Bantam yelled, "If'n you don't hand them over to me faster than I can spit."

Slowly the boy reached down and undid the straps on his skates. He pulled them off the bottom of his shoes and handed them up to Bantam, who looked at the skates a little puzzled.

"Make sure he's okay," Bantam said to the woman checking the boy's injuries. "You, young man, I do not want to ever catch you rolling down the town sidewalks again. Do you understand me?"

"Yes, sir."

Bantam, skates in hand, walked away. As he passed, he gave me a little wink and clutched his new toys a little tighter.

Chapter Twenty-Four

It was a warm evening breeze that met us as we stepped out onto the porch. Despite the darkening twilight, the heat clung, until the desperate end, up underneath the roof of the veranda. The three of us followed Slocum down the steps into the relative coolness of the street where the air was moving. We stood there with our hands in our belts while we attempted to figure out where we wanted to eat. Slocum's nose was high in the air, scanning for scent, as if he was ready to make his own direction towards food if we didn't move soon.

Around the corner to our left was the way towards town, a direct route from railway to the center of the city proper. The first couple of blocks were businesses designed for the traveler. We were getting fairly tired of the station area's food and could do with some real cooking if we had the opportunity. About the time we were giving in to letting Slocum follow his nose and we would tag along, Gina grabbed my arm. Her head was cocked like she was trying to pick up something on the wind.

"Listen," she said.

I stood trying to filter out the other noises of rustling leaves and creaking wagons and then . . . there it was. Singing. A voice rich and mellow wafted to us in and out as the breeze carried it past us only to snatch it away. I thought I could hear some type of stringed instrument.

"It's a songster," Gina said with admiration. "Whoever he is, he can sing."

Bantam stepped past me toward the sound.

"Medicine show. They used to come by the tent city outside of Kansas City where you found me."

I was a little confused.

"They sing to sell medicine?"

Bantam snorted.

"If that's what you want to call it. Flavored whiskey is all it is. They'll tell you it will cure anything: dandruff, stuttering, weak blood. But I drank some and I'm still short."

Gina started laughing.

"Yes, but you didn't care for awhile."

"Ain't that the truth," Bantam replied grinning at her. "I don't know about eating, but I do know about drinking. I'm walking that way."

He started to take off but I was a bit hesitant to follow him.

"Wait a second, that's away from town. We're going to just wander off chasing some music. What's in that direction?"

"Red-light district. Calico Queens. A whole lot of menfolk with money to spend on women and booze and hopefully food."

Gina spit once, something that I hadn't seen her do since we first met. I guessed her spirit had come around pretty full by now.

"Yes, there will be eatin' there," she said.

I still wasn't so sure but didn't want to be the anchor on this boat. Slocum was up front, standing with Bantam, and looking back as if to ask what was holding me up.

"Why do they call it a red-light district?"

"There are shacks with a lot of ladies down there doing business," Gina said. "When the train's in town there are a lot of railroad men relieving tension. If something was to come up, an emergency of some sort, the railroad would need to get hold of its boys mighty quicklike. So, to make it easier to find them, they hang the red kerosene lamps on the doors of the shack they're in."

I wasn't sure that information helped ease my mind any but I couldn't think of any reason not to go. My stomach was getting the best of me and Slocum was going to run off with Bantam no matter which way the deal came down.

"Let's eat," I said and we were off to find the singing medicine men.

We crossed the bridge over the river with its cool moist air. It was almost as if there was an invisible wall that lowered. Here we were one block from our rooms and the neighborhood changed dramatically. It had its ramshackle-looking buildings but no worse than some other areas of cities that I had seen. No, it was more like this area of town was darker, as if we were walking behind a curtain with very few lights. Except for the odd spot of color—a red lamp here, a brightly hued dress there, everything seemed dark gray. Either the businesses and signs had not been painted up or when things started fading away nobody saw a need to refurbish. Every place I saw color, it stuck out like a flash of lightning in a dark rainy sky. The red lamps that hung next to the doors of some of the shelters were small setting suns.

As we stood on the street, the music poured down to us from the other end. We could hear singing and then sales preaching. I could see the wagon all lit up with a multitude of lamps and a backdrop in bright colors that seemed to be trying to shake loose as it flapped in the steady breeze that shot down between the buildings. The costumes themselves seemed alive as the performers danced and sang, hoping in the end to sell enough *medicine* to make this stop on their never-ending journey profitable. Bantam watched for a moment before saying his piece.

"I know how this works," he offered. "They'll be bringing on the lovely ladies later. Good for them and good for this area of town to get the men all riled up. They'll sell some liquor and the men will saunter off to the shanty of their choice. That last part with the dancing ladies is always the best fun of the show. Right now, it's just Coon music and comedy. Bad comedy at that."

"So?" Gina asked.

"So, I say we've got plenty of time for some food before the grand finale."

"Now you're talkin', Short Stuff," Gina laughed.

"The food in this area won't be anything fancy," Bantam said. "But it will be affordable, filling, and probably tasty."

"That covers everything I'm looking for," I said.

"You might like to try the BS."

I turned to the voice beside me and was face to face with a left-handed wife who was painted to the nines. She was about my height and everything was either pushed up or tucked in. Even in the darkness I could tell that her pancaked face was scrapable, thick with makeup and her eyebrows a bright rhubarb wine red. Her clothes were garish with an oriental flair in color and design and the sequins could certainly have competed with diamonds.

"Pardon me?" I said.

"The Belle Starr. It's kind of reminiscent of her too, really ugly on the outside but quite nice on the inside. I'm headed there myself. We could walk together."

She looked about as if checking to see if somebody else was around. When she didn't see anybody, she seemed relieved. We were all staring at her when she turned back.

"You aren't from here, are you?"

We shook our heads and kept staring.

"Oh, I work and live here all right," she said and stuck out her hand. "Anne. Pleased to meet you."

I awkwardly shook hands very stiff and formal like some sort of a business arrangement.

"But just because you work here that don't make it safe. It's always good to have company at night. Somebody will knock you over the head in a second if they think you are loaded with Lincoln skins. Come on, it's this way."

We were hungry so we followed along beside her. I noticed Bantam gave a glance or two behind us during our short walk. I felt pretty confident in numbers. I guess I felt that if it was safe enough for a native of Laudanumville, it was good enough for me.

As we came around a corner there it was, **Belle Starr's Food, Firewater and Gambling**. The light that leaked out between the warped, gray, washed-out wallboards was the only adornment other than the signs. There was a smaller sign with an arrow near the door that said *Liquor in front—Poker in the Rear→*. Bantam chuckled but I didn't get the joke until later. I hesitated but Anne wrapped her arm about my shoulder and pulled me along.

"Come on, you'll like it, churchwoman. Sure, there are working girls there but I can guarantee you that it's much safer in there than it is out here." She cocked her head. "Besides, you're hungry, aren't you?"

"Yes, I guess so," I said.

"Good."

"I'm no prude, you know."

She patted my shoulder and moved us along inside.

"No, of course you're not," she said.

Small and claustrophobic, the smell of the restaurant's food fought its way through the smoke of what seemed like a thousand loosies being rolled and inhaled. There were tobacco makings and glasses on every table along with some of the loveliest platters of food I believe I'd ever set my sights on. Bantam, rubbing his hands together in delight, let out a yelp of pleasure and we were led to an empty table. When the waitress hit our table, Anne introduced us.

"New kids just passing through," she said.

And then whiskeys, coffees, beers, and dinners were ordered. After the waitress left, we sat there taking in the local scenery. Anne caught me looking at her. She gave me a very tired smile in return.

"That's a very pretty dress," I said.

"How do I look for my age?"

"I'm sorry," I said, "I have no idea how old you are."

"I've aged twenty years in ten and it wasn't the weather. Old enough not to have to learn new tricks. The ones I know have worked for me this long."

I turned away embarrassed. She touched my hand.

"No, it's all right. I know what I do for a living, so do you. I also know some people don't approve."

"It's not that I don't approve," I said to my lap. "It is just that I've never heard it spoken of quite so boldly before."

"I'm not ashamed. I'm still alive."

As she spoke she rolled a cigarette with one hand and killed her first shot of whiskey with the other.

"I've had my times good and bad. Laid thirty in one night at two bits apiece just to keep eating. I've done them three at a time and a good one all night long for nothing if I pleased. I've even had one die on me. Thank god he wasn't the grandest stallion in the barn. But it's all changing. As I get older I no longer taste as much sweet in life, but only the bitter."

She struck a match on the bottom side of the table and lit up the smoke.

"But nobody can say my life hasn't been interesting."

She looked across the table at Bantam.

"What do you think, Knee High?"

He was sitting across the table with his mouth open.

"I think you're an amazing woman," he said.

Gina broke into a husky laugh and slapped her knee. Our food arrived and we enjoyed the rest of our time with Anne. She spoke of town lore and who was famous and just about everything you would ever want to know. We told her our tales and where our undertaking was leading us. After our long journey and knowing we would have to get back on the train, it was a welcome diversion.

"We're going to go watch the medicine wagon after we finish eating," Gina said.

"Yeah," Bantam piped in. "It ought to be about time to bring the dancing girls out by then."

Anne pushed back from the table and put her cigarette makings back in her small hand clutch.

"Those grubs have been camped down there for a couple of days now. They must be making good money to be hanging on so long. They'll up and leave as soon as their Mormon tea runs out and they need to go make up another batch. Not a bad thing for my business either. The men get liquored up cheap, titillated by the dancing girls, and then come looking for a little love. Come to Annie! She's got as much lovin' as you've got money. I believe that supply and demand is what they call it."

We paid the bill and stood up to leave. I was full and it appeared that the rest of the party had stretched their bellies about as far as they could stand.

"Do you want to come with us?" I asked Anne.

"Thank you, but no," she said. "I believe I'll be heading back to work. I have to pay for that food I just ate."

We walked out the front and got our bearings. It wasn't hard to figure since the music was playing and the murmur of the crowd could be heard during the lulls. I stuck my hand out to Anne.

"It was very nice to meet you," I said.

She grabbed my hand and pulled me in for a hug.

"It was nice to meet you, Churchy. Any time you folks are in town you come see Annie and we'll break bread together."

She bent down and scratched Slocum on top of the head.

"You too, handsome."

There were smiles and laughs all around and we headed off in our respective directions. It was then that the music on stage stopped and the screaming started.

Chapter Twenty-Five

"It's coming from the direction of the medicine show!" Gina yelled and ran towards the commotion.

We started following her down the street when a rider burst out of the alley to our left whipping and lashing his large scrub, almost trampling Bantam in the process. His white long coat with flapping collar obscured his face and his hat was pulled down tight to his eyes. He was scooting like a burning bobcat with no thought of the people in his way. Slocum started barking. Bantam jerked to the side, throwing himself against the wheel of a buckboard, narrowly avoiding certain death. He was airin' his lungs with swear words and the rider was gone from sight before Bantam could pick himself up.

"Are you okay?" I asked.

"If that addle-headed barrel boarder ever comes back this way, I will be more than happy to knock a couple of holes in that face of his!"

"Yep, I guess he's fine," Gina said.

The screaming and excited talk from down near the bandwagon grew in intensity. As we approached, I could see that some of the dancing girls were huddled together crying. Some were being comforted by some of the menfolk. Many of the crowd had broken off and were up the alley, back towards the working girl shanties. With Gina leading the charge we made our way between people, shoving towards the front edge of the crowd to see what the commotion was all about. There was a space where the people stopped and whatever they were looking at was standing.

As I parted the sea of folks, I realized that nothing was standing, it was hanging. A woman probably in her twenties, although it was hard to tell from all the blood streaming down her, was suspended from the front door of a trug shack. The men were standing about pointing and spitting tobacco. The girl had been nailed to the door; her feet affixed about half a foot above the dirt, splayed spread-eagled with her belly ripped open. Her tranklements hung low to her knees pulling some of her inner organs out with them. Her breasts had been nearly sliced off but hung by the abundance of skin that was stretching out from her chest, slowly lowering their fatty mass toward the earth. She was a good-sized woman who had been attacked viciously. Slocum walked over and gave the scene a couple of sniffs. I whistled once and he joined me back where I stood.

"I've never seen anybody take that sort of a toweling outside of an Injun ambush," Bantam said. "I guess that leaves more room in the vaulting house. That's probably what those three over there are discussing."

He indicated the women standing to the side talking low amongst themselves.

"They're probably worried, like the rest of us, that they could be next," said Anne. "This isn't the first death we've seen. Some say its hired killing to drive the ladies away from the respectable town of Dallas."

With that proclamation, she swore and rolled herself up another smoke. The sheriff arrived and bulled between us, waving his arms and shouting orders.

"Everybody out of the way," he said. "Stay up by the buildings. Give us some room."

His deputy drove up in a wagon. The sheriff got right up to her and tried to pull the nails out of her with his hands. But it was to no avail. He turned and shouted up to his wagon driver.

"You got a set of pliers lying under the bench that I can pull these nails out with?"

The deputy stepped down so he could get a good look under his seat. He shoved a few things around but shook his head.

"Can't say that I do."

"Well, how about a hammer and I'll knock them on through?"

He went back to searching and the sheriff turned to the gathered crowd.

"Anybody see what happened here?" he asked.

"I come upon her," the girl from the trio who had been sniffling the loudest said.

The sheriff walked over to her. He leaned into her and softened his voice a mite.

"What'd you see, darling?"

"I saw her nailed to the door."

"You saw somebody nailing her to the door?"

"No. I saw her nailed to the door."

There was a pause while the girl and the sheriff stared at each other. The sheriff had taken all of the information there was to have from her. She continued to stare at him. He gave her a smile of resolution and turned to the crowd.

"Alrighty then, anybody else see anything?"

There was a general murmur through the crowd with everybody looking around at their neighbors. Nothing was volunteered.

"Really?" the sheriff asked. "There's a bigger crowd here than nickel night at the whorehouse and nobody saw anything, huh?"

Still nothing was offered.

"Well, I'm sure it won't take long before some scuttlebutt starts floating around. If anybody hears anything in the meantime, you be sure to let me or one of my boys know about it."

He gave the crowd one last look and snorted. I stepped forward.

"Sheriff, sir?"

He gave me a quick look up and down.

"What?"

"When my friends and I started running down here a man came riding out of the alley skedaddling about as fast as he could make his mount move."

"That right?"

"Yes, sir. He almost ran my friend, who is standing over there, right over. He seemed more interested in moving fast than where he was going."

The sheriff gave Bantam the same type of up and down that he had given me.

"I can see how he'd be easy to miss," he said.

This time it was Bantam who snorted. The sheriff looked back at me.

"What'd he look like?"

"Hard to say. It's dark and he was wearing a long white coat."

"Did he have a mustache?"

I shuffled my feet in the dirt, a little embarrassed about just how little I actually knew.

"Couldn't tell. He had his collar pulled up in front of his face and his hat pulled down tight. I couldn't see anything."

The sheriff spat some tobacco in Bantam's direction, causing him to take a step backwards.

"That right?"

"Simon-pure, Sheriff," Bantam said.

"Don't imagine you even saw as much as she did with ducking out of the way and all," the sheriff said.

Bantam frowned.

"No, not really."

The sheriff grunted and walked back to the door. He turned back to me.

"How did you know it was a man riding that horse?" he asked.

That was a good question, I thought. But all I could do was shrug.

"I assumed," I said. "The shape. The size. I don't know."

"Yep," the sheriff replied and went back to his bloody business.

The deputy of the buckboard walked over and sheepishly handed the sheriff a large rock.

"We don't even have a damn hammer, Travis? Christ almighty!"

He walked over to the whore and grabbed her wrist.

"Hold her arm right here," he said to the deputy who did as he was told.

The sheriff took aim and slammed the rock with a hard smack on her open hand. Two more smacks and the nail was pretty well punched through the flesh of her palm and into the wood of the door. Her hand still stuck to the door. He dropped the rock and grabbed her wrist with both hands.

"Let's pull it off. It's almost all the way through," he said.

The deputy leaned against the door to keep it from wiggling while the sheriff pulled on the hand. There was a ripping noise similar to the sound of tearing fabric. Then a pop as the arm came free from the door. Something fell from her hand to the ground and Slocum trotted over to investigate. The sheriff kicked at him with his foot.

"Will somebody get their damn dog out of here? This is official business."

I ran over and knelt down to grab Slocum's neck. He needed a tug or two to dissuade him from his curio, which I could see was a chunk of flesh. I turned to lead him back and when I stood up, I froze in place. Standing there in the crowd on the opposite side was the preacher man, Theophilus Barton Fanning. I doubt that name will ever leave my head. He looked a little different since he wasn't wearing preacher clothes but normal street wear. He half-smiled at me when our eyes met and I was stuck to the spot as sure as Job's wife. He acknowledged me with his eyes but remained stern as befitting the situation. Then he looked down as if the shame of the scene was almost too much for a God-fearing soul to bear. I turned, pulling Slocum with me, pushing behind Gina, removing myself from the scene. When I looked back Reverend Fanning was not to be seen.

"It's flesh," the sheriff said, looking at the object he'd picked up off the ground.

He held it up between his thumb and forefinger. The sheriff put the nubbin in his shirt pocket. He bent down and picked the rock back up. The dead girl was now hanging by one hand and both of her feet. The other arm dangled lifeless from her side. The deputy grabbed her other arm and held it steady for the sheriff who took a mighty swing at her palm. There was a loud crack when the rock hit but the nail did not move much.

"Christ on a cracker," the sheriff said. "She's nailed up there real good on this side."

Travis started laughing.

The sheriff looked at him.

"What?"

"More like Christ on the door the ways she's spiked up there."

"Yeah, that's funny, all right," the sheriff said. "You oughta write for the local paper."

He wiped his forehead with the back of his sleeve.

"Why the hell would anybody do this?"

The sheriff grunted and then took another wallop at her. This time the nail slammed right through her hand and into the door. Slipping out of Travis's grasp she fell forward, all dead weight, scaring the guys off to each side. With her feet only a few inches off the ground she ventured all the way down, her forehead plopping in the dirt. Her innards now hung down across her face. Her hands, with wounds like a strange stigma, lay palms up in the dirt. Her legs were bent awkwardly somehow just above her ankles and about a foot above where they were nailed into the wood. There was an audible gasp from the crowd and a couple of ladies attempted to shield the waifs from the grotesque sight.

"It's a warning," Anne said.

The sheriff looked at her. I could see in his eyes that he sized her up with some sort of familiarity.

"What sort of a warning?"

Anne stepped forward and looked up at the man.

"If he felt cheated," Anne smiled at him. "If he couldn't perform and felt belittled," she said holding that smile. "If he caught what he thought was his girlfriend bedding somebody else. It could be a million reasons. But it's most likely a message from our fine city fathers telling our kind to leave."

She turned to appeal to the crowd.

"We need more protection down here."

The sheriff looked down at her and then pushed her out of the way to get back to his work on the door.

"Then leave your clothes on," he said.

He leaned down and took a look at the hanging girl's feet. The nails were set through her ankles above the curve of the foot.

"There's no way I'm gonna be able to slam these nails through with a rock," he said shaking his head. "Meat and bone is too thick here. There's not one damn sumabitch that has a hammer around here?"

He was addressing the crowd with that last statement.

"Not sure a hammer would work anyway, Sheriff. It would probably just mash up the ankle. You know, make a mess of things," Travis said.

The sheriff stood up and brushed his hands off.

"Well, I can't just leave her there."

The deputy looked back at his rig.

"Sheriff, I've got a fire axe on the side of the buckboard."

There was a long pause of consideration before the sheriff spoke.

"I'm truly difficulted here but can think of no other solution. Go grab your axe."

Travis ran back to the rig and unhooked it from the sideboard. He brought it over and handed it to the sheriff, who balanced it in his hands, feeling its weight. Satisfied, he walked back and stood looking at the slumped-over figure. The sheriff turned and motioned to the deputy.

"You're gonna have to hold her up," he said, "or I won't be able to get a clear swing."

"What?"

It looked like the deputy had hoped to back away from the coming experience but he was being hauled back into it. The sheriff shook the axe at the girl.

"Hold her up!"

"I can't hold her by myself without standing in front of her and I'll be damned if I'm gonna do that while you're swinging that blade around."

The sheriff looked into the crowd and pointed his axe at a man.

"Isaac, get over here and help Travis a second. You hold one arm up and he'll hold the other."

The man stepped forward with a great deal of trepidation.

"Let's get it over with as I don't have the stomach or all night for this."

The two men each picked up an arm and raised the girl, leaning her back up against the door. Her guts slid off her face and plopped back down towards her feet. The men stepped as far to each side as they could and still hold her up. The sheriff took his swinging stance.

"She'll be down in a minute," he said and then Travis started laughing nervously.

For a large man the sheriff was fluid in his swing, bringing it back and then forward in one movement, without hesitation. I barely averted my eyes in time as I heard the thwack of the axe strike in her ankle and an audible groan from the crowd. I looked back up to see her one stumped foot still nailed on the door with the leg popped loose. The end of the stump was pointing up at me. The sheriff walked around to the other side. He scooted his feet in the dirt like a bull getting ready to charge and took his stance.

Waving his hand at the deputy, who was holding up the girl's arm directly to his right, he said, "Stand back as far as you can, Travis. I'm swinging with my odd arm so I'm feeling that my direction might be a bit off."

The deputy held the girl's hand with the tips of his fingers and stretched out as far from her as he could. This time the sheriff cocked the axe back above his shoulder dead still to bring it forward instead of the full swing. I watched as he swung the axe cleaving deep into her ankle, but not far enough to cut through.

"Hog spit," he said and with a couple of tugs pulled the blade free from the bone. He brought it back to another stop above his shoulder, took aim, and swung it. The axe hit just above the original cut like a chop from a tree trunk and managed to sink all the way through. The wedge-shaped body piece popped out onto the street and she broke free, collapsing on the ground before they could stop her weight.

"Pick'er up and toss her in the back of that wagon," the sheriff said, tossing the axe on the ground. "Make sure you also pop her feet free from the door and take them with you."

He looked around at all the people watching.

"I don't want any dogs eating them."

Anne scoffed. She stepped back up to him and pointed her finger in his chest.

"You and that bunch of old rats that pay you have wanted us out of here for a long time. They don't find us respectable in a Dallas sort of way. But we're the busiest section of town. You can't make laws about morality, Ephraim."

The sheriff took hold of her finger and moved her hand to the side.

"No, but I can enforce the laws that exist."

"And ignore the ones that don't fit your plans," she countered.

Slocum ran forward and grabbed the body piece that had flown out into the dirt. The sheriff kicked at him as he ran off to hide his treasure.

"Somebody get this damned dog out of here!" he yelled and walked away from Anne.

I whistled at Slocum and ran after him while Travis and Isaac gathered up the body and tossed it into the back of the buckboard. I grabbed Slocum near the wagon, pulling him out of their way. Then the deputy came back with a shovel and scooped up a pan full of dropped guts, dumping them in the back of the wagon. Using the shovel as a pry, he forced the edge between her foot and the door and was able to pop both of her feet off the door. Anne looked frustrated. She leaned in and gave me a hug.

"The longer I live, the more evil I recognize in the world," she said, looking at the bloody door, "most of it under the cloak of do-gooding. It's a damn shame. I thought people would learn."

She paused her speechmaking.

"It was nice meeting all of you. I hope you never forget Dallas."

"I don't believe we will," I said and we hugged again.

She gave us a quick wave and then headed off into Laudanumville to take off her clothes and have sweaty men climb on top of her for a couple of bits. The three of us stood in silence while Slocum walked back to the door and sniffed at the stain.

Chapter Twenty-Six

We sat on the porch for a long time, each of us reeling from shock. It had been almost like a strange part of the medicine show itself. But the violence began to tear and pull at us so we just sat and stared off into the distance. I could not see outside of my own skull. For me, the violence on this trip had been greater than anything I had ever witnessed in my own life outside of James's killing.

"How could he have hung her up there like that without nobody noticing?" Gina broke the silence.

I shook my head.

"I don't know. It would take at least a couple of *hims* I would guess. It took a few men to get her down. Although she might not have been killed until after they hung her."

"Nope," Bantam shook his head. "Even with a couple of fellers she would have been too hard to handle if she was struggling. She was a fleshy girl."

"Hmmm," Gina nodded and we slipped back into silence.

"Don't that cap the climax," Bantam said.

Slocum lay on the porch with his chin in his paws, his eyes moving back and forth between us as we spoke. I think he felt guilty for eating that piece of the girl. I was kind of hoping that maybe he was a little nauseous. After a while, Bantam slapped his thighs with his hands and stood up.

"I'm goin' to lie down. Might as well get this upcoming dreamin' out of the way. Can't say as I'm looking forward to it."

Not knowing what else to do and moving like we were in some sort of a trance, we all stood and shuffled our way to our beds. Sleep would only come from sheer exhaustion. Even Slocum lay on the foot of my bed with his eyes open. I closed my eyes for about ten minutes and then opened them back up. Slocum was still staring. At some point I collapsed into a kind of coma, dreamless and black, without reference points of time or space.

My waking came slowly. My hearing yawned first and gathered itself together in a lethargic manner, like the sound of a train that was arriving from a distance. You think you hear something way off on the edge of the world, a girl screaming, the loud whack of an axe hitting something solid, a crowd murmuring like a herd of cattle. Then slowly the sound grows, gathering body and soul, and makes itself recognizable. But as it arrived deeper and deeper in my slowly waking mind I knew it wasn't just a girl screaming. When the shouting and screaming began to register, my brain began to sort it out. It was the sound of fire popping and devouring dry wood. The smell of smoke hit me. When I opened my eyes, Slocum was staring at me, making a whining noise in the back of his throat.

I bolted up and looked about. It wasn't my room on fire and there was no intrusion of smoke. But light behind my curtains flashed orange. I rushed to the window and pressed my hand against the glass through the curtain. I felt no heat. My view was towards the side of the station house. I couldn't see any flames, but the wall glowed and flashed from flames just out of my sight line. I pulled on my pants and boots and opened the room door. As I stepped out into the hallway, Slocum shot around me and down the hall. It seemed I was alone.

"Slocum," I called. "Slocum, come here!"

I ran down to Gina's room. As I went to knock she jerked the door open.

"Slocum with you?"

"What? No."

"Grab Bantam," I said. "I'm going looking for Slocum."

She headed across the hall and I ran for the front door hollering for Slocum. As I rounded the end I could see the front door standing open and people running in the street.

"Slocum!" I shouted.

Behind me I could hear people racing down the hallway and Bantam saying, "What the hell is it?"

I kept moving out to the porch and stopped dead. It was pure chaos, shouting, people rushing, horses galloping, and the bright orange light flashing off of the side of the building across the street. I kept shouting for Slocum and ran to the end of the porch.

Looking towards Laudanumville I viewed a picture of Hell. The entire area glowed like a lava flow. The cracking and popping of burning timber almost drowned out the sound of the screaming. There was the length of a block between me and the beginning of the shacks, yet the heat from the flames made me sweat. It felt like my hair was curling from the blaze. A brigade was hauling buckets of water from the other side of the river. They were a waste of time and the tossed water seemed to evaporate before it ever reached its target. The buildings were dry. The snap and crepitating of the fire was as loud as cannon fire. Anybody trapped in one of those burning structures would surely be lost. I was almost as fearful for the people as I was for Slocum's life. Gina and Bantam ran up behind me as I stepped off the porch toward the blaze.

"What are you doing?" Gina yelled.

"I thought I heard barking. It could've been Slocum!"

"You've gone goslin, girl. There's no way you can get in there, if that is where Slocum ran off to. Why the hell would he run toward the fire?"

I kept moving toward the fire, looking for an entrance where the wall of heat might be low or already burned through.

"I've got to try," I shouted over my shoulder.

Gina grabbed my arm and spun me around.

"We can't go in there," she said. "We'll die."

"Then don't," I pulled away. "I didn't say *we.*"

I started moving towards the fire.

"Two ways to argue with a woman," Bantam yelled at Gina. "Neither one works."

He and Gina followed close behind as we searched the perimeter across the river for a place to break through. I could pick out the forms and shadows of people on the other side scrambling for their lives. Their screaming was matched by the whooshing of the flames in volume as they blew and danced. Bucket brigades were hard at work and another fire killer ran past us as fast as the four horses could pull it. Some people had fire grenades that they tossed at the flames along the base of the buildings but it seemed too little too late.

I saw what looked like an opening. When flames would twist to the side they created a clear shimmering shot right past them and into Laudanumville. Gina and Bantam came up beside me.

"We decided it was *we,*" Bantam said.

"Then we have to be quick because as soon as that flare closes back up it'll burn anything that happens to be standing there."

I pointed at the wind-driven parting of flames.

"Timing and speed, my friends."

The heat and my feelings of loss over Slocum were causing tears to pour down my face. Gina held my face to slow my thoughts and brushed the tears aside with her thumbs.

"Are you sure you want to try this?"

I nodded, unable to speak.

"Well," she smiled, "you keep crying like this at least your face won't burn."

I laughed a stupid crying snort and then we turned our attention back to the barricade of flames. Bantam began tearing his shirt off and pointed at us to do the same.

"Take your bandana or some piece of clothing off and we'll soak it in the river. Then wrap it about your nose and mouth so that you're breathing through it. Stay low when you run for the opening. Crouch down on the ground and you'll avoid a lot of the smoke. Let's go."

Stripping off various articles of cloth we made our way through the running people and horses to the river's edge where we stooped down and soaked them good. Then we tied them about our heads like outlaws.

"Tight!" Bantam yelled. "You're gonna be scampering and there's no way to use your hands to hold them on your face if we have to swim."

Two double-horse-drawn fire wagons raced behind us carrying hand pumps. Not only was our talk muffled behind the material but almost impossible to hear over the roar of the burning shanties. Bantam pointed toward the conflagration's opening and we made our way down into the river's flow.

The flames moved like sails that had broken from their mast moorings. They flapped together, making it impossible to see past them. Then they would open up wide offering a view of Hades. I could see a couple of bodies on the distant ground, smoking, unmoving. Then, quick as a blink, the leaping flames would snap back together and the opening was gone. Bantam motioned us down and we leaned in towards his covered mouth. He pointed at the flaming portal.

"That's where we're going in," he screamed in our ears. "First, we sink down in this river water as we cross, getting as wet as possible. Then we make a run for it and hope our timing is right."

We looked at him blankly, waiting for more. His eyes flicked back and forth between us.

"That's it. That's the whole idea."

He looked at us like we were dolts.

"Well, nobody else is offering up anything. Look, I don't know what we'll encounter on the other side. But we'll regroup there and play it by ear."

"Are you two sure you want to do this?" I asked. "It's my dog out there."

They took a last look at the shuffling wall of flames and nodded.

"Stay close. If we happen to get separated, climb up the other side and run past the fire. I don't plan on ending up on no meat wagon for some damn dog."

And with that Bantam smiled at me. Stepping away I walked into the edge of the river. I pulled the rag down off my face and cupped my mouth with my hands.

"Slocum! Slocum!"

The heat pushed at my eyeballs, making them water, and my lungs hurt from sucking in the hot air. But there was no sign of the dog. I turned back to the others and pulled my rag back up over my mouth, then nodded. I began wading in deeper, fighting the watery resistance for the other side. The two of them followed behind. We stopped and crouched down in the water, using it as a blanket to keep us wet and cool. Bantam pushed in between us.

"Get ready! The next time that wall of flames opens up, move your asses as fast as you can."

We pulled ourselves as close to the far bank as we could. The flames flapped and flailed, then they split open as if Moses had parted the Red Sea. We ran full speed towards something any sane man would have fled from. The bank seemed to stretch out in a strange dreamlike vista pushing the flames farther and farther in front of me. I knew in my heart I would not pass them before it jerked and sealed up in front of me. Time stopped.

Then, I was past and into Laudanumville proper. The wall of flames slammed behind me. I stopped and was immediately grabbed from behind by Gina. We turned and saw Bantam for a split second before the wall of flames closed. He was gone, obscured behind the blaze and smoke. I screamed and felt Gina's grip tighten about my shoulders. The air cleared and rolling towards us on the ground was Bantam. We ran forward, grabbed his arms, and pulled him back towards us until we were clear of the burn.

"Shit the bed," he screamed. "That was hot!"

Steam rose from the legs of his pants but otherwise he seemed intact. Part of his hair on one side was curly and one of his eyebrows was gone. He stood up feeling for his missing hair. He brushed at his face and head. Burnt hairs floated off into the air.

"Damn, that's a first. I'm glad I was wearing pants," he said. "I told you to stay low. That's the secret of fire."

I turned my attention to finding Slocum. I knew he wouldn't have run away from the room but only towards something. What that something might be was what I needed to figure out. There was a large WHOOSH and a crumbling of wood as a structure on the other side of the street collapsed. That helped us make up our minds as to which direction we were going to search in.

I shouted, "Do you think we should split up?"

Gina did a quick assessment of the scene.

"It might be faster and I'm for anything that helps us find Slocum and back across the river as soon as possible."

Bantam said, "I guess we're splitting up," and took off leaving Gina and I to each pick a direction.

"Meet back here as soon as possible," he screamed back to us.

He really didn't have to tell us to hurry. I was not only worried about Slocum's life but our own.

Chapter Twenty-Seven

I wasn't sure whether to think like a dog or if Slocum was thinking like a person. I was so panicked that I had to keep telling myself to stop and calm down, which was hard when there were people running and buildings collapsing all about you. I tried to think where Slocum would go and why he would go there. I knew he'd have a reason so I decided to backtrack our earlier visit to Laudanumville.

Smoke, flames, and a variety of moving objects made it impossible to see more than about a hundred feet. I kept shouting Slocum's name while ducking and dodging every time wood fell off of collapsing buildings, or horses and people ran into the street. I feared I would be crushed or trampled before I made it to where the medicine show had been. It was as good a place to start as any. The dead girl nailed to the door seemed to have been quite an attraction for him. I thought he might have headed back there. I was not doing well, thinking like a dog.

Somebody hollered and a horse ran past dragging a person whose foot was caught up in the stirrup. I shouted and jumped to the side where I bumped into a man running out into the street with his clothes on fire. I shrieked and pushed to the side, slapping at my clothes and hair. I was running blind now, tears streaming down my face and smoke choking my cries for Slocum as I stumbled towards the wagon stage. The smoke grew in volume but the flames were lessening. It was dense and dark. I was having a hard time breathing. I followed Bantam's advice and dropped down on the ground where there was a little more air. Now I was crawling on all fours. Acting like a dog even if I wasn't yet thinking like one.

The smoke blew aside at the same moment I scrabbled upon a charred and smoking piece of wood. I knuckled against it and my hand slipped inside the mushy texture. I saw a piece of material clinging to it and realized it was the charred body of one of the dancing girls. I jerked my arm away but her skin stuck to my wrist and pulled off of her body like pond scum wrapping about and dangling from my fingers. I flailed my hand about, screaming. The smell of burnt meat was gagging and I vomited at the same time. I stood up, stepping over her.

It was as if it disappeared. There was almost no smoke in front of me. The area had burned out. It was barely recognizable. I scanned the area for any sign of life. It was a circle of calm while Laudanumville burned around me. What was left of the medicine wagon stood off to my right. Pieces of canvas awning and some chunks of wood lay about unburnt, but most everything else had been devoured by the flames. Parts of the wheel hoops with spokes attached smoldered in testament to the ferocity of the heat. To the sides of the wagon were small piles that I took to be the remains of some of the performers or people who had been standing watching the show when they had been caught up by the crowd and the fire. Broken glass lanterns lay on the ground. Dry, paint-covered Osnaburg canvas and flames do not make a good combination. A little bit of rambunctious dancing and a falling light was all they would have needed to start the inferno. I was sure I knew how Dante got his imagery. I shouted for Slocum, hoping he had come here to this island of calm. I cupped my hands around my mouth and shouted again.

"Slocum!"

My gut hurt from sobbing and trying to breathe through the

smoke. I feared for the worst. The crackling of the fire combined with screams and shouting in the distance made me cave. I started crying, walking in circles, and waving my arms. I was sick and wanted to give up but I couldn't. Slocum was out there, maybe injured but certainly afraid. I had no idea of which way to turn. Where else would he go? And then I knew.

Anne.

She was the only other person Slocum knew around here. Although she hadn't told us where she lived, she had started off in the opposite direction from us when we had left the restaurant. It was a feeble lead. But any shot at finding Slocum right now was worth it. I gave one last shout for him, and then started back up the street towards where the restaurant had been located.

The fire had swept through this entire section of Laudanumville. Its edge was burning at about the halfway point down the block. The wind was blowing from behind me and carrying the smell of the fire down the riverbanks and up towards the railroad track. It would stop there, a natural firebreak.

As I began to cross back into the burning area, Bantam came running out from between two buildings. He was breathing like a locomotive and I could swear I saw smoke coming out of his mouth. He got up to me and dropped to his knees. I leaned down but was afraid to touch him in case he was injured.

"Are you all right?"

He took a few deep swallows of air, holding up one hand while staring at the ground. Bantam took one long deep breath and sat back on his haunches. He tipped his head back with his eyes closed. Soot was smeared across his face and his tears had washed little dirt streams across his cheeks. He took off his bandana and wiped his eyes.

"I'm sorry," he said.

I went down on my knees.

"What?"

He shook his head.

"I couldn't find Slocum. Not even a trace."

He opened his eyes and looked at me.

"I'm afraid . . ."

I refused to give up. I told Bantam my hunch about Anne, about her being in trouble because of the fire, about Slocum being a good dog able to find her by scent. Bantam was tired, dirty, and filled with failure. Slowly he stood up and nodded.

"I just wish . . ." Bantam said and he paused.

I turned and looked at him.

"What?"

"I just wish that at some point before I die I could be the love of somebody's life that way. Just once. To know what it feels like, even if I had to be a dog to feel it."

I smiled at him. We pulled our bandanas back in place and headed up the street towards the fire.

From where we stood, it felt like things had calmed down, until we made it about three-quarters of the way up the street. That was the line where the broom of flames was still finding dry tinder to burn. I could hear the popping of glass as windows overheated and shattered in their frames. At this end of town, the screaming had pretty much stopped as everyone had either evacuated or died. No life, no crackling of flames here.

As we battled through the smoke and debris, Bantam and I spread apart as far as we could and still keep each other in sight. We shouted Slocum's name, wishing that life would pony up for us just this once. Hoping that he would hear one of us. Bantam was gagging and coughing. I feared he was nearly finished with this venture. I could no longer hear myself when I tried to shout. The smoke had almost done me in. Our voices couldn't hold out much longer. As we failed to reach any volume, there came the sound of Slocum's name being shouted loud and strong. Gina stood in the clearing, waiting for somebody to return. Even though she was soot covered and breathing heavily, she still called out strong. Bantam went to laughing when he saw her dirty condition.

"You look like the dog's been hiding you under the porch," he said.

"Yeah, you're about as ugly as a burnt boot, yerself," she said.

Gina smiled when she saw us, knowing we were both okay. But her smile faded as she noticed that Slocum was not here. Gina looked skeptically around.

I took a deep breath and tried to call out again. My throat was raw and ripped. Bantam was no better.

"I can't."

Bantam was bent over and he looked up at us shaking his head. He too was throat dead.

"The river is to our left and you can cross it to safety now," I said. "I'll think no less of either of you but only remain grateful for your love and aid you have offered me. As a last connection to James my love for Slocum may go beyond normal. I understand that. It is not your burden to bear."

I listened to myself speaking, as formal as possible, to help remove any emotion from my voice that might cause me to break. A look exchanged between Gina and Bantam.

"My papa told me once that all women were broken," Bantam said. "He said my grandma was, my momma was, and even my sister was. They couldn't help it, beings as they were women and it came natural to 'em. I'm guessing this qualifies you for the club by chasin' a dog through a burning town of painted ladies and gettin' us to follow you. You've got gumption, lady. I'll give you that."

Another look between them and wordlessly they came to an agreement.

Together we turned and started walking toward the fire. I was panicking in my heart but couldn't let them know how close to the edge I really was. Gina stayed in the middle of the street and waved us to spread off to each side. She spoke loudly to be heard above the noise of the fire.

"Bantam, you take the Indian side and Peggy, you run the left. We've only got this one shot. So scream your lungs out with whatever you've got left but remember to pause in between to listen for a bark or yelling. We ain't got time to piddle so let's make this pass count."

We started our walk and screaming for Slocum. We'd shout his name and then pause. Then we would start walking again and do it all over. But as we dodged falling debris and tried to breathe through our neckerchiefs we weren't hearing any response.

"I'm sorry," I said. "We need to get out of here before we all end up dead."

A whistle from Gina's side of the street stopped both of us dead. She was waving us over.

"Listen!"

"What?" Bantam shouted back at her.

"Shut up and listen," she screamed.

It was then that Bantam and I heard the barking and the sound of a woman screaming.

Chapter Twenty-Eight

A large sheet of a wooden facade broke off a building in front of us and smashed into the street, sending up a brilliant shower of sparks. We bolted around it, dodging the flames and hot ashes, over to where Gina stood. She pointed into the burning building.

"I think it's coming from in there," she said.

I ran up as close to the heat as I could get.

"Slocum! Slocum!"

I was answered by a couple of barks.

"That's him," Gina cried.

Then a feeble voice crying for help.

"We can't get in this way. There must be a way around back through the alley," Bantam said. "I'll go around to the right and one of you run up the other side and try to find a way in."

I kept shouting Slocum's name to let him know we were coming. I had to go down two storefronts before I could find a cut through between the buildings that would allow me all the way in back. As I stepped into the alley I could see Bantam through the smoke, poking and prodding at the back of the building, trying to find a way in.

"They're in here, all right," he said. "I can hear them behind this wall but there ain't a back door."

The building next to theirs had an alley window. I picked up a large board from the ground and rammed it through the glass. Smoke escaped through the opening. I needed something to stand on as the window was too high for me to climb through.

"Bantam, let me hike you up to this window and see if you can't crawl through and find a way into the side of the place."

"It's as good a bet as any since I'm not finding a way in over here," he said.

I knew I wouldn't be able to pick him up so I leaned against the side of the structure and held on to the window frame. Bantam climbed me like a tree and up into the window. He hesitated, knocking out the shards of busted glass from around the edges, before clamoring off me and onto the frame.

"I can't see a damn thing in here. Black as pitch," he said.

Just then Gina appeared, having found her way around the building.

"Are they in there?" she asked.

"No. They're next door. We're hoping we can break through from here," I said.

"What's he doing sitting there?"

Bantam gave her a scowl.

"I'm trying not to impale myself on something by jumping blindly into the dark room. If you want to do this I will gladly trade places with you."

He turned and tried looking farther inside.

"I sort of wish it was burning a little bit in there since it would give me some more light to go by."

Then Slocum barked and I shouted back at him so he'd know we were still here.

"Here goes nothing," Bantam said and he pushed himself off the sill and into the building.

There was a lot of crashing and banging and a swear word or two I hadn't heard before. Then everything went quiet. Gina went up to the window and tried to see in.

"Bantam, are you all right?"

"I'm in a bad box here." The voice came from deep inside

the building. "I landed on something that hurt a mite but saved my bacon in the end. I think I'll be fine once I catch my breath."

"Can you see anything?" I asked.

"I can see that I don't want to do anything like that again. Now that my eyes are adjusting I can see the yellow of flames through some of the slats in the wall next door. I'm gonna try and get a fix on them. Slocum! Slocum!"

A woman's frightened voice and a couple of barks answered him. Bantam kept shouting.

"Anne, is that you?"

"Yes, oh, my God, yes! Who's there?"

"It's Bantam. You keep talking so as I can figure out exactly where you are," he said.

"Please hurry," Anne cried out. "The flames are getting close. We're trapped up against the wall. We've got the mattresses up in front of us to block some of the heat. But they're gonna catch soon. I'm not sure how much longer we can hold out with the smoke."

"I believe I've got them pegged," Bantam shouted back to us. "Hand me in the board that you used to smash the window out."

I handed the plank to Gina since she was taller. She slipped it in through the window and dropped it down for Bantam. It crashed and bounced about for a moment.

"I said hand me in the wood, not drop it on my head. Beef-headed woman."

I could hear him drag it across the floor and then bang it against the wall a couple of times.

"I think this is gonna work," he said. "Anne, move a little away from the wall so as I don't ram this into you when I break through. I'll have you out of here in a jiffy."

Anne's voice came from the other side of the wall.

"I can't move too far because of the flames. But don't worry about that. I don't care what you do, just do it fast!"

Then she broke into a cacophony of coughing and hacking. Slocum started barking again. There was a crash from their side and then they both went silent.

"Bantam, hurry! Please."

I could hear the banging as he slammed the end of the plank against the wall. Four, five, six times, nothing was breaking through.

"I'm in for it. Don't you worry any," he shouted, exhausted.

Three more hits and then the welcome sound of splintering wood met our ears. It's funny how the sound of destruction could be such a gratifying thing. I heard Anne scream as the wall busted in towards her. Slocum barked in panic and I was worried that maybe we were going to be too late. Gina had dragged a charred bench she'd found in the alley under the window. We stood up on it and looked inside the window. The flames from inside the building next door flared bright as it devoured wood on the backside of the wall. Bantam dragged a board across the room and wedged it into the hole that he had started. He slid it behind a loose board and tried prying it loose to create a hole. He just didn't have enough body strength to yank it free.

Gina hiked herself up over the windowsill and down on the other side. She landed with a *womp* that sent shifting boards scattering across the floor. The noise startled Bantam who jumped backwards, tripping on debris and collapsing in a heap.

"You scream like a woman," Gina said.

Bantam stood up, checking his arms and legs for injuries.

"Why didn't you tell me you were dropping in? I almost messed myself thinking the walls were falling on me."

Bantam scrambled to the wall and grabbed the board he had wedged behind the loose board.

"Take that end, Gina, and we'll try to yank it right off of the wall. Pull!"

They both pulled backwards on the plank and, as it rolled, open flames shot through the opening and then ducked back into the other building. It caused Gina to drop her end of the leverage board. She jumped back in and they gave it another try to no avail.

"Wait," Bantam said. "Let's slide the wood down and use gravity to help us pop this plank. When we're close to the floor we can finish pulling that wall plank down by hand!"

They slid the board down the inside of the plank, pulling it away from the wall. As it started leaning Gina became impatient and grabbed the top of the plank with her hands, throwing it to the floor. The orange glowing from the other side lit up the room and I could feel the heat even where I stood in the window.

Gina picked up a chair and smashed it on the floor twice, breaking it in pieces. She took one of the legs and tossed it to Bantam while she grabbed one for herself. Raising it above her head like a club she pointed at the charred wall. Bantam took one side of the opening while Gina began attacking the other with great ferocity. Within moments they had planks loose on both sides. I could see dark shapes moving on the other side and realized that Anne was kicking at the wall from the backside hoping to aid in its destruction.

The wall burst open with flames, wood, and bodies all pouring through in a flood of smoke. The heat drove everybody across the room. I could see some burnt flesh hanging from Anne's arms. Bantam guided her towards the window but seemed afraid to touch her for fear of injuring her more. Slocum came running through the opening with patches of fur singed. He was running with a noticeable limp. I leaned in the window with my arms outstretched.

"Gina, can you pick him up from under his legs and hand

him up to me?"

She scooped him up. Slocum was shaking and his eyes were wide black. I tried to stay calm so he wouldn't get more excited and start moving. She placed him in my hands and I scooped him against my body as much as possible. Gina gently pushed from below while I raised him up and over the edge of the window. Then she turned to Anne.

"I'll find something you can stand on to help you climb up and over," she said.

"Thank you."

Anne's response was very subdued. Her energy was starting to deflate. She was beginning to feel the pain of her burns.

Slocum's head lay to the side on my shoulder and he didn't take his eyes off of my face as I carried him. He made no sound but I could feel the shaking in his body. He jerked once when I moved my hands. I must have touched a bad spot. Still he made no noise. He constantly licked the front of his mouth. The soft part of his nose looked burnt to me. He needed water so I walked back toward the river as fast as I could manage. I was still damp from wading into Laudanumville earlier. I hoped that all the moisture I was feeling against me was merely his body pressing against my wet clothes and not blood. I didn't stop to look at him. I only wanted to get him out of here and back to the room. I was scared. The same emotions I had felt when James died flooded back.

I walked as fast as I could while trying not to jiggle him. He was heavy, but I swear I could have carried him all the way back home. My heart was pounding with each awkward step I took. I don't remember taking a breath. The sweat poured off of me. I stumbled and dropped to one knee. The motion caused Slocum to jerk and let out a soft lone whimper.

"Sorry, baby," I whispered.

Whether he understood it or not he quieted and laid his head back into my shoulder again. He was becoming torpid in his senses. I feared losing him. His breathing was shallow and quick. His eyes held a strange gaze.

I turned to see the other three stepping out into the street all under their own power. I had to hike Slocum up higher in my arms as his weight had pulled him down to a position around my lap where it was almost impossible to walk and hold him simultaneously. This shifting didn't cause Slocum to sound or jerk and that worried me.

The smoke in front of me was thinning. Flames were no longer in the vicinity. Smoldering structures shifted and died. Then the river ran before me like an oasis. I staggered to the edge and slowly waded into the cooling waters. I eased myself down in the water until the bath washed over Slocum. His eyes opened wide and his chin jerked up. I thought I could see relief accompany his awakening. He became lighter as the water supported him. He turned his head and began lapping at the river, taking in the cool refreshment. I supported him there until he had his fill.

I saw Anne and the others slowly crossing the bridge to my left. They walked close to her on each side, bracing her when she stopped, encouraging her with their words and presence. She only stopped briefly; then looking behind her at the devastation, she moved on. I stayed low in the water to make moving Slocum across easier and waded towards the far bank to meet them.

Gina came around and helped me up onto the bank while Bantam continued to walk with Anne towards our room. Although the fire behind us persisted, it had mostly been extinguished or burnt itself out. Smoke hung like heavy drapery over the entire area. In the street I could see the people laid out, cords of wood stacked, half-burnt, waiting for the flat wagons to come back and take them away.

I carried in Slocum and laid him on one of the beds. Gina began tearing strips of material off one of her undergarments to use as bandages. Bantam grabbed the basin and went for clean water. Anne sat on the edge of the bed, head down. Anne turned to Slocum on the next bed with tears in her eyes.

"Thank you, buddy," she said and began to sob. She was afraid to touch him, fearing he carried the same burns as her. "They heard you. They would've never heard me."

So I began crying, seeing the two of them injured so. Gina started welling up over the fact that we were all safe after running through Hell and back. By the time Bantam came back with the water, the entire room was a flood of female emotions. He stopped dead just inside the room staring at our group of crying women. The slack-jawed look on his face was worth a hundred dollars and I could not stop myself from laughing. I doubled over and the same contagion that started us crying now had all of us rolling with laughter. Bantam sat the basin as he both chuckled and snorted at the same time. The sound made us laugh all the harder. We would heal.

★ ★ ★ ★ ★

TRAIN TO YUMA

★ ★ ★ ★ ★

There are three things extremely hard: steel,
a diamond, and to know one's self.

—Benjamin Franklin

Chapter Twenty-Nine

James was buried with his badge pinned proudly to his shirt by me. The town had requested that I return it to the town fathers. I refused. He had died for it and he would have it. I had shined the metal until it was a diamond. Though he now lies in the dark, deep inside the earth, I believe the badge is a candle next to his heart, giving him vision in the next world. I like that tale.

I held a lot of beliefs early on after he was murdered but many of them slipped away as sanity, my new sanity, slowly returned to me. Now the little girl inside of me is gone. Now I believe in comeuppances. I believe in justice but it moves slowly. Now I believe in revenge and vengeance.

For the day of ***vengeance*** *is in mine heart, and the year of my redeemed is come.—Isaiah 63:4.*

Chastisement may be God's to hand out. But retribution will be mine. If it comes in a courtroom, I'm okay. If it comes from outside the courtroom, I'm okay with that also.

Even though I suffered through the pain of James's death, all the pain I have encountered since my journey's beginning would have been unimaginable to me just a few weeks ago. Gina's pain, Anne's pain, Slocum's pain are all different than mine. I saw how it has changed their lives. I realized how my pain has been the driver behind all of this. I seem to gather broken people.

I have been sheltered all of my life, from the world, from the pain of reality, hidden away in a very small world, partially of my own making. Had I, even as a young woman preparing to become a schoolteacher, have had the courage to ask why more often, I might have been a different person. I don't believe that I wanted to know.

Coming out from under the sleep of deep thought, I became aware that the methodical sound I had been hearing was Anne's breathing combined with the constant clacking of the train wheels. The fire was a day behind us now. She was a little out of it with the laudanum we'd given her. So she didn't protest too much when we kidnapped her. She had a wheeze and moaned occasionally in her rest with the pain of healing. Anne's burns were healing slowly. With the first day they had crusted over, growing a cover. But Gina made us remove that so that they could heal from the inside out. Slocum lay on the floor between the seats in a nest made of spare clothing. He has been cared for and bandaged and, like Anne, will one day be his own self. I, on the other hand, will never be my old self.

Bantam walked by me on his way to use the lavatory. He was scowling and muttering to himself as usual.

"Follow you through Hell and high water," he said directing it towards me, "and I'll be danged if I know why."

Gina's voice came from under her lowered hat.

"All water is high for you, ain't it?"

Bantam waved his hand in her direction.

"You're hilarious," he said and continued on his way.

I was watching Slocum follow everybody with his eyes without moving his head. A moan turned our attention back to Anne. Gina leaned over and checked the bandages on her arms. Leakage had stained dark portions of the wrapped areas.

"It's going to need a clean wrap and a salve if we're going to avoid an infection. We've also got to get some more food in her."

The conductor scoffed at us through his nose as if it were going to give him some sort of disease for him to be near us. He punched our tickets as far away as his fingertips would allow and only grunted to our inquiries for medical supplies. It was time for some down-home remedies.

"No dining car on this run, Gina. Otherwise I would grab butter or something from the galley to grease her wounds."

Bantam came scurrying up to us bent over. I thought he had been shot and reached out to him fearing he would drop. But he sidled up close to me and smiled. Out from under his shirt he pulled a towel. I took it and sat on the towel immediately to hide it from sight as the conductor walked past. He knew we were up to no good but I hoped it was just due to his disdain for our group. He passed by and I pulled the towel back out.

"Where?" I asked Bantam shaking it at him.

"Carpetbag. It was sticking out as I walked by. I snatched the towel quick and shoved it up under my shirt."

"That's stealing," I said.

Gina grabbed it from me.

"No, that's a bandage if you get it torn up and wrapped around Anne's arms before the owner realizes it is missing."

She winked at Bantam and he puffed like a rooster. Anne moaned again.

"I think I can get some grease off the coupling area between the train cars," Bantam said.

Gina nodded.

"Peggy, why don't you go with him? Try to get me something a little bit clean and maybe warm so that it spreads easy."

I looked around and found a newspaper left on the seat across the aisle. It would be clean enough to plop a dollop of grease on and bring back.

"Maybe we could get just a smidgen of grease off the end of the coupling where the caboose had been hooked," I said.

They had dumped the old caboose in Dallas and were probably picking one up down the line. In the meantime, the coupling from our car was sticking out naked behind us. I nodded my head.

"I'm worried that being at the end of the train, all the dirt has been throwing up behind us and sticking to the grease," Gina said.

We mutually agreed to try more towards the front of the train. Bantam started down between the seats with me right behind, carrying my paper. We went through the door at the end of the car and out onto the connecting platforms that covered the coupling between the two cars. With the help of the daylight reflecting up from under the train I could see how dirty the grease was there. It was worse than I had thought it was going to be. Bantam pointed towards the front of the train and we moved on.

We moved through the cars as far forward as we could get and stopped at the front end of all the passenger cars hitched behind the stock cars. We closed the door behind us to try and hide ourselves from prying eyes.

The noise was incredibly loud here with the rattling of the horse cars. We had to speak close into each other's ears to communicate. I knelt down on the iron tongue and peered around into the shadows of the coupling. I laid flat on my belly and stretched, trying to reach something we could use.

Bantam knelt next to my prone body with the newspaper, ready to collect anything I could swab. As I started to reach down into the darkness, the train rounded a corner. The cars swayed and separated. I jerked my arm back just in time as the two cars shifted in opposite directions, grinding between the platforms like a giant pair of scissors. I stared at Bantam with my mouth open in wonderment from the close call. We were up against something a little tougher than we had originally envisioned. I was sweating heavily as I scrambled back up into a sitting position.

"Those cars can make sausage out of your arm," Bantam shouted into my ear. "We're gonna have to be mighty fast. Spot the grease first and then make one quick swipe to get it."

I nodded, took a deep breath, and then lay back down on my belly. Peering into the jaws of the arm-eating machinery I could see where there was an excess of grease piled up. That was my target. I made a couple of tentative reaches, pulling back when the wheels clacked over a seam in the tracks. I was gun-shy. Nearly bitten once, my heart was willing but my courage wanting. I felt Bantam's hand on my shoulder and I looked up.

"I've got a better idea," he shouted. "You hold onto the back of my pants. I'll drop down. I'll grab some drippings and then you yank me back up."

"If our timing is wrong it will slice you in half," I screamed at him.

He smiled at me.

"If that happens let go of my pants."

We stared at each other weighing our options.

"As long as the train is going straight we're okay," I shouted. "If I feel us starting to round a corner I'll yank on your pants."

"Hand me that newspaper. Let's get gaited. I don't want to be down there any longer than I have to be."

Bantam lay flat over the bridging platform tongues and leaned over the side. He scooted up to the edge and angled his body around and underneath. He turned his head up sideways so I could hear him.

"Grab the back of my pants and hold on for dear life. My dear life."

I handed him the newspaper. He slid the entire upper half of his body over the edge of the walking tongue while I sat back on my haunches holding the prat of his britches with all my might. The cars rocked, sometimes together and sometimes apart as wind and dirt blew up from underneath. Bantam shifted, stretching himself as far as he could. Then, as if out of the jaws of some dark evil machine, Bantam's arm came up from the side with the newspaper wadded into a ball shape. I reached over with one hand and took it from him. I could feel the grease inside. I sat it aside on the floor.

I seized his drawers with both hands as I felt the car awkwardly begin sliding to my right.

We were headed into a curve in the tracks. His arms waved about as he tried but failed to help himself. He couldn't reach up high enough to grab anything for support. I didn't have the strength on my own to pull him up. He twisted back and forth. The car slid farther to the right while the one in front scissored off to the left.

"Quit wiggling around, I'm losing my grip," I shouted.

My hands were weakening. His pants began to slide away from his body and I knew I had lost him.

Without warning a pair of hands covered mine and the strength of two people yanked Bantam back up onto the platform. Bantam looked up behind me from where he sat on the floor. He was exhausted and frightened but clearly relieved.

"Thank you, stranger. I won't be lying when I say you helped save my life."

I felt the man stand up full behind me.

"I was glad to be of service," he said.

I turned and looked up into the face of Theophilus Barton Fanning.

Chapter Thirty

He smiled at me while I sat there next to a paper full of grease curd. Bantam was quick to his feet, though, wiping his hands on his legs. Once he had cleaned the lubricant off, he stuck out his right hand.

"I am much obliged for your kind effort in saving my hind end," Bantam said.

Theo chuckled and indicated the passenger car behind us with a crook of his thumb.

"Glad I could be of help. I heard the noise from where I was sitting," he said. "Sounded like quite a commotion."

Oh, god, so we had walked right past him on our way through. I had been too focused on my mission to pay attention to the people in the car. I took the moment to pick up the newspaper and give Theo a quick "thank you" before going back through the train to Anne. I could hear Bantam and him still talking when I walked away. Back at our seats I handed Gina the newspaper, which she unwrapped and scrutinized carefully. She put some on her finger and held it up to the window to see how the light shone through it. She nodded and smiled.

"I think there might be enough clean grease here to use for both Anne and Slocum," she said.

The dog picked his head up at the sound of his name, eyeing the newspaper expectantly as if I had returned with scraps from a dining car. Gina had already torn the strips for bandages from the towel. Anne was awake and gave me a sleepy smile as I held her arm out to coat with grease. Gina dipped two fingers in the lubricant. I twisted Anne's arm slightly to give better access to the burnt patch of skin, which ran in a fiery red streak along the underside. For a brief moment the lines at the corner of Anne's eyes deepened. The pain must have been excruciating.

Anne stared straight at me and never wavered as the grease made contact with her scorched flesh. She gave a sudden jerk, with a squinting of her eyes. Then she tipped her face up slightly as she took a deep breath. With all that she had been through, she was still a proud woman. I took strength from her. I held Anne's hand tightly, trying to offer a little bit of the support back to her.

Gina wiped the excess grease off on the newspaper and then picked up one of the bandage strips. She placed the beginning of the towel on the opposite side of Anne's arm from the burn and began wrapping it snugly about the limb. On the first rotation, the grease soaked through, turning the white cotton to a dirty gray, but with multiple coverings it all seemed contained. The other arm followed and upon completion, Anne sank back in her seat.

I took the grease from Gina and turned to Slocum. He knew something was up. His ears dropped and his chin plopped down on his paws. It was only the bottom shin area of his front legs that we could wrap. There wasn't much I could really do about the pads of his feet. He would probably lick at them. As they dried out in between lickings they would probably split, peel, and then heal back correctly. Keeping him calm would be my task. I was able to secure the bandages on his forelegs together with two safety-pins that Anne had stuck in her dress.

"Sometimes you have to give a customer a little extra prodding," she smiled.

I still did not understand her reason for having the pin but it put odd pictures in my mind. Slocum would have to be watched to make sure he did not chew at his leg burns. I figured that after a few days, I would take off the bandages and wash him clean. Everybody had settled back after the re-bandaging ordeal when Bantam showed up with Theophilus Barton Fanning in tow. I wished that the medical attention had taken longer so I would have had something to keep my hands occupied.

He stood there awkwardly while Bantam introduced him. Gina put her hand out demurely like she was the Queen of Sheba and he held it a moment too long, giving a tight head bow in her direction.

"A pleasure," he said.

When he reached for Anne's hand in greeting he saw the bandages and knelt down on one knee. He held her hand with both of his.

"I was very sorry to hear of your misfortune."

He nodded in Bantam's direction for having been told, what I assumed, was our entire history. Anne gave Bantam a quick glance and then returned to stare at Mister Fanning. He gently turned her hand to examine the extent of the damage on her arm.

"I do have a little medical training," he said. "Would you like me to examine the burns?"

"No, but thank you for asking. I just had my dressings changed," she said, indicating us as if we were Florence Nightingale initiates.

The only thing missing from her act was a European accent. She batted her eyes and sucked in a quick breath as if the pain was almost intolerable at that moment. He let go of her hand.

"I'm so sorry. I didn't realize that . . ."

"No, no," she interrupted and put her hand back between his, which were still outstretched. "It was an automatic reaction from the rough greasing and bandaging earlier."

She was good. I'll bet she'd made a lot of money at her work. He gave her hand a small pat and stood up.

"I'm glad," he smiled. "I would not want to cause you any more vexation."

I smiled to myself because, unbeknownst to him, he already had by letting go of her hand.

"I'll pray that you heal with expediency."

He straightened his vest and smoothed the tops of his pant legs. He wasn't wearing a collar of the cloth and I inquired about that. He hung his head a little in response.

"I am weak. There are times when I am too tired from the day's sojourn or ministering to continue on. I ask the Lord for strength but many times the flesh is weak and I hide from my obligations."

He gave the group a quick scan.

"But now that you know of my foible, please do not allow that to stop you from approaching me for any counseling during this trip."

He looked down at me and smiled.

"It was good to see you again, Peggy," he said.

I cringed. The others turned and looked at me as if I was hiding some dark secret. I scowled back at them.

"Good to see you also, Theophilus."

"Please. Call me Theo."

"Father Theo?"

"No, just Theo is fine. I'm a Methodist," he said and then nodded at the group.

He turned and walked away. Nobody spoke until he was out of sight. It was Bantam who broke the silence by clapping his hands together.

"Whooee! If that wasn't hog-killin' time. It was like being in a room full of unsalted schoolgirls."

We all glared at him and he quieted down. But as we turned

back to our own business, I could hear him chuckling under his breath. Gina gave a loud sigh and he took his mirth out of our hearing range. The rest of us kept still for the next hour or so as the train clacked along the tracks. The monotony of the sound put me to sleep and I was transported to the most beautiful church in heaven, the pastor of which was quite handsome.

With all of the events that had happened during this trip I was pleasantly surprised and pleased that the remainder of the rail ride was relatively smooth. The days passed while the healing process moved smoothly for both of the patients. I successfully kept Slocum from reinjuring himself. The bandages were soon removed and everybody got off the train and stretched at each and every stop. The sun felt good and the weather warmed steadily as we crossed the country. The green of the plains crops and grasses gave way to brown and black monuments of rock that spired into the cloudless blue eye of heaven.

There was plenty of time to think and read and sleep. I was becoming increasingly trepidatious with the approaching trial and the end of my quest. I even feared what would happen after this was over and our hearty band no longer had a purpose. Was it only the experience that bound us together or did we really feel for each other?

This train ride was soon coming to an end and outside the window was only dirt. No trees. No towns. Ugly and seemingly desolate.

In the distance I could see the dirt getting picked up by some light winds and dancing in circles before dropping back to earth. That was us. One by one we were picked up in the distance and danced about until being dropped here in the middle of our little clan. This coming morning it would be the end of the train line at Yuma and the ride for San Pueblo would commence.

★ ★ ★ ★ ★

San Pueblo

★ ★ ★ ★ ★

"It was considered the most dangerous route in the Hills, but as my reputation as a rider and quick shot was well known, I was molested very little, for the toll gatherers looked on me as being a good fellow, and they knew that I never missed my mark."

—Calamity Jane

Chapter Thirty-One

The wind was whistling as if God was trying to blow out a lantern. The dirt and sand that moved horizontally across the landscape forced itself into our eyes and ears and up our noses. We pulled our bandanas over our faces and looked like a band of bank robbers as we led the horses down out of the cattle cars. They fought us, pawing and whinnying, partially from trying to turn away from the blowing grit and partially because they were getting their ground legs back after having had the earth constantly moving beneath them during the train ride. We had help from the local stableman who ended up tying rags about the horses' eyes and leading them one by one away from the chugging train and into the wind-free stable.

"Is there a storm approaching?" I shouted at him as we were walking in.

"No. This is Yuma," he said. "It always blows in Yuma. You'll get used to it."

"No, we won't," Bantam said. "We're leaving tomorrow for San Pueblo."

The stableman put two of the horses in one stall and Gina's in another. He forked in some hay and showed us where the grains were for their feed bags. Then he sat back and watched us as we cooled them with water and settled the animals into their home for the night.

"I couldn't help but notice that there are four of you, not counting the dog there," he said pointing at Slocum. "Only three horses. There's too much distance to San Pueblo for any horse to ride double, especially a horse that hasn't been ridden for some time," he said noting the skittishness of the mounts.

"Nor would I put my friends or their horses through that trial," Anne said, stepping forward. "Do you happen to have a capable mount for sale?"

Gina jumped in.

"Anne, do you ride?"

"Riding is my specialty." She smiled a quick smile at Gina and turned back to the man, all business. "Well, do you?"

He looked her over, trying to get a bead on her beneath her layers of clothes. Then he made a sound deep in his throat and shook his head. Then he turned and walked over to the area where he kept his stable bills.

"I do not. But I heard talk in the saloon the other day that one of the folks in the area had an extra beast or two. His horses have always been sturdy and responsive. Perhaps if your . . . man . . . friend there were to go into the saloon and ask for Logy."

Bantam gave him that look that meant he would have loved to shoot him on the spot. There was a pause while he gathered himself and then he turned back to Anne and smiled.

"Ah, Miss Anne. This is a man's job that must be done."

The stableman snorted a dismissive sound and Bantam gave him a quick look before turning back to Anne.

"And beings that I am also a mite parched from all this dirt blowing about . . ."

Another snort and another look.

"I would be more than glad to take on this duty for you."

Anne laughed and gave a light bow to Bantam.

"Thank you, Bantam. Make sure you find me something sturdy as I'm no wilting garden flower in girth or stature."

The stableman was picking at his teeth with a sliver of wood when he spoke.

"Logy will try to dicker with you but hold fast. Make sure the horse is broad to carry your things and the lady here. He'll need to be at least fifteen hands."

Bantam almost growled when he turned to the worker.

"I am familiar with horses."

"Fine with me. It's your call. I was just tryin' to be helpful. Didn't want her to end up with some kind of pony ride."

Bantam started to run at him when Gina wrapped her arm about his shoulders as he ran past. She held fast and pulled him back to the group.

"You have a duty, Bantam," she said. "This is no time to get into a cockfight."

He straightened himself, regaining his composure.

"Thank you," Anne said. "I am much obliged for your efforts."

"Oh, one last thing," the stableman said, sucking air through his newly cleaned teeth. "I don't know where you are from but around here we would never pay more than one hundred dollars for a horse, not twice that like they do in Texas."

"One hundred dollars! That's outrageous," Bantam shouted.

The stableman shrugged.

"We're in the Arizona Territory here so we get a few more horses down from California than the Texans do. But still there is a scarcity of them to a degree."

Bantam looked over to Anne.

"Do you have those kinds of Lincoln skins?" he asked.

"I do," she said. "Look away."

Bantam scowled but turned his head. Anne lifted up the hem of her dress and rolled it upwards over her thighs to a hidden inner seam. She picked it open and removed a small bunch of bills. Then she rolled her dress back down and looked up to see Bantam watching her.

"Well I'll be plummed," he said.

Anne smiled. "Now go and do me proud."

Bantam turned and scurried out the door of the stable.

"One last thing," the stableman shouted, turning Bantam around. "Logy is crazy and in your case, he would just as soon step on you as work out a horse trade."

Bantam pointed at the stableman.

"I will be returning with a mount. Then you and I will speak."

He left while the stableman went back to picking his teeth. He was quietly laughing to himself. Gina was looking out the stable door while staying out of the wind.

"Peggy, what do you say we go across the street to the sheriff's office and ask for directions and maybe a few pointers? Now that we're within riding range, he may have a feel for what's going on in San Pueblo."

"Not a bad idea," I said. "Would you mind telling my friend where we went when he gets back?"

"Wouldn't mind a bit. But this little lady best stay here with me anyhow," he said nodding at Anne.

"Why's that?" Anne asked. Our stableman was not turning out to be her favorite person.

"Well, Half-Sack might do an all right job in buying you a horse but unless you're intending to ride bareback you're gonna have to try out a few of my riggings."

Anne weighed the thought for a moment.

"You two go over there and see what you can find out and I'll take care of business here. Besides, Bantam will be back shortly."

A snort sounded from behind her as the stableman walked over to a large door and slid it open. I could see rigs and pieces of saddlery piled in there and hanging on the wall.

"Shortly is right," he said. "Ma'am, would you care to step over this way and see if we can't interest you in a saddle for your horse?"

"My, where did you get this entire inventory?"

"Well, ma'am," he said. "Some people don't end up having the money to pay their bills. Being the fine fellow that I am, I am willing to sometimes dicker and take things in trade."

He gave her a smile that stopped Gina in her tracks. But Anne waved us off and went to look at saddles. Gina led the way to the sheriff's office she had spotted. We turned our heads away from the wind as the sand continued to pelt us unrelentingly.

The wind had been blowing so hard we couldn't hear any sound from the office prior to us opening up the door and walking in. We were just happy to have the weather behind us. But as soon as we stepped in, we could hear the shouting. The sheriff was facing away from us yelling at a prisoner inside one of his cells.

"You gonna give me a hard time, Riley?" he yelled. "I pulled your ass out of that drunken fight before that monstrous moose ripped your head clean off. It's late afternoon and you're in till morning, so quit airin' your lungs at me and sit down."

The man stepped up and held on to the cell door bars. He pulled his face right up between them, the metal squishing his cheeks together like he was going to whistle. Blood ran down the side of his face and I couldn't tell if the missing teeth were a recent altering of his looks. He'd been beat, all right.

"Sheriff, you've got no right."

The sheriff took the side of his metal drinking cup and smashed it against Riley's fingers, trapping them between it and the bar. He let out a yell like he'd been bit by a bear and backed up, waving his hand around in the air.

"You broke 'em, goddamn it," Riley yelled. "You broke my fingers! You had no call to do that!"

"I told you to shut up. At this moment you're lucky to be alive, you addle-headed turd," the sheriff yelled back and turned around to face us.

We were obviously a surprise to him but his anger easily turned to a phony, oversized smile. He snatched the hat off of his head and held it over his heart.

"Why, ladies, what can I do for you?"

There was a moment where we just stared at each other and the only sound was the whimpering of Riley in the cell. The sheriff cleared his throat and, taking a step towards us, held out his hand.

"Wood," he said. "Rocky Wood. Sheriff Rocky Wood. At your service."

I started to speak when Riley let out a mournful cry.

"You done smashed them in a couple of places! I may never be able to rope again."

Sheriff Wood spun around.

"You're not going to be able to think neither 'cause I'm gonna rip your head off if you aren't quiet. I'm not farting around."

He turned back around and gave us that toothy grin again.

"Sorry, ladies. Now what were you saying?"

I held out my hand, which he took daintily and let drop.

"Peggy."

"Pleased to meet you, Miss Peggy," the sheriff said.

He looked over to Gina but she just stood there silent. When he didn't get a response, he looked back to me and cocked an eyebrow.

"There are four of us altogether, who will be traveling to San Pueblo. We thought we'd check in and see if you could give us any tips or advice about riding from here to there. Anything we might need to know that maybe a . . . a seasoned gentleman, such as yourself, may be able to pass on to us in terms of forewarning or guidance."

Another death moan emanated from the jail cell and our conversation came to a complete stop. I could see the sheriff's shoulders tighten up along with his jaws. But he said nothing and merely paused before answering me. I had a feeling he was on his best behavior in front of "the ladies," which wasn't all that good. He took a deep breath and let it out slowly before continuing.

"Are there four of you ladies, then?"

Gina snorted this time.

"Not really," she said.

"There's one man among us," I said and gave Gina a sideways glance to let her know that I had better finish this conversation.

The sheriff pondered this over.

"Still, three ladies and one man is a very dangerous way to travel," he said. "The distance between here and there is not insurmountable. The country is fairly barren, but there are thieves, heathens, and all the deadly beasts of the world that Satan himself could conjure up to populate this little personal section of his habitat. But you could make it on a straight two-day ride with the four of you and some luck."

Another melancholy moan from Riley and the sheriff sat down at his desk and closed his eyes for a moment, rubbing his temples. He didn't look over at the cell but tried with all of his power to ignore the whimpering.

He stopped and looked back up at me.

"Are you well armed?"

"Well enough," I answered.

"Is your mission to San Pueblo of such importance that you are willing to risk your life and the lives of your friends?"

Now, Gina answered up.

"Yes, it is."

"Suit yourself," he said.

Riley started crying and Sheriff Wood spit and pointed at the cell.

"Now, I can't take that," he said. "It's almost over."

He stood up and took his gun belt down from the peg on the wall. He spoke as he buckled it up about the base of his protruding belly.

"All I can offer you is my blessing. May you be safe," he said and I felt like some preacher had just tried to flamboozle me and then passed the collection plate.

Wood eyed us a moment and shrugged his shoulders. He put his hat back on his head and adjusted it with a sort of cocky tilt. He seemed to think much of himself.

"I've known men like you," Gina said.

He smiled.

"I'll bet you have, ma'am, I'll bet you have. Probably quite a few of them. And I have known ladies like you."

More sobbing came from the cell. The sheriff had finished with our conversation. He tipped his hat to us.

"Good day, ladies, and good luck."

We walked out and shut the door behind us. Gina was nigh on to exploding. She brushed at the annoying sand flying in her face.

"He is as useless as tits on a boar," she said and we started across the street.

A loud bang rang out from inside the sheriff's office. We froze in place. Passersby turned and looked in the direction of the sound and then continued on. Nobody seemed to care. Gina looked at me.

"I believe that Riley won't have to worry about that hand healing up."

She marched back towards the stables.

"Like I said, I've known men like him. Authority is a dangerous thing, especially when it is worn by an unconscionable man."

Chapter Thirty-Two

Harsh. That was the land, the wind, and the people who seemed to survive in this godforsaken place. My eyes all bound together with dirt and my own tears. The wind made them gush water like a primed pump. I couldn't wait to get back inside the four walls of the stable. Sweaty grit clung to my face and neck, drawing lines on the wrinkles like netting across my skin.

Anne was standing on the far side by an empty stall. There was a full rig hanging on the half wall as if she was going to ride that instead of a horse. The stableman was over in his alcove fooling with some papers, not looking up. Gina looked the saddle and leathers over, flipping parts of it up and looking underneath. At one point she even took a piece of a strap and smelled it. Then she bit on it. She saw me watching her inquisitively.

"I can tell if there's been anything cheap in the tanning. It's like tasting bad whiskey. Can't tell you what they use but I can tell you that it ain't right."

She dropped the strap she was holding and looked at Anne.

"These seem fine. You did yourself good, girl," she said. "Did you get a decent price?"

Anne glanced over at the farrier.

"Could have done better," she smiled.

"Really?" Gina looked at her.

Anne smiled. "For now."

"What about a horse?" I asked.

"Bantam hasn't gotten back yet. We'll see what Bantam brings home and go from there. Did you get any information from the sheriff?"

She caught us off guard. Gina shrugged and stuck her hands in her pockets.

"He's like most men you and I have probably had run-ins with. Likes to hear himself talk, knows more than anybody else, and if you get in his way, he'll kill you. He's got some heft but not many brains. Best we get ourselves together and leave that highbinder to his own devices. He's trouble."

"Well then, maybe we should just scout about for a place to eat and sleep," Anne said.

I piped up. "I don't know. This is the type of town where somebody could wake up dead. Gives me the jitters."

Anne went over to the smithy.

"I'm leaving my rig here," she said, staring right at him like a bullet from a carbine. "Make sure nothing happens to it."

He looked up and caught her heat. Then she waved at us and we followed her out the door. Though it was daytime, it had darkened precipitously and the air had begun to hold water. Clouds were gathering on the close edge of the northwestern sky. Heaviness lay in their bottoms, weighing each one down as the wind slowly dragged them across the heavens, scraping the tops of brown dirt hills along the way. We kept our faces pointed away from the wind and looked for signs of food and lodging as we pushed down the wooden sidewalks.

Gina pointed at the saloon.

"Even though I could do with a drink, I think we'd better let Bantam do what he set out to do without any interference from us."

"Besides," I said, "he could probably do with a little time away from us." I started to laugh. "I know I could."

That got a slap on the shoulder from Anne and a bark out of

Slocum as he watched us play fight. Anne rubbed the side of his head as we walked.

"Seems like somebody else could use a bite to eat."

Gina put her hand up to shield her eyes.

"I don't care where we eat as long as it's indoors."

Once we found ourselves an eatery with satisfactory vittles we spent a good hour or so eating, talking, and washing the dirt out of our throats with our choice of favorite beverage while Slocum shared the scraps and handouts we offered him. They had rooms upstairs and we were grateful to not have to look any further. The couple who owned the place sent one of their kitchen folks down to Bantam and took him a note about where we were spending the night.

In the morning we would retrieve our mounts along with Anne's new child and load up on supplies before heading out on the road (more like a wide trail from what I was beginning to pick up) to San Pueblo.

When I saw James's murderer again, I had no idea how I would behave. It would feel good to see justice served. James was a lawman and the law would serve him in the final hours of his story. There was a calm about that which seemed to envelope me as if James himself was standing behind me.

Tonight, before going to sleep, I sat on the side of the bed and looked at the palms of my hands in the lamplight. The angle and hue of the glow darkened some of the lines, made them deeper and seemingly longer.

I jumped, startled, when two hands enveloped my own, pointing them palms skyward. Gina smiled at me.

"Do you want to know?" she asked. "It's what we do, us gypsies. We read your life in your hands."

"I'm not sure."

"Yes. That's always the question."

Gina sat on her knees on the floor.

"It is not so detailed. I can't tell you that you will die today. I can't say riches are yours for the taking. It's more like waves upon the beach. It's little layers of information combined with other pieces of information. You have a bent for one thing or the other and that I'll be able to see. It's more 'can' than 'will.' "

Gina let go of my hands and smiled at me.

"The power of your life still belongs to you. It's not a predestined thing given over to some higher power. That's why you have a brain and a heart. They both control you in different ways but with some help and understanding you can learn to control them to your best advantage."

I shrugged.

"If it doesn't give you answers what good is it?"

She picked my hands back up. She flipped them over once and then flipped them back palm up.

"It gives you a meeting place, Peg."

"What?" I shook my head. "I don't understand."

"A gathering place. Once you know what your possibilities are and what your stumbling blocks might be, it allows you to pull together all of your resources, all of your internal treasures of mind and heart to use as a combined force against obstructions and things that may pull you away from your center. Sunlight bounces off of a store window or off of the water and into your eyes. But it's not coming from the window or the water. It all starts with one bright spot that throws that light out into the world, the sun. In your life you are your own sun. Just like the sun, the further from your goals the more windows, mirrors, and waters bounce your original light in different directions. To read your palm is to offer you a chance to see your original life's intent before it starts getting reflected. The decision about what to do with that information is yours."

I nodded.

Gina held my right hand between both of hers.

"Maybe now is not the time. It will only mean something to you. There is time. We'll do it later because much of what I will tell you is meaningless to me. When you have fewer things to deal with."

She stood up.

"Good night."

And with that she left the room, shutting the door behind her. I sat and pondered my hands in the lamplight.

Chapter Thirty-Three

From where I sat on Horse, I could see the stableman pointing in the direction we had to go. I was too far away to hear what he was telling Anne but his gestures made it quite obvious. When he had finished speaking she mouthed "Thank you" and then rode over to join us in the group.

"Good-lookin' mount," I said.

Bantam was a little puffy with pride.

"I told you I knew what I was doing."

"Thank you, Bantam," Anne said and patted the neck of her horse. It was a clay, cream colored with a black mane and tail. "I think this will do fine."

"Yeah, well I had to sacrifice the entirety of my night to the evils of alcohol."

Bantam smiled. "I'm havin' to put up with a little barrel fever this morning. But somehow I'll make it through."

He laughed and tightened up the reins on his horse. Swinging it about in the direction we were to head, he started the last leg of our journey.

"Well, let's go see Judgment Day," he said and gave us a wagon-master hand signal to follow him.

A couple of days and we would be into San Pueblo. Sheriff Bannon would probably be surprised to see me arrive with an entire band of *inadaptados,* including one little fella who thought he could rule the world. We all swung around and fell in step behind Bantam. Slocum, glad to be back on the open road, was running along the side of the trail and sniffing in the weeds like he had done when the two of us had first set out from home.

The morning was warm and the sun bright, the kind of day that would get vicious hot without too much provocation. There was not a cloud in the sky or our moods until we rode past the sheriff's office and Wood walked out the front door and stood leaning against a porch pole watching us pass. He didn't say a word, the expression on his face did not change. A wooden matchstick stuck out from the corner of his mouth and he used his tongue to play with it, flicking it back and forth. There were dark sweat circles already peeking out from under his armpits this morning. Maybe they were left over from yesterday or the day before. The two of us stared at each other as we rode along. Further on, the shopkeeper, where we'd bought supplies, waved at us through the window and Gina waved back. Wood took note from where he stood and the shopkeeper got on with his business. Sometime later, we would look back on this moment as one filled with hope and determination.

It had been too long since I'd ridden any distance and it took me some time to get my derriere adjusted into the motion of Horse. All those days of sitting on a train bench curves your spine or spreads something within you in the wrong direction. Horse rose and I dropped, then I rose and he dropped. Yep, this would take a minute and I knew I would feel it at the end of the day. I felt the anticipation rise inside of me. I forced it back down and tried to look at the country around me as we left Yuma behind.

This was a foreign land compared to Missouri. Sand and scrub seemed to be the only features of this scraggy territory. Rock outcroppings jagged and pushed towards the sky, giving ledges for lizards and rattlesnakes to bake lazily in the heat. Still the wind, that damn wind, picked up the sand and threw it in our faces and the horses' eyes like tiny serrated bits of broken glass. I pulled Horse to the side of the trail, behind a rock, and jumped down. Although I had on a bandana about my face, I pulled a second one out of my saddlebag and shook it out. Gina rode up beside me.

"What are you doing?"

I poured some water on it, then began tying the cloth to the top of the bridle above Horse's eyes. I kept working while I answered her question.

"I need some kind of tog or material over his face to keep the sand out. Otherwise he'll blow his eyes out before we get five miles down the road."

I wrapped it under and tied it off to the center strap between his eyes. It would flap in front of him and darken his sight some but it would also keep a lot of the sand out of his eyes and he would still be able to see. Gina nodded.

"That ain't a half bad idea," she said and jumped down to begin working on her mount. "He keeps turning his head away from the wind but then he can't hardly see where he's going anyway."

The day proved challenging with the headwind and the heat. Much to our delight, it blew itself out or stayed behind us in the general area of Yuma so that by afternoon we could remove the bandanas from the horses' eyes. We rode steady but not hard enough to put needless wear on the mounts. Sometimes we moved side by side and sometimes single line depending upon the trail. Not much talking, mostly lost in our own thoughts, keeping our eyes open for Apaches or a bushwhack of any sort. It felt like we were making good time and the entire party appeared lighthearted and calm. The sun and air seemed to offer a freedom, which each of us was drinking in.

Though I was at the back of the pack, I saw Bantam pull up and stare down at the trail. Gina rode up beside him and they conversed for a moment. Then Bantam continued down the trail followed by the group. Gina held to the side and waited until I was even with her and rode with me.

"A good size group of riders were through here today."

She nodded at the ground and I saw the horse manure and excessive amount of tracks.

"Fairly soft. They're crossing the trail here and heading up there into the brush."

She pointed off to my left and I could tell where the grass and bushes had been parted.

"They're headed the same direction we are but off trail. Means they know the country and where they're going. You're in the back of the basket here so keep your eyes wide open. I don't want anybody to get the bulge on us."

"Not a problem," I said and did a quick look about and behind me.

Gina slapped my shoulder and rode back up ahead of Anne. I followed behind, shifting around in my saddle, certain we were being watched. Luckily, we didn't encounter anything else unusual the rest of the day and eventually found a great little spot to hunker down for the night. By the looks of it, it seemed like this was a natural area for most travelers to stop on their sojourn. A creek trickled nearby. The mesquite and sage proved to be nice cover with enough distance not to ignite should a breeze arise while the fire was crackling.

The sounds of the animals outside of camp changed as dusk gave way to evening and the darkness began to close down around us. We ate and fed our mounts, then laid back to relax for the night. Bantam was a little antsy.

"Sure wish I had a jar of that hooch I was peddling right about now," he said.

"Seems to me that was what got you in some trouble in the first place, I think we barely escaped with our lives."

"The fact that you were in that tent didn't help any. That gorilla had designs on you."

Anne was digging around in her saddlebags. She laughed.

"It's hard to get used to a new piece of luggage."

Bantam snorted, not wanting to let the earlier remarks go.

"I had them right where I wanted them. If we'd stayed on and fought back we would have been fine."

"Sure we would have," I said. "We would've ended up like that last person on the Pena de Muerte."

"What's that?" Gina asked, chewing on a piece of jerky she had dug out of her bags.

"Bantam had a tent in this nasty blackleg encampment selling jars of Everclear," I said. "The place was nothing but trouble."

"I made good money there," he countered.

"Anyway," I continued, "there was a mud alley that ran behind these main street tents. It was where a lot of the fights, robberies, and any other kinds of deals you can think of took place. It was called Pena de Muerte—Death Penalty. Rightfully so, if you ask me."

Anne looked up from what she was doing.

"I'm sure there was what fine gentlemen refer to as a hook shop in among those tents."

"I pitched my place of sales right near it," Bantam smiled. "Figured I'd get some easy business with it being so close. The boys need to drink."

"And the ladies too," Anne said and held up a bottle from her bags.

"Lawd," Bantam said and stood up.

Anne waved him over.

"Never travel if you aren't prepared for the trip."

She looked at the rest of us.

"Anybody else care for a gut warmer?"

It looked real good to me and I figured it couldn't hurt. The trail made a person mighty thirsty.

"I'm your huckleberry," I said and scooted over to join them.

Then Gina joined the group.

"By gummy, there ain't no sense in me sitting by myself and sober."

So we socked together in a circle and began drinking and jaw-jacking. There was only the one bottle to share but plenty of conversation to go around. We laughed and talked and took the day's edge off with Anne's gift. Then, as the night drew its cloak around us, things became a little quieter and the conversation turned nostalgic. Bantam, with the help of the liquor, couldn't hold back his thoughts any longer. He took a breath and released the thought. He looked at Anne.

"I have to say, I appreciate the little gift that you are sharing with us, so please don't get me wrong here. But I was wondering how does somebody, lovely as you are, become involved in your end of the business?"

Anne looked at him over the neck of the bottle.

"Thank you, but I believe the blossom is off the rose in my case. Still, men will lay with anything and anybody. Why? Do you have a problem with my chosen occupation?"

"Not at all," he said, smiling. "Men like me are mightily grateful for gals like you. I'm just wondering why or what? Why not a teacher or something safe?"

Now it was my time to snort.

"I was a teacher and I'm sitting at the same campfire with the rest of you all. A lot of good it did me."

Gina laughed and slapped me on the leg.

"I thought about it," Anne said, looking at me. "Things happen. Circumstances change. I'm not even sure I was smart enough for it."

"Oh, I'll bet you are," I said.

"You know, I always made more money than most of those around me because I'm a redhead, not because I'm so smart."

"No kiddin'," Bantam exclaimed.

Anne laughed at him.

"Easy, Bucko," she said. "I've worked with some of the best in the business and they showed me the ropes. I've swung hips with the likes of Legs Diamond, Hambone Jane, Sarah Sackum, Tit Bit, Sweet Annie, Black Pearl, Smooth Bore, Fatty McDuff, and Cotton Tail, who was a natural blonde, mind you. Cotton and I had quite a rivalry outside Fort Darning for a while. In turn, I've passed some of that knowledge on to help the next demimonde with her life.

"Some got into this line of work purely as survival. Some were escaping their family where they had a father who used them as a towel to wipe their willie on. They thought that they may as well make some money with that space between their legs that caused them so much pain. Some were trying to provide for their family and some were just plain stupid. Everybody's got a story and every story is different. Yet, after a while, they all start to sound the same.

"There's a lot to learn and it ain't easy. I've seen 'em come and leave the profession quick enough from disease or gettin' beat to a pulp. Even with the best of precautions, you can't be sure that somebody ain't hiding a rot in their lap or an angry attitude when they get to drinking. A lot of it is luck. I'm still here so I guess I was a lucky one. It's better if you're with a house of some sort. Life alone on the town is a tough way to go."

She took her swig and passed the bottle on. Some of it dribbled down her chin and she gave a laugh as she wiped it off her face with one finger.

"So, what do you do when life is finished giving you the looks that will get you paid? Some of us start our own business or ladies house or get married to our last rich trick and don't look back. Some move away and hitch up with somebody who has no idea of where we've been. Everybody has a past they keep inside. Anybody tells you they don't are a liar."

Gina listened intently and locked eyes with Anne as she spoke. The floodgates had opened and her story just poured out of her.

"Then there are those of us who can't take it when their time has come to shut the door on their living. I've seen many die by their own hands. It's sad. But that's what life is, ain't it? Sad? Many of us can't write or read and have nothing else. They can't work anyplace else. What business would hire an ex-whore?"

Gina took a drink as the bottle passed and sent it on to me. Bantam wiped his mouth with his sleeve.

"Which one of those women were you?" he said.

Anne thought about it a moment.

"I don't know. Maybe a touch of all of 'em, I guess. But I think I was more of an adventuress than anything else. At least that is how I like to think of myself. Couldn't fence me in and I had to have my own way, with everything. I guess that's the stupid part. I probably could've done better. Que sera."

She waved the bottle in the air.

"It was intended as a temporary solution to my problems from the very start and here I sit on my fat ass with wrinkles and bad breath."

"I think you're lying a little too," I said.

Anne looked over at me and squinted her eyes.

"About what?"

"Regrets. I think we all have some regrets if we think hard enough."

She looked at me in a flicker like she could kill me. I assumed this was a woman who did not cry often, at least in front of others. But she cried now, helped by the liquor and the ability to feel comfortable enough with people to let down her guard. She could be herself and not be vulnerable. A quiet choking sound in her throat was the only noise while she looked away.

Gina took the nearly empty bottle from Anne and leaned back watching the internal reconstruction happening in front of her.

Anne turned back around and looked at each of us individually across the flickering flames, ending with me. She lingered a moment and then invited us in to her circle with her body movements. There was a ghost story about to be told. Like any good ghost story, the audience was already apprehensive about what it was going to hear. We were already frightened of specters. Because we believed in ghosts, our own haunted lives, but listening to Anne's story would delay the inevitable moment when we would have to look into the mirror reflecting our own evils.

"When you are young and beautiful on the frontier," Anne began, "your life is very different from the average citified youth who is sashaying towards womanhood."

Bantam stood up and brushed off his pants.

"I think I should retire. Tomorrow's going to be a long day," he said.

Anne reached out, grabbed his arm, and yanked him back down to the ground.

"You will stay and you will listen," she said curtly.

Chapter Thirty-Four

"I wed at the age of fourteen as a way to get out of a home where my uncle, that's what my mother made me call him, would force me to have sex with him. I think that if I had not escaped from that situation, I would've killed him and my mother too. I found a tinker heading to the frontier. I married him quick-like and left on a wagon clanging with pots and pans.

"How I felt about him didn't matter. Whatever my life would be with him was better than what I had. He was willing to take me as I was. If I had not jumped at that chance, I would be dead now."

Bantam tipped the bottle all the way up, sucking in the last bit of liquid. He tossed it to the side in the darkness. Gina watched him and then rose and went to her saddlebags.

"Dog fleas," she said. "If we're going to be spitting out our past, I guess I'll break out some more tarantula juice."

"Oh, yes," Bantam practically shouted.

Gina stopped and pointed at him.

"You calm down. You get the bottle last in line with the gulping you've been doing."

Bantam scrunched back down on his haunches while Gina dug the bottle out of her bag.

"Go ahead. Keep talking."

"It was okay," Anne said. "He was fine but kind of demanding. He liked his daily life and his sex in a frequent manner. I was happy to unload it on him since he treated me right in every way as long as he got his daily dose."

"Wow, every day, huh?" Bantam said.

Gina passed him by and knocked the back of his head with the full bottle of liquor.

"Let the woman talk," she said and sat down next to me.

Bantam rubbed the back of his head, pouting.

"He was good too and taught me things that a man likes, things he'd picked up on the road." Anne continued, "He also taught me things a woman likes and tried to offer me as much pleasure as he could."

She laughed, thinking back.

She leaned in to us, "He taught me how to spray a stream myself. That little trick has netted me more money than almost anything my repertoire has to offer. I learned my basics with him.

"Then outside of Collinwood, Kentucky, we were attacked by a pack of lowlife dirt boys. I escaped but the tinker was killed. After that I was lost and wandering about until I found my way into a town a little outside of Mammoth Caves. I wasn't skilled enough to be a seamstress or teacher. The war was on and I needed some money and to get out. I scavenged behind the buildings in the garbage for food."

Bantam nodded. "I had seen that kind of thing where I was doing business when I met up with Mrs. Thomas."

"Yes, it was a lovely area," I said.

"What usually happened was that the local law would find me," Anne continued, "take me back to jail, have their way with me, and then put me out on the road outside of town with a warning to never return. Last time they actually put me on a coach and I was able to get farther west than I'd ever been.

"I was without skills, except one. Eventually I found myself in a vaulted house making good money for the madam and myself. I moved up the ranks in a hurry and in time became a madam myself. I was riding high right about then. That could have been my best time.

"In time, the do-gooding politicians called on me. I got a wagon and with my best girls ran one of the first traveling cat wagons going from mining town to logging town. I was moving further west all the time. I opened many a new settlement, helping them prosper I am proud to say. Although I will never be recognized for those achievements."

She laughed.

"I had money, friends, influence, and eventually a mansion. Being a redhead was a special gift from God. He'd smiled on me . . . that once. Now I sit here today drinking this varnish and packin' my savings sewn in my clothes."

She held up the bottle that had been passed to her and took a good swig.

"Thank you, Jesus!"

She saluted the sky with the bottle, drank a good long drink. and then passed it over to me. She wiped her mouth with the back of her hand and burped like a cavalry horn. I followed her lead on taking a swig of my own.

"Then I lost my girls and house," Anne said. "The road took its toll. My red hair began to dull. Wrinkles began to chase each other across my face and extra flesh filled my body. The young taut body gave way to a softer cushiony experience for the customer. Mind you, there are those who prefer that mastery with a satin feel. I gave them that along with a lifetime of experience of pleasing a fella. But the monies were less and the customers were fewer on the road. Eventually I ended up in the crib in Dallas where you found me."

She winked at Bantam. After taking a sip, he set down the bottle, which was being watched over very carefully by Gina.

"Then that horrible fire," Bantam said.

Anne turned and looked at my dog.

"Slocum saved me. I'm thankful to him."

She looked back at us, her eyes glistening.

"And to all of you," she said.

She grabbed the bottle back and took a major shot. Her eyes closed, with her head tilted back, she enjoyed its long hot run down her throat. When it had washed, she took a deep breath and opened her eyes.

"And that, my new dear friends, is my sad tale of woe."

"You get to start over again. Now you can be just a person," I said.

She looked at me from where she stood and extended her leg towards the fire.

"You mean instead of a whore?"

She wasn't angry when she said it.

"No," I said. "I mean just a friend."

Anne brushed her dress as if straightening it and then the river began to flow from her eyes and down her face. She looked at me.

"Real glamorous, huh?"

I smiled at her.

"I don't know if I can start over again," Anne said. "At my age, I don't know if I've got the energy or the desire."

Gina piped in.

"Weigh your alternatives," she said.

"Been there?" Anne asked.

Gina spit a shot of tobacco between her teeth and into the fire.

"In my own way."

I heard the whiskey slosh in the bottle behind me and turned to get a sheepish look from Bantam, bottle in hand. He slowly set it down and stood up.

"Can I turn in now?" he asked looking around.

Anne raised her head up and looked at him standing

awkwardly there. She began to giggle and Gina began to laugh and then I joined in. Anne waggled her hand at Bantam.

"Yes, yes. Please take yourself to bed," and she began to laugh even harder.

Chapter Thirty-Five

Bantam was in a talking mood the next day as we rode the sun higher into the sky.

"I've told these tales of myself so many times, both drunk and sober, that I really can't remember which ones are true and which are fables. I'm not sure it matters. I will tell what I remember to you, as I remember it, to pass some time on this godforsaken trail."

We were riding side by side enjoying a flat wide area of the wagon road. The sun was heavy and I had to keep wiping my brow so the sweat would stay out of my eyes.

"They must be really entertaining stories," I said, "to keep people spellbound and listening."

Bantam looked at me and smirked.

"When you've been drinking some, delicious drink sold by me and are being told fantastical tales by a laughing midget with a sense for the theatrical, it don't take much to attitudinize you into staying around listening and drinking some more. After a while, they forget how long they've been listening and how much they've been paying. Once they were cornered, they were mine."

He laughed and rubbed his palms together.

"You three lovely ladies have not been drinking anything stronger than Gina's preparations of our newfangled coffee. Though it is thick and somewhat dizzying first thing in the morning," he scowled at Gina, "I believe it serves to make you more coherent, not less. Putting that fact aside, I will do my best to shed some light on the darkness of my past, some of which Mrs. Thomas already is aware of. Yet she invited me along on this excursion nonetheless."

I looked at Anne who was frowning dubiously at me.

"I wouldn't exactly call it invited," I apologized. "He's the one who did the inviting himself."

Bantam took off his hat to wipe his forehead and bowed at me from his mount.

"An invitation is an invitation, just the same," he said. "I thank you for it."

I rolled my eyes and smirked at Anne.

"My date of birth is unknown, even to me," he said, clearly enjoying a captive audience. "But it never mattered. If one of you suddenly discovered your birth date was different would it really change anything about you?"

Gina nodded her head.

"It wouldn't change who we are. But when we looked to the stars for guidance, it might explain some things about us that we didn't understand," she said.

Bantam dismissed her.

"I've never looked to anything outside of myself for guidance," he said.

"I know what you mean," Anne said. "I'm glad there's only one trail in and out of this lost town, otherwise I might be afraid to let you lead us. You can learn from other people's experiences without having to live them. I learned a lot from others."

Bantam dismissed her also.

"While your life has turned out so well," he smirked.

"And yours is any better?"

She was irritated and didn't hide it.

"Nope, that's the point. We all have something of a mess going on here with ourselves. Now if you'll be quiet for a moment, I'll let you know where I was derailed and maybe you can learn something from somebody else's experience, again."

Anne took a deep breath and looked away. Bantam continued with the fable of his life.

"Not only do I not know when I was born, I'm not sure that the first parents I recall were really mine. Since that time, I've been passed around like last night's bottle. I can only assume it was the same for me in my younger days.

"Adults realized I was duerg long before I knew. I am sure that nobody wanted to be saddled with an extra mouth to feed that would probably never be able to take care of itself. All take and no return. So at the age of about 13, under no restraint or objection mind you, this dwarf left his current family and waddled out into the world."

"That hurts," I said.

"I could have joined a traveling show or a circus as an exhibit."

He raised up his arms and pushed himself standing in his stirrups like a ringmaster.

"Ladies and Gentlemen. Welcome to the circus of the simpleton dwarf."

Nobody said anything but rode along silent, waiting to see where this particular tale was heading.

"But I couldn't do that. I escaped from no self-worth enforced by others and I was not going to enslave myself with the same problem. I needed to work, to prove to others and mostly myself that I could hold my own, anywhere, with anybody. I also needed to eat. My first job along the way was as a piss-pot tosser at a hen emporium. I would crawl under the bed, grab the pot, which was usually filled with most anything you can think of, and dump it, return it, and be out the door without causing a stop in the action. That was important. You had to know how to sneak quietly to get the job done right."

"Yes, it is," Anne responded. "That's the job and it is important. I'll give you that."

He squinted his eyes and took a moment to look around before continuing.

"One day there was a high-falutin' customer in a room having his dalliances with a house girl. I could see he was kind of rough with her but that was none of my never mind. I slipped in and grabbed the pot as I was wont to when he stood up, accidentally placing his foot on the edge of the pot, upsetting it and tossing the contents across his lower leg. He was angered and grabbed me by my arm, swinging me to the side."

Bantam acted out the scenario as best he could while riding a horse.

"He began shouting at me, leaning down and smacking my face a little. I shied away and tried to tell him how it was an accident and I was sorry. But he told me to hobble my lip.

"He stood back up and turned to the girl who was sitting on the bed with the sheets pulled up, a look of terror in her eyes. He started laughing and spun back around. He told me to stand up. Then he stuck his business in my face and said I was just the right height to finish what his charge had begun. I stood frozen, inches from what looked like an eaten-up member of ravaged flesh. His impatience got the best of him and he grabbed the back of my head and shoved my face into his crotch, yelling all the while for me to apologize. I pushed away and pulled my gun out, firing immediately at face level. My face level. He doubled up and fell over on the very pot he had already spilt. I turned and ran to my room where I hid under my bed.

"I found out later he had died. The girl stood up for me claiming that she'd seen it and it was in self-defense. It was the only reason I wasn't arrested. However, the madam didn't believe I was good for customer confidence and sent me on my way with some money in my saddlebags and a couple of day's rations."

We rode in silence for a little while. I watched Slocum run alongside. It was hot enough to melt a fence post and as the riding became more familiar to Slocum, he quit running crazy like a snake, pretty much sticking to the trail alongside the horses where the ground was a bit flatter and easier to navigate.

"That was when I quit trying to work for others in a law-abiding manner," Bantam said. "Although my size is a detriment in many ways, it's also something that I can get to work for me in times of need. I hide better, fit into places better, and because people are too busy looking at me and not listening, I can convince any yack of damn near anything.

"I had traveled back and forth across the landscape, cheatin' and stealin', not worrying about the folks I hurt or trouble I caused. I hornswoggled any and everybody I could. I kept it up until Sheriff Thomas nabbed me for theft. That was how my ways ended."

I laughed.

"You were busted trying to sell stolen pots and pans to me."

"I didn't want to travel very far with them," he said. "They were whapping and, beings the size I am, hard to carry about. I tried to dump them on the first person I came across. Didn't know you was the sheriff's wife at the time."

"You found out shortly."

"Indeed I did," he smiled. "Indeed I did."

"Anyway, I had been caught many times before and slept nights in the local hoosegow but this time I was sent away by the court. Prison is not the place you want to be when you're a little guy like me. I was nervous as a cat in a roomful of rockers."

He paused, looking at the heat shimmering in front of us.

"Yep," he said slowly, "it's not the place you want to be."

He grimaced and went someplace else in his head for a moment.

"When I came out, I was transformed. Not converted to God mind you. I make tracks from that kind of thing. But I knew that if I didn't change and ever went back to prison I would probably die inside. I was lucky to get out when I did."

"I'm still skeptical," I said.

Bantam nodded at me.

"So what did you learn?" Anne asked.

"What?"

"When you were out there, you said you learned a lot of things."

"I learned how to not come out on the little end of the horn in most situations. I learned how to eat off the land a lot. I learned how to make Indian soup in a buffalo paunch."

"I'm always up for a new recipe or two," Gina said. "So how do you make the soup?"

Bantam looked at her to see if she was serious. He must have concluded that she was because he went on to explain Indian soup to us.

"You take the paunch of a buffalo and you clean it out real good. Wash it clean."

"That's assuming you have the buffalo paunch to spare," Anne piped in.

"Assuming," Bantam said glaring at her. "Then you get yourself a hefty rattler and you cut off the head."

"What about the poison?" I asked.

"Cut it back from the face at least a middle finger's length," Bantam said. "And cut off the tail piece too. Then you boil the mid part until the meat falls right off of the bone."

"Eww! What's that taste like?" I asked.

"Almost like fish," he snapped.

He was getting impatient with us. We were having fun watching his frustration grow.

"Then you put it in the buffalo paunch along with some of the buffalo meat."

"You would probably have some of that if you had the buffalo paunch," Gina said.

"Probably." He eyed her for a moment and then continued. "Then you add some wild onions and other vegetables you dig up on the prairie and a couple of gallons of water. You tie up both ends."

"With what?" I asked.

"Anything!"

He had to take a deep breath before continuing. I couldn't tell if he was red in the face from the temperature or exasperation.

"Then you place it in a kettle and boil it. When it's done it will keep for a long time and is about the size of a saddlebag."

"How do you know when it's . . ." Anne stopped mid-sentence.

Bantam glared at her until she looked away. He cleared his throat and continued.

"When you're traveling and stop for the night, you just toss it on the fire until it's good and hot. Then open up one end and pour it out on your plate or reach right inside. Now here's the best part. When you have eaten all the contents, you can eat the paunch. That's the best part all flavored up like that."

"Sounds terrible," Gina said.

"Yeah, I'm not parcel to innards either," I mentioned.

Bantam gave us a harrumph and rode on a little ahead of us for a while. I really didn't know what the big deal was. So I shouted up to him.

"Hey, if I'm ever on the verge of starving, I'd eat it to stay alive!"

He didn't turn around but waved me off. At least I think

that's what he meant. Anne rode tight beside me.

"So, if I was in the middle of the prairie or desert, starving with no food and I saw a buffalo, do you really think I'd bother to make some kind of silly soup? Damn if I wouldn't be eating chunks of meat raw off that buffalo instead. One doesn't have to be thundering smart to figure that out. Besides, why would I be hauling some boil pot around with me . . . to make Injun soup? You think the Injuns carried a pot around with them?"

We laughed together and then quieted down. Bantam kept the lead while we rode singly or together behind him depending upon the width of the trail. It was late in the afternoon when Bantam rounded a corner at the top of the ridge. He stopped his horse and sat there staring.

"Tarnation," he said.

We had left the Fortuna Foothills behind us and were now looking at the Galiuro Mountains rising up out of the flat of the desert. In front of us lay a very beautiful valley, the Aravaipa Valley, run through with the Aravaipa Creek. There was green and there was water and it was a welcome sight. Above the basin in a hanging valley sat the town of San Pueblo. There were plenty of buildings, at least a block, to promise a soft bed and cold drink, maybe even a decent meal. Even Slocum, tongue hanging out and dripping, seemed to perk up.

"After riding that trace for the last two days, I could go with easing myself down in those cool waters," Bantam said.

Gina agreed.

"A bath would be nice."

"How far do you think?" I asked hopefully.

"Ain't much," Anne said.

"Two whoops and a holler," Bantam chimed in. "We're not going to get there by sittin' here gazing at it."

He nudged his mount and started down the trail.

Chapter Thirty-Six

The trail continued, gradually dropping, until it bottomed out at the water. I had never seen anything so refreshing in my life. A creek splashing a musical tune of *come drink me* dancing along the craggy valley bottom. Bushes and trees stood on either side of the stream. Tall grasses with their green slender reeds shot up, framing the water. After the desert scrub, that creek and its girdling of verdure was a refreshing sight. I couldn't resist dismounting and walking down to the water's edge. I sat on its edge and began to remove my boots for a cool foot dip when Anne shouted.

"Whoa, whoa, what are you doing?"

"My dogs are swollen and barking. I thought I'd dip them for a minute and cool down."

She pointed up to the hanging valley lying out above us. A few buildings could easily be seen against the trees.

"The town's right up there," she said. "If you pull your boots off here, you'll never get them back on."

I spun about and splashed the cool water on my face. Then I soaked my bandana to put around my neck. I tied it about me in a knot, feeling the joy of some of the cooling water running down my chest and back. I mounted up. We swung the horses about and rode on down the trail until we came to a bridge, crossing high and long over the creek.

"Bridge seems a little like overkill, don't it?" Bantam said as we tread over it.

"I'll bet they get some damn good flash flooding through here," Anne said. "I remember the way that river outside of our Dallas tenderloin would swell up when there wasn't nary a rain cloud in sight. It would have come down some place miles away and suddenly everything near the river was washed up and out the spout."

She paused.

"I guess it did its job washing out some of the vermin, both animal and human. For that I was grateful."

We crossed the bridge and looked down at the rushing water below us. I felt cooler all the time. A spray rose up off the splashing of the rocks and was carried along by the breeze. No wonder they had built a town here. It was a beautiful spot, an Elysium, high enough not to get flooded out and close enough to have a never-ending water supply.

I believe we were all in awe as we made our way up the inclined trail to the town. That trail became the main street, actually the only street, although there were a couple of offshoot dead-end roads. At the end of one these was the sheriff's office. It was a small building not much larger than a shack. I could see an extension on the back, which I presumed was the jail cell. I could not believe this podunk building was housing the man who murdered James.

Such a beautiful setting and such a nothing town. I had seen a saloon so there must be a spot to put us up. We pulled up in front of the shack and Bantam rode up beside me. I sat and looked at the building. The thought of who was inside was making me sick to my stomach.

"You sure this is the pokey?" Bantam asked.

"Sign says Sheriff's Office. What else could it be?"

Bantam stared at the building with me. The odd feelings running through me at that moment silenced me. It seemed like the end of the trail and the reliving of my nightmare. We stepped down and tied our horses to the single rail out front. It was small so Anne and Gina tied their mounts to ours. The door sat at the front of the building right on the dirt. We walked up to it and pushed it open.

The interior was dark. The only window was next to the door and covered with a dirty sheet. Through an opening in the back wall we could see a couple of bars to a cell. A little daylight crept in from there. We left the front door open for what light it provided and walked towards the back. A voice low and calm spoke to us from the darkened room.

"Stand still. Do not turn."

We stopped, stopped breathing it felt like.

"Drop all weapons on the floor."

I could feel Gina behind me and I was afraid that she might get her knickers in a knot and do something rash. She wasn't all that good with taking orders. Anne must have felt the same way since she piped up before things jacked up any further.

"We don't want any trouble."

"There won't be any trouble," answered the deadpan male voice, "as long as you drop your weapons on the floor."

We began unbuckling our belts and dropping our weapons. Slocum spotted whoever was speaking from the darkness and began that low rumble that started deep in his chest.

"Who owns the fice?" the man asked.

I started to turn.

"Ah, ah, ah, no turning," the man said.

I stayed still.

"He's mine and he's a damn fine dog," I said. At least I could still stick up for my family. "He'll mean you no harm as long as you don't appear to be a threat, Sheriff Bannon."

There was a pause.

"Who am I speaking to?" he asked.

"Margaret Thomas, widow of James. I've come a long ways."

Another pause.

"And who are these with you?"

Gina turned and faced him in a quick movement.

"Gina Bochinscu. I'm a friend of Peggy."

"Really?" he said.

He pushed the door shut with his foot. The latch fell into place, locking us in.

"And how long have you . . . been a friend of Peggy's?"

"Since I stink like a man," she said straight-faced.

I snickered.

"You too?" He looked at Bantam.

"Same goes for me, Boss."

Sheriff Bannon sat for a moment. I could see what little light there was reflecting off the barrel of his pistol as he wiggled it towards Anne.

"And you, Missy? Turn around," he said.

Anne turned slowly and faced him.

"How long have you been friends with Miss Peggy?"

Anne took a step forward.

"Ever since the four of them saved my life by putting theirs at risk."

"Four?"

We had confused him again.

"Slocum," I said. "The dog."

He looked at Slocum, watching his sides move in and out with every rumble.

"That mongrel moves on me he's dead. So keep him to yourself."

Roy holstered his weapon and reached up, pulling the sheet aside. The light through the dirty window revealed a filthy little office with a chair and a table, not even a desk. Sheriff Bannon was long enough that it looked as if he had to fold himself to fit in the chair.

"What a shithole," Bantam said.

"It's what I got," he said without looking over. "Have yourselves a seat."

We looked around but there were no chairs.

"Where?" Gina asked.

"Oh, yeah," he smiled at her, then looked back at me. "Are these traveling companions here for any reason outside of completing the little circus we have going on around here?"

"You wired me," I said as flatly as him.

"I did indeed," he said and pushed himself up from his seat. "Sorry for being a little brusque but things are kind of testy around here. Your husband was a sheriff so you must have been the intelligent one in the marriage. Being a sheriff is a worthless job, unless you can get one in a place that nobody will ever find you; then it's a virtual paradise."

He indicated his surroundings.

"It ain't all that nice getting here," Bantam spoke.

Bannon walked up to him and leaned down.

"That, my little friend, is the beauty of it. This lovely place may stay lovely longer than most because nobody wants to make the trip to get here."

He walked across the room to the connecting doorway to the jail.

"No mining. No railroad. No reason to come here except not to be somewhere else. One would think it was ideal. Then one day some flannel mouth smoothie comes riding in looking for a reason to lay low. I usually don't poke or pry. Most cases they come in and get a breath of fresh air. Once they've relaxed a little, taken a bath, and realized they aren't going to be bothered too badly, they become bored. At that point, they have two options. They can try to find some fun here, which means they are out of luck. Or they can move on.

"But sometimes a jackaroo stays too long and gets too drunk.

About that time, he starts to talk too much. It got me to thinking about some old posters. I did some digging in my desk drawer."

"You don't have a desk," Anne said.

"Right there next to the table," he pointed.

There was a wooden liquor box filled with papers next to his table. I pushed on the wet bandana around my neck and sent trickles of water down my back. It distracted my thirst for a moment.

"Anyway," Bannon said, "I pulled them up, and eureka! There was a picture of our current tenant. He had, among other things like robbing banks and trains, shot and kilt a sheriff. That would be your husband, Mrs. Thomas."

I nodded.

"I just couldn't let that slip. Who'd give justice to me if it were the other way around? So I had to lock him up. I got in touch with the district and eventually arrangements were made for the circuit judge to come here on his next pass through Yuma."

He looked at Bantam and then turned back to me.

"He probably won't like coming down here any more than you did. That's why it's taking so long. Mrs. Thomas, I was surprised when I got word that you were coming. Didn't expect it."

"I kind of had to," I said.

He nodded his head.

"You've got your reasons, I suppose. Things do get delayed out here, though. It doesn't look like the judge will be here for a month yet. The weather will be starting to cool by then. I can already see the leaves changing on the higher elevations. We don't get much snow here due to the way we sit. I hope you packed your woolly undies in case this thing drags on."

Bantam was starting to work himself up.

"Just what are we supposed to do around here for a month?"

"Relax, I guess," Bannon said. "Why? You got some place you're supposed to be?"

Bantam stopped and stared at the sheriff. Then he turned his head, snorted, and walked away. Bannon looked us all in the eyes.

"I guess I've saved the worst for last."

"What is that, Mr. Bannon?" I asked.

"Our man back there," he hitched his head indicating the jail cell, "doesn't work alone. There's a gang."

"I already knew that, Sheriff," I said. "I was there."

"Right. Well he claims they're going to break him out."

"That's all beer and skittles," Bantam said. "How do they even know he's here at all?"

"Says he told them how long he'd be away too. It's past time."

"Is that the reason for your high security measures, Sheriff, like the dirty sheet on the window?" Gina asked.

Bantam snorted again.

Bannon said, "I ain't interested in dying and they're truly a bad bunch."

A loud pounding at the door made us all jump and Bannon swung his gun around at the wood. We all dropped to the floor and began picking up our weapons.

"Who is it?" he shouted.

"Bradbury," the voice returned.

"Aw, hell," the sheriff said. "Everybody, relax."

He holstered his weapon and opened the latch. A lean man in his later years stood there. When he stepped in, I noticed a wagon was parked in the street behind him loaded with rusted metal. He wore overalls or at least pants with suspenders over a plaid work shirt. His pants were short like he was walking up in the mountains. He noticed me looking at them.

"Breeches," he said. "Walking pants."

Satisfied with his explanation to me he snapped his suspenders and dust rose from his shirt.

"I've finished with Charlie Halloway's," he said. "You sure you don't want one on the office?"

"Nope, Brad. I'd just as soon let it burn and build a new one, or maybe just move away. But thanks for asking."

He spit out the door.

"Check with me next time you come through."

"Will do," Bradbury said and gave us a salute.

"Nice to have met you folks."

He was back out the door.

"Who was that?" I asked.

"The seller of lightning rods," Bannon answered as he shut the door behind Brad. "We don't get a lot of snow around here but we get some hellacious rainstorms."

He sat back down.

"Like I say, I don't know if or when this retaliation might take place. I can't be too careful. I'll show you where you can get a room and food as it seems you might be staying a bit."

"I guess that only leaves one thing then," I said.

Bannon asked, "What's that?"

"I'd like to see who you've got in there."

"Follow me," he said and turned and walked through the doorway into the jail annex.

There were two cells and a figure lay on the bed in the closest cell, sleeping with his hat over his face. Sheriff Bannon clanged his keys against the metal bars and the prisoner sat up, losing his hat in the motion. He looked at the sheriff, then turned and looked at me. There was a grin on his face. I caught my breath with my hand against my chest and stared into the face of Theophilus Barton Fanning.

CHAPTER THIRTY-SEVEN

He sat up in the cot and placed his hat back on his head. His white tombstone smile was both ingratiating and disarming. I was speechless, my head swimming with half sentences and unformed thoughts. He stood up and gave a quick bow.

"I am so glad to see that you and your friends navigated here safely," he said. "I was a little worried about Sheriff Wood's reception. We call him Peckerwood behind his back."

"Preacher?" Bantam asked.

I turned to Sheriff Bannon with a quizzical look on my face. He looked back and forth between us.

"I get it," he said. "It's the setting. You didn't expect to see your religious friend here behind bars. Well, sometimes these Holy Joes go bad . . . most of the time they start that way if you ask me."

Theo looked at the sheriff with a hurt expression on his face. The sheriff turned back to me.

"But that ain't what happened in this case," he said.

He reached over and swung the jail cell door open. It hadn't been locked. "Mrs. Thomas, I'm aware that you two know each other but I would now like to introduce you to Burton Alvord."

"You can call me, Burt," Theo said.

The sheriff continued.

"Burt here is an ex-lawman, an apple-pie shot, and a damn fine tracker should we need that particular skill. He's also a good friend. We've known each other for years in and out of business."

"What's he doing here, Sheriff, and why the act?"

I was beginning to anger over the deception.

"Well, in case you haven't noticed, Mrs. Thomas, I'm a little short-handed around here, especially when it comes to dealing with an infamous outlaw, let alone an entire gang. Burt volunteered . . ."

"After he wired me with the problem," Theo butted in.

"And then he came a runnin'. I told him to come in disguise in case he ran into anyone suspicious on his way in. I have no idea if and when these cohorts may show up to exhume their fellow scum."

I was flabbergasted.

"But he knew we weren't any outlaw gang!" I said.

"How?" Theo stepped forward. "I'd never met any of you before."

Bantam jumped up on this one.

"You thought the gang might be made up of three women and a dwa . . . a Lilliputian?"

Bantam pointed at the sheriff.

"How the hell protected are you feeling with this addled-headed man as your partner?"

The sheriff shrugged.

"We just figured it might be best if he didn't break cover. Remember, I wasn't expecting Mrs. Thomas to actually make the trip. I sure as hell didn't expect her to bring other folks with her! So you weren't really in my plans when Burt was on his way."

Then it hit me.

"Wait a moment. Where is this outlaw you captured that the gang is going to break out?"

The sheriff pointed past Theo to the second cell. We had

been so wound up about our reverend that we had not looked beyond. The people parted like the Red Sea. A large man sat on the edge of the bed with his head down. I took a couple of steps toward him. Gina grabbed my arm but I shook her off. I walked right up to the bars and stopped. He raised his head slowly and I watched the flicker of recognition in his eyes. He smiled, many broken black spaces where teeth belonged.

"Hello, Tulip," he said.

I felt flushed red like I was standing in the desert sun. I had to grab hold of the bars to steady myself. He stood up and took a step towards me. The sheriff and Burton each grabbed one of my arms and pulled me backwards. The prisoner stood on his side of the bars laughing while they slid me well out of his reach. They pulled me around the corner into the office and sat me down in the chair. I could hear him laughing in his cell. The sheriff stood in front of me looking down.

"You trying to get yourself killed?"

I didn't answer. I was staring past him to the other room.

"Look at me!"

I looked up at his hard, angry face.

"He'd just as soon snap your neck as spit on you. Don't you ever try something like that again!"

"Partially your fault, Roy, for letting her in there close," Burt said.

"It is. Hell, yeah, it is. I just never thought she'd do something stupid like that. Jesus!"

I brought my focus back into the room. It took me a second to gather my thoughts. I stammered when I could speak.

"I'm sorry, Sheriff. I know better and I apologize."

I shook my head trying to clear my thoughts back out. Such a long time had passed since I had lost James. When I stood up, I felt them shift around me like they were going to grab me should I try to get back into the jail. I waved them off.

"I'm fine. I'm fine."

My own personal gang was looking at me. It seemed like even Slocum was giving me an evil eye. I walked about in a small circle, bringing all my thoughts into headquarters.

"When did you say the judge would be getting here?" I asked the sheriff.

"Three or four weeks."

I watched my group watching me.

"Then I guess you'd better show us where we can put up, because we've got some waiting to do."

"Are you sure?" the sheriff asked.

"Yes, I'm good. I'd like to lie down a bit."

The sheriff nodded and opened the door.

"I think that can be arranged. I'll pull a couple of favors."

"I've never been on this end of a trail," Bantam said as we exited the office.

Gina stepped outside and looked up at the sky.

"You know, Sheriff," she said. "With you not buying one of those lightning rods, we might get lucky and he'll be holding on to the bars when one of them strikes."

The sheriff laughed.

"You never know," he said. "God's ways are a mystery to man. Say, one of you wouldn't happen to have some reading material, would you?"

Bantam patted his back pocket.

"I have one here all beaten and rolled up but still readable. I've read it fifteen times probably."

"Well, it's new readin' to me," the sheriff said.

Bantam handed it to him.

"It's yourn."

We walked down the peaceful street, looking at tree-colored mountainsides. A breeze floated past barely strong enough to cool me down. Below us, the stream rushed along smacking its crystal waters over smooth rocks. It was deep looking in the middle and promised the possibility of some good fishing. To the casual observer, everything around San Pueblo looked perfect. We had no idea about what was coming.

Chapter Thirty-Eight

We settled in, and after a couple of days had fallen into a routine of sorts. Bantam enjoyed practicing on his roller skates over every flat surface he could find. Only once did he lose control and end up in the creek at the bottom of the hill. I sent a telegram to Jenny back home letting her know of my arrival in San Pueblo. I caught Anne, our *city* girl, taking some long walks and spending time sitting in the woods breathing in the invigorating crisp air. There were definite signs of the cooler temperatures to come as Sheriff Bannon had indicated. Gina found herself a copy of *A Tramp Abroad* by Mark Twain at the general store. Reading was not her best talent and I saw that she struggled with some of the pages. But the last time I looked, she was pretty well through it and seemed to enjoy the fight.

I spent a lot of time thinking about what I was hoping to prove by being here. My life as a potential schoolteacher had been mind-numbing. I had chosen it as my occupation merely because I could and it was available, not because I had any type of predilection or propensity for the bairns. A herd of children of various ages all clamoring for my attention had gone from something I felt tolerable about to a nasty, loathsome idea. I could never say that aloud as the other good people of my town would have shunned me completely. They would have taken their children and I would have been jobless before I even got started.

But then James came into my life as he traveled through. A

chance meeting, a whirlwind courtship, and the clouds of misgiving and fear were blown away. I was like jetsam caught up in his tornado. I was spun around and landed right where he put me. From that point on, I thought of nothing but us. I only wanted to wake up every day and be with him.

We were married only to make things proper before moving to Missouri. I wanted to be with him more than I had ever wanted anything in my life. Our friends and family wished us the best, came to our vows, and then tossed us one of the loudest charivaris as to awaken the Seven Sleepers. They banged pans and fired guns for what seemed like hours. We laughed and pulled pranks on one another and became as intoxicated as stinkweed. It was a great joy, a time I'll never forget. Then the two of us rode away from the festivities and towards the Missouri border to spend our new lives together. It was all too fast, but it was good. Our life together was as one person, one care, and that was to see the other happy. Being next to James, conversing with him, even sharing work with him gave me life. His presence made my soul smile. It was all I ever thought I would need.

When that ended, when . . .

It was late night two days before the judge was supposed to arrive. We had gotten word from Yuma that he had shown up there that evening. I was lying in my bed when I heard somebody kicking up a row outside. There were gunshots, yelling, then the sound of wood snapping and collapsing. Fearing boulders or some such were rolling down the mountain I jerked my clothes on, then Slocum and I hightailed it out onto the street. Dust still rose from the commotion, yet I was hard-pressed to see what had made all the noise. I could see Gina in front of me as she ran into the sheriff's office, shotgun in hand. Behind me I could hear Anne screaming, "What is going on?"

As I ran into the interior of the office it was dark as pitch but moonlight shone in from the jail and I made my way straight through. A figure lay on the floor outside of the second cell. I could tell in a glance it was Sheriff Bannon. Gina was just rolling him over, face up, as I come into the room.

"Any sign of Burt," I asked.

"Not yet but he could have gone with the wall," she said and nodded toward the cell.

It was then that I noticed that a large chunk of the back wall was missing. Timber and debris lay stretched out on the ground all the way back, about fifty feet to where the edge of the cliff behind the jailhouse sat. Beyond that things just dropped off into the darkness below.

I shouted, "No, no, no."

Anne and Bantam came rushing in followed by some of the townsfolk. By now a lamp had been lit and cast pale light and long shadows across the room. Anne leaned down next to Gina.

I heard Gina tell her, "He's gone."

In the wavering darkness, the black puddle that spread about him spoke for itself. He seemed to have bled out in a hurry.

"Tarnation," Bantam said. "They took it all, the whole damned wall."

We all looked up at the gaping hole in the back wall. Three ropes were tied to the window bars and left behind in the culprits' desire to escape the law. They had obviously tied them to a wagon and pushed it over the edge into the abyss. The weight of the wagon dropping into space pulled out the window and part of the cheaply constructed wall from its fastenings. A piece of axle was still tied to the end of one of the ropes that lay on the ground. It must have ripped free of the wagon as it went over the edge. Beyond that we couldn't say. It was dark. There was no need to venture near the precipice.

Burt came around the busted edge of the back wall. He was

breathing hard and all sweaty, apparently from running as the night was cool. He tried to speak but had to lean over for a moment to catch his breath. Hands on his knees he pointed out of town.

"They took the road up into the mountains," he gasped. "They must be familiar with the territory since they knew we wouldn't risk following them at night through that terrain."

As he caught his breath and straightened up, he saw the body of Sheriff Roy Bannon. Gina was beginning to cover him with a sheet she had pulled from the cell bed. It immediately soaked bloody upon touching him. You could see the agony cripple Burt's body as he bent down and touched his friend's boots. He squeezed his eyes shut for a moment, pulling a long breath through his nose.

"Damn, the killing always starts just when life begins to get good."

He didn't pull the sheet back off Bannon's face. Standing up he looked at Bantam.

"Tomorrow I go after them," he said.

"Tomorrow we all go after them," I replied.

He stared at me as if to protest when Gina stood up and Anne sidled over to join the group. I'm certain our faces reflected the intent in our hearts.

Bantam looked at the three of us.

"Tomorrow we all go after them."

Burt nodded his head.

"I hope you can stand for yourselves. I don't have the time or desire to be a caretaker or wet nurse.

"Understand this, he won't be brought back easy and there will probably be some bloodshed. But I probably can't do it alone and there's nobody else in town to take."

"So what do we do next?" Bantam asked.

"Tonight, we pack whatever provisions we can carry on the

mounts. We leave first crack of daylight."

He looked over at the storekeeper who had come in with others during all the commotion.

"Winthrop, see what you can do to help us out. If you can, organize a burial for Roy and maybe figure out how to run this town."

"Not a problem, Burt," Winthrop said. "Ain't that much to it."

"Also send word to Yuma. May as well save the judge a trip. I'm sure we'll be back sometime, one way or another, no matter the outcome. I just don't know when."

He addressed himself to the group struggling to get a look from the doorway.

"If a couple of you fellas would help me move Roy over to Doc's office that would be right nice."

Burt turned back to us.

"Meet me at the stable with the daylight and we'll be on our way," he said.

Then Burt, Winthrop, and some of the other men of the town gathered up the sheriff. They gently carried him out the door over to the doctor's office. There he would lay until burial.

The rest of the night was spent sleepless, packing all the things that I had unpacked with our stay in town. Some of the items seemed superfluous to what we were about to do and would only end up as extra weight that would get dropped along the trail somewhere. So those items I left behind. I could move a little leaner and quicker. I've learned what was excessive and now leave it in my wake. My journey may have been extended by this turn of events but I wasn't going to let it hold me from my endpoint.

I was ready before daylight. When I could stand it no longer and possibly made believe that I was seeing light in the sky, I moseyed my way out to the street and down to the stable. I entered to the surprise that I was the last of the group to arrive. The others were there cinching straps, repacking, and tying up their hen skins behind the saddles. We would need those bedrolls for many a night I feared.

"I could sure use an Arbuckle's right about now," I said.

I shrugged and began putting Horse together and preparing him for a full day's ride. The blacksmith had already heated his pit. I saw a broken iron wheel hub set to the side that was probably his first order of business. Anne strapped a feed bag on to her horse and backed away smacking her gloves together, letting the straw dust fly.

"Well, that ought to do it," she announced.

"What time did you all get down here?" I asked.

I threw my saddle up on Horse and realized that my arms were getting stronger from doing this many times. When I first left the ranch, it was all I could do to lift the saddle up on Horse's back so that I could finish pushing it up and on. But now it was one swift slinging motion.

"I got here about twenty minutes ago and the others were already here buckling things up," Gina said.

I bent down and gave Slocum a hug around the neck. Breathing open-mouthed he gave me a quick kiss before I could fully pull away. Burt came walking in right about then with a wicker basket and a pot of coffee.

"Lenny thought we could use something to help us start our morning. What we don't finish eating here can travel with us."

"That was very nice of him," I said.

"Yep. Come get a cup of black. It might be awhile before you get some more."

We were all about complete on what we could do to get ready, mostly itching to go and waiting for a tad more daylight. So we grabbed cups and biscuits and sat down on the bales. Bantam pulled a bottle out and offered it up.

"Anybody want some corn juice to wake them up?"

Bantam poured a little in his own cup and Burt reached out his hand.

"I could do with a finger of that," he said. "It makes the bitter a might bit sweeter."

He poured it in the empty cup and then added the coffee. He stirred it with his finger and then licked it off. It looked like it tasted good but I wanted to be as clearheaded as possible for this trip.

"What do we do when we find them?" Anne asked.

I saw she had caught Burt off guard.

"Huh?"

"What do we do when we find them? More of them than there are of us."

"That's true," Burt said. "Hopefully we'll have the element of surprise on our side. Then we bring them back for trial."

He took another sip of coffee.

"I haven't thought it all through entirely."

"Great plan," Gina exclaimed and flapped her arms against her side. "We say *Boo!* Then we tell them to hold still while we tie their hands and take their weapons and lead them back here for trial. Figure we'll just put them in jail and ask them real nice-like to not run away through the missing back wall?"

"Something like that," Burt said.

He reached out and took the bottle from where it was sitting and added another dollop to his coffee. He looked up at us as he stirred with his finger and then licked it off.

"I want to kill them," I said.

Burt stopped in mid-suck.

"What did you say?"

"I'm tired of playing. I need this to be over. I want to kill them," I said. "Over is over the way I see it."

"You can't just go out there and shoot them dead," Burt said, his voice raising an octave.

Bantam jumped up. He was on fire.

"Who's gonna charge us? Sheriff Roy Bannon? Shoot them from afar and let them buzzards have 'em."

"There is justice in this land, as savage as it is," Burt yelled. "I will not allow it. Some of those people now riding in that gang may not be responsible for earlier crimes."

Anne shook her head and walked as she spoke.

"Birds of a feather," she said.

"What?"

"Birds of a feather, Burt. Ain't you ever heard that? When I was a calico queen, I was at fault for everything that ever happened to anybody because of whoring. I didn't even have to be in the same state and it was my fault. Goddamn it! These are not noble citizens of our fair country. They are murderers and thieves. I'm for killin' and being done with it."

"Peggy, you were here for a trial. You believed in it."

"Yes, I did, Burt," I said. "I was all for it. I came halfway across this country to go to trial. When I got here, I was told that he was just being nice inviting me to attend. He really didn't mean it. But I would have seen it through, all the way. Your way, with a trial and all, I was ready to endure that. It just isn't going to happen now. Do not . . ."

I walked up to him and put my finger in his face. I was shaking inside from anger and hurt. I could not have stopped if I had wanted to.

"Do not get between them and my rifle," I said.

I sat back down before the shakes could drive me to the ground. Gina came over and sat beside me for a moment, rubbing my shoulders and looking at Burt, daring him to speak. He said nothing but I could tell he was stewing in his own self-righteousness. I looked up at him.

"Maybe you're the one who shouldn't come along on this ride," I said and turned away.

"Could be Indians kilt them," Bantam said. "Nobody'd know the difference. Not like there would be an investigation anyhow for a bunch of sidewinders like them."

Gina leaned in to me and whispered low.

"I'm with you, Peggy."

I was calming down now and I smiled at her.

"Thank you."

"I've killed before, honey, and I'd do it again if I had too," she said. "It isn't an easy way to go. But sometimes it's the only way."

She stared dead at me now, expressionless.

"What do you mean?"

She squeezed me tighter for a moment.

"There he was, my husband, down there in the patties and pies," she said and stood up. "If you all will excuse me I believe I have to relieve myself before we get going."

I watched her walk away from us. She never ceased to surprise me.

Chapter Thirty-Nine

Burt led the way out of the stable and down the street. Our one packhorse was tied to his and carried the extra supplies we managed to pull together in the brief time since the jailbreak. We three women rode in the middle with Bantam bringing up the rear. After our little blowout, everybody was quiet. The air was crisp and cool, helping to keep our eyes open. The last thing we could afford to do was not be on our guard all the time. None of us had any idea how long this would take. We were walking straight into the caliginous opening of a tunnel that could turn out to be the barrel of a gun.

At the crossroad, we turned away from the creek and began the long ascent into the mountains. I knew it was only going to grow colder. I buttoned my coat across my chest in anticipation. The only sounds were the snorts and heavy breathing of the horses and the light biting breeze rattling the leaves in the Arizona ash trees, which were just starting to get a yellow tinge to them. The sky was cloudless and the morning sun, though bright, did not have the power to warm us.

I could see the top of Burt's John B, every now and then, bobbing up and down. But I had both of the women and the packhorse between him and me so most of the time on the twisting road he was hidden from my sight. He must have stopped as the line of horses came to a halt like the folds of an accordion. I leaned out from my saddle trying to see what was going on. Slocum stood next to Horse breathing hard from the climb even though we hadn't been pushing any speed. We had been at it for about a half-hour or so at this point. Bantam came up along my other side.

"What?" he asked indicating the front of the line with a nod of his chin.

"Not sure," I said. "Daniel Boone must have seen something or we're lost already."

"It's a single road. So as much as I find your sharp remark humorous, I have a feeling he's seeing something."

He nudged his horse and rode up past the rest of them to the front. I could hear the male mumblings as they conversed. I took the moment to talk to Slocum, and pat Horse on the side of his face. They concluded their conversation up front and Bantam rode back.

"Well?" I asked.

"Looks like our original crew joined with some others. They stepped over each other's prints so we can't quite tell how many there are. It's just a guess at this point."

"Am I supposed to?"

"Supposed to what?" he asked.

"Guess."

"Somewheres between eight and twelve is our best figure."

I looked forward to the other two ladies who had crowded back toward us to listen. Gina spit and then looked at me.

"That's a lot of garbage in one pile," she said.

"Do you mean that as a real play?" I asked Bantam.

"Dead serious."

I could tell that Burt was just sitting and waiting for our move. I knew my decision.

"I'm still going but you don't have to come," I told them.

"I'm still not convinced Bantam can count," Gina said and rode her mount up behind the packhorse.

Burt gave her a little nod and then looked back, watching to see what the rest of us were going to do.

Bantam smiled at me.

"She's not so wise as I was starting to give her credit for," he said and smiled.

"I'm still here too," Anne said.

Except for an occasional widening of the trail, this was single-file riding. It snaked and climbed its way higher and higher. Somewhere near the tree line we swung into a large flat area that could fit us all. The crest looked about ten minutes away. We would have hit the top and looked around if there had not been a small waterfall here offering some cool clean drink. Slocum and the horses were glad for the pause. I was not too far behind them in topping off my water bag with the rest of our group. Bantam filled his canteen, took a large drink, and then refilled it. He walked away from the water, securing the cap, and headed over to his horse near where Burt was standing.

"I guess your plan kinda went flyin' away back there at the junction," Bantam said.

He slung the canteen around his saddle horn, tying it down.

"How'd you figure?" Burt asked.

"Well, I believe we have to acknowledge the corn here and realize there's no way that two men and three women are going to apprehend an entire retinue of killers and drag their behinds back to trial. In fact, there's no reason to since there isn't any law back there. You're only riding point because we don't know where the hell we're going and aren't the best trackers in the world."

"So you need me," Burt said.

"I'm not too sure."

Bantam looked down at the ground from the tracks our small group had left in the soft dirt.

"But I'm starting to believe even a blind man could follow

the tracks, so far," he said.

Burt walked out to the trail and a few steps up, to read the marks of the horses in front of us.

"There's a bunch of them and a fight's a fight," Burt said. "I'm just not kin to murder."

He walked back and pulled himself up on his mount.

"Let's move and see if we can't get down into the valley," he said.

We rode out and headed up to the crest. The panorama was breathtaking. With such a massive terrain before us, searching for a group of riders was like trying to find an honest man in a game of saloon poker. But we all kept scanning the land. It was tough and the variety of features that mark up the landscape made it hard to pick out individual objects.

"There," Burt said and we all looked in the direction he was pointing.

It took a moment. Then I saw it. A cloud of dust rose up a little ways and hung just above some trees at the far end of the valley. It was right at the base of the next line of mountains.

"That point right in front of them is the only pass within a day's ride either side to get through those mountains," Burt said. "They are headed south towards Mexico. Once they get over that range they'll have the choice of continuing on in or moving west towards California or east towards New Mexico Territory."

"So we have to follow them through the pass until we can figure which way they choose?" Bantam asked.

"Yep, no way around it. If we decide to take a guess and go one way or the other to cut them off and choose wrong, we could lose them for good."

"Best thing we can do is not let them know we're behind them," I said. "With such a small town and the sheriff dead, I doubt they'll think anybody is on to them unless we give ourselves away."

"Then let's go," Gina said. "We're wasting time."

She spiked her horse and took the lead on the downward slope. We fell in line behind her, glancing to the next ridge, keeping the dust cloud in sight as long as we were able. It was a long ride down and a longer one across the valley floor to the next climb.

"We're probably gonna want to camp someplace on the far end of the valley floor or partway up the mountain," Burt said. "That way they won't be able see our fire or smoke."

"That's if we camp," I said.

Burt turned and gave me a sharp look.

"I know you're anxious but you can't push the stock that hard if you want them to hold up."

We rode quiet for a while. It was warming up as we descended into the valley. I looked over at Slocum. I could see the muscles in his shoulders had strengthened. All that walking was making him one strong cur.

"You know," Burt said. "If they head into Mexico, I'll have to bow out. I think you should also turn back in that instance."

"A little hitch like that isn't going to stop us. I'm not wearing a badge," I said.

Burt stared straight ahead as he spoke.

"It's a tough place down there. That group in front of us could be the least of your worries if you head south. I'm just trying to use a little hindsight first."

"I'll take it under consideration," I said.

"Folks?" Anne said. "I think I hear something in the brush to my right."

Gina pulled up and we all stopped, remaining silent. I unsheathed my Winchester and I noticed the others had their weapons naked also. Something large was moving slowly along, snapping through the greenery. Then, all was still. We glanced at each other. Bantam slowly moved his horse around behind where the noise had been coming from. With a loud grunt three javelinas came out running as fast as their little piggy legs would carry them. Anne pulled a bead on them.

"Don't shoot!" Burt yelled.

In that pause, they disappeared and were gone into the shrubbery. Bantam rode up angry and all red-faced.

"What the hell?" he said. "That's some good eating!"

"We've got food!"

"For now, most of it dried pemmican. We could have saved that and eaten fresh today."

"For the sake of your belly, you'd give us away?" Burt said. "Who do you think is going to hear the echo of those shots across the valley?"

Burt spun his horse around so he could look at all of us.

"Every move is important," he stared right at me. "Everything we do is important. So think before acting. *Think!*"

"Hey, I'm an adult," I shouted back. "You don't need to speak to me like I'm a child!"

"Really?" he said. "So, have you been on a manhunt before?"

"No."

"Have you ever tracked anything?"

"A lost cow."

"So then, don't tell me how to speak to you about a life and death situation. I'm interested in keeping us alive."

With that pronouncement, he kicked his horse and rode on down the trail. Bantam gave him a "Harrumph" and spit. We looked at each other and then slowly followed after him.

"Hurry it up," he shouted from in front.

Nobody asked to stop for a long time. Nobody spoke for a while. Eventually we pulled up for the night to save the mounts and Slocum. Burt felt fairly sure that they had probably crested the hill at some point. So we started a fire, made some coffee, and relaxed in anticipation of the next day's ride. The smoke would dissipate before it crested the top of the mountain. By this point in the evening, we were at least mumbling at each other.

Chapter Forty

From our elevation, the desert stretched out as far as the eye could see. Although the Mexican border was about ten miles straight out from the base of the mountain, I knew we were looking well into the country. It was late morning by the time we had ridden over the top and started down the scree slopes at the shoulders of the desert. The haze and shimmer of the heat made it difficult for anything but general viewing across the dancing landscape.

"I sure could use a pair of those binoculars I hear the army is using," Bantam said. "I can't see a dad-blamed thing except hot and more hot."

It was like an entirely different world on this side of the mountain. Cactus and scrub were the only vegetation to speak of and any animal life would only be vicious. I would be too if I had to live out here all the time. Gina took a swig out of her canteen, which was duly noted by Burt.

"Just wet your lips and tongue at this point. I'm not familiar with this terrain so the water may be far apart."

It was soon after we hit the crease in the land where mountain meets earth that the trail diverged into the four compass directions. Wagon ruts went east and west as a supply route along the base of the mountain. Without knowing the distance, we at least knew there was civilization to both sides. No real wagon marks continued south into Mexico but the trail flattened out and the ground was covered with hoofprints galore. The Outlaw

Trail. With the sheer number of prints there was no way to be certain which ones belonged to our group.

"Well, that really balls things up," Burt said.

Anne seemed to be studying the landscape closely.

"Let's think this through," she said.

"I think that whatever we decide will be a lick and a promise. It's just a guessing game," Bantam interjected.

"No, not really," Anne said. "I've spent a lot of time studying men. Most of the time they take the path of least resistance."

Burt shrugged.

"All right, professor, give us one of your life lessons."

"Well, we have four directions to choose from. We can eliminate the one we came from. With an educated guess on Burt's part, we don't believe they thought that anybody was following them. Since they weren't running from the law they wouldn't have any reason to head into Mexico."

"That eliminates two," Gina said getting into the exercise.

"So now we have east or west," I added.

"Everything we've known about them and their marauding was east of here, right?" she asked me.

"Far as anything I've heard."

"So, in this godforsaken country where water and shade is so very important, the unknown is to the west. I say they went with what they knew. They headed east."

Burt looked at her.

"I'm impressed."

"Thank you."

"But you could be wrong."

"I could be," she said. "You got a better way of figuring it?"

He thought for a moment.

"Can't say that I do."

We turned our horses and started east.

"Looks like I'll be with you folks for a while longer," Burt said.

Tucson was the next town of any size and it would be a welcome sight when we arrived there. Fort Lowell was just east of Tucson. It had been built there to keep an eye on the Apaches. We would try to get any information about the group that we could and offer up any information of our own.

As we rode, Burt spoke of one of the former gang members, who was now dead, a fella by the name of William Whitney Brazelton.

"He was somewhat famous for robbing stagecoaches all over the Arizona and New Mexico territories," Burt said. "One time he robbed a coach carrying a newspaper editor name of John Clum. The sheriff of Pima County at the time, a certain Charles A. Shibell, did not take too kindly to this happening in his area as he thought it might make him look incompetent if Clum printed it up, so he formed a citizen posse to track the desperado down. They shot Brazelton down near the Santa Cruz River."

"The area seems to have been no stranger to violence," Anne said.

Burt shook his head.

"Nope. There was also the fairly recent killing of Frank Stilwell who had been accused of Morgan Earp's murder. He had been found lying in wait for Virgil Earp and his family at the train station in Tucson and was shot dead by brother Wyatt and his boys."

We were on our third day of riding.

"When do we reach someplace where there are other people?" I asked riding up alongside Burt.

"Within the next couple of hours, we will be descending upon Villa del Craneo Quemado por el Sol. It kind of rolls off of your tongue. In the old days, if riders coming up from Mexico made it here, they could say they had ridden with God. *Ca-*

balgando con Dios. They would have spent a week or two trying to cross the Sonora Desert. For them it was a welcome sight."

"It wasn't all that fun for us," Gina said.

Burt nodded.

"True, but at least we had a trail to follow. Many of them would have been following stars and the sun in hopes of arriving somewhere. That's how it got its quaint little name."

"What does it mean?" I asked.

Anne answered from the rear.

"Village of the Sun-Baked Skull."

"Charming," Bantam said.

I heard a whimper from Slocum and I figured he was probably feeling the same way we were. The sizzling sand couldn't be much of anything but agony on his feet. I was sure he'd be glad to stop.

The buildings that sat up out of the desert dirt were about as inviting as skunks in a school house. The structures were unevenly made and the bosque woods they were built from had sun-faded to a brittle white/gray. But they were shelter and shade, if nothing more. The constructions totaled five in number with one of them being a stable and another having a large, crudely written word across the front of it—*Liquor.*

A small stream ran past a good distance away across a flood plain from the pueblo, creating the haven for the mesquite.

"They could've built the place a little closer to the stream," Gina said.

Burt didn't turn to her as he spoke.

"When it rains out here, the water falls so hard it doesn't have time to soak in. It rushes along like a stampede, clearing everything in its path. Had they built themselves any closer to the stream they would have been washed away in the flash floods. Maybe they have been once or twice before they got it figured out."

As soon as we tied up out front of the drinking place, Gina and Anne rushed around back to use the outhouse. That was a touch of civilization for them. Slocum and I had taken care of business earlier on the trail while the men sauntered over out of the way to relieve themselves. Once we had gathered ourselves back together, Burt led us through the half-hanging doors and into the smallest saloon I had ever seen.

Two tables and a short end bar welcomed us inside the darkened interior. Light came in through the window holes since there were only frames with no glass to fill them. That probably accounted for all the sand and dirt that covered darn near everything in the place. Some of the tables had clean swipes across them. Some of the chairs, by the looks of them, had mostly been wiped by the seat of a visitor. As we stood gaining our eyesight back from the change in light, the bartender stood up from behind his work station with a double-barreled thumper aimed in our direction.

"Bye," was all he said.

"But we just got here," Bantam growled.

I could tell the barkeep hadn't noticed Bantam, as the gun dipped down and up trying to figure out the best way to cover all of us.

"I don't need any more of the same."

"Same what?" Burt replied.

The bartender gave us another look-over but kept the gun pointed our way. Anne stepped forward. I put my hand out to stop her but she brushed me away.

"This ain't the first time I've had a man point his barrel at me," she said. "What are you so afraid of? We aren't here to hurt you. We've traveled a long way and need to get out of the sun."

He considered what she said.

"So, you ain't with that last bunch?"

"We ain't with anybody 'cept ourselves," Burt answered.

"How can I be sure? There's a gang of you. You could just be the rest of those snakes."

Bantam shook his head.

"I'm tellin' you we aren't. You can call us anything you like but that ain't us. You can put your boots in the oven too, but that don't make them biscuits."

Gina laughed at that one and it was the steam release on the situation. The barkeep considered things a little more. He put the weapon under the back counter where he could get at it if he had to.

"I'm sorry folks but it was a little rough. I feel lucky to be alive. Poorer, but alive."

"They took your money?" I asked.

"Yes, ma'am. Broke a few things and stole some of the hooch."

This part spurred Bantam.

"You got any tongue oil left?"

"I do but it's more costly now that there is less of it and some time before more arrives."

"I don't give a tinker's damn what it costs. Just set us up."

The bartender looked at us.

"The ladies too?" he asked.

"Everybody," Bantam said.

"But we have a rule about ladies in the bar."

We stood there and stared at him. I could tell he was fumbling, trying to get out from under this one.

"I guess that in this case . . ." he said. "And it is a special type of circumstances here . . ."

We nodded.

"We could make an exception to the daily rules and allow you parched souls to all drink together."

Burt watched him as he poured drinks for all of us and then

sat the bottle back on the bar. We picked up the shot glasses in unison and gave a salute.

"Still alive," Gina said.

A quick downing of the turpentine and the glasses slammed back down for refilling. I saw Slocum standing in the doorway watching us.

"Come here, boy," I said and turned to the bartender. "I'd like some water for my buddy."

He handed me a bucket, which I filled three-quarter full with water from the pump in the yard. When I sat it down on the floor Slocum didn't even pretend. He went right to the bucket and starting slurping.

"You can use that pump out there for your horses too," the bartender said.

"Much obliged," Burt said. "Can you tell me what these fellas looked like who robbed you?"

"Not only can I tell you what they looked like, but I can tell you who they were. I knowed them the minute they came in. Must have been fifteen of them. They was all wearing light-colored long coats."

I must have gasped inadvertently as everybody turned and looked at me. I mouthed the word *fifteen.*

"Another thing," he said, "there was two women with them. One was part of the gang. She was a hard Belle Starr kind of girl, Maud Davis. Didn't say much but when she did, they listened. She seemed to be partnered with Black Jack Christian. He's the tough fella with the pockmarked faced. They were real close, like they were eating supper before saying grace. The other woman was an Apache squaw, pregnant, full as a tick. I think they were keeping her as insurance against running into any of those savages."

"We're hunting them."

"Injuns?"

"No, the gang."

"Good luck with that."

"They say where they were going?" Burt asked.

"East. I heard them talking that they were going around Tucson instead of through it as it was running tight these days. Seemed as if they'd had a run in there before."

Bantam downed his second shot.

"Damn, they can get lost up in there in those hills real good if they know the land," he said.

"Oh, they know it," the barkeep said. "They've been doing damage from here to the Mississippi for years. Everybody with a bank, stagecoach, or rail line knows about the Black Jack Christian Gang. William Christian runs that bunch of thugs. They're also called the High Fives. Christian, himself, is sometimes called 2-0-2 because he's a big man.

"Don't underestimate Maud Davis either. She's a petticoat doctor without the petticoats. She cleaned a bullet out of one of the gang right here on the bar. Knew what she was doing with that knife too. Although she wasn't too gentle about it. Bad attitude. If I never see that bunch again, I'll be happy. Probably rode up towards Skeleton Canyon."

After finishing ourselves, we walked the horses down to the stable where we fed and watered them, then spent the night. That straw felt softer than a fat lady's bosom. I was out hard within minutes. You could have burnt the barn down around me and I would've never known it.

Chapter Forty-One

The scream was blood-curdling. Had I been in the loft instead of on the ground, I would've fallen out. It was Burt and the cry was followed by an entire epitaph of swearing. I grabbed the Winchester beside me and scrambled to my feet. Looking over the wall, I saw Burt lying on his back holding his foot and mouthing a blue streak. On top of that he was beginning to redden quite noticeably as he rolled about on the floor. In between swearing he was trying to give directions.

"The boot! The damn busted boot! Oh, my foot!" he cried.

Then he continued on with his wordage. We three ladies rushed over to help him while Bantam went to investigate his boot, which had been flung some distance out into the middle of the stable. We stripped off his sock, not a pleasant job in itself, and looked to the wound. His entire foot was red with streaks shooting up his leg. It was starting to swell and was almost too tender to handle. While Anne and Gina worked on Burt, I looked to see how Bantam was coming along. He approached the boot with caution and gave it a nudge with his foot. A brownish scorpion about three inches long walked out of the top of the boot. His tail was raised in a menacing stance that said *I've done it once and I'll do it again.*

I jumped back instinctively and knew I would be living with the vision of this little monster with multiple legs. It moved almost like one of those new wind-up toys that jerks about while the elastic loosens up. Bantam looked around for something to attack it with.

"Keep an eye on him," he hollered.

"You don't have to tell me," I said.

He ran over to the wall and grabbed a shovel leaning against the wood. I was wishing he could move quicker because even in that short time the little devil had scrambled on those many legs and was headed for a pile of straw to hide in. I beat him there and kicked it out of the way while yelling at Bantam the entire time.

"Here, here! He's over here!"

Bantam raced over and slammed the flat of the shovel down on top of that bug like a safe falling from a second story window. Either not trusting his own strength or maybe out of fear for himself, he slammed it a few more times until it was barely discernible where the body ended and the segmented legs began. He held up the shovel and looked at the bottom and then wiped it across the straw to disengage body mush.

"He's having a bad reaction," Gina shouted.

By the time the two of us turned and got back to them, I could see the milky white around the edges of Burt's mouth. He was doubled over in extreme pain. He was propped up. The leg was kept down from his heart to slow the run of the poison but apparently it hadn't helped all that much.

"I need some cool damp rags," Gina said to Anne, who rose up and hurried out the door.

"Cut it and suck the poison out," Bantam said.

Gina waved him off.

"No. This isn't a snake bite. Just getting that poison in your mouth will cause your tongue to swell and teeth to ache."

Burt started to twitch and jerk. He was in a bad way and becoming worse. Bantam found a thick piece of leather used for reins and brought it over.

"Open your mouth and clamp down on this," he said.

Burt bit down, his teeth sinking well into the hide. Spittle flung out of his mouth as his head shuddered to and fro. It reminded me of the giant bull we used to have on the ranch who slung snot and spit from side to side as he ran. The strands hung from the corners of Burt's mouth giving a slick coat to the leather, punctuated by his agonizing growls.

"Look out," Anne said as she pushed past Bantam with a couple of rags and a bucket of water.

The barman followed close behind in his trousers with the suspenders up over his under-johns. Anne wrapped the wet cloth around Burt's foot, squeezing only as hard as she was able before he would call out and jerk his leg away. The barkeep knelt down. He held the leg while studying Burt.

"It's a backlash to the poison," he said looking up at me. "Honestly, he should be fine. He'll work his way through it. Gotta keep the compress on him. It will take a day or two until he's all the way back 'cept for the painful foot. That'll take longer. But the nausea will leave him by nightfall."

I looked at Gina. We both connected, knowing that we could not wait a couple of days or we might lose Black Jack and the bunch forever.

"You sure?" Bantam asked.

"Seen it before," he answered.

"How are you at handling him for a few days if we give you a bit of money?" I asked the bartender.

"Unless you're staying, there ain't much choice, is there?"

"You seem like a good guy. I feel like I'm leaving him in good hands?"

My voice rose at the end like I was questioning my own idea. Burt glanced up at me in his agony. I looked about at the others for support.

"We're a group of four plus a packhorse. Once he recovers he'll be able to catch up with us no problem. Right?"

Just about then, he let out a moan and tightened up his knees towards his chest. The barkeep stood and walked over to another stall.

"Well, we've got to get him inside on a bed. I'll grab this wheelbarrow and all of you help me lift him in. Then roll him inside and we can put him on the bed."

We each grabbed a corner and lifted him up and into the wheelbarrow. He grunted and yelled as the barkeep rolled him over the uneven ground. He remained curled up to help cushion himself against being slammed about. There were a couple of wooden steps into the doorway behind the saloon where the barkeep lived, so we took him out of the barrow and carried him awkwardly through the opening. Anne banged her hand against the doorframe letting go of his shoulder. He shouted again as he dropped and smacked against the floor. But we gathered him back up and made our way into the main part of the room. We put him down on the bed and he let out a long sigh.

"Where are you gonna sleep if he's in your bed," Gina asked.

"It's only going to be a day or so," he said. "It won't be the first time I've slept lying on my own bar. If one of you could grab that cold compress, rinse it out and bring it back to me, I would surely appreciate it."

"I'll get it," I said and started back to the stable.

"Be careful," he said, stopping me.

"Why?"

"There ain't just one. That was most likely a bark scorpion, common to this territory. If there's one, there are twenty. Be easy turning anything over or riling up some straw. They like dark places."

"Thanks for the warning."

"Not everybody reacts the way he did but they can get you real good. As you leave here and go after those hounds running their bellies through the brush, keep your eyes wide open. Between the snakes, scorpions, and Gilas you could go down a number of ways. That's without even bumping into savages. Your friend was lucky it happened here and not out in the desert plains."

As I walked back out to the stable, Slocum rose to come with me.

"No," I said turning on him. "Sit right there."

The last thing I needed was for him to get stung.

I went out to the stable and gingerly picked up the rag off the ground with two fingers. I doubted they had any time to crawl underneath it, or that they even liked the damp, but I was taking no chances. Once it was free and clear I shook the ground off it and then went over to the pump in the yard. I beat that handle until the water running out was steady and cool. I rinsed off the rest of the dirt and brought it in clean.

The barkeep wrapped Burt's foot up snugly and then gently laid his leg back down on the bed.

"We gotta go," Bantam said. "We're losing time. He can catch up with us."

I kept looking at Burt, not wanting to leave him behind.

"Yeah, I guess you're right," I said.

"I know who some of the gang were," the barkeep said, and he began counting on his fingers. "Beside Black Jack Christian and Maud Davis, you had William Nilie, Cole Estes, George Musgrave, and Harvey Logan. Nasty bunch that have been riding together for years. Now that they have hooked up with those others, there's no telling. Every one of them is a curly wolf and you could come back dead."

We finished getting ourselves and our mounts together and finally, with packhorse in tow, we pulled up in front of the saloon to say our goodbyes. Burt could not come out to greet us so there really was not much to do. The barkeep had a final word.

"At some point, they are going to jump trail. Don't know if you'll want to follow them then. They know this land like the Indian they're draggin' around with them," he said. "You follow them into the chaparral and I believe your life expectancy will drop to zero."

"I've got no choice," I said looking down from Horse.

The barkeep nodded.

"I understand your drive. I just question your smarts."

Bantam pulled up beside me.

"These fellas are on the prod. They've kilt we don't know how many, robbed hardworking folks of their life savings, and performed egregious acts upon humankind. They need to be stopped. We've come this far, I believe we're in for the scad."

"Why don't you leave that up to the law?" the bartender asked.

Bantam swiveled around on his saddle scanning the horizon.

"Don't see any. Only one I know of is lying in yer bed," Bantam said.

"They'll kill you."

"Maybe. Maybe they will."

With that simple proclamation from Bantam, we turned our mounts and rode off to find trouble.

Chapter Forty-Two

That wind we had lost a little ways outside of Yuma seemed to have found us again. Although not as strong, we feared the tracks of the outlaws would disappear from the sandy soil. Sage and scrub bounced across the trail in front of us like racing tumbleweeds. Once Slocum got used to them he began to play as they crossed, snipping and biting at them. I'm not sure what he would've done if he had accidentally grabbed one. A sudden gust hit me full on and I turned my head away to keep the dirt out of my mouth. It was then that I saw the remnants of a group of horse tracks heading up and over the hill to our left.

"Ho, everybody," I shouted out.

The group stopped and I pointed up the hill.

"I think this is them."

I turned Horse and began following the tracks off trail.

"You sure you want to go there?" Bantam asked.

I stopped and turned back to them.

"We've been riding all morning and this is the first group of tracks we've spotted off the trail."

"How do you know it's not Injuns?"

"I don't," I said. "It looks like the horses are wearing shoes. But I'm hoping to see better sets of tracks on the breech side of the hill. If they're far enough in front of us their marks will be wiped away by the wind. We could end up riding all the way into Tucson without seeing anything and miss them completely."

I began riding up the hill. They followed behind me. I kept

facing forward but spoke loud enough so they could hear me.

"When you come over that knob, stay to one side or the other. I don't want these tracks messed up until I can get a better look."

I was making myself wonder since I had never before in my life tracked anything more than a stray cow. Now I was playing Indian guide and leading us through the wilds after a bunch of scum. The tracks were all scrambled together with no real definition. I don't know what I was hoping for as I came down the side of the hill away from the wind but I found it. I stopped Horse and then jumped down and crouched to get a good look at the prints. There were some mighty clear tracks of well-shoed horses. Sure, it could have been a bunch of Indians with stolen horses. But in my mind, the odds were that these were our boys.

"What are the two lines all the way along?" Anne asked.

"I'd say they are pulling a litter with them," Gina said.

Bantam scratched his chin.

"So one of them is sick or injured," he said. "That's to our advantage. It'll slow them down."

"They ain't sick," Gina said. "The barkeep told us. The squaw was pregnant. There's no way she could keep up riding or walking. That's why they're pulling her."

"Depending on how far along she is, we could gain on them."

Gina looked at the country from where she sat on her mount.

"I think that when she becomes more of a burden than a shield, they'll just leave her, if there is any heart among them . . . or kill her if there ain't. Those boys have proved they aren't right in the upper story," she said, tapping her head. "Her days are numbered any way you look at it."

We followed tracks when we could decipher them in the hard ground. Our food was beginning to run a little tight. We had crossed some good water on the second day and refreshed ourselves. The distance between them and us was guessed at until the third morning when we spotted smoke rising in a light trail about half a mile in front of us. Being that close reenergized us and we immediately fell into a stealth way of approaching the campsite.

While still hidden behind the mesquite, we dismounted and tied off the horses to the scrub. We formed a semicircle, approaching the smoke so that we could come at it from a variety of angles. Maybe make them believe we were stronger in number. As we peered over the last barrier of brush it was evident that we had missed them so we walked on in.

The smoke was merely the remnants of this morning's breakfast. On the way in, Bantam stepped in something and was busy scrapping his boot on a nearby rock. He started airing his lungs about the human beings who relieve themselves this close to a campsite.

"Are you all right?" I asked.

"I am just in apple pie order," he replied sarcastically.

"They just may cut that squaw loose sooner than later," Gina said.

"Why do you say that," Anne asked.

Gina pointed at the campsite.

"They're running out of food."

"How can you tell?"

"The shells there are from desert tortoises. They spend most of their time underground, which means these folks would've had to dig for them. Not a fun thing in this heat. You'd only do it if you had to."

Bantam walked up.

"Does that mean we're near water?"

"Not really," Gina said. "They can go damn near a year without drinking. They get most of the water they need from the plants they eat."

"Do they taste good?" I asked holding up a cleaned-out shell.

"Don't know. Never ate them," Gina said. "But I know that they just build a fire and toss them on it alive to roast. Then you dig out the meat from the shell with a stick or your finger. Another thing . . ."

She looked at the prints leading away from camp.

"We're gaining on them. Tracks are deeper and fresher. They're moving slower, not thinking somebody is after them. It would also keep the stress on the horses low. If they come out the northern side of this thing, say up near the Silver Bell Mountains where they can bag themselves some Bighorns, they could be free and clear."

"So what does it say in the cards?" I asked.

"It says we need to catch them before they reach the Silver Bells," she said, "or we'll have lost them again."

Anne piped up.

"There's mining going on up there. I've had boys who'd been employed there in the past."

Gina continued.

"They can get horses and rest and money. That opens up everything wide for them including leaving a few more dead bodies behind."

Bantam looked at the tracks leading away.

"So how far is that?" he asked.

"About a short week, I think," Gina said.

"Then we've got five days, everybody," I said. "I'd like to reach them and put an end to this."

We walked back to our horses and mounted up. I rode next to Gina.

"Any water in those Silver Bells?"

"Wells maybe," she said. "All you'll have to do is pump it out."

"Then let's go get them."

I nudged Horse with my heels and we led the way, following the tracks they left us as a guide. They were so careless, being that blatant with where they were going. I thought for a moment about whether the tracks were left on purpose. But it didn't add up for me so I didn't say anything to the others.

The timing was correct and it was on the second day after turning off the trail that we found our prey. Funny thing, thinking of them as prey. Hunting, as in hunting a man, is not that different from hunting any large animal. I was more emotionally involved in this but I was hoping it would be my first and last manhunt. It felt like they were taunting us, daring us to follow them into the wastelands and scrub. Each mile made me angrier. Each day infuriated me that they had the intent to escape.

The hills before us rose up in a circle leaving a bowl in the center. The next rise beyond was only about a hundred yards from the hill we were on and there were no signs of tracks climbing them. Bantam silently signaled us to stop and we dismounted before cresting the top.

"Ain't that far away," he said softly to us. "With all of them horses, these tracks we've been following would've been easy to see going up the other side. I don't trust just riding over the top. So let's go have us a look."

A woman's scream echoed up from the base of the knob and we instinctively dropped. A small growl rumbled inside Slocum and I bumped him with my hand to be silent. Following Bantam and moving in a crouch, we ascended to the ridge while Anne stayed back and held the horses. Near the top we dropped flat to our bellies and crawled in the sand to the edge. We removed our hats and peeked over the rise.

They were there.

They'd made camp and dug a couple of firepits, evidently

still unaware that we were on their backs. At least we had that. There were about a dozen of them laughing and talking. Some were wearing their dirty long riders and some had their coats off, not needing them while they were in the heat that was captured down in the bowl. The entire shoot looked like a bad bunch in my head. A couple of them still looked familiar after all this time. I was able to give a couple of them names from what Burt had told us. Black Jack William Christian fit his description to a tittle. Maud Davis was there. Boils sat with his back against the rock wall sweating like he was squeezing water from the wash. The ones with the long white hair and a skinny jake looked like the two oldermost. I couldn't tell much about the others.

With the way the sound resonated up from below, they could have been sitting right next to us. Black Jack stood holding the squaw with one arm while she wiggled and thrashed trying to get away. He reached around and slapped her hard to settle her down.

"How much are you willing to bet, Harvey?" Black Jack shouted. "Let's put your money where your mouth is."

"I ain't put my mouth there . . . yet," Harvey said.

They all started laughing like it was the funniest thing in the world. A skinny guy walked toward us and we ducked down not wanting to be sighted by accident. Slowly we looked back up and saw he was relieving himself, paying no attention to the ridge above his head.

"He seems to be an odd stick," Bantam whispered. "Doing that in view of the women."

Gina smiled. "One of them ain't much of a woman and I don't believe he cares what the other one thinks."

"Maybe she ain't far enough along to tell, Jack," Harvey shouted back.

"Oh, I think she is," Jack said, and with his free hand he

grabbed her clothing near her throat and ripped them off the front of her body in one motion.

She screamed and tried to cover her nudity with her hand. The entire group broke into laughter and whistles. The skinny one who had been watering the ground walked over to help Jack keep her hand away from covering her body. He grabbed her free arm away and then ran his hand around her breasts squeezing and kneading them like she was a cow back on the ranch. He shook his hand getting some liquid off.

"Nice titties, boys," he said. "They're all round and full of milk, just the way I like them."

Then he danced his hand across her belly, ending with it up between her legs. She turned her head away and kept screaming.

"And it's feeling pretty deep in there."

He turned back to the others.

"Maud, you're a woman. Do you think she's far enough along?"

"Thank you for noticing, you pismire, Nilie," she said. "She is looking pretty full to me and she smells ripe from here."

Nilie pulled his hand out and smelled his fingers.

"She does smell ripe, don't she?"

He licked at her neck and shoved his hand back between her legs. She jumped up on her toes struggling but he bit her neck hard, settling her down.

"I think I could use me a drink of milk right about now."

He twisted her arm behind her back and latched onto one of her breasts with his mouth while she struggled against both of the men. He brought his face free and looked at the group for approval. Their laughter turned him back to leeching her milk.

"Hoo-wee, even a savage's titties are fun to suck on," he laughed.

"Well, by every measure we have before us, she seems far

enough along," Black Jack shouted. "Harvey, place your bet."

"I say ten that it's a boy," Harvey said and he reached into his saddlebag next to him and pulled out some bills.

"I'll see that and add another five that it's a girl."

The voice came from a red-peeling blister face.

"Oh, God," Gina said. "Please, no."

Her eyes were riveted to the sight below. The men in the group continued betting and shouting while the woman screamed and screamed. She tried to bite at Jack's hand but he knuckle-busted her in the mouth and I could see the blood even from where I lay. Maud stood up and walked over to where they held the Indian. On the way, she scooped up the bills that lay in the sand in front of the men, handing them to Jack. She held her arms up and the gang quieted down.

"All bets are in boys. No changing your minds now!"

She reached behind her back and withdrew an Arkansas toothpick from a sheath. The blade looked to be almost a foot long.

"Watch your hand!" she screamed and Nilie yanked back his fingers from between the Indian's legs. It was replaced with the knife held two-handed, and then jerked in an upward motion slicing her wide open. It stopped, sticking in the bone. Maud had to saw her way up to a point just below the hang of her breasts. The Indian shouted and collapsed as a washtub of blood, water, and baby poured out onto the sand. Nilie danced around crazy, cradling his hand.

"You got me, you stupid bitch!" he cried.

"Shut up!"

Maud bent down and tried to pull the baby out from under the squaw. She was still squirming and Maud couldn't get a good grip on the baby's wet slimy skin. Jack kicked the eviscerated squaw off the child so Maud could grab it. She sliced the stretched umbilical cord and held it up by the feet. She then splayed its legs apart and grabbed his crotch area to display it to the gang.

"There's his dingus, Harvey," she said. "Collect your money."

I hit William Nilie in the cheek and took off a piece of his face. It was enough to make him ugly but not enough to kill him. He ran about in crazy circles screaming like a child. When the gun let go, everybody jumped.

Gina took a bead on one of them. Gina let go a shot that shut him up permanent. They all started scrambling.

I would have gotten off a third shot but Bantam knocked my barrel down to the dirt.

"What the hell are you doing?" Bantam shouted.

"I couldn't watch it anymore. I just couldn't."

He turned his anger on Gina.

"You just may have killed us all with that second shot. They sure as hell know where we are sitting. Back to the horses. Hurry!"

I looked back down to the firepit. They were all running, like ants from a destroyed hill, for their weapons and pointing up at our position. Gina looked at me and then ran down to the mounts. Bantam and I were right behind her. Anne was frantic and trying to hold the skittish animals from running.

"What happened?" she asked. "What's going on?"

Gina grabbed her reins from Anne.

"I wounded one and Gina killed the turd," I said. "But the rest of the bowel movement is heading our way."

It didn't feel bad at all. I spurred Horse and we ran like the Devil himself was after us. Bantam was right. We may have sent us all to Hell with that one impulsive act.

Chapter Forty-Three

By the time they climbed the ridge, we had a good start going. I kept swearing at myself as we beat the horses to their limit. There was no way we were going to outrun them once everybody was on open ground. I knew it was hopeless. Behind us and coming over the rise were the first riders of the pursuing gang. Their horses were bigger, more muscular, and used to this ground. We were dead.

"There," Bantam shouted and pointed off to our left.

Jagged spires and rock formations shot up out of the earth. I had read about the badlands and how outlaws were able to escape from the law by riding into their maze. This looked like a smaller version of that description, but enough hiding places for our needs. Boulders sat on the edge of cliffs and crags while precariously overhanging slag provided the jagged entryway. It was dangerous feeling that at any minute something could come tumbling down on top of us. We swung towards the rugged walls and just needed a little bit of divine grace to wing us inside there before they caught up.

Outside on the trail into the earthen monuments, Gina swung around and slid out her rifle. The others rode past but I pulled up beside her. Slocum ran over the rise with the silhouettes of Black Jack's bunch not far behind. He came up beside me and stopped for a breath.

Gina cocked the weapon and smiled at me. She pulled bead on the approaching outfit and took a moment to find her target.

I could see her finger slowly tightening on the trigger. Then whang! It whistled as it fired. The front horse stumbled and fell, throwing its rider into the cactus and scrub. The others immediately scattered to each side.

"Aim's low. I think I blew the horse's knee out, damn it," she said. "I'll fiddle with the sights."

The three of us turned and rode into the maze to catch up with the other two. They had waited along the way, with Anne at the first major turn and Bantam at the next. From that point on we rode together. The ground was a hard dirt dusting on rock. We left no tracks to follow and we seldom slowed, keeping a pace while twisting and turning. We seemed to climb and drop with each turn adding to the labyrinth confusion of the trails. Slocum stayed right with us. I was praying constantly, asking for forgiveness for Gina's and my impatience. We had been so wrong to endanger the group for the sake of a stranger.

"Make sure all of your weapons are fully loaded," Bantam sang out. "There may come a time when you will not have the luxury of reloading."

Gina brought her rifle back up to capacity and I saw Anne double-checking her handgun. We were still moving, digging in as deep as we could in the stony maze, hoping that we didn't double back and come on them. We were lost ourselves. Our aim was to disappear and have a chance to pause, catch our breath, and rest the mounts. We stopped after what seemed an interminable amount of time. I offered up water in my cupped hands to both Horse and Slocum. In the end, I drank a little myself; it was more like wetting my mouth, saving what I could for my animals in this barren realm. Then I plopped myself down on the ground next to Bantam with my back against a stone wall. Anne wiped her forehead with a bandana and left a clean streak across her brow.

"Any idea where?" she asked Bantam.

He shook his head.

"Not a clue."

"Damn, it's hot," she said.

"Heat stays right down in these crevasses. Once the rocks heat up, they just keep putting it out."

"I don't see much green," Gina said.

"I don't see any green," I remarked.

Bantam was digging at his nails with his knife.

"I wonder if they're as lost as we are. They may know their way through this Hell."

"I hope not," I said. "If they do, we're dead."

"Thanks. I feel better," Anne said.

Bantam switched hands. He wasn't nearly as coordinated in this direction but he was getting the job done.

"I don't imagine they do," he said. "This isn't some place you ride through for fun. But I do have a plan."

Gina put her hands on her hips.

"Do tell."

He wiped the knife blade off on his pants and put it back in its sheath. After inspecting his workmanship, he gave her a sideways look and continued.

"We lay low until night and then we creep ourselves out of here."

Anne spoke up.

"How do we know which direction to go? The rocks are blocking our sight lines and we really don't even know where we are."

"That's true," Bantam replied. "But we know where we were headed."

"Towards the mining camp," I said.

"Right."

"Great. I'll look for an arrow that says mining camp this way," Gina said. "We can just follow that."

"Almost. We know the camp was north and east of where we were. We follow those," Bantam said and pointed to the sky. "We fix on a star or pattern in the direction we want to go and keep riding towards it. We get out of here the same way a ship crosses the sea."

It was not a bad idea. It was hope.

"Once we get outside of this playground, we stop and figure out where we are and what to do next," I said.

So, without a better plan, we waited for the darkness to blanket us, hoping that in the meantime, we wouldn't hear the sound of their horses rounding the rocks. The trail went down on either side and gave us the longest view we could hope for inside of that earthen puzzle. But the view wasn't much more than about a hundred feet in either direction. The sun had moved enough to offer one side as a little shaded. We sat there in the coveted shadow, pretending it was slightly cooler.

"I need to tell all of you that I'm sorry, more than you can imagine," I said.

In the silence you could have heard a snake slither. Leaning back against the stone Bantam spoke from beneath his pulled-down hat.

"I wish you'd shot sooner," he said. "But I wished you had better aim. Then we wouldn't have needed that second shot. I ain't ever seen anything quite like that and you know from where you found me Mrs. Thomas that I have seen some awful things, including some strange ways that people have cashed in their chips. You caught us by surprise. Had I known you two were going to fire I could have volleyed along with you and dropped a few more of those scum where they sat."

Anne took a warm drink from her canteen.

"You two just had a moment, that's all. Unfortunately, it made the rest of us scramble. They hurt a woman. Getting all righteous about something can blind you. Emotions can kill you. So you learn to harden."

She reached over and touched my leg.

"We've cast our lots with you and I'm willing to finish with you."

She sighed and looked about at this ragtag family surrounding her.

"What is behind me has shaped my thoughts and feelings. I have no idea what is in front of me. But I have learned that it is what is inside of me that matters. I've spent a lot of time alone being surrounded by people that didn't matter a tinker's damn. Now it's different. I'm glad to spend a portion of my time with you folks."

She laughed.

"Just remember that Shakespeare said, *He's mad that trusts in the tameness of a wolf, a horse's health, a boy's love, or a whore's oath.* I have to say that he was a right smart fellow."

She put the cap back on the canteen and leaned against the wall to wait. I looked at the others not knowing if they were awake or sleeping. They lay resting with their eyes closed, conserving energy.

I jerked to consciousness to see everybody rousing and jumping up. Gina was waving her arms and shouting that she could hear horses coming. We scrambled for our mounts. I could feel the vibration of their impending arrival. The stone walls projected and bounced the clatter of the horses. The sounds were terrifying as they seemed to come from everywhere at once. We had to choose a direction in which to flee and from where we sat, we had a choice. Pick a trail and head off on its twisting back. It was as sure a thing as the roulette wheel.

Chapter Forty-Four

We were disorientated, outgunned, and outnumbered. We scrambled and jumped onto our mounts.

"Let's ride!" Gina shouted.

We spurred our horses and flew down the trails. In the confusion we split up and rode off in different directions.

"Gina." I shouted at her as she rode down another trail thinking we were behind her.

She rode directly into the gang as they rounded the corner. Their guns were raised and she stopped, putting up her hands. I started to swing Horse around but Anne grabbed his hackamore and held me up.

"We can't help her from here. Get out and regroup."

They fired a shot at us, which took a chunk of rock out of the wall spraying shards all over Slocum. He jumped behind Horse with his tail tucked. I saw the back end of Bantam as he rounded the corner on another trail.

By this point they had surrounded Gina and were taking her weapons. Anne and I rode off around the corner and out of sight. We needed to work our way back around and find Bantam. I was afraid he'd run into the gang and that would be the end of him. Self-preservation first, we were no good to the others if we were dead.

"You know," Anne said as we continued to ride, "it might be best to hole back up and wait for nightfall like we had planned."

I said, "Maybe we can locate Bantam in the meantime."

We covered another couple of twists and turns and felt far enough away to stop. We needed to find a way to conceal the horses and sneak our way back over the rocks to wherever they were holding Gina. As the sun dipped below the tops of the highest peaks, I saw something amazing between the rock spheres: land. Rolling desert land. It led out to a far horizon at the end of my eyesight. We had ridden ourselves to the very edge of these badlands.

"We have the option to leave now if we so choose," Anne said. She looked out at the vista in front of us.

"We may find a spot to tether the horses out there and then work our way back in on foot. Can't be more than a mile back in to where they are. With the sun starting to slide, this may all work in our favor."

Anne looked up and down the trails.

"All we have to do is figure which one takes us out," she said, "And mark it as we go, so that we can find our way back in."

I picked one and we started riding. Anne moved up next to the wall at every junction and scraped a spot on the wall. We rounded a turn and looked out across the Sonoran Desert.

The saguaro and organ pipe cactus seemed to reach out to us, welcoming us to wide open rolling desert with a breath of fresh hot air and the option of freedom. A thick growth of vegetation squatted about a quarter mile off to our right, which meant a spring-fed marsh and a drink for all of us. Slocum beat us there and was already lapping at the water when we arrived. We drank, filled our canteens, and tied up the mounts. I made sure my pistol was loaded with a full belt of extra rounds and slid my rifle out of its sheath. Strapping my canteen around my waist, I was ready to go. Anne was right there with me. I looked down at Slocum.

"You want to stay with Horse or come with me?"

Water was dripping from his tongue and his breathing had

slowed considerably. He turned a couple of circles, as if making up his mind, took one last lap of water, and then lay down as if to say, "I'll guard the horses." The two of us began the trudge back into the maze, hoping to find Bantam and rescue Gina.

The temperature on the ground was about ten degrees cooler than the badlands. The day waned and a slight breeze skipped the ground but the stone walls back inside baked at us like a hearth. It felt hotter than our first time through. Shadows were beginning to slide to the tops of the rock and creep slowly downward. We trudged back up the path we had come out of by following Anne's markings. The hard ground seemed hot as the walls, baking our feet through our leather soles. We tried not to make any loud noises as we trudged up the inclines. Every noise was magnified off of the stone cliffs and bounced about. Their sounds had not come to us yet. With a group of that size, we would be hearing them soon enough.

We stopped about halfway up the incline against a shaded wall and wet our mouths. We sat for a breather, catching our wind. I envied Slocum back at the pool. The shadows were deepening and longer, crossing the trail at various points. I was a little afraid of what the blackness of the night would bring.

We picked up and moved on, determined to climb the rest of the height. All sound rose up and we'd be able to hear something once we were above them. As we met the trail's summit, we were able to look out over a foreign landscape. It was even different from the last time we were here. The sun blasted the peaks from eye level this late in the day, making them look brick red and one-sided. Their backsides were dark as the spaces between them that plummeted down into the skinny nooks and canyons.

The sound of horses and loud talk rose up to us out of the depths, circling and bouncing off the peaks, challenging us to find their origin. Sometimes we could make out distinct and individual words but mostly it was a massive blur of sound, as if standing outside of a large gathering and hearing the hubbub through the walls. At its loudest points, when the conversation wasn't swirling around us, it seemed to come from our left. So we focused in there and began winding ourselves off in that direction. There was no sign of Bantam but Anne and I couldn't wait for that rendezvous as we had no idea how much time Gina had left.

"This might be a great way to pick off a few," I said. "We spot them from above and fire with our long guns. Then we move. By the time they figure out which trail leads to us we've changed position. We keep doing that until the odds are a bit more favorable."

"It's worth a try," Anne said.

Slowly, honing in on their sounds, we made our way towards them until we were close. We began creeping to the edge on the rim. There, we were able to look over and see them below us. They were riding slowly. Gina, hands tied to the saddle horn, was in the middle of the pack.

I waved Anne down the rim.

"Try and get to the next viewing spot on the trail to draw a bead."

She scuttled off. There was a little time from where I sat as they were making a long bend in the trail directly below me. If she wasn't ready by the time they began moving out of sight I was going to shoot on my own.

"I hope you feel as ripe as you look," one of the men shouted at Gina. "I love a woman with some flesh and you look like you have enough for all of us."

They all laughed but Gina did not change her posture or acknowledge their taunts. Maud and Black Jack rode up front, without looking back.

I was hoping Anne was settled in as they were about to disappear around a curve. I needed to inflict a little damage before they did. Figuring Anne would try to pick off somebody on one end of the line or the other, I drew a bead on one of the riders in the middle. I was hoping this would throw some confusion into them.

I pulled down on a skinny gringo in the middle and followed him as he rode. My finger tightened on the trigger. A shot rang out. It wasn't mine. The last rider rolled from his saddle and slammed his head against the wall, crumpling at the bottom. I fired but in the confusion my target moved and I missed. I reloaded. They all spun around and were looking at the ridge tops. One pointed up to where I was lying. I put some lead in his throat. His hands wrapped around the bottom of his beard and the red ran out between his fingers. I could see him vomit blood even from my perch. But as he died, I knew it was too late. The others had seen where we were. Black Jack shouted orders and a couple of men raced down the trail to reach us. Maud rode back and grabbed Gina's reins. She pulled her around the corner and out of sight.

"We will kill her slowly," she shouted up at us.

I scooted backwards from the edge and stood as Anne came running. We kept moving, looking for a new place to hide. Our best bet was to conceal ourselves and let the riders go past. Two more of their guards were down. But that still left about a dozen for us to deal with. We had no idea which way they might come riding at us so we kept running down the trail looking for some rocks to duck in behind.

We stumbled upon an outcropping that veered out from the edge of the cliff. There was a space to tuck in beside it. We had worked our way around enough so that looking down to the canyon floor below us, we saw the caravan of thieves. They all sat on horseback except for a fat man with broken teeth. He held Gina with his arm around her neck, holding her down by his belly. He shouted out and his coarse voice banked against the walls and echoed.

"Tulip! Hey, Tulip! Look at what I've got!"

He twisted his arm and her face pointed skyward. It was red from the sun and his chokehold. She gurgled and spit, gasping for a breath.

"I have your friend," he shouted. "In fact, when we're done, we will all have had your friend."

He laughed a deep, dirty, belly laugh.

"She misses you," he continued, "and has invited you to watch the show. She likes me the best and said I can go first and last."

He pulled her head back down to about belly height and punched her several times in the face.

"She likes it a little rough."

Beside me I could hear Anne grunting. I put my hand on her and pointed below.

"Two of the riders are not there. They're up here someplace trying to find us," I said. "You can't move or you'll give away our position."

"But Gina," she said.

I couldn't answer her. Looking down I could see the ground beneath Gina turning dark.

"She is so excited that she has wet herself," the fat man said. "She wants me very badly."

Bent over, she got a hand free and slammed it against his groin area. He screamed and doubled over but didn't release her. With the weight of his body pinning her, he punched her several more times with his fist. Two others jumped off their horses and helped him stand up. They grabbed Gina, retied her hands, and forced her back up on the horse. When it was over, the pig looked back up at the walls.

"We're going now," he said. "I hope you can find her. You can have all the pieces you can find. There is only one piece that I want."

He climbed up on his mount and the troop rode off. We backed out of our perch, shocked and frightened.

"That's it, isn't it? They want us to come after them so they can kill us all."

"Yes," a male voice answered and we turned to find the two riders standing there with their guns pointed at us.

"Throw your weapons over the edge," one of them said.

There was no option so we did as we were told. You could hear the rifles clatter and bounce against the side of the walls as they dropped into the canyon below. He wiggled his gun at me.

"The pistol too," he said. "And the belt."

I unbuckled it and dropped the leather at my feet.

"Kick it over," he said.

I turned away from him and kicked the rifles. The pistol and belt followed over the edge. In that same instant I pulled my own little pig sticker from my pants, spun, and threw the knife at the talker. I remember hearing his scream as the flash from the other fellow's pistol blinded me.

Chapter Forty-Five

I thought I could hear a bell clanging incessantly somewhere off in the distance. The banging of metal rolling over and over in the deep fog I was grouping through. This was followed with a layer of pain that felt like there were a thousand knife points being pressed into the side of my head. It was sharp and steady. I struggled to send messages from my brain to my muscles. Initially I failed miserably but gradually the cogs and drive rods in my body's machinery connected with one another. A huge collaborative effort took place internally and I was able to push at my body from the inside out. As it was, I shouldn't have wasted my time. Nothing happened.

I could neither move nor pick my face up from the hard earth. The very effort sent lightning bolts of pain coursing across my jaw and down my neck. Surely my heart was going to stop from this intense exertion of fighting the pain. I opened my eyes. Lying on my left side everything was off-kilter. My lashes brushed dirt back into my eye but I couldn't move to clear it out. I squeezed it shut and held it tight, peering only from my right eye.

Night had fallen and I wondered how long I had lain there. I didn't know why I wasn't dead. I began to pull the puzzle pieces of my memory together. Where was Anne? Where was anybody? I moved my right hand flat across the surface of the ground, feeling the pebbles and grains of sand. The sensation in my fingers was there, even the palm of my hand. Slowly, ever so slowly, my feelings and movements were coming back. I forced my legs to scissor and knees to bend. I was not paralyzed. I braced myself against my left shoulder, which I was lying on, and rolled myself over on my back.

Oh, God that hurt!

I lay on my back, catching my breath, staring up at the stars with my one good eye. I patted myself down the side and found that my canteen was still attached to my pants. I unhooked it by feel and slid it up and onto my chest. I opened it and poured the warm water into my eye. A second try and whatever dirt had been lodged under my lid was gone. I shared some water with my mouth and ran it over my lips and tongue.

Slowly I moved my right hand across my body and touched the left side of my face. It was sticky with earth and blood forming a gritty layer on my skin. Painful to the touch I knew the stickiness was blood. Tenderly I tapped around and discovered part of my ear was missing and the skin and meat of my cheekbone were no longer there. It felt like the froth around Horse's mouth after a good run. I assumed that a few of the hard bits that felt like gravel were small pieces of bone or teeth shattered and tossed aside. Pain shot through my face and its flash blinded me. In that instant I remembered seeing the muzzle and the explosion that had dropped me.

They must have left me for dead. I thought they may still be right. I did what I didn't want to do. I sat up. Things swirled. I turned and leaned on my forearm, vomiting onto the ground. The nausea helped take my mind off the old pain. Lovely. While I was in that position I poured some of the canteen water on my face hoping to minimally clean up. Putting the top back on, I leaned forward and crawled over to a wall. There were enough crags and handholds to pull myself up. One more bout of nausea while clinging to the wall. I took the time to catch my breath. I didn't have the strength of a baby.

I was sweaty and stormy but the clouds in my head began clearing. Everything was physically downhill from where I stood. To my side lay my hat, which I picked up and put on hoping it might aid in keeping my brains inside my head while protecting what was left of my ear. I took a stumble step and then another. Pretty soon it was almost like walking, gravity helping me move down the trail. While I moved about, things started to clear.

I had no guns and no knife. Horse was, hopefully, still tethered at the water hole with Slocum. It was a long way and I was pretty sure that I couldn't make that walk but it was my only hope.

The pain was dulling with every step and the fog behind my eyeballs was slowly lifting. I'd quit bleeding while I lay on the ground and as I touched the wound, I could feel the crusted blood. My drying face felt tight. The skin pulled and strained along the side of my cheek when I opened my mouth to drink or take a deep breath. I was starting to focus on my situation and ignore my slamming headache.

I still had water. Stopping every five or ten steps was helping my strength to return. I was moving slowly enough in the darkness not to trip over anything. Walking was taking a lifetime and by the time the night was weakening to the gray of morning I had rounded the last turn and was moving down the slope towards the desert. The clump of trees that hid the mounts and Slocum lay dead ahead. I concentrated with a singular vision on that one sight and forged ahead with no walls to stop and lean against. I only fell once, which didn't hurt, but the getting up practically killed me.

It was do or die time.

I was greeted by Slocum, who sensed enough not to jump up on me in welcome. Both horses were still there. Black Jack and the boys had not ventured this far from the stone maze. I dropped to my knees and I fell face first into the soothing water.

I could have drowned and been happy at that moment. I swished my head back and forth hoping to remove some of the clotted blood and packed-in dirt. I stood up and went over to Horse. We had to ride. Slocum was itching to run so I untied Horse and swung him back around towards the rocks. So here we were—Shadrach, Meshach, and Abednego, heading back into the fiery furnace. Dead or alive, I still had friends in there.

We hadn't even made the trail heading up, when Slocum took to barking at something off about a hundred yards. I pulled Horse up and looked. I couldn't see it. He took off running and I had no choice but to follow. Slocum stopped his barking. He pulled up at a rock. But as I got closer, I realized it wasn't a rock but a person. It was somebody flat on their back in the dirt. Her head stuck out of the rocks that had been piled on top of her. But it wasn't just somebody. It was Anne and as I jumped down from Horse I could see the red welts covering her face and neck. She had been buried flat over an ant nest. It appeared that a shallow ditch had been carved out in the dry desert earth and she was laid in it covered with rocks. She was facing upwards into the blazing sun. An army of insects crawled across her skin and clothing. She was crying and moaning in pain. The ants were crowding on the moisture from her eyes and the insides of her nostrils. I brushed at the ants until I had knocked most of them aside. Then I lifted my canteen to her lips and let the moisture run across her mouth and tongue.

"Anne, I'm going to get you out of here," I said slapping at my legs. "When I get enough of the rocks off push your way free from underneath."

"You can't."

Yes, I can. Just bear with me."

"You can't," she screamed at me. "Listen to me! They bound my hands to my feet underneath me, I can't push. The woman cut me. She knew where and how. I'm bleeding to death while

I'm being eaten alive by these goddamned ants."

Now I was crying with her.

"No! No! Maybe the weight of the rocks against you has slowed the bleeding. I'll help you."

I began to dig around her with my hands and fight the ants at the same time.

"Shoot me, you whore! You think you're such a prim little schoolteacher who was married to a sheriff. You're a fake. You're just as lousy as the rest of us. Now kill me, you piece of shit!"

I stopped digging. She was screaming for relief and sometimes screaming incoherently because making noise was the only relief she could find. I slapped at my side while bawling.

"I don't have a gun! I don't even have a knife."

She leaned her head back and screamed at the sky. It was a long agonizing wail that broke off into coughing. She tried bashing her head up and down on a rock.

"Just hurry. Please."

She stopped and stared me dead in the eyes. Her voice became lower; it was hard to hear her. "I'd kill you," she whispered slowly. "I would kill you."

I looked around, crying, searching for anything. I saw a rock and picked it up. It was jagged and about the size of my fist. I fell back next to her and raised my arm.

"Do it. Peggy, do it," she said.

When she spoke my name, I knew I couldn't.

"I can't," I cried.

"Yes. You can."

She spit at me and I crumpled.

"No. I can't."

I could do nothing while she slowly died in agony before my eyes.

The stinging on my legs and feet woke me to fight. I stood and began swatting at the ants with my hat. Then I turned to swat them away from Anne's face. I needed to stop the torment.

"There." She cried out. "There. Use your hat."

"What?"

"Take the band off the crown of your hat and slip it around my neck."

I looked down, trying to picture it as a weapon of death. I pulled the band away from the crown and tossed the hat to the side. My hands shook. It took two tries to slip the leather over her head and around her neck.

"Now pull from the back."

I took a deep breath and grabbed it with both hands. I had to look away as I pulled. I heard her begin to gurgle. The side of my leg was braced against her shoulder and I pulled as hard as I could. The noise of her choking didn't stop. I wanted her to die. But she lived and I was running out of strength. When I dropped the band, she started coughing and spitting.

"It's not working," I said.

"You're a pitiful marm," Anne spit out.

"I've been shot. I'm weak."

"Get a stick."

"What?"

"A thick stick."

I got up and stumbled towards the water. There on the ground I found what I needed. I returned and knelt next to her pouring some water on her face and brushing at the ants, digging at them with my finger just inside her nostrils. I picked up the canteen.

"Do you want some water?" I asked.

"No. I want to die."

I dropped the canteen and showed her the stick.

"Now put it between the hatband and the back of my neck."

I had to do it from the side. I did it slowly. I didn't want to scratch her. It was stupid. I wasn't thinking straight. There were ends of the wood sticking out top and bottom. She was taking long, deep breaths. A few more and she was ready.

"Okay. Twist it and don't stop, no matter what. Don't stop."

I twisted it once and the band tightened on her neck. I gasped involuntarily. She looked at me letting me know I had to continue. A loop was formed around the stick and I kept turning it slowly. I was fighting myself from stopping. She stared at me the entire time. The squeezing of her throat making tears roll down her cheeks as her face turned red.

"I love you," I sobbed.

Anne smiled and it turned into a grimace as I twisted. Her eyes bulged and she began to gag. I stopped and she shook her head violently, vocalizing some noise from deep down in her throat like an animal. I looked away and continued to twist as hard as I could. I prayed the leather hatband wouldn't snap. When I could no longer turn the stick I held it in place while staring off at the desert. My arms jerked with her struggle. Eventually she quit making noises. I don't know how long I continued to hold it, an eternity. When I stood up there was no movement from Anne. I started towards Horse and I refused to look back at her.

Chapter Forty-Six

The shot rang out kicking up dirt near my feet. I jumped and ran for Horse. Laughter came from up on the cliffs above me. I realized they had been watching me go through this ordeal.

"You bastards," I shouted at the walls.

Another shot whistled past me as I leapt up on Horse. I scanned the rock face until I picked out the figure, a black spot against the burnt ridge landscape. Whoever it was stopped and shot again. This time a bullet rocked Anne's head and sent a red spray into the air. Their laughter rang boldly down from above, an evil God with a thirst for killing. I was sickened. I raced to the rise to get out of their sight line and from underneath them. I would find them and kill them.

Once into the maze I had to find my way to their encampment. I was sure that their lookout had informed them that I was back inside the pillars. I had to find Bantam. Since my discovery of Anne, I was afraid their anger had turned towards Gina. I was so filled with anger, rage, and nausea that it nearly kept me bent over. The rock ground revealed nothing. If it hadn't been for the wall marks that Anne had made, I would have been totally lost. Once I had reached a certain point I veered off from the trail hoping to find Bantam.

What I came upon was more than I could have anticipated. Rounding a corner, I found myself facing their camp. I yanked Horse's reins and did a quick scramble back behind the wall before we were seen. I looped his lead around a cropping and snuck my way back over for a sight line. I swear I was almost close enough to reach out and touch one. They were eating, arguing, and cleaning their guns. One of them was facing away from me, buck naked with his unmentionables in his hand. He stood next to the fire shaking his loose clothing over the flames. I could hear the ticks snap and pop as they dropped off the material into the burn. He was scratching and rubbing his legs and groin, trying to brush off any strays.

"I'll feel much better once I get out of this heat. These peckerwoods are eating me alive," he said.

Maud looked at him over her shoulder with disinterest.

"We'll all feel a lot better once you get someplace where you can take a bath," she said. "Your horse smells better than you do."

She got a laugh out of a couple of the guys. I watched her. To me, she was the dangerous one. She had the power. She wandered over into the shadows and knelt down with her back to me.

I realized she was talking to Gina.

Gina shook her head a couple of times and then looked up, right at me. Her eyes widened and her body stiffened but she caught herself and dropped her head so as not to give herself away. Her hands were behind her, so I figured she was tied. I was on my own unless I located Bantam. Looking at the way they were laid out, with a gun I could take out about three of them before they found cover or came charging at me. It would also put Gina in danger.

If shooting broke out, there had to be a fast way to free Gina. It helped that she knew I was here. We might find a way to work together to get us out of this situation. I told Slocum to stay with Horse and managed to creep my way a little closer along the craggy rock on the right, remaining hidden from their sight. A hand covered my mouth from behind. I froze. I turned my head around and looked up into the face of Burt. He pulled his hand away once he saw the recognition in my eyes.

"What are . . . how did you find us?" I said too loudly.

He shushed me and we hunkered down behind the stone.

"Once that scorpion poison worked itself out of me, I was only about a day and a half behind you. The overland tracking was easy since there were about fifteen horses heading in the same direction. It was easy to move faster than the group. Where I lost time was in here on the hard ground. When I saw Slocum's butt I knew you had to be nearby. Thank God he knows me or he might have alerted the entire camp by barking."

He peeked out at the campsite before us.

"It's just the two of us, huh?"

I nodded my head and brought him up to date on Anne's death, a missing Bantam who may be dead, and the capture of Gina. His face stayed sober while I related the entire story.

After a moment of quiet he asked, "So what's the plan?"

"I don't have one, yet," I said.

"Far as I can tell one of us will have to create some sort of diversion, start them moving in one direction while the other one frees Gina."

"Any ideas on how we're going to do that? I don't have a weapon."

Burt took the saddlebags off his shoulders and opened one of the flaps. He handed me a pistol and pulled out a couple sticks of dynamite.

"I think these doggies will do the trick. Once they blow, that group over there will be all horns and rattles, but they may be scattered enough for us to make a move. I'll attempt to plant them about and see if I can't make some noise."

I nodded.

He stuffed them back in his bags.

"I'll put as much fuse as I dare to give me a little time to head back here. Be ready when you hear it blow."

Burt took one last peek at their camp.

"Why is that fella with the table muscle naked?" he said.

"Just shaking ticks out of his underwearings," I said.

"Oh yeah, they will eat you up," he replied and scratched without thinking. Then he scampered around the rocks and out of sight.

I looked across the way at Slocum wondering how he was going to react to the explosion. I checked the pistol. I began to creep forward trying to edge myself closer to get as much advantage as I could steal. I had made a mental waybill to keep track of how many of them there were. From what I could tell, we were dealing with an even dozen. My main objective was to grab Gina and get out of there.

The explosion felt like it was right on top of us. Chunks of stone bounced and bounded off the walls, ricocheting from all directions. The second explosion was immediately after and was far worse since the bouncing stones came from out of the smoke of the first explosion. Eyesight was limited. Breathing was tough. People were coughing and shouting and then the gunfire started. Scooting across the opening to where I had last seen Gina, I stumbled over a body that had either been shot or bashed with a rock. I didn't stop to inspect him. Somebody grabbed my arm and I spun about to face the naked man with the potbelly. He was looking at me sort of stunned. I placed my pistol on the side of his head and pulled the trigger. Some spray breezed me but I didn't slow my pace. I kept moving and began shouting for Gina.

Another crud appeared behind me from the cloud of smoke, evidently notified by the sound of my voice. He lifted his gun. A shot rang out. The insides of his skull pushed themselves out through his face, showering me with blood. I looked up through the drifting haze to see Burt perched on a ledge about ten feet up. He waved at me and then shouted.

"Go. Go."

I turned back and continued my quest, gun drawn, shouting.

"Gina!"

"Here!" came the response and I caught sight of her being pulled around a corner.

More shots rang out and gang members dropped to the ground. Then a gun blazed not far from my head and I turned to see Burt double up. As he fell, he deliberately pushed himself out from the wall as far as he could and dropped from the ledge. The outlaw he targeted underneath him may as well been hit by one of the boulders. Burt's shooter stepped up next to me still looking at his prey to see if it was alive. With all the smoke and confusion, he hadn't noticed me hunkered down on the ground. I stood up with my barrel at the bottom of his chin and discharged the pistol. The lower part of his face flapped up to his forehead. When it settled back down there was no nose or even an eye on my side. He crumbled like a house of cards.

I was covered with blood and bile. I could taste death. I wiped blood from my eyes and ran as best I could to the rock corner and stopped. I didn't want to meet a rifle head-on. Peeking around, I could see Maud Davis pulling on Gina, who was struggling even though her hands were still tied behind her. I ran towards them while shouting.

"Let her go, dammit!"

Maud immediately moved Gina by the neck, spinning her around and facing me with the human shield. She placed her gun directly against Gina's ear. Behind me the commotion continued but by now it was all voices and no guns.

"Pretty strong language for an ex-sheriff's wife."

Gina struggled against her. Maud shoved the barrel hard against her ear.

"You keep moving," she hissed, "and you'll be missing the

top of your head."

Gina stopped pitching and stared at me. Maud was grinning real large, showing me her full mouth of tombstones. She motioned with her shoulder in the direction where Burt lay.

"You figured you and your friend would just pop in here, take us out, and ride away with your *girlfriend*?"

When she said *girlfriend,* she jabbed the pistol hard against Gina's skull. I could hear it clunk against the bone from where I stood. There was a whimper from Gina and then she bit her lip.

"So this is almost like a family reunion ain't it? I'm awful sorry I don't have any punch and pie to offer you." Grins came easy to her. "Seems like me and my boys are killing off your friends and relatives every time we meet."

She began backing up the incline leading out of the bowl, pulling Gina with her. I took a step towards her.

"I'm a good enough shot," I said. "You keep moving up that ramp and I'll drop you."

"I believe you're wrong."

She took another step backward and nodded at my weapon.

"Set the pistol down and then turn around slowly."

I knew who it was behind me and after setting down the gun, I slowly turned to face him. He had a couple of his friends. Along with pus pimples was Maud's toy, Black Jack, and one of the other fellas. They may have been all that was left. I had no way of knowing. I could hear moaning from somewhere but I didn't know if it was one of the gang or Burt. I had no weapon and from what I could tell, no chance of living much longer.

For the second time in my life I was in the wrong place at the wrong time. Seems like both times portended death.

They motioned for me to start walking back the way I had come. As I passed them, they gave me a little shove just to reaffirm who was boss. When I approached the camp area I could see Burt still lying crumpled where he had dropped. The fella underneath him had his head cocked at an odd angle. There was no hope.

"Why don't you just shoot me?" I asked.

"We will," Black Jack said.

"Don't let these bastards win," Gina shouted out behind me.

I heard a slap and tussle on the ramp. Then came a whoop and holler instantly recognizable as Bantam. I turned in time to see him lurching down the incline above Gina and Maud. His hat was tied around his neck and flopping behind him. There was a kerchief tied to each wrist and they fluttered out flag-like from his spread arms, looking like a poorly feathered bird-of-prey. He was screeching at the top of his lungs. He slammed into Maud with his shoulder and shoved her to the side. She careened off the incline and smacked on the dirt below. He almost followed her but caught himself and continued down the rock incline. Gina dropped to the ground.

I thought my eyes were deceiving me until I realized he was wearing his roller skates. He had a pistol in both hands and when he wasn't trying to balance himself he was pointing them in our direction. My captors stood stone still facing Bantam, completely amazed. He flew at us, wobbling and wavering, as he shouted and fired, all the while trying to keep upright.

I ducked to the side. Bantam hit one of the outlaws in the leg and he dropped next to me. I grabbed a rock and beat the side of his head into mush. Black Jack and Boils had regained their senses and got off one round each before Bantam smashed head-on into them. A bullet from Bantam hit Black Jack in the arm. He turned in pain as Bantam began rolling and fighting with his partner. I grabbed my pistol and ran to Gina. She was trying to untie herself.

A shot rang out and we both dropped. Black Jack had his pistol raised for a second attempt but I got mine off first. My shot skipped off the rock wall near his head and he turned and ran. Bantam stood with his gun pointed down at Boils, who still lay on the ground. As he looked up, Bantam stepped on the side of his head with his skates, turning his face back into the dirt. Bantam fired twice. The body jerked and settled. Then Bantam kicked off the roller skates and left them beside the body.

Gina ran over to the fella I had lain out with the rock and took the gun from his dead hand. She lit out after Black Jack. I heard scrambling behind me and looked back to see Maud surmounting the trail up into the rocks. I fired two rounds. One hit her squarely in the back and she dropped like a rag doll, tumbling back down the slope. I rushed to her and kicked the weapon out of her hand. She looked up at me, squinting through the dust and the heat.

"It doesn't hurt," she said and smiled at me.

Bantam walked up beside me, gun naked. He watched for a moment and then put it back in his holster.

"You killed my husband."

"Oh, him," she grimaced. "My boys did that."

"It was your call," I said.

She smiled.

"Yes. It was."

Maud tried to move her body but somewhere between her head and her legs the signal was getting crossed.

"My back," she said. "Everything is numb. I can't move my legs."

I looked up above our stone cathedral and watched the vultures circle lazily overhead.

"Do you have some water?" she asked.

I looked at her, lying there, baking in the sun.

"Yes," I said and didn't move.

After a moment she nodded her head and coughed.

"Your husband was easy. He was no dead shot. So we took him out."

I nodded at the hole I'd put in her spine.

"I guess that kind of aim runs in the family."

Then I turned and started walking away from her.

"Where are you going?" she shouted. "You just gonna leave me here, bitch? I can't move."

Gina came back around the corner.

"Black Jack grabbed a horse and hightailed it out. He'd been hit in the arm but I'm sure it wasn't deep."

"Maybe he'll come back for you," Bantam said to Maud.

"I know Black Jack. He'll hunt you down," she said directly to me. "Why don't you finish me off, you chicken-shit quim?"

She attempted to drag herself but without something to grasp on the hard incline it was a futile effort.

"I like it better this way," I said.

Maud looked up at the circling birds. I turned away.

"That lick-finger Nancy husband of yours should rot in hell!"

Gina, Bantam, and I began our walk back to our mounts while Maud lay on the sunny rock, slowly baking, awaiting her death. As we gathered our dead she continued to scream at us. It echoed and bounced among the spires like an animal in distress.

My worst times were yet to come. We had two people to bury, friends, compadres who saved our lives and believed in justice. I had yet to tell Bantam and Gina about Anne. She'd been a good friend and a decent human being who knew more about love and friendship than I could imagine. We would bury her by the oasis with Burt next to her.

We would let the others rot where they lay.

Chapter Forty-Seven

I look at James's place on the hill through the curtains and think of the double mounds that lay near a beautiful oasis in a godforsaken corner of the Devil's desert. The stage watering and saloon house on the border had earned a certain amount of notoriety from our ordeal and is now a regular layover for travelers and dime novel devotees. So much so that a hotel of sorts has sprung up naming the area Scorpion Sands.

The rest of us are here. Outside of the bumps and bruises associated with the endeavors of the past, my grievances are few. I have learned to hold my anger better. In most cases life has followed the course of most nature and corrected itself as only time can do.

The district judge, upon arriving in San Pueblo after the death of Sheriff Bannon and finding our posse in hot pursuit of the Christian gang, took it upon himself to appoint a new sheriff to the town. In turn, that lawman organized the local citizenry and rebuilt the jail in order to hold any undesirable who might happen upon his town. It is a beautiful arcadia in the heart of Hell and I would be sorely upset to see it in ruin or disappear. If ever I were to find myself back in that area of the country, I would make it a point to visit. I sincerely hope that I never will.

There is a bark from Slocum and I can hear Bantam telling the dog to get out from underfoot. Gina wanders no more and has put down tendrils deep into the soil here. We are family and maybe have been since we connected those many months ago.

Even though she is building herself a new colorful wagon, it has no wheels. She feels more at home sleeping there. Bantam seems to enjoy the hard labor, sweat, and stability that comes with having a place of one's own. I have added their names as seconds to the property deed.

Although a time may come when once again I venture from this homestead, I don't hasten the arrival of any such passage and am quite content to remain where I am. Drinking Gina's latest blend of coffee, not quite her original and not quite American, combining whatever we can get, is baptism enough. The whiskey helps smooth the rough edges of the black drink and makes it palatable although we tell her how delicious it is. If that is to be my biggest complaint, then the rest of my life will be good.

Those two, along with others who are no longer with us, saw my growth as a human being and it is to them I owe my life. I no longer feel trapped in a home carrying the ghost of James. Although I still go up the hill and speak to him, I realize that I am speaking to myself. May this halt any speculation perceiving me as a crazy old woman. That situation has been rectified and I would honestly contemplate returning to try teaching, if it weren't for the damned children everywhere. Months ago, I was frightened to leave and now I'm not sure that I want to self-impose any encumbrances at all. Time will tell.

As I have put pen to paper and related my tale, the ending is somewhat bittersweet. It is closing the book on memories and acquaintances that I have curried along the way. It is a feeling that once my personal quest was completed, they no longer live, and in closing the book they, like the memories of them, begin to fade and turn to dust. We do live longer than our days but only as long as we are remembered. Once those who knew us also pass on, we become ancient mythology. It is so strange that moments that mean so much while they are happening can, in turn, mean so little to current life.

I don't believe that Black Jack ever came back for Maud. Too scared of dying, I suppose. Most bullies are cowards. I'd received word that a posse hunted down Black Jack and his new gang and killed them. Their bodies were placed on display for all to see. There was never any mention of a woman. The place where he was killed is now known as *Black Jack Canyon.* The resting place of Anne and Burt has no title. Thirsty travelers, lost in the shimmering desert, may find life in the spring waters near where they lay and that may be legacy enough.

The sharply eroded buttes, stone pinnacles, and rock towers that make up the final resting place of Maud Davis has become known as the *Screaming Woman Spires.* It is said that at night when the wind changes and blows between the formations, it sounds like a woman screaming. If ghosts are memories of atrocities past, the screaming will continue for a long time.

ABOUT THE AUTHOR

Del Howison is a Bram Stoker award–winning editor and author. He has been nominated for a half-dozen awards including the Black Quill and the Shirley Jackson Award. His work has appeared in dozens of books. In 1994, along with his wife, Susan, he opened the world-famous horror store Dark Delicacies in Burbank, California, which has been inducted to the Rondo Hatton Hall of Fame. He has also served on the board of trustees for the Horror Writers Association.

The employees of Five Star Publishing hope you have enjoyed this book.

Our Five Star novels explore little-known chapters from America's history, stories told from unique perspectives that will entertain a broad range of readers.

Other Five Star books are available at your local library, bookstore, all major book distributors, and directly from Five Star/Gale.

Connect with Five Star Publishing

Visit us on Facebook:
https://www.facebook.com/FiveStarCengage

Email:
FiveStar@cengage.com

For information about titles and placing orders:
(800) 223-1244
gale.orders@cengage.com

To share your comments, write to us:
Five Star Publishing
Attn: Publisher
10 Water St., Suite 310
Waterville, ME 04901